MW01267958

DAY OF THE DOG

DAY OF THE DOG

MARK SALVI

DAY OF THE DOG

iUniverse books may be ordered through booksellers or by contacting:

iUniverse
1663 Liberty Drive
Bloomington, IN 47403
www.iuniverse.com
1-800-Authors (1-800-288-4677)

ISBN: 978-1-4917-7373-4 (sc)
ISBN: 978-1-4917-7460-1 (hc)
ISBN: 978-1-4917-7372-7 (e)

Library of Congress Control Number: 2015914078

Print information available on the last page.

iUniverse rev. date: 01/21/2016

Acknowledgment

A thank you to my family and friends who supported me and encouraged me to complete this book.

My girlfriend, Beverly Bates My mom, Lenore Crandall

My stepdad Ralph Oakes

My sisters Lori Stanley, Lisa Granger, and Deb Adler

My Kids Zack Salvi, Chelsea Salvi, Krystal Fowler, Steven Peer

My brother Brian Salvi, brother in-law Red Martindale

My friend James Paddock

A special thanks to Lori Lewis, Danny Lewis, and J.K. Grantham. for their help and hard work in the editing process.

Day of the Dog

Prologue, world events

China & Russia, Islamic groups (ISIS, Al Qaeda)

The time is January 2020 and racial tensions are on the rise throughout the US. Curfews and martial law have been called for in over a dozen cities around the US. But outside the trouble spots, life in the US is mostly normal for now. Due to the lack of US students, universities and colleges have opened their doors to more foreign students. Now most of the student body of the major universities and colleges in the US are Chinese and Russian. Most US college-age people are involved in protests for one side or the other. They have set their education aside for what they consider to be more important issues, depending on which side they agree with: black, white, gay, or straight. To protect the US military and government from bad PR with the American people, the government has accepted peacekeeping forces from the United Nations. These peacekeeping forces are made up of Russian and Chinese soldiers.

Russia and China have been working with America to improve the US education system (at least publicly). The US is their marketplace, so a better educated US population is a better market for their factories and sale of their electronics. Russia is also helping with our space program by sending scientists and engineers to work at NASA to build rockets for space exploration.

In Washington, political correctness becomes top priority. Concern for our global image causes our government to be reactive rather than proactive to national and global crises.

The US government puts a stranglehold on the media by passing laws that affect the FCC and how the IRS taxes public broadcasting. Using the federal agencies, the FCC and the IRS, gives the government unlimited control over what the news media can report.

It was at this point when some unexpected events took place. The Islamic terrorist groups ISIS and Al Qaeda infiltrated the US the same time as the Chinese and Russian students. They launched their attacks on the US with dirty bombs of nuclear and biological nature.

The United States government and the US military are caught off guard by these events, and are unable to help or protect the people of the United States.

The simultaneous combination of all this had unexpected effects, horrifying everyone around the world. Everything dominoed rapidly. Electrical power and communications were lost. The violence spiraled out of control. Then people started getting sick and dying by the millions nationwide. America went dark to the rest of the world. The violence and disease spread out across the world, touching all nations. The lives of the surviving human race were now changed forever.

Introduction

United States Strategic Command Offutt Omaha, Nebraska.

Sgt. Mason O'Reilly was a strict STRATCOM USAir Force First Sgt. and proud of it. He was proud of his sharply creased coveralls and the blue scarf at his throat and the white gloves. He was proud of the 9mm on his hip.

It was late afternoon in Omaha. Today had been hot and Mason glanced at his watch again. Just as he did the RC-135V/W swept out of the sky and down the runway and taxied over to the unloading area where Mason waited. The first man out of the plane was a colonel presently stationed at Offutt. Mason recognized him. The next man fit the photograph security had furnished. They came over to the jeep.

Mason said, "IDs, please."

The Colonel took his out without a word. Republican Sen. Thomas Kane of Texas frowned. "I just came in on the general's plane with your own colonel."

Mason said, "Yes sir, but I need to see your ID."

Kane nodded, amused. He took a leather folder from an inside pocket then grinned as the sergeant came into an even more rigid position of attention. The card was Kane's Air Force reserve officer ID and showed him to be a Lieutenant General. "That," Kane thought, "ought to shake the kid up."

They got into the jeep and drove down the runway past the specially equipped E-6B Mercury Boeing 707 code-named Looking Glass Plane. There were three of those planes, and one was in the air at all times. They carried a strategic air command general officer and staff.

Back at the end of World War II, SAC headquarters was put in Omaha at the center of the US. In 1992, the facility received upgrades, and the name was changed to United States Strategic Command. It was again upgraded in 2002 to include the Department of Space Command. It was now referred to as STRATCOM. The command center itself was built four stories below ground and reinforced with concrete and steel. The hole was supposed to withstand anything, but that was before ICBMs. Now there were no illusions. If the big one went off, the hole was doomed. That wouldn't keep STRATCOM from controlling its forces, because Looking Glass couldn't be brought down. No one except its pilots ever knew where it was. If Looking Glass should crash or be compromised, military control would be handed over to the two TACAMO planes; one out in the Atlantic and one in the Pacific. Next in line would be the Navy's AWACS Planes. There were one or more of these with each naval task force.

Mason ushered the senator into the big brick building and up the stairs to General Fred Harrington's office. The office had an old-fashioned air about it, with leather covered wooden furniture and a huge desk. There were display cases of US Air Force models; WWII fighters, B36 bombers, B-52s and missiles of every description. There were three telephones on the desk: black, red, and gold. A portable unit containing a red and a gold phone stood on a table near the desk. The phones went with the general in his car, to his home, in his bedroom and even in the latrines. During his tour of duty as commander in chief strategic air command, he was never more than four rings from the gold phone and never would be. The gold phone reached the president, the red one went downhill from Harrington to STRATCOM's CIC floor (command and control systems floor). They could launch more firepower than all armies in history that had ever been employed.

Gen. Harrington waved Sen. Kane into his office and joined him in conversation. Standing by the big window overlooking the runway Gen. Harrington asked, "What the hell brings you out here like this? What couldn't we settle on the phone?"

Kane asked, "How secure are your phones?"

Harrington shrugged, "As good as we can make them."

Kane said, "Maybe yours are all right, you've got your own people to check them. I'm damn sure mine aren't safe. Officially, it's what I told you: I need some help understanding your budget requests."

Gen. Harrington said, "Uh huh. You want a drink?"

Sen. Kane said, "Whiskey, if you've got it here."

"Sure," General Harrington replied as he took a bottle and two glasses out of the cabinet. He brought the whiskey to the coffee table and poured a shot In each glass. "Okay, just what is this all about?"

Sen. Kane said, "The civil unrest. The Russians and the Chinese wanting to be so helpful."

Gen. Harrington's face went blank. "What about it? The president and his administration have Homeland Security on top of the rioting and civil unrest and they're both jumping through hoops to stay friends with the Russians and the Chinese."

Sen. Kane grimaced. "Homeland Security couldn't control a bingo game at a retirement home, much less get control on the civil unrest and rioting that's going on across the country. I'm very suspicious of the Russians and Chinese wanting to jump in and be so helpful to us in our quote-unquote 'time of need.'"

Gen. Harrington said, "I agree with you but I take my orders from the president of the United States. The Chinese hold most of the US debt. If they should demand payment of that debt in full, it would destroy our economy, sending us into economic collapse. The Russians and the Chinese have worked up a plan to help the US pay off its debt. That's the official word out of Washington anyhow. The civil unrest is not a military matter. What can I do about it? Nevertheless, that's all civil and political matters. The Russians and

Chinese have not made any aggressive military actions. Therefore, my hands are pretty much tied. We're at DEFCON4 because of this civil unrest. I cannot heighten that state without some military cause or order from the president."

Sen. Kane said, "I know there's a lot more going on behind the scenes, but I don't have any proof. Governor Carry feels the same as I do, and that's why he is nearby at the Texas border and now at odds with Washington. I am just asking you to have your best people in all the right places."

Gen. Harrington said, "Governor Carry has put me and the military in a very tough spot. The president is not happy with Texas at the moment. I do not know how this is going to all play out with Texas, but for now we're taking a wait-and-see attitude. What bothers me the most is the Russians and Chinese being friendly and *working together to help us*. All leave has been canceled and extra personnel have been added to the duty roster. That's the best I can do."

Sen. Kane said, "This administration has taken political correctness to an extreme. Profiling a threat is strictly forbidden. Words like Islamic extremists or Muslim jihadist cannot be used in a public forum. If a group of Arab men go into a mall and shoot the place up yelling 'Jihad, Allah is great' before they blow themselves up, the news media cannot report that incident as being carried out by Islamic extremists or Muslim jihadists. If they do, the IRS will call an audit on them and the FCC will suspend their license until the completion of the audit. If a 200 pound, 6 foot tall black man robs a convenience store and then disappears into the crowded city streets, the police have to question and search suspects by a random criteria vs. the profile of a 200 pound, 6 foot black man. I'm worried that in an effort to protect our global image, dangerous people are going to slip through the cracks. You do what you have to do to protect your forces and the United States. Remember that you have friends in Washington."

Chapter 1

Dahlonega, Georgia

Pre-Event.

It was January of the year 2020 in Dahlonega, Georgia, a small rural town in the mountains of northern Georgia. My family and I moved here five years ago from upstate New York. We were looking for a community that was more in line with our values and lifestyle. The people of Dahlonega have old-fashioned Christian values and a country lifestyle. We bought a log cabin on a dead-end road where we only had a couple of neighbors.

As I was sitting in my living room watching TV, I looked over to my wife and said, "The holidays are finally over. Now I can watch the news and relax without having to worry about running here or there to get this or that. Life can get back to normal."

I turned on the news, popped the cap on a beer and kicked back on the couch. The news anchor came on with breaking news. Rioting had spread to most metropolitan cities across the U.S. The president would be coming on TV to address the current problems with all the rioting and racial violence.

My wife asked, "Mark, why are you watching the news? It's nothing but gloom and doom."

I replied, "Well it's good for us to keep up on current events so we can prepare to bug out or prepare for some kind of survival on our own."

"You're always going crazy with all that survivalist stuff. We're all right; we are miles from the nearest city, and all of that violence isn't going to affect us here. Why worry about it?"

I said, "Well, it's better to have it and be ready for it, than not to have it and not be ready for it when you need it."

The news continued with stories about martial law being called for in numerous cities across the country. Atlanta, which was only 65 miles from us, was one of them. Then the news anchor said, "The president is now ready to come on with his announcements."

The president walked to the podium and proceeded to tell us about all the violence in the different cities across the nation. In addition, he said that he was going to have to take drastic measures even though he didn't want to. He was going to have to institute curfews and martial law in some metropolitan and densely populated areas. More restrictions and curfews could follow if the violence did not cease.

The Drive To Work

It's a 30 minute drive on Georgia 400 to the city of Cummings, where I worked as a maintenance technician for a plastic injection molding factory, 9 PM to 7 AM, four nights a week.

I told my wife that it was time for me to get ready and go to work. "See you in the morning." I gave her a kiss and hug.

I went into my ten year old son Zach's room. As usual, he was playing one of his video games. I came up behind him and began tickling him. He started laughing and said, "Stop, dad, stop! You're messing up my game!" I gave him a hug, and told him I was off to work.

I grabbed my travel bag and my 9mm Beretta. I checked the rounds in the magazine and went out to my truck. As I started the engine, I noticed my gas gauge. My tank was getting low. Damn, I was going to have to stop and get gas on the way in tonight. On the way to work, I saw large numbers of police sitting in different locations. I got off the highway near work to go to the minimart for gas. I saw several large groups of people hanging around. In the minimart where I stopped to get gas there was also a large group of people, and they looked to be on the rowdy side. After getting out of my truck, I grabbed my Beretta and put it in the back of my pants in a way that the crowd could see that I was armed. As I started to pump the gas, several from the group broke off and came my way. I stopped pumping the gas and I turned to face them, reaching my arm behind me to grasp my Beretta. They stopped and looked me over. They saw that I was standing my ground, reaching for something behind me. They turned and went back to their group. I guess they decided I was not an easy target.

At work, my coworkers had lots of stories about incidents that happened to them on their way into work. One coworker was attacked by a crowd and didn't make it in to work. Two other coworkers were stopped in roadblocks by police and questioned about their firearms that they had with them. Everyone was scared and worried. Some of my co-workers said, "We are taking our lives in our hands just driving to work now". Production was slow and uneventful that night.

In the morning, I left work and headed home. I saw the evidence of violence that had happened in the area overnight: burned out cars, trash in the streets, broken windows, and boarded-up storefronts. I made it home safely with no noticeable events. At home, I talked with my wife and son for a while and sent him off to school. Then I went to bed for some sleep.

Work Night Two.

I woke up about 4 o'clock in the afternoon. As I was fixing my coffee and waking up, my wife told me about the news flashes that had been on TV all day. I got my coffee and went to my computer to check things out and see what was going on. As I browsed through the news websites, there were lots of website issues. It looked like half of the news websites had been hacked, and the internet was unreliable. I went to the TV to see what news I could find there and turned on CNN. The same old news stories were on about the violence. I couldn't get any local up-to-date information.

As my wife was cooking dinner, I went to inventory my survivalist supplies and organize everything to see where I was short. I made up a list of miscellaneous items that I needed to add to my supplies. Zach complained that the internet kept going out, and that he couldn't play his video games. My wife said dinner was ready, so we sat down and tried to get some news.

The local news was finally on and had numerous stories of violence around the area. They also said that the governors of several states were calling for martial law in the metropolitan areas of their states. Locally, Atlanta was one of the cities where martial law would be enforced, starting that night. Roadblocks and checkpoints would be set up at the entrances of most cities where violence was occurring. Travel would be restricted in those areas. Anyone carrying firearms into a violence-stricken area would have those firearms confiscated. Curfews were being set in violent areas from dusk until dawn. They gave a list of cities and areas with curfews, but did not detail areas with the roadblocks or where they were confiscating firearms.

I switched over to Fox News network. The news reporters there were complaining about restrictions on what they could report concerning violence, the response of authorities and how they were handling the violence in certain areas.

It was time for me to leave for work. I hopped into my truck with my gear. On my way into work on the highway that night, I saw a lot of military vehicles. I exited the highway near the factory. Within a block from the highway, I came to a roadblock checkpoint. The police officers approached my vehicle and asked me to step out of the vehicle. I went to the back of the truck and waited. Two officers stood talking to me while another looked through my truck. One officer asked if I was armed or had any firearms in my vehicle. I replied, "Yes, I have a handgun for self-defense, due to all of the violence in the area." They said they would have to confiscate my handgun and told me not to bring any weapons to this area again. There was nothing I could do; I had to surrender my handgun. At work, my coworkers reported having had similar issues happen to them on their way in to work. The management came out and stated that things were slowing down, and that we shouldn't count on a full workweek in the weeks to come. The work night was uneventful.

On my way home, I was stopped at the same checkpoint and questioned, but was not asked to get out of the vehicle. On the way home, I continued to see more military vehicles on the highway. When I got home, I told my wife what had happened. I was really pissed that they took my handgun, because the 9mm Beretta was my only concealable handgun and now I was down to my .44 Magnum revolver, which is big and bulky, and a .22 revolver that I did not feel was adequate for a self-defense weapon. I didn't know what weapon I was going to carry with me to work from now on. Well, I had to go to bed and get some sleep. I'd worry about it after I got up.

Work Night Three.

I did not sleep well worrying about the events that had occurred yesterday. I got up around 3 o'clock, fixed my coffee and started waking up. I checked the Internet and found it was totally down, not working at all. I clicked on the TV to check out the news channels. They covered the same old stories about the continuing violence across the country, such as police and protesters clashing, having shootouts, how many people were being shot and arrested.... But one report caught my eye and was interesting. It was about a clash between National Guard troops and local police forces. I hoped to get more information on this report, but the regular newscast was interrupted by an emergency broadcast about the expansion of martial law in the Atlanta area. It would now cover the urban areas outside the city. Regular military troops were now being used in some areas to replace the National Guard where martial law had been instituted.

The regular news then continued with the story about NASA and the Russian cooperation in deep space exploration. NASA would be launching six rockets. Two from Cape Canaveral, two from Houston, and two from Los Angeles. Once in outer space, the rockets would separate from their boosters and connect to construct a single large interstellar space craft with a new ion propulsion system in order to explore distant planets and the universe. NASA expected to start receiving photographs and data from the spacecraft in about one year.

It was about this time the phone rang. It was work. I answered the phone, and they told me that there would be no work that night and to check back the next afternoon. Due to the violence and protests in Fulton County, area traffic was restricted and night shift work had been canceled until further notice.

I said to my wife, "Well, it looks like we are starting to be affected now. I guess we'll need to go to Walmart, grab up whatever supplies we can and hunker down and dig in for a little while." We continued watching the news and then popped in a movie to kick back and relax for a while. Then we went to bed. We'd see what tomorrow would bring.

Day Four.

The next day we got up and got ready for a supply run to Walmart. I got my list of needed supplies. I decided to go to the bank first to get cash because I was guessing that the credit cards wouldn't be working at the stores due to the Internet being down and all the other electronic communication problems. My wife said she was in the middle of doing laundry and wanted to stay home and finish. She asked me to go on to Walmart without her. I got in the truck and headed to Walmart. In the store, I saw it was packed with people going nuts, buying up all kinds of things, everything that they could get their hands on. It was a real challenge fighting the crowds of crazy people. Nevertheless, I managed to grab some supplies, canned goods, flashlight batteries, duct tape, bottled water. I even got some ammo (shotgun shells, buckshot, turkey loads and a couple boxes of slugs). Then I got the heck out of there. Back home I unloaded the truck and told my wife about all the crazy people at the store. We'd need to get ready for self-dependence here at home.

I did a reassessment of my supplies. I combined some of my packs to conserve space: my hunting pack and my bug-out pack. I got to thinking about all the stuff I heard on the news and decided that sooner or later they would be coming around to try to take away my guns. I knew I would need some guns for self-defense, so I decided to keep them handy. I only had three handguns left after my Beretta was confiscated. My .44 Magnum Smith & Wesson, my .22-caliber revolver and a .44-caliber old army cap & ball black powder revolver. I also had a good paintball gun that I knew, if loaded with jawbreaker candies, would put a hurt on someone. Therefore, I decided to keep the paintball gun loaded with jawbreaker candies handy. I didn't think they'd take away my pump pellet gun, either. I also had two .22 caliber rifles, one bolt action Mossberg, a Ruger 10/22, a Ruger model 77 in .35 Whelen caliber, a 12 gauge Mossberg model 835, a 12 gauge Ithaca model 37 deer slayer and a 9mm MP5. I decided to keep the .44 Magnum by my bed. The .22 caliber I would keep out in the kitchen for my wife to use in an emergency. The paintball gun I'd keep by the front door loaded with the jawbreakers candies. In the gun cabinet, I'd leave the pellet gun, 303 British, one of the .22 rifles, a .50 caliber black powder rifle and some ammo for each. The other guns I would take down to the basement.

Our basement had a dirt floor, and there was a workbench down there. I thought I could move the workbench and dig a pit in the dirt floor and put a cabinet or wooden box in there with those guns and then set the workbench back on top of the hole. I decided I'd better hide all my reloading equipment, supplies and the extra ammunition. I'd dig another hole in the basement floor in another location for that stuff. I got to work doing this little project.

After taking a shower and getting cleaned up from the work,

my wife said that dinner was ready. We sat down to check out the news and see if we could get any more information on what was happening.

The big event on the news that day was about Texas. Texas had petitioned Congress to secede from the United States. Texas had closed its borders to all non-residents, including federal representatives. Oklahoma, Arizona, and New Mexico were talking about joining the Texas coalition. Texas was placing the Texas Rangers on all roads leading into their state. Homeland Security and the president had ordered military troops to the Texas border. Texas Gov. Carry said that he didn't want any trouble or violence with the United States; he just didn't feel that the government was handling the violent problems in the correct manner. He believed that the state government could do a better job of protecting the rights of the citizens of Texas. He announced that any police actions or power brought against the Texas Rangers or the territory of Texas would be responded to with force.

All non-residents of Texas were being asked to leave. Military soldiers who were stationed within the borders of Texas and were not residents were being given the option to become residents and stay in Texas, or to surrender their military equipment and leave. The president of the United States stated that all military equipment inside the borders of Texas belonged to the United States of America, not Texas, and that Texas must surrender that equipment to the United States of America. Fox News said that they would keep us up-to-date on breaking news concerning what was going on in Texas.

Fox News was also reporting that Homeland Security was setting up two kinds of camps. Some of these camps were detention centers for those citizens who had been arrested for violent acts and protesting. Others were FEMA camps, where peaceful residents could be moved "for respite." The announcement stated: "For a list of areas that are being evacuated, go to homelandsecurity.gov or call the number that is scrolling across the bottom of your screen. Citizens that need to evacuate or need assistance evacuating can contact Homeland Security for help. FEMA camp locations are listed on our website at homelandsecurity.gov. Homeland Security and other authorities in the suburbs and rural areas are restricting travel. Citizens who need food and other supplies will be able to get them at supply centers being set up by Homeland Security. All stores and businesses will be closed until further notice in all problem areas. Homeland Security and Red Cross representatives will be going door to door with surveys for the medical needs of the people in the household. They will be handing out pamphlets at the food service centers to get a list of people who need medicines and the types of medicines that they need. All of this is due to martial law rules and regulations being enforced by Homeland Security and is for the safety of the citizens of the United States of America. Anyone caught traveling the roads after sunset or before sunrise will be arrested and taken to a detention center. Stay tuned to Fox News and the emergency broadcast channels for updates on developing events in your area."

Then the news went off the air, and tickertape information scrolled across the screen about violence in different areas around the country.

"Wow, things are really getting bad now," I said to my wife. "I think I need to call my sisters in New York and my brother in Savannah and see how they are faring through all of this. I'll find out what's happening in their areas. We really haven't been in close contact with each other since our parents died a year ago."

I called my brother in Savannah first, and his wife answered the phone. I was using the cell phone and the connection was very garbled, so I decided to use the landline and see if that was any better. I called back and I was able to hear my brother's wife better. She told me that my brother had been reactivated into the Army Rangers and was not at home. She was very worried and scared about the situation and all of the violence in her area. Everyone was restricted to their homes and not allowed to leave.

I told her, "Well, I would come and get you, but it's a five hour drive from here to Savannah and I'm not sure that Homeland

Security would allow me to drive that far. You're just going to have to hunker down and do the best you can for now. I'll come and get you as soon as I can. Maybe Brian will be able to do something for you sooner. I need to call my sisters Lori and Lisa in New York and see how they're doing. I'll get back to you when I can."

There was a lot of clicking sounds on the landline phone, but other than that I was able to hear okay. I called my sister Lori. She only had a cell phone. It was very garbled. I could hardly understand anything she said. I gave up trying to call her and I tried my sister Lisa. I was able to get her, and she said no one's bothered her or come around her place. "Being so far out in the sticks, it may be a while before anybody comes around my place."

She was not near any cities or towns, and due to the roadblocks and travel restrictions, they were pretty much just staying home. I told her to get ahold of Lori and get Lori over to her house and then just stay put.

My wife's family was killed in an earthquake in California a few years ago. She didn't have any family to call. I said to my wife, "Well, I guess tomorrow we'll go into town, check out the food service center, and see what kind of news we can pick up there."

So for the rest of the night we sat at the table playing cards, and our son stayed in his room playing video games. He still couldn't play online. He was taking everything fairly well.

Around 9 o'clock at night, I went outside and made a perimeter check around our house, making sure everything was okay. All looked fine. I fed the dog and went back into the house. Just as I was getting ready to set my perimeter alarms around the outside of the house, I heard a knock at our front door. It was our neighbor Jim, from across the street. He looked a bit anxious, and I asked him to come in. I asked what was up? He was in the Army reserve. He told me that he had some important information for me.

He said, "As you know, I'm in the Army reserve, and I was reactivated. Shortly after I reported for duty, I discovered things were not exactly right anymore. They were asking us to invade neighborhoods, fire on American citizens and kick down doors.

We were to confiscate any firearms that we found, arrest anyone that had any type of information about or associations with the protesters or were involved in the violence that's going on around the country. This looked too much like Nazi Germany to me. So, first chance I got, along with several other soldiers, defected and returned to our homes and families. We need to be very cautious and suspicious of any authorities, especially Homeland Security."

I told him that the next day we were going to the food center, and we'd see what kind of information we could get while we were there. He said that probably was not a good idea, especially for men. Nevertheless, his family also needed food and other supplies. He recommended that we send our wives and keep watch from a distance. "Maybe up on Crown Mountain near the water tower. We can see the town center from there."

I agreed, and we decided to send our wives down together. We would watch from a safe distance, where we could possibly rescue them, if necessary. At 10 o'clock the next morning, we would initiate the plan. He went back home.

I set the perimeter alarms. They were just homemade devices, with lightweight strings and cans and wires that made noise that sounded an audible alarm if somebody tried to enter our house or disturb our vehicles. I also had an electric fence charger that I hooked up to our vehicle so if anyone tried to steal our gas, they would get a good zap. The fence charger was solar powered and charged a battery that would run all night. We went to bed and wondered how things would go the next day.

Day Five.

We got up around 7 AM. My wife started cooking breakfast and I clicked on the TV to get the morning news. Fox News had breaking news of military forces and police forces having conflicts in some suburban and metropolitan areas. While the local police forces were attacking a group of violent protesters, the national guardsmen who were in the area sided with the protesters and fired on the local police force. The local police force retreated and called in a regular Army military unit to defend them. The regular Army military would not fire on the national guardsmen, and the national guardsmen would not fire on the regular Army military. That just left a standoff, both sides trying to figure out what the other side was going to do. Word of this spread to other National Guard and regular military units across the country. As of that moment, there were several other National Guard and regular military groups across the country in standoffs in cities across the country. The president and secretary of defense were calling for calm and the unification of our forces.

Homeland Security had recruited the NSA, FBI, TSA, ATF and other federal agencies as enforcers in curbing violence and other problems around the country. Homeland Security had equipped them with military vehicles and firearms. All citizens were being asked to remain in their homes regardless of where they lived. All reserve and National Guard personnel who had not already been called into active service were now being required to report to their units for duty. Any service members who did not report to their duty stations within 24 hours would be considered deserters. The United Nations had offered to send peacekeepers here to the United States. They would be Russian and Chinese soldiers due to the conflict of interests of US military forces being required to fire on their neighbors, friends and family. Then the news went on to describe other events where people were being rounded up and put in the FEMA camps and detention centers all over the country. Texas, Oklahoma, New Mexico and Arizona were still in a standoff with the United States.

Then the news channel went off the air and tickertape started scrolling across the screen with bits of information. One of the tickertape news bits scrolling across the screen said that the news media was not being allowed to show the arrival of Russian and Chinese soldiers on US soil. "Public Notice: the Russian and Chinese soldiers are under the command of the United Nations and are not an invading force."

I went out and secured my alarm system, and then Jim came over from next door. We talked and decided not to tell the girls about our plan. We were just going to say that we were sending them to get some food and other odds and ends from the food service center and to get any kind of information pamphlets that were being handed out. We also told them not to give out any information about where we lived, how many people there were in our household and warned them not fill out any of the questionnaires. We tried not to scare them anymore than they already were. The authorities were not bothering women and children. Our wives took our sons and they went off to the food service center. Jim and I hopped in my truck and went to the top of the hill overlooking the town and food distribution center. I brought my binoculars and .44 Magnum. Jim also brought binoculars and was armed.

As we approached the top of the hill that overlooked the town where we were going to observe our wives, we noticed some official looking vehicles up there and suspected that Homeland Security also had some lookouts there. I pulled the truck into a residence driveway. There didn't seem to be anybody home, so we just left the truck there and went on foot to the top of the hill, watching out for any authorities that might be in the area. We saw a couple of guys in Homeland Security blue uniforms. But they were just standing by their vehicles talking, so we easily avoided them and stayed out of sight. We found a good position to observe the food service center and our wives. Down below there was a big tent set up and a large crowd of people. The line of people leading to the tent was extremely long. As our wives got closer to the tent, we noticed some people handing out pamphlets and our wives took them, as we had asked.

It was about this time when a disturbance broke out near the tent. We watched closely and noticed two men wearing turbans on their heads yelling something. The crowd of people by the tent moved to get a better view of what was happening. Then the two men that were yelling suddenly blew up. The explosion wasn't very strong, but there was a cloud that looked like white smoke or mist coming from the explosion area. All of the people down there scattered and ran for their vehicles, our wives included. After seeing that our wives safely made it to the car and out of there, we picked up our things, went to my truck, and headed back to the house to wait for them.

Jim said that it looked like some kind of chemical explosion, maybe even biological.

The wives came down the road and pulled into Jim's driveway. Jim and I ran over there to meet them. As soon as our wives and kids got out of the vehicle, Jim told them to stand by the car and not move. Jim got the garden hose and started spraying them down. It was a bit chilly outside, and they started screaming at Jim. "What are you doing?"

Jim told them to turn around. "I'm washing you guys off! There was a chemical explosion down there, you could be contaminated with chemicals or a biological agent. I'm trying to wash it off. You hold still!"

Jim said, "Okay, everybody in the house, strip those clothes off and put them in plastic bags. Get new clothes on after you take a shower. Be sure to wash thoroughly!"

As our wives and kids got cleaned up, I went outside to talk to Jim. He was standing outside by his car, looking at some of the pamphlets that the girls picked up at the food service center. The pamphlets were mostly questionnaires with lots of personal questions: where we lived, how old we were, how many people were in our household, if we any firearms in our household, and what medicines we took.

At about this time, the dogs started barking for no reason that we could see or hear. Then they suddenly went quiet. Too quiet. We looked at each other and both thought, *what the hell is happening now?* Jim's wife came out of the house and said that all of our electricity was out. We looked at each other and at the same time said "EMP!"

I went back to my house and Jim went into his. At our house, the power was also out. Zach's video game console was also dead. I checked my cell phone and it was dead too. I went outside, jumped in my truck and turned the key. Nothing. It was dead. Well, it was definitely an EMP. There would be no TV, no radio, and no more news I guess.

My wife said, "Mark, what are we going to do now without any electricity?"

I said, "I don't know, but don't panic, we will survive. We'll just have to wait it out for a bit and see what happens."

My wife said, "Well I guess we'll fix some lunch. The gas stove still works, but we'll have to light it with a match."

As we sat eating our lunch, we heard a vehicle outside and looked up. There was a Homeland Security Van and an ambulance. One ambulance attendant and one Homeland Security officer came to my house, and the other two went to Jim's house. When I asked them about the electricity or a possible EMP, they said the power should be back on shortly. Just stay tuned to the radio and TV. I didn't bother to ask the dumbasses how we were supposed to do that without any electricity, but I kept my mouth shut. They offered no other information. They wanted information from us. One of the questions they asked was if anyone was near the food service center when the incident took place earlier. I thought it was okay to tell them that my wife and son were there. They examined both of them. They took blood samples from each of them. Then they left some questionnaires like the ones my wife picked up at the food service center and said they'd be back tomorrow.

My wife was scared and said, "What the hell was all that out about?"

I said, "Don't worry about it; it's just government red tape crap."

I thought to myself, "I'm thinking they know a lot more than they are telling us." But I didn't want to voice my concerns to my wife and scare her even more, so I kept this to myself. My wife always saw the world through rose-colored glasses; the bad things that happen on the news only happen to other people and other places. Not here, not to us. As evening approached, the power did not come back on. There was nothing for us to do, so we decided to go to bed. My wife got out her digital-readout blood-sugar device that she bought for her and Zach to keep track of their blood-sugar levels. I went outside, set the perimeter alarms, and checked on the dog. Then I went in the house to go to bed.

My wife said that the digital glucose meter was not working. She had to use the old one to check their levels. She added that we needed to get more insulin.

I had never thought about the high tech digital medical devices being affected by an EMP before now. That was not good at all! What about people with pacemakers?

Day Six.

I woke up around 6 AM. My wife was still asleep, but felt hot and sweaty, so I decided to wake her up.

I asked her, "Are you okay?"

She answered, "No, I'm not feeling very well. I'm cold, and I ache all over."

"Okay, I'll see what kind of medicine I can find for you, and I'll go check on Zach." I went to Zach's room to check on him. He was the same way, sweaty and hot. I didn't wake him, but I returned to my wife and told her about Zach. She said that she would move into his room so that it would be easier for me to take care of them both. I agreed that it was a good idea. But I had information that I wasn't willing to share with her at that time. I did not believe there was much I could do for either my wife or my son. They both needed professional medical treatment, and the only way I was going to be able to get that for them would be to protect myself and keep myself healthy long enough to at least get some help for them. If I was going to protect myself, it would be easier if I keep them quarantined in Zach's room. I got rid of the blankets and stuff from our bedroom. It might be too late for me already, but I had do what I could and hope for the best. I gave them some aspirin, a couple more blankets to keep them warm, and a bottle of water each.

I put on some rubber gloves and a facemask, got the bedding off my bed, and put it into a plastic garbage bag. I took the garbage bag of their clothes from yesterday and the bedding from our bed down to the back yard to burn them. As I was down there, preparing a fire pit to burn the clothing, I got bit by a damn spider. It hurt, a lot! Immediately my leg turned red and started to swell up. I thought it must have been a black widow that bit me. I got the fire burning hot and went up to the house to get some first-aid cream for the spider bite. The power was still out, and the phones did not work. There was nothing more I could do except wait for the Red Cross people to come back.

It was late in the afternoon when I was lying on the couch, not feeling so well myself, when there was a knock at the front door. It was the Red Cross EMT that had visited yesterday.

He said, "You're not looking so good."

"Yeah, thanks a lot. I'm not feeling so good either, and my wife and son are a lot worse. They're in this room over here."

I sat in a chair at the kitchen table and waited for him to come back out of Zach's room after examining them. When he emerged, he said that he had given them some medicine and left some more on the nightstand by the bed. Then he checked me out, and I told him about the spider bite.

He looked at it and said, "Yeah that does look like a black widow that got you. I'll give you some antibiotics for it. You should be okay in a day or two. I'll be back to check on all of you tomorrow. I have a lot more people I have to go see and check on right now. Take care, and get lots of rest."

I wasn't feeling good at all, so I went and laid down on the couch. I fell asleep and had some wild dreams. At one point, I even fell off the couch.

Day seven.

The next thing I knew, it was morning. I wasn't feeling any better and could hardly move. I knew I needed to check on my wife and son. I tried to get up, but I just couldn't. Then I saw images of people and felt myself being moved. I went in and out of consciousness.

Chapter 2

Lyndon B. Johnson Space Center Houston Texas.

Two scientists, Борис (Boris) Zakharov and Анна (Anna) Salko, were on "loan" to NASA's Houston Control Center from Russia.

Republican Sen. Thomas Kane of Texas was at the Control Center for the launch of the deep space rockets. Sen. Kane was meeting with the chief scientist of the deep space program. Chief scientist Boris Zakharov and chief engineer Anna Salko were explaining the stages of the launch to Sen. Kane.

Boris, a tall, heavy man with hair that was graying at the temples, spoke with a thick accent. He was saying that a space craft large enough to carry all the test equipment and propulsion sections into deep space would be too large to launch from a single rocket. Instead, two smaller rockets would be launched from each of three locations: Kennedy Space Center in Florida, George C. Marshall Space Flight Center at Redstone Arsenal in Alabama, and Armstrong Flight Research Center, Edward Air Force Base, California.

Anna, a short woman who was as wide as she was tall, said, "Once each of the rockets are synchronized in orbit around the earth, the satellite in the nose cone will detach. Each will be controlled from their respective control center to engage and hook up with its partner, creating a single large spacecraft capable of deep space travel."

Public relations officer, Capt. Heinz said, "Senator, another amazing aspect of this launch is the propulsion system. No liquid or solid fuel will be needed for this deep space exploration. We're going to use ion propulsion powered by the solar panels. We'll be able to observe the launches from the video screens here and then see the trajectory of the rockets as they achieve their orbit altitude over here on this screen." As he said this, he walked over to a large console where a man in a utility uniform was manning the instruments.

The countdown began in a tinny, mechanical voice: "Ten, nine, eight, seven, six, we have ignition, five, four, three, two, one and we have liftoff."

Capt. Heinz pointed. "There you see the trajectory of the rockets." He paused. "That's weird. The trajectory should be at East and West parallel to the equator. The trajectories are not right."

Boris said, "Excuse us. We have to check some instruments."

Boris and Anna beat a hasty retreat toward the exit. The tech Sgt. guarding the exit stopped Boris and Anna, saying, "No one is allowed to leave the control room at this time."

Capt. Heinz yelled, "Sergeant! Hold those two."

Suddenly, the video screens went blank and the lights went out. Battery-powered emergency lighting and reflective exit signs were the only lights in the building.

Sen. Kane said, "What the hell is happening?"

Capt. Heinz said, "I'm not sure, but I suspect our Russian comrades had something to do with it. Sgt., do not let them get away. Everybody outside."

Everyone headed for the exits or the main lobby. Outside there was total chaos. Fires and explosions could be seen in the distance. People were either wandering around in total confusion or running in panic.

Technical Sgt. Crandall handcuffed Boris and Anna to chairs and Capt. Heinz began questioning them. Neither Sen. Kane nor Capt. Heinz had the time nor the patience for proper interrogation, so they began to get rough with Boris and Anna. Finally, Boris and

Anna submitted. "It does not matter," smirked Boris. "It is too late to stop it anyhow."

Boris and Anna said that the plan was to undermine the US economy so that the Russians and her new allies, the Chinese, could take control of the United States of America without going to war.

In his heavily accented English Boris bragged, "The Chinese and Russian students are really here to incite riots and protests to a point where your economy is brought to a standstill. Then China and Russia will send in peacekeeping forces to help control the violence."

"You see, this has already happened. We are already here on your soil. After the students did their job, we, the scientists and engineers of Russia, were sent to NASA to build rockets for deep space exploration. Yes, we build rockets, but the rockets disguised as deep space exploration were really non-nuclear E.M.P. tactical missiles that have detonated over most of the US, knocking out all your power and communications. Now Russia has the United States of America in iron grip. You lose, United States."

Capt. Heinz and Sen. Kane got enough information from Boris and Anna to confirm Boris' words. The Russians were behind an EMP attack on the US.

Sen. Heinz said, "We need to get in touch with the governor and notify the military immediately."

Capt. Heinz said, "All of our communications are down and none of our vehicles work. No one is going anywhere."

Sgt. Crandall thought for a moment. "An EMP would not affect the older vehicles, correct?"

Capt. Heinz agreed. "That's correct, but where are we going to find any?"

Sgt. Crandall said, "The auto pool is not very far from here and they have some old Jeeps and trucks there. Maybe we could get one of those running."

Capt. Heinz found some security officers and had them take custody of Boris and Anna. Sgt. Crandall took Capt. Hayes and Sen. Kane to the motor pool. With some help from the mechanics there, they were able to get two of the older military jeeps running.

Sen. Kane turned to Capt. Haynes. "We need to get a message to Gov. Carry and the rest of our military as soon as possible."

Capt. Haynes frowned. "With communications and transportation down that's going to be very difficult."

Sen. Kane asked, "Are there any planes around here that we could use?"

Sgt. Crandall said, "There's an old B-23 Dragon that's been converted to a transport plane in one of the hangers at the airstrip. The mechanics believe it will still operate, but we'll need a pilot to fly it."

Sen. Kane nodded. "I'm a pilot, and I've flown a wide variety of planes. I'm sure I can figure it out."

Capt. Haynes said, "I'm also a pilot, and I've flown the larger transport planes myself. Let's give it a shot."

When they got to the motor pool, Sen. Kane told the mechanics about the Russians and the EMP attack. He wrote a quick note to the governor and handed it to one of the mechanics along with his Senate ID badge, telling him to deliver this to the governor ASAP. He said, "This Senate ID badge should help authenticate the letter and get you in to speak with the governor."

Then, Sgt. Crandall took Sen. Kane and Capt. Heinz to the hangar where the B-23 Dragon was being stored.

At the hanger, they were able to find some of the tarmac crew, who helped them fuel up and get the plane ready for flight. The B-23 Dragon was a plane from the Cold War and its electronics were hardened against EMP attack. Capt. Heinz took the pilot seat, Sen. Kane took the copilot seat, and Sgt. Crandall took the navigator's position.

They taxied down the runway and took off without tower control or radar. Due to the fires and devastation of the crashing commercial flights in the area, they were forced to take a westerly course. This enabled them to make contact with the Pacific TACAMO plane. Bringing Rear Adm. James Taylor up to date about the Russian EMP attack, they then returned to Johnson Space Center in Houston. Rear Adm. Taylor then gave orders to the Pacific submarines to fire an EMP attack on Russia and China.

Islamic terrorists, already having a strong foothold in Europe, launched devastating attacks all across Europe. At the same time, the canine flu was sweeping across Europe and spreading to the rest of the world.

In the Middle East, the Palestinians and the Israelis suddenly realized there were no human powers capable of intervening. This time the war would go on until a conclusion. The regiments of Israel, Jordan, Syria and Saudi Arabia were on the march. There were no jet planes and little fuel for tanks. There would be no ammunition resupply. This time the war would not end, even if fought with knives.

Looking Glass, Hummingbird One.

Aboard the Looking Glass somewhere over the United States.

Red warning lights flashed across the electrical communication panels indicating satellite communication failure. "Hummingbird One to Neptune One, Hummingbird One to Neptune One, come in, over."

The communications officer said, "General, we've lost communications with STRATCOM and all our military forces in the continental United States, including the president and vice president. We've lost communication with our satellites, and it'll be another four hours before another satellite gets within range. Our navigation radar is out; air and ground radar is unreliable. We only have communication with the Navy's TACAMO plane in the Atlantic, and we only have enough fuel to stay airborne for one more hour."

"Damn it!" Gen. Harrington shouted. "Tell me what the hell is happening. Did someone nuke us?"

"No sir, no missile launches were detected and no nuclear blasts were detected before our radar went out. The only missile launches we know about were from NASA. The deep space exploration rockets launched 10 minutes ago. Two from Kennedy

Space Center Florida, two from Marshall Space Center, Redstone Arsenal Alabama, and two from Edwards Air Force Base, California.

"From our last intelligence reports, the communications said multiple suicide terrorist nonnuclear detonations occurred across the country. The offending groups were ISIS and Al Qaeda, backed by North Korea, Iran, Yemen, and other Islamic extremists in Middle Eastern countries."

Gen. Harrington said, "We need a tanker up here to refuel us."

"Lt. Col. Mullen says we have no contact with the air bases to call for a tanker. The Navy refueling tankers are too far away and too small to do us much good. Auxiliary aircraft like refueling tankers are most likely not EMP protected."

Gen. Harrington was calm and in command. "Move our alert status to 'cocked pistol DEFCON1.' This appears to be an EMP attack. Alert the Navy and any subs that you can contact with fire orders on North Korea, Yemen, Iran, Afghanistan, and Syria. Code word 'broken arrow,' authentication code, 'Hummingbird.' Tell Rear Adm. Ted Pickett of the Atlantic fleet that Hummingbird One is going down. He has command. This is going to be a manual override fire order. The president, vice president, and the rest of our government's status is unknown. We do not have the time to find the next government official in line to give us the launch codes."

He turned from the communications officer. "Okay boys and girls, we're going in for a manual landing if we can find a clear area big enough to put this bird down. Hang on to your butts!"

The communications officer said, "General, at any given time there are over 7,000 planes in the air over the US. Half of those planes will be either landing or taking off from airports. An EMP would disrupt all their controls, navigation, communications and radar. Air-traffic control will also be out. Every airport in the affected area will have multiple plane crashes and collisions. The other planes still in the air, including private aircraft, news helicopters and most military aircraft will all be crashing down."

Gen. Harrington shook his head. "The damage and loss of life will be unimaginable. Just think of all the planes crashing into populated areas. Fires and explosions of proportions beyond imagination."

Gen. Harrington face changed from sorrow back to being in charge. "Tell the pilot to look for some place for us to land other than an airport."

Looking Glass had gone down in the Allegheny National Forest, Pennsylvania, 12 miles north of the town of Pigeon. Most of the crew were killed or severely injured. Lieutenant Colonel Jack Mullen was a tall thin man in his late 40s, clean-shaven with short, salt and pepper hair, and had a professional Air Force career personality. He quickly took stock of the devastation around him. He could see Technical staff Sgt. Rebecca Williams, an attractive young woman in her mid-20s with shoulder length auburn hair and a shapely figure. She always had an outgoing, friendly personality. It had taken a while for the rest of the team to accept her, but she had proven herself capable of any task and had earned their mutual respect. FBI agent Greg Forster was a rough, muscular man that gave the appearance of a barroom bouncer. He was in his late 40s with a crude but professional personality. He was sitting up, and looked in pretty good shape, considering. NBC news reporter Todd Adams was in his late 20s. He had long hair, wore a leather jacket and was always friendly; he really knew how to get people to open up to him.

Mullen had no idea where they were. They would have to wait for rescue. The survivors gathered to discuss the situation. Todd looked around at the wreckage and summed up the situation. "This is it. All the injured have died, including Gen. Harrington. We're all that's left."

Lt. Col. Mullen said, "I guess that leaves me as the highest ranking officer in charge." Sgt. Williams was putting a bandage on Mullen's arm. Mullen said, "It's a miracle that any of us survived this crash."

Agent Forster said, "Maybe were not as lucky as the others. Now we get to starve or freeze to death in the middle of fucking nowhere."

Sgt. Williams frowned at Forster. "The only reason we survived is because the pilots dumped all the remaining fuel before we crashed so the plane didn't explode. They gave us the best chance of surviving that they could. Let's not throw that away."

Lt. Col. Mullen said, "As long as the weather holds we can use the supplies from the crash to hold up here for about a week. We need to start gathering up all the supplies we can from the wreckage and get a fire going."

Agent Forster snorted, "How the hell do you think we're going to get a fire going, rub two sticks together like Indians?"

Todd said, "I'll start getting some wood together to build a fire."

Sgt. Williams said, "I'll help you."

Lt. Col. Mullen said, "Forster, you and I will start going through the wreckage and gathering all the supplies."

Then the group all met back at the crash site next to the fuselage that they were using for shelter.

Lt. Col. Mullen said, "We gathered food and clothing from the wreckage. There was quite a bit of freeze-dried food in the galley which survived the crash. We also found pots, pans, and some silverware, so we can cook and heat this stuff up. We have about four gallons of water. After that, we'll have to melt snow. We have some coveralls from the guys who didn't make it. They're not too badly damaged, so we should be able to dress warm enough for this weather as long as it doesn't get too bad."

Sgt. William said, "Todd and I found several armloads of firewood, but we are going to have some trouble getting it going because it's all wet and covered with snow."

Agent Forster said, "Yeah, all of this is great, but do any of you have matches or a lighter?"

Todd said, "You know smoking was not allowed on board Looking Glass. So, there was no need for matches or a lighter."

Agent Forster said, "Fucking great because of the no smoking rules. We have no way to start a fire. So were going to freeze to death out here."

Lt. Col. Mullen said, "Chill out Forster! We'll get this figured out."

Todd said, "I found my survival pack, and I have a few things in there that we could probably use. I have a fire starter kit in there. It's only flint and steel, but I think I can get a fire going with it."

Todd started clearing the snow away from the area in front of the fuselage that they were going to be using for shelter. Then he started breaking up small sticks and pieces of bark and laying them in a pile. He took the flint and steel and started hitting them together, sending the sparks on to the small pile of sticks and bark.

Agent Forster said, "Well, big shot news reporter, it doesn't look like your caveman skills for starting fires is working out very well."

Todd said, "Everything's too cold and wet. I need something that's dry and will catch easily from the sparks."

Sgt. William suggested, "How about some pocket lint, will that work?"

Agent Forster said, "Hold on, maybe I can get you some bellybutton lint too."

Lt. Col. Mullen controlled his rising anger. "Forster, unless you've got something productive to contribute, shut your face!"

Todd said, "Yes, Rebecca, the pocket lint should work, gather me up a small bunch of it."

Todd took his flint and striker and the sparks caught on the pocket lint. With a little coaxing and some care, Todd had a fire going in a few minutes. They stacked the other wood close to the fire so that it could dry.

The survivors spent the next five cold days and even colder nights in the forest waiting for a rescue. Their doubts were growing. There had been no sign of rescue. Mullen was thinking that in order to survive, they were going to have to find their way out of the forest on their own. On the sixth day. Lt. Col. Mullen voiced his concerns. "It doesn't look like a rescue is going to be coming for us anytime soon. We need to start hiking out of here."

Agent Forster said, "And in which direction would that be?"

Todd said, "As long as we can keep walking in a straight direction we should come to a road within a few miles."

Forster said, "Okay, that sounds great. I hope you've got a compass in that bag too."

Sgt. Williams said, "In boot camp we had training on how to find our way by using the sun and the shadows." She picked up a stick and two rocks. She put the stick in the ground in a sunny area and placed one of the rocks at the tip of the shadow.

Agent Forster said, "I'm no outdoorsman, but I know you can't follow your shadow like a compass, because the sun and the shadows move."

Sgt. Williams said, "But we can use the movements of the shadow to determine which direction is north. In about ten minutes the shadow will move, and then I can get a bearing."

Ten minutes later, she placed the second stone at the point of the shadow. She then placed her left toe at the first marker and her right toe at the second marker and pointed straight ahead of her. "That," she said, "is approximately North."

Lt. Col. Mullen said, "Okay, let's say you're right, and that's north. How does that help us to determine which direction we should go?"

Agent Forster said, "We have no idea where we are and if we take off in the wrong direction, we could be walking for miles before we come to any signs of civilization. If we knew where we were, that would help us determine the right direction. It may be only a couple of miles to civilization if we choose the right direction. Choose the wrong direction and we could die of exposure or starvation before we find anything."

Sgt. Williams nodded. "I know we were over Pennsylvania when we crashed. But where in Pennsylvania we are at the moment, I do not know. Like agent Forster pointed out, if we pick the wrong direction we could be hiking for days before we find any civilization."

Lt. Col. Mullen said, "I think we should go East. East will take us toward the coast. The closer we get to the coast the denser the population. Therefore, the greater our chances are in finding civilization."

The group gathered up some supplies and prepared for the hike out of the forest in search of a town. Each put together a small survival pack with extra ammo, food, and water. Lt. Col. Mullen had a Glock 19 and a FN SCAR-L, Sgt. Rebecca Williams had a 9mm Beretta, M9 92FS, and an M16A4, agent Greg Forster had a SIG Sauer M11 and an M4A1 carbine, Ted Adams had a Beretta M9 and a Remington M870 pump 12 gauge shotgun. Agent Forster picked up a large, secure briefcase and handcuffed it to his wrist.

Todd asked Sgt. Williams, "What is that?"

Sgt. Williams said, "That's the TACCOM case. It contains the last orders from the general, launch code information and command procedures for our nuclear weapons. Whenever we establish communications with our military, Lt. Col. Mullen, being our highest ranking officer, will use the information in that case to authenticate our status and issue new orders as necessary."

Agent Forster said, "Don't even think about looking at it, big shot news man. I would have to kill you."

Just within earshot of Sgt. Williams, Todd said, "I'm sure he would lose a lot of sleep over that too."

After hiking eastward about four miles, the group came to a highway.

Agent Forster said, "A road. The first sign of civilization. I'll be damned! But I see no road signs. What road is this?"

Todd walked down the road a short distance and found a green mile marker sign. After studying the numbers on the sign, Todd said, "This is route 66, and by the numbers on the mile marker sign, I believe the closest town to be south of here."

The group decided that south was as good a direction as any, so they started hiking. Lt. Col. Mullen and Sgt. Williams lead the group south along Route 66 with agent Forster and Todd Adams brought up the rear. Along the way they found several abandoned vehicles, but no signs of people.

Todd said to Agent Forster, "Are there many women in special service?"

Agent Forster was looking at Sgt. Williams' rear end as she

walked alongside Lt. Col. Mullen. Forster said, "Yeah there's a few women in the special service, but they don't look as good as Williams does in that uniform."

Lt. Col. Mullen glanced back at Forster and Adams, then said to Sgt. Williams, "Would you take up the rear of our position, please?"

Agent Forster said, "Well now, Williams, you get to check out my ass now."

Sgt. Williams said, "Yeah, and if I happen trip on a stick, I just might shoot you in the ass for being a jerk."

Lt. Col. Mullen said, "Okay, knock it off and stay alert. We're coming into the town now."

They had been hiking about six miles when they came to a small community. The road sign outside the town said, "Welcome to Pigeon Pennsylvania, population 967." The group saw the occasional residence and an industrial complex, but no signs of people until they came to the Pigeon lodge and general store.

At first, the townspeople were suspicious of the group. They seemed not very trusting or friendly toward government or military personnel. Lt. Col. Mullen told the others in the group not to tell anyone that they were from the Looking Glass plane. Eventually Lt. Col. Mullen convinced the townspeople that they were no threat. The good people of Pigeon took in the survivors.

United States Strategic Command.

Red warning lights flashed across the electrical communication panels and the satellite communication failed. In the command center, the commanding officer picked up the red phone and said, "General Briggs, we've lost contact and communications with Looking Glass. All satellite communications are down to all our military forces in the continental United States, including the president and vice president. We have power, and all of our equipment is functioning normally, but there are no incoming feeds or communications from the outside. No missile launches were detected and no nuclear blasts were detected before our radar went out. The only missile launches we know about were from NASA. The deep space exploration rockets launched 10 minutes ago. Two from Kennedy Space Center Florida, two from Marshall Space Center, Redstone Arsenal Alabama, and two from Edwards Air Force Base, California."

"From our last intelligence reports, the communications said multiple suicide terrorist nonnuclear detonations occurred across the country. The offending groups were ISIS and Al Qaeda, backed by North Korea, Iran, Yemen, and other Islamic extremists in Middle Eastern countries."

Gen. Briggs said, "Move our alert status to 'Cocked Pistol DEFCON1.' This appears to be an EMP attack. We are supposed to be protected against this. Why is it that we cannot contact anyone?"

Maintenance officer Capt. Munro said, "We are protected and hardened against EMP attack. It's the rest of the world that is not protected. That's why we can't contact them. They can't hear us. The reason our satellite communications are down is because the equipment on the outside of this facility is new high tech stuff which wasn't hardened against EMP attack. It can easily be repaired by sending some crews to the surface, but we'll only have contact with others that are EMP protected. Any upgrades made after 1992 are not hardened against EMP attacks. Congress didn't think EMP hardening was a high enough threat to include in the budget."

Gen. Briggs said, "The president was aboard Air Force One flying to Florida for a fund raiser golf tournament. The vice president was aboard Air Force Two, returning from California. Do we have contact with either Air Force One or Air Force Two?"

The CIC officer said, "Communications with Air Force One and Air Force Two are down, status unknown."

Capt. Munro said, "The president's Air Fleet, Air Force One, Air Force Two, and both helicopters, are newer than 1995 which means they are most likely not hardened against EMPs."

Gen. Briggs said, "Fucking great! We're under modern-day attack and stuck blind down here because of budget cuts! Get maintenance crews on the problem immediately. If communications cannot be established in the next 24 hours with our missile silos, they'll go under automatic fire orders. We'll need to send a team to the surface to see what's going on and try to establish communications."

The CIC officer said, "At any given time there are over 7,000 planes in the air over the US. Many of those planes will be either landing or taking off from airports. An EMP would disrupt all of their equipment. You can also count air-traffic control out. Every airport in the affected area will have multiple plane crashes and collisions. Any other planes in the area will all be crashing down."

Gen. Briggs said, "We need to send a crew to the surface and get our communications back. Have First Sgt. O'Reilly take a maintenance team to the surface immediately." To himself he thought, "If Looking Glass is still in the air, they are experiencing the same things. They have the same equipment, and the crew has had the same training as my crew here. We have to reestablish contact."

First Sgt. Mason O'Reilly took his maintenance crew, Pfc. Frank Walker, Specialist Krystal Carter and Specialist Matthew Stevens, to the surface. They couldn't budge the main entrance door to the hole, so at the surface level, the team had to exit through the service access tunnel. The group stepped outside into a world of fire and devastation.

The team had to erect an antenna for communications. As they were working to complete the task of installing the antenna and wiring it, an SUV came speeding up the highway and crashed into a power pole. A woman got out of the van and came running toward them screaming, "Help me, help me!"

Specialist Carter left her work and headed in the direction of the frantic woman. Sgt. O'Reilly said, "Carter, come back here and finish your work!"

SPC Carter said, "That woman and those people need help."

Sgt. O'Reilly said, "We are at war and under strict security guidelines. We're not here to help anyone. Do your job!"

SPC Stevens said, "I'm going with Carter. We have to help them if we can."

Sgt. O'Reilly said, "Leave them and get back here to your duties. That's an order!"

Pfc. Walker said, "Sergeant, they are the technicians and we need them. I'll go see what I can do for the woman and the people in the van. That way Carter and Stevens can continue working on the antenna."

As Sgt. O'Reilly and the maintenance group approached the SUV, two men in Arab garb came out of the van and grabbed the woman. One of the Arab men yelled, "Praise and honor be to Allah. Death to the infidels!" Then they and the woman blew up in a white cloud.

The surprise and the shock wave from the blast knocked Sgt. O'Reilly and his maintenance group to the ground. Pfc. Walker yelled, "What the hell was that?"

SPC Carter asked, "Is everyone okay?"

Sgt. O'Reilly looked around and said, "Everyone seems to be okay. Now let's get back to work."

SPC Stevens was still shocked. He asked, "What was all that?"

Sgt. O'Reilly said, "Like I told you, we are at war. Those were Islamic extremists. The ones who've attacked the United States. We're lucky we weren't closer. We could've been killed. Now we need to complete our mission and get back in the hole!"

With the antenna completed, the group returned through the service tunnel, carefully securing the entrance. At ground level, walking down the hall past the visitor center, Specialist Carter stopped at one of the vending machines. She took some coins out of her pocket to buy a Kit Kat bar.

Sgt. O'Reilly said, "Carter, what the hell are you doing?"

Specialist Carter said, "I'm just getting a Kit Kat bar. They don't have any in the machines down the hole." Reilly shook his head.

The group continued down the hallway to the elevators. Taking the elevator back down into the hole. SPC Carter started eating her candy bar.

Upon exiting the elevator at the main subterranean level, they heard alarms and saw flashing lights. Several guards rushed the group, aiming their weapons at them and ordering them to remain where they were. SPC Carter dropped her candy bar onto the floor of the elevator.

Sgt. O'Reilly exclaimed, "What is this?"

Staff Sgt. of the Guard said, "First Sgt. O'Reilly, your team set off the contamination alarms. You and your team will have to report directly to decontamination."

A 4-man team in hazmat suits arrived and took the maintenance crew to Decontamination Area One. The decontamination doctor told Sgt. O'Reilly and the maintenance team that they had been exposed to radiation and an unknown biological agent.

Capt. Munro arrived for a status report in Mission Briefing. Still in decontamination, Sgt. O'Reilly gave his report to Capt. Munro. Sgt. O'Reilly described the fire and devastation of the airbase. He then described the events surrounding the crash of the SUV and the explosion of the Arab men. He also reported that the antenna, transmitter, receiver, booster, and communication lines had been installed and should be fully functional.

Dr. Evans of Decontamination Area One reported to Captain Munro that Sgt. O'Reilly and his team were exposed to low-level radiation and an unknown biological agent, most likely from the suicide bombs that were detonated by the Islamic terrorists.

Capt. Munro said, "Dr. Evans, have these soldiers been decontaminated and are they safe to continue with their duties?"

Dr. Evans said, "The radiation levels that they were exposed to are not high enough to be life-threatening to the maintenance team or to us. The biological agent has been cleaned from their bodies on the outside, and decontamination is complete. What physical effects or sicknesses they may encounter, I do not know. We'll keep them here under observation for 24 hours."

Capt. Munro said, "If there's any change in their condition inform me immediately. I need to take this information to Gen. Briggs. First Sgt. O'Reilly, you and your team are going to be here for a while, so get comfortable."

When he heard Captain Munro's report, Gen. Briggs asked,

"Now that the antennas is up, how long before we have some communications?"

Capt. Munro said, "The EMP would have taken out all satellites in line of sight from point of detonation. Meaning most of the satellites which were in the northern hemisphere over the United States will be inoperable. The other satellites, which were on the other side of the globe out of line of sight protected by the earth, should be okay. They'll be in our communication range in approximately three hours."

Gen. Briggs said, "With the president and vice president status' unknown, that leaves things up to us. What do we know about who attacked us?"

Col. Hayes said, "We don't know for sure. All we have are the usual suspects. What we do know is that Islamic terrorists have taken advantage of the EMP attack to launch attacks of their own."

Capt. Munro said, "The origin of the EMP attack and who ordered it would only be a guess."

Gen. Briggs said, "I'm going to give a fire order on ISIS and Al Qaeda in Syria, North Korea, Iran, Yemen, and Afghanistan. Then we will hold off until we get more information on who is behind the EMP attack. This is going to be a manual override fire order. The president, vice president, and the rest of our government's status is unknown. We don't have the time to find the next government official in line to give us the launch codes. Codeword: 'broken arrow,' authentication code, 'rabbit hole.'"

Capt. Munro typed the fire order code into the transmitter: broken arrow, Foxtrot, Oscar, Sierra, Neptune, Kilo, Indian, Yankee, Alpha 1, Zero, Niner, Zulu, rabbit hole.

Gen. Briggs said, "Continually broadcast our status and request the status of other government and military facilities. Of course, this needs to be encrypted, and I also want it in Morse code on short wave bands. Now we wait, and God help us."

As a K-9 unit was checking the elevator area, one of the dogs found the remains of the Kit Kat bar and started eating it. The next day Sgt. O'Reilly and his team became sick with flulike symptoms.

Apparently, the decontamination and quarantine was not 100% successful. Some of the guard dogs in the K-9 unit got sick and mutated, attacking their handlers. The disease escaped, spreading to all the personnel in the hole. Less than 30% survived.

Chapter 3

Post-event Day??

I woke up and looked around. My vision was a little foggy, and my head was a little dizzy, but I was still kicking, at least for now. I sat up and let my vision clear up a bit. I saw some bottles of medicine on the nightstand and a note. The note said, *I hope you're feeling better today. I'll be back to check on you tomorrow. There are some antibiotics for you on the nightstand. If you should wake up, take some.* At the bottom of the note it was signed *EMT Bob.* I saw there was a bottle of water there with the medicine, so I took the antibiotic as Bob instructed. I said to myself, 'Well, I need to go and check on my wife and son.' I got up a little weak in the knees, and I staggered a bit, but I was able to walk. I got to Zach's room; there was a note on the door. It said, *Sorry to inform you of this, but your son and wife have passed away. Due to the circumstances of the times, I did the best I could by burying them out in your backyard. My condolences, EMT Bob.* I looked out the back window and saw two fresh graves and wooden crosses. I closed my eyes. With a sigh, I said, "Thank you, EMT Bob."

I looked around trying to get some idea on what to do next. My head started to clear. I tried to think of what my best move would be now. I guess to drink some more water and find something to eat would be a start. I sat and drank half the bottle of water, and I started to feel a little bit better. I decided to go and take a shower and get cleaned up. I was a mess. EMT Bob could've at least put a diaper on me. Yuck! As I was taking a shower, I noticed that the water pressure was getting low. The power had still not come on, but the water was gravity fed from the water tower on top of Crown Mountain, a few miles from here.

It was time to kick into survival mode. I was going to have to think about a long-term survival situation here. Over 30 days, maybe six months, even a year, I couldn't be sure. I started filling up jugs with water before the water ran out. All I had were five empty jugs to fill. I would have to find some other water containers or hope that the water lasted for a while. On that note, I had to survey my surroundings and get myself up-to-date on what was going on. The gas stove was still working, so I heated up a can of soup and started going through some of my survival gear. That's when I noticed the .22 revolver was missing from the drawer in the kitchen. The paintball gun was also missing. I went to the bedroom. My .44 Magnum was missing, too. Crap! I went to my gun cabinet. The only guns left in there were my black powder guns. All my ammo and guns are missing. I thought, "Well, I guess I'll have to go dig up my stash and hope that they didn't find it." The soup hit the spot and I started to feel much better.

I went down into the basement. Nothing was disturbed down there, so I moved the workbench and started digging up my gun supply. I brought my guns and ammo upstairs and started looking stuff over, making sure everything was okay. I inventoried everything: 12 gauge model 37 Ithaca Deer Slayer, ammo, five boxes of slugs five rounds per box, five boxes of 00 buckshot five rounds per box and I had five boxes of turkey loads 10 rounds per box, five boxes of birdshot 25 rounds per box. I had my model 835 12 gauge Mossberg Ultra Mag, my 9mm MP5 with 200 rounds of ammunition, and my 35 Whelen with five boxes of ammo. I still had my reloading supplies and equipment with enough to load another few hundred rounds of ammo. I had five cans of black powder for the black powder guns. I had about 500 bullets for the .50 caliber rifle and I had 500 rounds of 240 grain for the black powder pistol and 1000 caps. My gun and ammo supply seemed to be okay, but I was without a handgun. I was a little limited on being discreet. I got some gear together to go next door and check on Jim.

I loaded the old army revolver, a black powder cap & ball gun. It was not the best weapon, but with the 240-grain lead bullets, I had confidence it would do the trick. I grabbed my Ithaca loaded with 00 buckshot. I grabbed two boxes of slugs and another box of buckshot which I put in my pocket. I felt the shotgun would probably be the best weapon for me to take to check things out because I was still a little weak and unsteady. I added a few light items to my travel pack like rubber gloves, dust masks, and garbage bags. Then I went outside and checked the perimeter of my house. All seemed normal with one exception. My dog was missing. The cable from the dog run near the clip that attached to his collar was broken off. I wondered how that broke? At least he got loose, so then he could fend for himself while I was sick. Maybe he'd come back home soon.

I walked across the street to Jim's house. All seemed quiet… but there was no sign of life anywhere. I looked in a window and everything seemed to be normal. I walked around the perimeter of his house. I did notice that out back he had some 55-gallon blue plastic drums. I made a mental note that these could be useful to catch rainwater. I went to the front door and knocked. I saw no movement and didn't hear any noise coming from inside the house. I tried the door, but it was locked. Then I noticed some symbols on the garage door. It looked like the symbols that I saw on TV after natural disasters. I believed these symbols were the same that Homeland Security used to let people know that the house had been checked, and what they found there. But I wasn't very familiar with the symbols, so they meant nothing to me. Then I looked back across the street toward my house and saw similar symbols written on it.

I retrieved my lock picks out of my pocket and started to pick the lock on the front door of Jim's house. It took me several tries, but I eventually got the door open. I cautiously went inside and looked around. The first thing I noticed was a foul odor, but nothing else seemed out of place. I went from room to room checking all the closed doors. I found nothing unusual, but noticed he had a gun cabinet in his office. I went to the gun cabinet and tried the door. It was locked. It needed a key and a combination. Maybe I could find the key somewhere. I came upon to the door that lead to the garage. It was locked too, but from the inside. I unlocked it and looked inside. Jim's cars were there and all looked normal.

I went back in the house and decided to investigate the upstairs. I went to the top of the stairs. Straight ahead was a bathroom; the door was open. To the right, back along the stairs, was a walkway. There were two doors that were closed. On the left was the same thing, a walkway that went back along the stairs and two doors that were closed. I assumed these doors lead to bedrooms.

I decided to check out the doors on the right first. I went to the first door and checked to see if it was locked. It wasn't, so I slowly opened it and peered inside. This seemed to be Jim's son's bedroom. I went in and looked around. Everything seemed to be normal, and nothing was out of place. I left the room, closing the door behind me, and went to the next door. The door wasn't locked and I opened it slowly and looked inside. This looked like it could be a spare room. There were boxes and items stacked around the room. I glanced around and decided it would take a long time to go through the boxes and stuff that were in there. I'd have to come back to it later.

I went to the first door on the left. The door wasn't locked; I opened it cautiously. As I opened the door a strong, foul odor hit me in the face. There was definitely something dead in this room. It seemed to be a large master bedroom. The lighting was poor, but I could see the outline of bodies in the bed under the covers. I backed out of the room and put on rubber gloves and my facemask. I went back into the room and I moved some of the blankets with the barrel of my shotgun. I saw three decaying bodies. I assumed these bodies were Jim, his wife and his son. There was nothing I could do for them.

I decided to search the room and the rest of the house for any items that were of use. Clipped to the underside of the nightstand I found a 9mm Browning. I checked it out, and it was loaded and functional. I clipped it to my pants and continued searching. In one of the dresser drawers, I found two boxes of ammo for the 9mm and two boxes of 5.56 mm NATO rounds. Under the bed, I saw a gun case and pulled it out. There was an AR15 bushmaster rifle with three extra magazines and some other attachments. Nice find! There was a large walk-in closet and I checked it out. There was mostly clothing, some of which was military, but the odor from the decaying bodies had permeated them and made them undesirable. I found nothing more that was useful upstairs. I went downstairs to search that part of the house. I went to the gun cabinet first and checked it out, but I wasn't able to get it open. I'd do a more thorough search for the keys later. I went to the kitchen and searched through it. In the corners there were some canned food and drinks. I found boxes of cleaners and other miscellaneous items that I then dumped out. I put the canned food and drinks in the boxes. Then I set the boxes and the guns that I found upstairs on the couch in the living room. I went out to the garage and looked around there. Tools and things like that were in the garage, but nothing that was immediately useful to me. However, there was a wheelbarrow. That would be useful. I took the wheelbarrow into the house and put all the stuff I found in there in the wheelbarrow and took them all to my house.

I was still a bit weak and tired, so I was going to have to rest and prepare myself something to eat. I would wait on doing more investigating - maybe tomorrow. As nighttime approached, I went outside to set my perimeter alarms. While out there, I noticed some strange animal noises that I'd never heard before. But when I shined a flashlight around through the woods, I couldn't see anything. I went back inside the house and went to bed. We'd see what tomorrow would bring. Well, maybe then EMT Bob would be by, according to his note.

Date: Tomorrow. (2 Days)

I woke up near daylight. I looked at my watch; it was 5:30 AM. My digital watch quit working, so I was using a windup analog watch. I set the time on it by the clock in the kitchen that ran off a battery. I got up, had coffee, and made some breakfast. My bread was stale, but it wasn't moldy, so it was okay to make some toast with it. I had to make the toast by heating the bread over the burner on the stove. I was eating my breakfast and looking at the guns I got from Jim's house. The AR15 had a lot of oil, even some Cosmoline still on it, and it didn't look like it had been fired. I'd probably need to sight it in. I'd have to test fire the 9mm Browning, also. I wasn't very familiar with the weapons, so I would practice with them a bit. I was somewhat apprehensive about doing much shooting because it might attract some unwanted attention. I decided I'd go down to the end of the road and check out my other neighbor's house. I'd never met the guy that lives there, but Jim said he was an officer in the military. I was guessing that he had probably been activated and was now on duty somewhere, so he wouldn't be around, and I would go down there and check out his house to see what kind of useful items an officer might have.

I got my gear together and started the hike down to the officer's house. It was about an eighth of a mile to the end of the road, and the driveway that continued up to his house was about 100 yards long. On the walk down everything seemed to be normal. It was a bright sunny day with birds singing, squirrels chirping, and insects buzzing: all the normal sounds of spring.

As I reached the officer's driveway I noticed there was a vehicle. As I got closer I recognized it as an ambulance. It was the same Red Cross ambulance that the EMTs drove when they came to my house. As I approached the ambulance from the rear driver's side, I saw what looked like a body on the ground.

I cautiously approached, keeping my eyes open and surveying the surrounding area. I edged closer and saw that it was a body. It looked like it had been torn apart! Yes, the clothing was ripped, and pieces of the body and its flesh were torn away. I saw a lot of dried blood and tracks all around. The tracks seemed to be from some kind of animal. I went around to the other side of the ambulance. The door was open, and there was another body on the ground there. This body was the same: clothes torn to pieces and chunks of flesh were missing. I looked up at the house. The front door was open.

I approached the house cautiously. I got up onto the front porch and saw there were a lot of tracks, dirt and debris leading in and out of the front door. They were smudged, so it was hard to pinpoint exactly what kind of tracks they were. I looked inside the house and saw that everything was in shambles. I decided to enter the house. I did so cautiously, with my shotgun ready. I smelled a strong, pungent odor. The house seemed to have the same floor plan as Jim's house. I knew that both houses were built by the Army for soldiers to stay in while they attended the Ranger camp. I searched downstairs, being careful not to make a lot of noise or disturb anything. I opened the door that led to the garage; there was no vehicle in the garage. I found nothing of interest or of use downstairs.

I proceeded upstairs. I noticed on the stairs that there were many tracks where something had been going up and down. As I examined these tracks more closely, I saw that they resembled canine tracks. They were too large to be coyote tracks, and I didn't know of any wolves being in this area. They had to be from a domesticated dog. I reached the top of the stairs and saw that all the doors were open except one. The second door on the left was the one that was closed. At Jim's house, that door led to the back of the walk-in closet off of the master bedroom. That pungent odor was much stronger up here. I decided to use the same search routine that I used in Jim's house, so I searched the doors on the right first.

I went to the first room and looked inside. There were posters on the wall of sports figures and girls. I assumed this was a teenage boy's room. The room was in disarray: the bedding was pulled off the bed and thrown on the floor, and clothes, old blankets and shoes were thrown about everywhere. I entered the room to take a quick look around. I tripped on something large and solid on the floor under the blankets and clothing. I moved some of the clothing and blankets aside with my gun barrel, and the odor of something putrid hit me in the face. It was a body. I pushed the blankets back over it and left the room, closing the door behind me. As I closed the door, I had to move stuff out of the way to get the door closed. This caused some noise. I heard shuffling and other noises coming from across the hallway. I quickly turned to look into the rooms on the other side. I could see nothing. I remained still, watching and listening. After 5 or 10 minutes with no apparent noises, I decided to go to the next room.

This room was also in disarray. It was the same as the other room, clothing, blankets and dresses were scattered all over. It was a total mess. From observing the items in this room, it looked like it was a girl's room. I entered the room and made a quick search, being careful not to step on anything or anybody this time. There were no bodies or anything of interest in this room. I left this room and closed the door behind me. I closed each door after searching the room, just in case I missed something in the room that might sneak up on me. Also, if I came back to this house in the future, and the doors were open, I would know someone or something had been here.

As I walked up toward the top of the stairs and across to the rooms on the other side, a board creaked under my feet. At this sound, I caught a flash of movement straight-ahead and heard a vicious growl. The next thing I saw were blazing eyes and flashing teeth coming at my face. I quickly swung my shotgun around and fired from the hip. The blast caught the creature in the chest and knocked it away from me, dropping to the floor. I was startled, and my heart was about to jump out of my chest. As I was looking at this thing that I had just shot, I heard another growl and some movement. There was another coming my way from out of the room. I had time to shoulder the shotgun this time. I fired quickly, the blast dropping the creature in its tracks before it could get close to me. I cautiously approached the creatures to examine them. They seemed to be canine, in nature anyhow, but not like anything I've ever seen before. Their bodies were shaped a lot like African hyenas, but they had short black hair, and their heads were shaped like pit bulls. Their tails were long and more like a shepherd, and the front feet were large with long claws. Well, whatever these things were, they were dead now, thank God. Good, and I hoped there were no more.

I entered the master bedroom and explored it cautiously. In a pile of blankets in one corner of the room, I saw something moving. I approached with caution. Whatever it was, it was a lot smaller than the things I had just killed. As I got closer and moved some of the blankets aside with my gun, I noticed it was a litter of puppies. Puppies? Puppies from the creatures I had just killed? Damn, zombie dog puppies! Hey, I guess that's what I'll call these things: zombie dogs. I didn't know what to do with the puppies, so I just continued to search the room. I found no bodies, but there were human bones and torn clothing. I found a .22-caliber pistol in the dresser drawer and a .32 Walters in the nightstand. There was also some ammo for each. I decided to use the .22 pistol to shoot and kill the puppies. This I did with no regrets.

I continued my search of the house. The door to the walk-in closet was closed. I carefully and cautiously opened the door and peered inside. All seemed to be okay. Everything was neat and orderly. I assumed those creatures had never gotten in there. I found a lot of military clothing, backpacks and duffel bags. I checked the size and it was my size. How about that? Even the boots were my size! I loaded as much of it into the backpacks and duffel bags as I could and headed outside.

As I was walking by the ambulance, I started thinking that if the ambulance had a lot of medical supplies, and it still worked after the EMP, I could drive it to my house. That is, if I found the keys and could get it started. I walked around and checked the ignition switch. The keys were not in it. Damn! I'd have to check the bodies for the keys. I went to check the first body on the driver's side. As I was examining the body and checking the pockets, I noticed the nametag. EMT Bob. Then I stopped and thought for a minute. If this was EMT Bob and his body looked like this, it had to have been here for quite a few days. His note on my nightstand said he would be back to check on me tomorrow. How many days had EMT Bob been dead? How many days had I been sick and unconscious? What day was this? These were questions I didn't have time to contemplate. I said to myself, "You need to get your shit together, Mark, and get your head screwed on straight."

I found the keys to the ambulance. It had three quarters of a tank of gas. I turned the key, and it started right up. Yahoo! I loaded the stuff from the officer's house into the back of the ambulance. I dragged the bodies up toward the house so that I could turn the vehicle around. As I got in and was turning it around to return home, I noticed something in the woods off to the side of the house. It was an older model Chevy pickup truck. I stopped the ambulance, got out, and walked over to check it out. It didn't look like it was in that bad of a condition. Maybe I could get it running at a later date. It would be less conspicuous than an ambulance to drive around in.

I drove the ambulance toward my house and pulled it into Jim's driveway. I opened the garage door of Jim's house and pushed his car out of the garage. I drove the ambulance into the garage. I closed the garage and put cardboard over the windows so no one could see in. I thought that if certain types of wrong people came around, in this day and time, an ambulance full of medical supplies was a valuable commodity. I thought, "I'll need to keep that hidden and safe." I took the stuff that I found and brought it into my house.

I started cooking some dinner and going through my spoils. After eating, I went outside to set my perimeter alarms. Then I went back in the house and started cleaning the guns and gathering all my supplies to get ready for a longer trip the next day. I might venture into town. As nightfall came and I got ready for bed, the strange animal noises and howls that I had heard the night before were again outside.

Chapter 4

Day of the Zombie Dog

Prologue

Islamic extremists had been posing as foreign college students and were able to steal biological specimens from college laboratories to create biological suicide bombs. Others had acquired chemical and radioactive materials to include in suicide bombs. The terrorists worked in pairs. One carried a biological suicide bomb, and the other carried a chemical or radioactive dirty bomb. The terrorists didn't care about what they were mixing or how they were mixing it. They had inadvertently created a deadly mutant disease. This disease, which became airborne, infected any humans that came into contact with the spores. Like most airborne diseases, this one had spread rapidly. Domestic dogs trapped in houses after their owners had died fed on the bodies. The disease then mutated the dogs into a new canine species later to be known as the zombie dog. The disease would become known as the Canine Flu.

Without electrical power, densely populated big cities became increasingly dangerous and uninhabitable. The panicked people of these big cities made a mass attempt of escape into the countryside, spreading the disease as they went. The country people, recognizing the danger of this mass exodus, formed militias to force them people back into the cities. This also scattered the city people into small groups throughout the countryside. Large militant gangs were formed in the cities for survival. The leaders of most of these gangs were the worst of our society. The city people who were forced back into the city were forced to either join the gangs or be killed by the zombie dogs.

The surviving country people formed small militias to protect their communities from the zombie dogs and to keep any outsiders out.

The Russian and Chinese peacekeepers realized the severity of the situation and for their survival and mission, seized the opportunity to take control of small cities which held viable resources. Working together, they hoped to gain valuable portions of the United States.

The United States, already in a state of martial law, went into total collapse. Government and law enforcement vanished due to the lack of electrical power and communications. The military, Russian and Chinese peacekeepers were all overwhelmed by the panicked population and were unable to maintain any civilized order throughout most of the country. Most of the key leadership personnel in the government, military and peacekeeping forces, succumbed to the canine flu. Without leadership, electrical power or communications, the people panicked. The panicked people unknowingly infected and spread the canine flu to otherwise unaffected areas across the country. This also led to the spread and mutation of canines coast-to-coast. Man's best friend was now man's worst nightmare. The zombie dog.

Back in Dahlonega, Georgia.
Survival Day Three.

I was awakened by a noise. What was that? It was my perimeter alarms! I got out of bed, put on my pants, slipped on some shoes and reached for the gun on the nightstand. The 9mm Browning felt a little light. I grabbed my headlamp, clicked on the red light and noticed there was no magazine and no round in the chamber. After cleaning the guns last night I had forgotten to reload them. I was still not at 100%, and I got tired and weak easily. The only weapon I had loaded was a .44-caliber old army black powder revolver. Well, the old black powder gun would have to do. I strapped on the holster, grabbed my high intensity LED light and looked out the windows on the north side of the house. I was only using the red light from the headlamp so as not to alert anything or anyone to my presence.

I couldn't see or hear anything. The noise came from the north side of the house, near my vehicles. I decided to go out the back door onto the back porch to investigate the perimeter alarm noises that I had heard. The back porch went the length of the back of the house and had a railing all the way around with a gate at each end. From the back porch I was able to see the whole backyard and both the south and the north sides of the house. The railing and gates would protect me from being seen. Therefore, anyone or anything that was out there would have to come over the railing or through the gates to get to me. I had battery-operated audible alarms on the gates. The back door was a sliding glass door and didn't make very much noise when it was opened.

I opened the sliding door carefully, looking out onto the back porch in both directions with the red light from the headlamp. I saw nothing. I waited and listened for about three minutes. Then I stepped out onto the back porch, closing the sliding door behind me. While I was out investigating, I didn't want anyone or anything entering my house. I went to the north side of the house where the vehicles were and looked around with the red light. I saw nothing and heard no more noises. That seemed odd. There were no noises at all, not even nighttime noises from tree frogs or insects. It was completely silent. I disconnected the alarm from the gate at the north end of the porch. I opened the gate and walked toward my vehicles. That's when I noticed that some of the strings with cans tied to them that I used for my perimeter alarms were broken, and the cans were lying on the ground. I shone the red headlight around the vehicles, looking to see if I could see any signs of what broke my perimeter. Then from behind me, I heard a growl and saw something move. I quickly turned around and pulled the hammer back on the black powder revolver. From the red headlamp light, I saw one of the zombie dogs standing there looking at me. The dog cocked its head to one side and wagged its tail. Keeping the black powder revolver aimed at the zombie dog, I said in a medium toned voice, "What the hell are you up to?"

At the sound of my voice, the creature growled and charged. I fired at the zombie dog, which was less than 20 feet away, striking it in the torso. The zombie dog yelped and fell to the ground. I cocked the hammer on the black powder revolver, ready for another quick shot. The zombie dog was lying on the ground kicking and twitching. I approached to within five feet and fired another shot at the creature's head. The bullet struck the creature in the neck just below its head. The creature made a few more quivers and then stopped moving. Good enough, I thought, "it's dead." I cocked the hammer, readying another round. I approached the creature and cautiously kicked its feet and legs. No response. There was a broken tree branch lying on the ground near me so I picked it up and poked the creature a couple of times with the branch. There was no response from the creature so I assumed it was dead. Then I used my LED light to look it over more closely. I noticed that the creature had a collar on. I looked at the collar more closely and noticed that it looked familiar. This collar belonged to my dog! It even had the snap from the dog run still attached to it. This creature was my dog at one time! Well, I knew what happened to my dog now. I decided there was nothing I could do with the body of the zombie dog in the dark.

I decided to reattach the perimeter alarms near my vehicles and go back into the house. I reset the gate alarm, went into the house, and secured the back door.

Now that I was awake and my adrenaline was pumping, I wasn't going to be able get back to sleep right away. I decided to load up my guns now, seeing that I had forgotten to do it before. I had a battery-operated lantern and a pretty good supply of batteries. I got the lamp out so that I could see. Then I started loading up my weapons. I loaded the Ithaca up with some buckshot and stood it in the corner near the kitchen table. I grabbed the clips for the MP5, loaded it, chambered a round and laid it on the table. I grabbed the clips for the 9mm Browning and loaded them too, putting one in the gun and chambering a round. I brought the MP5 and the 9mm Browning with me into the bedroom. I leaned the MP5 against the wall by the bed. I took the 9mm Browning out of the holster and put it on the nightstand. Then I went back out into the kitchen and loaded up the .22 pistol that I got from the officer's house. I put that in the cabinet by the kitchen sink. I loaded the magazines for the AR15, chambered a round, put the safety on and leaned that against the wall by the Ithaca shotgun. I only had 50 rounds for the AR15, so I would have to see what I could do about acquiring some more ammo. I then decided to go back to bed and try to get some sleep.

Survival Day Four - 6am.

The sun coming through the bedroom window woke me up. I looked at my watch. It was 6 AM. I got up, put on my clothes, and went out to the kitchen. I grabbed a kettle to heat up some water for a cup of instant coffee. I turned on the water faucet and only a couple of drops of water came out. I said to myself, "Well, that's the end of showers, I guess." I filled the teakettle with my bottled water. I set that on the stove to heat up and thought about what I was going to have for breakfast. I checked my bread and was it not only stale, it was getting moldy now. I tossed the bread in the trash and went to look at my food supply. The only thing I saw that I had for breakfast was some Mountain House dehydrated foods. I thought, "I guess I'll get to try those out now." I grabbed a pouch of ham and eggs and brought it out to the kitchen. Sitting at the table drinking my coffee and eating my Mountain House breakfast, I thought about what I should do.

As I sat there, the reality of my situation hit me bluntly. When I started preparing for a survival situation a few years ago, I did not imagine anything like this. I imagined something more on a natural disaster scenario. Even an invasion by a foreign power, I thought that I would still have my wife and son, and maybe other people around. But in this situation, I was all by myself. Not even my dog was with me. I loved that dog. I'd have to go out and bury him in a bit. I was trying to decide whether or not I should just hunker down here and wait for other people to come and find me. On the other hand, maybe I should pack out and go look for other human life nearby.

I was 45 years old. I wasn't in tiptop physical condition to begin with and now I was recovering from an illness with limited food supplies and medical attention. So I decided that making my house into a base camp and going on short excursions to some of the nearby towns would be my best bet for now.

If that's what I was going to do, I would have to get the house more organized and habitable for the circumstances I had to live under. This meant I would need a continuous source of water and food.

I looked around and saw the boxes of supplies I had gathered from the neighbors' houses and other things stacked up in the kitchen, living room and my office. I'd start by organizing all of the stuff and putting it somewhere secure. If someone came around here while I was away, everything was out in plain sight, easy for them to take.

I hadn't been in my son's room since I read the note on the door. The note was still there. I just hadn't been able to bring myself to the realization that my wife and son were gone and would not be coming back. It wasn't a job I was looking forward to, but I figured I'd have to go in there and clean the room out. I needed to make it into a secure room to store my supplies.

I went to my son's room, opened the door, and looked in at all of Zach's stuff. The bed and the medical things left over from when EMT Bob was caring for my son and wife would all have to be burned. I took a deep breath. I'd start by putting on my hazmat gear, cleaning this room, throwing everything that is in there out, and burning it. Then I'd put up some shelving so that I could keep better organized. My supplies would then be easier to inventory. This project took me about three hours. I'd also need to build a strong secure door to lock it up. I remembered seeing some lumber and carpentry tools over in Jim's garage. I'd go over there and get some stuff to reinforce this door and door casing.

I got ready to go to Jim's house and realized that walking around here was not as it used to be. I would need to be equipped and armed at all times now. So I dressed up in some camo gear. I brought my tactical knife, 9mm Browning, and a small survival pack: rubber gloves, facemask, and garbage bags. I went outside and got the wheelbarrow. I figured I could use that to carry tools and supplies back to my house. Maybe when I was over there I could do a quick look for the keys to Jim's gun cabinet. I walked over to Jim's house and the first place I went was in the backyard. I dragged up a couple of those blue plastic 55 gallon drums and took them back across the street to my house. I then went into the house and started looking through some of the drawers and stuff in the downstairs rooms for the keys to the gun cabinet. I found a key ring with some keys on it and went to the gun cabinet to try them. None of the keys fit. I needed to stay focused on my project and to not get side tracked, so I went out to the garage. I found some lumber, a screw gun, some long wood screws and a battery drill that still worked. I loaded that stuff in the wheelbarrow to be brought back to my house later. I closed the door on Jim's house and tried the keys on the key ring in the front door lock. One of the keys worked, so I locked up. At my house, I reinforced the door casing and the door to my son's room. I had a heavy-duty dead bolt lockset that I installed on the door. My supplies were more secure now.

Next I needed to address the water problem. I took the two drums out onto the back porch. The backyard was about six to eight feet below the house and the entrance to the basement was down there also. I set one drum at each end of the porch. Then, I went back over to Jim's house and got one more drum. I brought that drum over and set it in the middle of the porch near the railing. I arranged the eve spouts so that they would drain into the barrels, catching the rainwater. I cut a small hole in the side of the bottom of the middle drum. Then I fastened a toilet reservoir valve to the inside of the drum. I tied some parachute cord to that and attached a little roller to the top of the barrel, then dropped the rest of the parachute cord down to the ground below. On the outside of the barrel, I attached a vacuum cleaner hose from a shop vacuum to that same hole. I found a garden can with a sprinkler thing on the end. I cut the sprinkler's stem off and duct taped that on to the other end of the vacuum cleaner hose. I then dropped the vacuum cleaner hose and the sprinkler spout through the railing and down toward the ground from the porch. If this worked right, when the barrel got full of water, I could go down there and stand under the sprinkler and pull the parachute cord which would open the valve. The water from the barrel would then provide me with a shower. No hot water, but a shower nevertheless. Okay, now all I had to do was wait for some rain and I'd have water. I had plenty of water filters for my purification system. They were one-gallon pitchers with a filter in them. It was called the pure system. I'd be able to filter the rainwater for drinking water. I had enough canned food, dehydrated food and bottled water to last me about a month. I was sure we'd get some rain in that time to provide me with more water. I'd need to restock my food supply and keep my eyes out for more food as I explored the towns around this area.

It was late afternoon now, so I decided to have myself something to eat. I contemplated ether or not I should go down to the officer's house and try to get that old truck going. On the other hand, I could hike up to the water tower and observe the town for any signs of life. Since it was after 4 o'clock in the afternoon, I didn't believe I'd have time to do anything with the old truck. I'd leave that project for tomorrow. I'd just get some gear together and hike up to the water tower. It was about a 3-mile hike, I should be able to get there and back before nightfall.

I got out some of the military clothing I took from the officer's house and put it on. I decided to wear my hunting boots versus the military boots because the hunting boots were already broken in and comfortable. I strapped on the 9mm Browning, tactical knife, and binoculars. I also decided to take the Ithaca shotgun with me, loaded with slugs. I didn't have much ammo for the AR15 and the MP5. The 9mm was good for close combat, but it couldn't match the range and power of a rifle or shotgun. On this trip, I wasn't really expecting many close combat situations. The Ithaca, loaded with Brenneke slugs, was effective to about 100 yards and would compete with most rifles. Even an enemy with an armored vest couldn't stand up to a 12 gauge shotgun slug blast at close range. I also had a little hunting tool called a game finder. This was a heat-sensing device made to help hunters find deer that were wounded or lost after being shot. It read the difference in temperatures in the surrounding area. It would pick up a heat source like a living body or a recently killed one. I had successfully used this device to locate game during hunting season. If I suspected there was any danger in the woods, along the road or any other place, I was betting the game finder would tell me if there was a sizable heat source like a zombie dog or person hidden from my sight. I put together a small pack for a day hike: a compass, two bottles of water, rubber gloves, facemask, garbage bags, duct tape, parachute cord, zip ties, two packs of peanut butter crackers and some extra ammo. The road that I lived on was called Trail Road. This led to Crown Mountain Road. Going uphill about two miles would bring me to the water tower. Going downhill about another 3 miles would get me to the main road leading into town, but then there were about three more miles on the main road before town.

I secured my house and started the hike to the water tower. Everything looked and seemed to be normal. If it wasn't for the lack of traffic and man-made noises, you'd think it was just any other day. The road did have some minor debris in it: leaves, pine needles and things like that. Usually this stuff was brushed away by traffic. No other signs of any kind of disaster on the hike so far. There were three or four resident homes along this route. I wasn't going to take the time to search each home, but I'd make a quick sweep around each one for any signs of life. The first two residences that I checked were locked up and had the Homeland Security symbols on the front. All the houses were closed up. No one was around and there was no noticeable damage. I continued on and noticed something in the road about 100 yards ahead. It looked like a dead animal on the side of the road, which was not unusual for this area. As I approached, I saw that it was a deer, but this deer didn't look like it had been hit by any car. It was torn apart and there wasn't much left. Animal tracks around the kill looked to be those of the damn zombie dogs. I'd need to keep on the alert for those. I checked out two more houses on the way, but nothing unusual stood out. I came to the resident's house where Jim and I had pulled into the driveway to observe the town just before the shit hit the fan. I checked the house out, and it looked the same as it did when Jim and I were here. No one was around. The water tower was about 100 yards from here, and I continued on. No Homeland Security assholes were guarding the water tower. I crouched down and worked my way to the edge of the hill where I could observe the town. I did not want to silhouette myself up there where anyone or anything down in the town would be able to see me.

I could see the town pretty well from here, and it looked to be deserted. There were some pillars of smoke coming from several buildings, and I saw a lot of abandoned vehicles. Some of these had been burned. I took out my binoculars and searched the area more closely. The town looked like a war zone. There was no one around and no activity that I could see. There were some military vehicles near the courthouse. These vehicles had some of their doors open and many windows were smashed. It didn't look like there was any active military presence there. To really find out what was going on down there, I'd have to go down for a closer look at another time. It was getting too late today; it would be dark before I got there. I'd make that a priority for tomorrow… checking out the town.

I got up and started the hike back home. Just before I got to the intersection to my road, I heard a vehicle coming. People! But friend or foe? I quickly ducked into the woods out of sight. I wanted to see who they were before they saw me. Up the road came a late-model pickup truck. Two people were in the cab, and two people were standing in the box overlooking the cab, holding rifles. They had beards and, by the way they were dressed, I assumed they were some of the local hillbillies who lived around here. From my encounters with the locals in the past, there was about a 50-50 chance that they could be friendly or dangerous. I was dressed in military clothing so they would assume that I was a soldier. Most of the hillbillies around here did not have a very good relationship with the military or authorities. So by flagging them down, I would probably not be received very well. Four were armed, to one of me, so I thought I'd just stay out of sight and let them pass. Well, at least I knew there were other people around. How many and what their dispositions were was still unknown. But just knowing there were other people made me feel a bit better. It gave me hope that I might be able to find some friendly people, eventually. We humans, being social creatures, like to have some company. The rest of the trip was uneventful, and I made it back to the house.

Nighttime was approaching so I set my perimeter alarms and went into the house to fix some dinner. You know, I was going to get real sick of eating Spaghetti-Os and dehydrated food. At some point, I was going to have to see what I could do about my diet. I set my camp lantern on the table while I ate my dinner and made a list of goals I wanted to accomplish in the next few days.

To-do list:

- I need information on what's been happening and going on around the country and in the area.
- I need transportation to travel to towns and other populated areas.
- I need to see if I can find out if just North Georgia is affected or the whole country, or the whole world?
- I need to see if I can find other humans. Friendly ones preferably.
- I need to see if I can rig some kind of electrical power. It'll probably have to be solar or wind.
- I need to see if I can find the exact date. I still don't know what month or day of the week it is. My only working watch just gives the number day, and I'm not sure that that is even correct. My battery operated wall clock does not give a date either.
- I need to take my emergency radio to a better location where I may be able to get some reception, possibly up by the water tower on Crown Mountain. My emergency radio was buried in the basement with my guns and other survival supplies and that seems to have protected it from the EMP.

Tomorrow's goals: Check out that old truck down at the officer's house and see what I need to get it going. If that's successful, I can use it to go into town and maybe gather some more supplies to accomplish my other goals. My weapons are loaded and strategically placed throughout the house now.

I decided I'd go to bed and see if I could get some sleep. I set my battery-operated alarm clock for 6 AM. As I was taking off my clothes and getting into bed, I knocked my flashlight off the nightstand, and it rolled under the bed. I got down on the floor and looked under the bed for it. I found the flashlight, but there were some other items under there too. I turned on the flashlight and saw that it was my paintball gun and pellet gun. Yeehaw! I wonder if EMT Bob put them there? I'd just leave them there for now.

Survival Night Four - 1am.

I was awakened in the middle of the night at about 1 AM by loud noises outside: barking, howling, and squeals. I quickly put on my clothes and shoes, grabbed the 9mm Browning, my headlamp and LED flashlight. The commotion seemed to be coming from the backyard. I had a one million candlepower spotlight that still had a charge. I took the MP5 and the spotlight, opened the sliding back door and stepped out onto the porch. I shined the spotlight in the direction of the noise out behind my house. I saw a frightening sight. A pack of a dozen or more zombie dogs were attacking a wild hog. Among this group of zombie dogs was one that was different. It was much larger and had a reddish color, rather than black like the others. As soon as the light hit this one, it looked at me and disappeared into the woods. Half of the group finished killing off the hog, and the other half disappeared into the woods.

My perimeter alarms at the north end of the house went off. I turned quickly in that direction, spotting several of the zombie dogs charging in my direction. I dropped the spotlight and brought the MP5 to bear on them. I quickly fired about five shots in their direction, hitting one or two of them. This stopped the charge and gave me time to shoulder the weapon for more accurate, follow-up shots. But the spotlight was out, and I only had the headlamp light to see with. I saw movement, but I couldn't get an accurate shot on any of them. Suddenly my perimeter and gate alarm on the south side went off, and I turned, looking to the south end of the porch. Another charge of zombie dogs was coming from that direction. I fired several shots their way, hitting two more of them, stopping the charge, but now I was outflanked and being forced to retreat. I opened the sliding doors to my house and retreated inside.

A few years back, on the outside of the glass, I installed a metal gate that I could pull across the glass. I pulled the gate across and secured it. Then I closed the glass doors and secured them too. I put down the MP5 and grabbed my trusty Ithaca shotgun, which was loaded with 00 buckshot. In the dark at close range, this would be a more effective weapon against the zombie dogs. My perimeter alarms all the way around the house were going off. Through the windows, even in the dark, I could see the zombie dogs moving around my house, barking and howling. My house was completely surrounded. The zombie dogs dug and banged on the doors and walls all around the house, but they could not find a way in. I tipped the kitchen table on its side and flipped chairs over in the doorways leading into the kitchen. This put obstacles between me and any zombie dogs that might break into the house. I holed up there in the kitchen where I could see the other rooms, windows and doors. This was the best defensible position if any of the zombie dogs should be able to break into the house. The zombie dogs barked and howled for about 45 minutes or so and then everything went quiet. I stayed alert, watching and listening for another 15 to 20 minutes. Then, with caution, I got up and went to the doors and windows to look and listen outside. I saw and heard nothing. I decided it was not safe to go outside to reset my perimeter alarms. I braced the kitchen table against the glass backdoors and used kitchen chairs to brace the front door. All the windows were already secured and locked. I went back to bed, but I slept with my clothes on this time.

Survival Day Five.

I was not awakened again until 6 AM when my alarm went off. I got up and put on my shoes. Grabbing the 9mm Browning, I went and checked all the windows and doors of my house. All looked to be secure. It was daylight now, and looking out the windows, I saw no sign of the zombie dogs. I put the kitchen back in order and put on some water for some instant coffee and instant breakfast. I cautiously opened up the back door and looked out onto the porch and backyard. The gates entering my porch from both the North and South were broken but repairable. My perimeter alarm system was not damaged and could be reset. The pig that the zombie dogs killed was no longer in sight; they must have dragged it off to eat. No bodies of any of the zombie dogs that I shot last night were around. I knew I hit a couple of them, but I wasn't not sure if I killed any. The leader, or alpha dog, of the pack must be that big red one. He seemed to be a smart son-of-a-bitch, because he called his pack off the pig and sent them to attack me. They out smarted and outflanked me, forcing me to retreat with their attacks. Having to deal with them was going to be dangerous. I was going to have to rig up a better, defensible position out there on the back porch so that I wouldn't have to retreat next time. I had no location where I could launch an offensive attack against them; I was stuck playing a defensive role. When it came to the zombie dogs, a defensive role was a losing one, and I didn't want to be on the losing side.

I ate my breakfast and then took my coffee with me as I made minor repairs to the gates on the back porch. I'd have to see if I could find or build full height doors at the end of the porch to make it more defensible against the zombie dogs. I went back in the house and started getting my stuff together to go down to the officer's house. I'd be working on that old truck today, so I would need to take a weapon with me that was small and light. The MP5 would probably be the best choice for this task. I put together my pack and dressed the same as I did for the hike to the water tower. I secured my house and walked down to the officer's house.

Nothing looked disturbed from the last time I was there, the front doors were still closed, and the EMTs' bodies were still on the front porch of the house where I left them. I walked over to the Chevy truck and checked out the area that I could see around to make sure everything looked safe. I saw no signs of danger, so I started my investigation of the truck. It was a 1979 Chevy Silverado, four-wheel-drive with 31-inch off-road tires; it also had a wench in the front bumper and a trailer hitch on the back. A few minor dents and faded paint, but the box and body seemed to be solid. It looked like the guy used it for a wood truck because in the box were pieces of wood, wood chips and bark. I opened the driver's door and looked around inside. I pulled the hood release, got out and popped the hood. The V-8 engine looked okay and all seemed intact. I checked the oil and antifreeze and it all checked out. I did a more thorough check of the inside the cab. Nothing in the glove box, but in the ashtray, I found the keys. I put the key in the ignition and turned the switch. The dash lights came on and the gas gauge moved to a full tank. I turned the key to the start position; the truck made a groan, the dash lights dimmed, and then all I heard were clicking noises. I knew my luck wouldn't hold out. The battery was dead. The truck was a four-wheel-drive standard, four speed on the floor. If I could get it up the driveway and push it downhill, I might be able pop the clutch, but there was no way I was going to be able to move it from there to the driveway.

I got out and looked around the backyard. In a metal shed, I saw a utility trailer and a large object covered with a tarp. Humm. I went to the shed and looked at the large object under the tarp. I pulled back the tarp and saw that it was a boat. It was a 17-foot deep V bass tracker with a trolling motor, fishfinder and a 75 hp Mercury outboard motor. Nice boat. Well, this thing must have a battery in it? I climbed in and opened the battery compartment. Yes, there were two batteries there. I'd have to go up to the garage and see if there were any tools that I could use to remove one of the batteries.

In the garage, there were various mechanic tools, carpentry tools, and odd and end household repair items. I started by going through the toolbox. I found the tools that I needed to remove the battery, and I also found a multimeter to test the batteries. I went back to the boat and tested the battery with the multimeter. I wanted to make sure they had a charge in them before I went to the trouble of removing them. Both batteries had 12.2 V. That was a good sign. Maybe I could get the truck started with one of them. One battery was a deep cycle marine battery, and the other was a regular battery. I removed the regular battery from the boat. I put the tools in my pocket and carried the battery up to the Chevy truck.

Wow, that's a workout carrying a battery without handles. They are heavy suckers! I removed the old battery from the truck and put the boat battery in. I went to the cab and hit the key. The engine turned over a few times but didn't start. I didn't keep cranking it because I didn't want to drain the battery. I'd have to find some way to get it started without draining the battery.

I went down to the other shed, but it was locked with a padlock. I gave the padlock a good hard whack with a hammer, and the lock came open. In the shed there were two lawnmowers: a riding mower and a push mower. I looked around and saw a 2 gallon gas can. I picked it up and felt that it had some gas in it.

I brought the gas to the Chevy truck. I removed the air cleaner and dumped a little bit of the gas down the carburetor. I went to the cabin and hit the key again. The engine turned over a few times and then started, ran for a few seconds and quit. Dammit! I repeated the process, and this time the engine stayed running. I left the truck running and went back down to the shed. I put the tarp back over the boat and then closed the shed. I went back up to the truck, put the air cleaner back on and closed the hood. I hopped in the cab and put it in gear. As I let out the clutch, gave it some gas, and rolled on up to the driveway. Cool, now I had some transportation, so I could go down and check out the town and maybe find some more supplies and information. I drove the truck up to my house and backed it into the yard and shut it off. I went in the house to cleaned up and got my gear together for my expedition into town.

First Time to Town.

Now that I had transportation, I'd be able to take more gear with me. I'd take my emergency radio to the water tower first and try to get a signal from there. I also wanted to make another observation of the town with my binoculars to see if anything had changed since the last time I checked it out. This was going to be an urban environment where the dangers could be human and/or zombie dog. This would require a new skill set of tactics, weapons, and gear. The AR15 would probably be the weapon of choice for the urban environment. I needed to test fire it first.

I went down to the backyard with the AR 15. Fifty yards was the max range I had to test fire the AR15. I set up a target out there and sat on the ground holding the rifle with my elbows resting on my knees. I fired three careful shots at the bull's-eye. I shot a nice kissing group, but it was about a half-inch low. I made a quick adjustment to the sights and fired three more shots. Dead on. A nice group, all in the bull's-eye now. I got back to the house and started loading my gear into the truck. I added some extra water and snacks to my pack, and I took the wheelbarrow and put it in the back of the truck upside down. I put a crowbar and hammer in the cab along with my emergency radio. I fired up the old truck and headed for the water tower.

The only thing I noticed that was different from last time was that the doors of some of the resident homes were now open. The hillbillies I saw in the old truck that day must have searched those homes for useful items. At the water tower, I turned the truck off. I grabbed my binoculars and the emergency radio and cautiously approached the edge of the hill overlooking the town. The town looked basically the same as it did before: like a war zone. I took out my emergency radio and started trying to tune in a station. I was still only getting static, but on one frequency, I was getting a Morse code. That was promising, but I didn't know Morse code well enough to know what it was saying. I thought I saw some movement on Main Street, so I took out my binoculars for a better look. I saw a woman and a young man, possibly a teenager, pushing a market cart full of items up the street. As I was watching them, the hillbillies in the old truck came out of a side alley down the street and headed toward the woman and teenager. The woman and the boy ran into one of the buildings nearby. The hillbillies stopped the truck and the two in the back jumped out to pursue the woman and boy. The other two drove off with the truck down a side street. I continued watching. The two hillbillies that went after the woman and boy were then dragging them out of the building. The other two in the truck came back. They threw the woman and boy into the back of the truck and drove up toward the town hall. I couldn't see all of what was happening from where I was, but I knew it didn't look good for them. I picked up my stuff and headed for my truck. I decided to go into town and see if I could find out what happened.

As I got to the outer edge of town, I saw that trying to drive around there was going to be difficult. There were lots of abandoned vehicles in the road. There were downed power poles, streetlights and other debris making it difficult or even impossible to drive through most of the streets. I saw an open carwash nearby and decided to drive the truck in there and leave it. The carwash would hide it from sight and was only about four or five blocks from the courthouse. I'd go the rest of the way on foot and stay out of sight until I could make a better assessment of the situation.

As I worked my way up the streets, staying close to the buildings and as much out of sight as possible, I took note of my surroundings. I saw a lot of what appeared to be the remains of bodies or pieces of human bodies. I bent down to observe a boot with a leg bone sticking out of it. I noticed the bone had teeth marks. I believed this to be the work of the zombie dogs. I hoped this person was already dead before they got to him. At the second intersection, I saw a lot of vehicles off on the side of the road, on the sidewalks, with their doors open. I noticed that these vehicles were riddled with bullet holes. I saw a lot of empty shell casings on the ground in this area, also. I continued on and came to the market cart that the woman and boy were pushing. I saw most of the items were only clothing; there were also two backpacks. The backpacks were small, so I grabbed them and attached them to my pack.

I made it to the courthouse and saw one of the hillbillies walking around out front. As I watched, I saw there was adequate cover from the south side to approach the building without being spotted. The hillbilly's vehicle was parked near the north corner of the building on the grass. I made my way to the south side of the courthouse, near the front corner. The hillbilly was out front, standing by a tree smoking a cigarette. He was only a few feet away from me and didn't know I was there. I took a link of clothesline rope out of the side pocket of my backpack. I wound a couple loops around each of my hands, leaving about a 2-foot span between them. I quietly approached the hillbilly from behind. When I got within two feet of him, I quickly slipped the rope over his head and around his neck. I then turned my body so we were back to back. I squatted down and pulled hard, flipping the hillbilly over my back. He landed on his face in front of me. I jumped on him, slamming his head into the ground hard. He was not moving, so I assumed he was either unconscious or maybe even dead. Taking no chances, I used some parachute cord from my pack to bind his hands and feet. I dragged him over to the left side of the building into some bushes and left him there. He had a lever action rifle leaning up against the tree. I took the rifle and tossed it into the shrubs in front of the building. I also took off my pack and stashed it in the bushes by the front door.

I approached the front door of the building, looking in through the glass doors. The reflection of light on the glass made it difficult to see inside, but I could see down a long hallway, and no one seemed to be there. I carefully opened the front door and entered the building. I heard loud voices coming from the end of the hall. I quietly moved down the hall in that direction, looking into several offices along the hallway. No one was in any of them. I continued. At the end of the hall, I saw there was a large room with stairs going up to the second floor. Near the middle of the room, I saw the other three hillbillies, the woman, and the boy. The boy had been beaten badly, and one of the hillbillies was standing next to him. The boy was a teenager with short dark hair and a medium build. The other two hillbillies were taunting the woman. She was crying, and her clothes had been torn. The woman appeared to be in her 30s with a petite build and shoulder length dark hair. I watched and waited for an opportunity to do something to rescue them without any more harm coming to them, if possible. The boy was lying on the floor moaning and groaning, obviously in a lot of pain. The hillbilly by him was not paying much attention to him; he was more intent on watching his buddies torment the woman. I couldn't hear what the two hillbillies were saying to the woman. From their actions, it appeared as though they were working up the courage to rape her. The woman wasn't answering any of their questions. She was only crying and shaking in fear.

One of the hillbillies pushed the woman, and she fell to the floor. This was my opportunity. I shouldered the AR15 and took two quick shots at the hillbillies standing over the woman, striking them both in the torso. They yelled and fell to the floor, bleeding badly and kicking. The woman scurried away from them quickly. I turned and fired at the other hillbilly by the boy, but I only winged him in the arm. He pulled up a shotgun to fire at me, but he yelled and missed me, because the boy on the floor bit him in the leg, giving me an opportunity for another shot. My next bullet struck the hillbilly in the chest, and he fell to the floor. I stood up and started to approach the woman and boy, but I was grabbed from behind, and my AR15 was knocked out of my hands.

The hillbilly I left outside was not dead and came at me from behind. He had a good chokehold on me. With my left hand I grabbed the tactical knife strapped to my left leg. I pulled out the knife and stabbed him in the leg. He yelled and let go of me. I spun around and turned to face him. He was partially bent over, holding his leg. I kicked him hard in the face with my hunting-booted right foot. He went down hard to the floor, and I drew the 9mm Browning. I fired three quick shots into his chest. I picked up my AR15 and holstered the 9mm. Watching the other three hillbillies I had shot, I approached the woman and boy. I asked if they were okay and told them it was all right, and that I wouldn't hurt them. All four of the hillbillies seemed to be dead.

The woman and boy were huddling together, looking frightened. I put my AR15 down on a bench and again told the woman that I wasn't going to hurt her or the boy.

I said, "Come with me, I need to get you guys out of here to safety. Can you walk?"

The woman said, "Yes, I think we can."

On the way back out of the building, I noticed the hillbilly that grabbed me from behind had a box of 30-30 ammunition sticking out of his pocket. I grabbed that and took the woman and boy out the front door. Once outside I grabbed my pack and the lever action rifle. I told them I had a truck a few blocks from here and once we got there I'd take them to safety. They agreed to come with me. The woman noticed that I had her packs attached to my pack and asked me about that. I told them about how I saw them from the water tower, and I knew that those packs belonged to them. I had grabbed them on my way to the courthouse. She thanked me and took them from me. As we passed her market cart, she grabbed a few more items. Then we went to the car wash and got into my truck. Then we headed out of town, back to my house.

They did not talk much on the drive back to my house. I told them that they were the only people other than the hillbillies that I had seen. The woman replied that she had not seen very many other people either, but she seemed unwilling to elaborate any further. When we arrived at my house, I invited them in, putting on a pan of water to heat up for them in order to wash and clean up. I poured the water in the sink in the bathroom and gave them washcloths, towels and soap. They had clothes and stuff in their backpacks. I put on some water for coffee for me and the woman and grabbed a couple of cans of soup from my stock to heat.

After they washed and changed into some clean clothes, I invited them to sit at the table and have something to eat. I saw that they took a pretty good beating. They didn't seem to be seriously hurt, though. I handed each of them some aspirin and a bottle of Gatorade. Then I sat down with my coffee to eat with them. I finally got them to talk a little bit.

I said, "I guess I should introduce myself. My name is Mark Antonio."

The woman said her name was Susan Miller and the boy's name was Robert Miller. I called him Bobby; he was 16 years old.

Bobby asked me if I had seen any monsters.

I said, "You mean the zombie dogs?"

Susan says, "Yes, zombie dogs. That's a good name for them."

Bobby said, "They only come out at night, you know."

I said, "Yeah, that's the only time I've seen them."

Susan said, "Three days ago they attacked us and killed my husband and Bobby's sister Suzanne."

"I'm very sorry to hear that."

Bobby said, "My father killed a few of them before they got him."

Susan said, "Yes, your father got us to safety before they got him and your sister." She turned to me. "We've been locking ourselves in an upstairs room of the photo studio that my husband and I used to own, every night, hoping that they wouldn't find us."

I said, "I'm sure it's been a rough time trying to survive down there in town."

Susan said, "Yes, we had to hide from the zombie dogs at night and run from those mean men every day. My husband was doing the best he could to protect and take care of us. Three days ago, those men were patrolling the streets, looking for us all day long. We had to stay hidden, and we were running out of food and water. That evening, we went out to get food and water, and we were attacked by the zombie dogs. As we were running for our lives back to our hiding place at the photo studio, my daughter tripped and fell. My husband told us to keep running, that he would get her. He had a small caliber rifle that he used to shoot some of the zombie dogs that were attacking her, but there were just too many of them and no way for us to save them. I see that nightmare every time I close my eyes. The screaming, the blood, those vicious creatures tearing the flesh from their bodies while they were still alive."

Susan put her head in her hands and start crying. Bobby put his arm around her, comforting her, saying, "You still have me, mom, and we have each other."

I said, "It must've been horrible. We are safe here though, and together we can protect each other. Have you seen any other people?"

Susan replied, "Yes, there are a few more groups of men like that. They come through town daily."

I asked, "How many?"

Susan said, "There are two or three different groups. Most of the time I only see four or five at a time. I'm not sure if they're all from the same group or if there are different groups."

I asked, "Have you seen any military or any types of authorities?"

Susan shook her head. "No, Homeland Security and the military took everyone from the FEMA camp that was not sick to some other location weeks ago. I havn't seen any of them since."

I told her how I had been sick and how I woke up to the disaster. Susan told me that her family was sick also. Only she and her daughter had been well. They faked as if they were sick so they wouldn't be taken away by Homeland Security. After a few weeks, her husband and son recovered around the same time I did.

Susan said that some of the locals and Homeland Security had shootouts in town when they were trying to take people away. When the military backed out, so did Homeland Security. They left everyone else behind. It seemed there were not many people left, at least around here. I agreed.

I told her and Bobby that I had made my house a base camp, and each day I would go exploring further away, and that I wanted to go to Gainesville or Dawsonville next. They said that they would like to get away from here and find other people, too. I needed to make this a more defensible home base, so it was important that I go back to one of the neighbors' houses and get some materials to reinforce the gates on the back porch.

"Do you want to come with me?" From the expression on their faces, I could tell they'd had enough excitement for one day. I told them, "Well, you can stay here and rest if you'd like. I'll only be gone about a half an hour. I'll lock up the house and you'll be safe here until I get back." They agreed to wait at the house.

I took the truck and went down to the officer's house. In his garage were some building materials and a couple of old screen doors. I loaded the materials in the back of the truck and brought them back to my house. I went out on the back porch and had Bobby and Susan help me. We hung the doors and reinforced the door casings. Then we added barbed wire and lattice boards to fill in and strengthen the screen part of the doors. The wood and barbed wire should make it more difficult for the zombie dogs to get through it, and at the same time it would allow me to see through and shoot through the door if necessary. With that project done and nighttime approaching, I went about the task of setting my perimeter alarms. Then I went in the house to start cooking us some dinner.

As we were eating, I asked Susan and Bobby if they knew how to fire a gun. They said they had a basic understanding of it but didn't have any training or much experience.

"Well, I guess that's what we'll have to do tomorrow. I'll show you two how to handle a gun safely and how to defend yourselves. I'll defend you as best I can, but it would be much easier if you both knew how to handle firearms and could help without shooting each other or me."

They agreed this was a good idea and looked forward to the training tomorrow. I offered my bed to Susan and Bobby and told them that I would sleep out on the couch where I was better able to keep an ear tuned for the zombie dogs or any other problems that might occur in the night. I brought them into the bedroom and showed them the paintball gun.

Bobby said, "Now that's one gun I know how to use." I told him that it was loaded with jawbreaker candies, which were much more powerful than normal paintballs. Bobby and Susan both laughed at this idea, but they agreed the jawbreakers would be a better offensive ammo than the paintballs. I secured the house and strategically placed loaded weapons around the house in case the zombie dogs came back.

Chapter 5

Night Five/Day Six.

I provided Susan and Bobby with a battery-operated lantern and showed them how to use it in case they needed to get up, use the bathroom or for any other problems that might occur. As they got settled into bed, I prepared mine on the couch. I had another small camp lantern that I could use here on the coffee table. I put my LED flashlight, headlamp, and a 9mm Browning on the coffee table within easy reach. I got in bed and turned out the light. I lay there thinking about the previous events and what was to come. I now had two more mouths to feed, so that cut my supplies in half. I would need to do some scavenger hunting in town and at some of the neighboring homes to see what kind of food and water supplies I could be find. Also, I needed to see what we could do about finding clothing and stuff for Susan and Bobby. I drifted off to sleep, mulling over these issues in my head.

Around midnight I was awakened by loud noises and flashes of light. It was only a thunderstorm. The rain was coming down hard. I thought to myself, "Very good. Hopefully the rainwater will fill the drums I put out on the back porch and that'll solve some of our water problems." I drifted back to sleep.

A bit later, I was awakened by a loud crash and screaming. I grabbed the flashlight and the 9mm Browning and ran into the bedroom where Suzanne and Bobby were. They had the lantern on, so I was able to see what was happening. A zombie dog had crashed through the bedroom window and was trying to attack Susan and Bobby. Bobby was keeping the creature at bay with the paintball gun, firing it as fast as he could. The jawbreaker candies being fired from the paintball gun were obviously painful, creating an effective deterrent, stopping the zombie dog from charging straight in on Susan and Bobby. I quickly took aim with the 9mm Browning and fired five shots into the creature, killing it. I went to the dog and kicked it a couple times to make sure it was dead. It appeared so, but the bedroom window was broken and rain was coming in. There was a possibility of more zombie dogs entering the house this way.

I pushed the dresser away from under the window and then asked Susan and Bobby to help me with the bed mattress and box springs. We stood these up on end and pushed them against the window. Then with Susan and Bobby's help, I moved the dresser against the box spring and mattress, holding it against the window. This would have to do for tonight. It would hold until tomorrow, when we could do a more permanent repair. I then took the flashlight and went to the other rooms and looked out the windows and doors, looking for any more of the zombie dogs. By the flashes of lightning, I could see most of the outside of the house. I could see no sign of any more zombie dogs.

I went into the closet where I kept my camping supplies and got two tent cots for Susan and Bobby to sleep on. I started setting them up in the bedroom.

Bobby was dismayed and said, "We're not going to still sleep in here, are we?"

I stopped and looked at him and Susan. They were both shaken and very frightened.

I said, "Okay, I'll set up the cots in the living room near me. That way I'll be right next to you all."

Susan's face showed her relief. "Thank you, that'll make us feel much safer."

I set up the cots in the living room where I had been sleeping.

I grabbed an old blanket and rolled the zombie dog's body in the it, dragging it out onto the back porch where I threw it over the railing into the backyard. I would take care of the body tomorrow. I secured the house, then closed and locked the bedroom door in case any of the dogs got through the window again. I told Bobby, "Good job with the paintball gun. You sure put a hurt on that monster."

He laughed and said, "Thanks! I was scared as hell and thought we were dead. Thanks for coming in and killing it." He was a pretty tough kid. It was good that he was talking about it. A lot of people would be in shock.

Susan said, "We really need to know how to use firearms so that we can defend ourselves in situations like that."

I told them, "After breakfast tomorrow morning we'll start training." We all settled down and went back to sleep. The night continued uneventfully with the exception of the thunderstorm, which woke us up a couple of times. We got up around 7 AM.

Day Six, Firearms Training For Susan and Bobby.

The thunderstorm had passed, but it was still raining outside. It was just a light drizzle. I put on my shoes and clipped the 9mm to my pants. I went into the bedroom and checked on the mattress to make sure that it held up against the window. It looked alright, but it was going to take the mattress a long time to dry out. It might even be ruined. There was also a lot of glass, blood and sticky jawbreaker candy pieces in the carpet. I wasn't sure I knew how to clean it up. I went back out into the kitchen where Susan and Bobby were sitting at the table. "Well, I guess I'll put on some water for coffee and breakfast."

Susan said, "A coffee sounds good!"

Bobby said, "I'll have a coffee, too." His mother gave him a look but didn't say anything.

I asked Bobby, "How do you take your coffee?"

He thought for a second and said, "In a cup."

Susan and I both laughed.

I said, "Well, Bobby, we'll try two sugars and cream, how's that?"

He replied, "Sounds good to me."

I said, "I hope you guys like dehydrated food because Mountain House dehydrated food is all I have for breakfast."

Susan replied, "I'm sure that'll be just fine."

I got three cups, fixed our coffee, and handed Susan one and Bobby one. I took the third one. Susan and I both watched Bobby intently. Bobby took a sip from his coffee, shook his head and made a face.

Then he took another sip and said, "Good, just the way I like it."

I prepared the breakfast meals and we sat down to eat.

Bobby said, "This stuff is pretty good."

Susan said, "Unique, but I still like fresh eggs and bacon."

I said, "Yes, but I don't think we'll be having any of that anytime soon. Sorry."

Susan said, "Don't be sorry. We're grateful; this stuff really isn't all that bad."

I got the Sheridan Blue Streak pump pellet gun and brought it into the kitchen. I told Susan and Bobby that we would now start the firearms training. First, they needed to learn about the parts of a firearm. I started with the small calibers and single actions and we worked our way up from there.

"This is a .22-caliber pump pellet gun. It uses compressed air that pushes a pellet down the barrel at high velocity."

- "The caliber equals the diameter of the projectile or bullet."
- "All firearms have the same basic parts, or components. It's important to know the terminology and understand how each piece works in order to safely handle and use a firearm."
- "The end of the firearm where the bullet exits the barrel is called the muzzle. You need to remember to always keep the muzzle of your firearm pointed in a safe direction. This is the 'danger end' of the weapon. Do not forget this."
- "At the other end of the barrel is where you put the bullet, shell or cartridge. In this case it's a pellet. This part of the barrel is

called the breach or chamber. The chamber is designed to only hold the correct caliber and type of ammunition the firearm is designed to fire."

- "This pellet gun is a single shot bolt action." I showed them the bolt. "You lift the lever and pull it all the way back until it clicks. This cocks the firing mechanism."
- "This is a pump pellet gun. The forearm of the stock comes out like this when you pump it back toward the barrel. The more times you pump it, the more powerful it becomes. Also, the more times you pump it the harder it gets. This weapon is only good for small game hunting, like squirrels, rabbits or target practice. I don't believe it would be effective against the zombie dogs or other people, but it could still seriously injure a person, so you still need to be careful with it."
- "The wooden part is called the stock. The front part where you hold one hand is called the forearm piece. In this case, you also use that to pump up a charge in order for it to fire."
- "The back part of the stock is called the butt and grip. The grip is where you hold your hand when shooting it, like this near the trigger. The butt is the part that goes against your shoulder; it's always good practice to make sure the butt is tight against your shoulder before firing a weapon."
- "The trigger is what fires a weapon. The metal guard going around the trigger is, of course, the trigger guard. Never put your finger inside the trigger guard until you are ready to fire the weapon."
- "Near the trigger, or action part of the weapon, you will normally find the safety. Always keep the safety on until you are ready to fire the weapon. But just because the safety is on does not make the weapon safe. A safety is a mechanical device, which can fail. The only safe weapon, loaded or unload, is one that's pointed in a safe direction."
- "The sights are what you use to aim the weapon. In this case, this weapon has a peep sight. It is called that because the one here at the back has a small hole that you look through, or peak

through. The front sight is a post. When looking through the rear sight, you align the post in the center of the hole. This gives you the correct sight alignment. You want the bull's-eye of the target sitting on top of the post in your sight." I drew this out on paper.

- "Hearing protection is another issue. You need to wear earplugs when practicing with firearms to protect your hearing. Of course, you won't need that for the pellet gun, and you won't have time for it in a firefight. But for practice we will always wear hearing protection."

"We will be using this pellet gun for practice because it doesn't make noise and I have a lot of pellets for it." Then I got the Ruger model 77 35 Whelen out. Being a bolt-action rifle, it had very similar features to the pellet gun, but it was equipped with a scope and had an internal five round magazine, which I explained to them. I took each weapon, one at a time, explained all of the features, and showed them how to load and unload it safely.

The rain had stopped and the sun had come out. I stepped out onto the back porch and looked in the barrels. They were each over half full of water. Nice! Now we didn't have an immediate water crisis to worry about. I told Susan and Bobby that I needed to go out and bury that zombie dog body then I'd set up some targets for us to do some firearm practice. As I was digging a hole to bury yet another zombie dog, I was thinking to myself that this was getting old. I was going to run out of places to bury these damn things soon.

After burying the zombie dog, I set up a target for Susan and Bobby. After some practice with the pellet gun, they were both able to understand the sights and were fairly accurate with the weapon. Next, I got the .22 Ruger and brought it outside for them to practice with. This weapon had iron sights, but they caught on quickly and achieved accuracy with a short amount of time. I explained that the larger calibers would probably not be good weapons for them, due to the excessive recoil. I let them fire a few rounds with the MP5 and the AR15. Then I got out the 30-30 that I took from the hillbillies. I test fired this weapon, and it seemed to shoot well. It was a 30-30 Merlin lever action. This gun had little bit of recoil, so I let Susan and Bobby each fire a shot with this so that they understood recoil.

Susan liked the 30-30 and said it made her feel like she was back in the old West. I told her she could have it if she wanted. Of course, Bobby liked the MP5 and the AR15, but to his disappointment, I issued him the 10/22 Ruger.

I then explained the parts of handguns, including how to load, unload, and fire. We fired a few rounds with the .22 revolver and the 9mm Browning. When Bobby took the 9mm Browning he started to hold it sideways to shoot it.

I told him to stop. "You don't hold a handgun sideways like you see on TV and movies. You can't accurately hit anything that way. Trying to be cool will only get you killed, so hold the weapon properly, the way I showed you."

He held the gun properly, and after a few shots, he was able to hit the target. Then I told him to hold the weapon sideways and see how well he did. He not only missed the target, he missed the whole backstop. I told him, "See, you cannot hold on to the gun properly or achieve a proper site picture holding it sideways. Whoever came up with that idea is a dumbass and didn't know anything about firearms." I told them that I didn't have any handguns to give them at this time, but maybe we would find some at a later date. To myself, I was thinking that they would need a lot more training in how to handle a handgun before I trusted them with one so as to not shoot each other, or me.

I told Susan and Bobby that I needed to look over that broken window and the rest of the windows around the house. I needed to make all of them more secure. It seemed like every time I made something more secure, those damned zombie dogs found a way around it or some other weakness in my defenses.

Susan said she'd go back in the house and clean up the things from breakfast.

Bobby came with me. I went to the north side of the house where the broken window was to look things over. I disconnected the electric fence charger from the vehicles and took down my perimeter alarms on that side of the house. Bobby asked, "What's up with all the strings with tin cans tied on them?"

I explained about the perimeter alarms and how they worked.

Bobby answered, "Oh, cool!"

As I was doing this, I wondered how the zombie dog got through the window without tripping any of the perimeter alarms or getting shocked from the fence charger that I had attached to the vehicles. He should have received a shock similar to what birds got when they sat on high-voltage wires. I looked around and decided that the zombie dog must have jumped up onto my wife's car and then my truck. From there he was able to jump through the window, into the bedroom. By jumping onto the vehicles, he was not grounded, so he didn't get shocked.

I still had quite a bit of barbed wire and decided to put that across all of the windows of the house. Bobby and I completed this task and then went into the house.

Susan was heating a big pan of water on the stove and had also cleaned the kitchen and the bathroom.

I asked, "What are you heating the water for?"

Susan said, "I found some cleaners that I think will work on the carpet in the bedroom to clean up that mess. I'm heating water for that. I used the water from the rain barrel to flush the toilet and clean up the kitchen."

I said, "Okay, thank you. Good job."

Susan said, "We have to work together to keep this place clean, livable, and safe."

I liked her thinking and agreed. I was grateful for the help. I said, "Yes, it's going to take teamwork for us to survive in this day and time."

Bobby and I went into the bedroom and moved the dresser, the mattress and box springs out of the way so Susan could clean the carpet. Then, Bobby and I started searching for materials to repair the window.

Bobby said, "Can we use the plastic carpet guard you have under your chair in the computer room to put in the window?"

I said, "Yeah I think we can. Good idea, Bobby."

We set to work on the task. We took the mattress outside and placed it on the back of my Toyota truck where it would get lots of sunshine and hopefully dry out. Susan cleaned up the glass, jawbreaker candy mess and most of the blood from the carpet in the bedroom. By the time we were done, it was early afternoon and we sat down to eat some lunch and discuss what our next goal might be.

I said, "Now that there are three of us living here in this house with a limited supply of water and food, we will have to be somewhat conservative. In the daylight, Bobby and I can go outside to pee and we'll only use water to flush the toilets when we have to. For cooking and drinking, only use the water from the water jugs that are marked 'filtered water.' Don't drink the rainwater from the barrels or from any other water without filtering it first. The water could contain bacteria that'll make you sick."

"I know you guys don't have very many clothes, so we'll have to see if we can find some more clothes that fit you."

Susan said, "I saw some women's clothes in the bedroom closet. Some of that stuff fits but most doesn't. I hope you're not upset with me because I went through your wife's things?"

I answered, "No, I am not upset. If there's anything there that you can wear you are welcome to it. My friend Jim and his wife lived across the street. There may be more clothing items that'll fit you and Bobby over there. We'll go over and see what we can find. However, I have to warn you that they died in their bedroom upstairs. Their bodies are still there and the odor was pretty bad the last time I was in there. Now that I have you two here to help me, if you would, I'd like to take their bodies outside and bury them. Then we can air out the house so that we can spend more time in there searching for things we need."

Susan and Bobby looked at each other apprehensively. Susan said, "We'll try to help you bury your friends, but I'm not sure how much our stomachs can stand."

I said, "I think I know a way for us to tolerate the odor, and I then can wrap the bodies up myself without help. That way you guys don't have to see them. I just need help carrying them outside. We'll need to take the bed and bedding outside and burn it, also."

"It's a dangerous world that we live in now, so we're going to have to change the way we approach even everyday things. This means we don't go outside without being armed. We do not leave the yard without our survival gear. We'll take our backpacks and equip them with needed items. When we go over to Jim's house, I'll teach you how to clear a house. I know the layout of the house, and I don't believe there is anything dangerous in there right now. It'll be a good place for training. I'll give you the hand signals and speak them for your training. But if we ever enter an unknown building, you'll have to learn the hand signals, because we cannot speak nor alert anyone or anything to our presence until we are sure the place is safe."

I had them get their packs and empty them out. Then I added the survival items to each pack: parachute cord, rubber gloves, facemask, two bottles of water, energy snacks, fire starter kit, extra ammo, duct tape, first aid kit, and other miscellaneous items. I explained that this was the minimum amount of survival items they needed to keep in their packs at all times. Never leave home without them.

I gave Bobby the Ruger 10/22 and some extra ammo to put in his pocket. I gave Susan the MP5 and some extra ammo to put in her pocket.

Susan asked, "Why not the 30-30?"

I replied, "Because for this exercise the MP5 is lighter, shorter and easier to maneuver around inside a building. Its design is better for a close combat weapon. If we were going into town where you might need to shoot at a longer distance, the 30-30 would probably be better."

I took the AR15 with the extra clip. As we left the house, I locked the doors and made a quick check of the perimeter. I instructed Bobby and Susan that we must never leave the doors open anytime we go outside, and that we should always lock up, even if it's only across the street. We didn't want anyone or anything entering our safe house unbeknownst to us. When we were in the house we would always keep the doors locked. This is what would keep our safe house safe.

"The training starts now." I told them. We approached the house in single file, going from cover to cover. We entered the house in a tactical manner. "Whenever you come to a doorway with an open or closed door, always stand to the side and look into the room before entering. Never stop or stand directly in a doorway. This silhouettes your body and makes you an easy target. For opening a closed door, the person on the handle side releases the latch. The person on the hinge side pushes the door open all the way to the wall. If the door doesn't go all the way to the wall, look through the crack between the door and the door casing to make sure no one is hiding there before entering the room. Enter the room quickly, moving to one side or the other of the doorway. Scan the room corner to corner, high and low, looking for any movement or anything out of place. Take up a position to one side of the doorway and do a more careful search of the room before committing yourself completely into the room. When walking through the room, stay to the sides and out of the middle of the room if possible. Check all places large enough to hold a person before going on to the next room."

We cleared each room downstairs before continuing upstairs. There we came to the door of the master bedroom and stopped.

We could smell the odor of death outside the room, but it was just tolerable. When I opened the door, the smell that came out was overwhelming, so I reclosed the door. After a bit of choking and gagging on all our parts, I said, "Okay now it's time for the nasty part of the job. Sling your weapons over your shoulders and never put them down out of your reach."

Susan said, "I don't think I'm going to be able to do this."

I said, "Hold on. I have something that'll help."

I took off my pack and reached in for handkerchiefs and facemasks. I handed these to each of them. Then I pulled out a bottle of Vicks VapoRub.

I said, "Take the Vicks and rub some on your nose and upper lip. Then put on your facemask and cover your face with a damp handkerchief. That should dull the odor enough to keep you from gagging."

I entered the room alone first and opened the windows. I then grabbed the bedding and rolled it around the bodies. Susan and Bobby were able to enter the room without gagging. The Vicks was working. They helped me get the bodies outside. We went back into the house and got the mattress and box springs. We brought them outside also. Bobby and I started digging a grave, and I had Susan start a fire pit to burn the mattress and box springs.

With that project accomplished, we went back into the house. Susan found some aerosol cans of air freshener and started spraying it around the upstairs rooms. Between the air freshener and the windows being open, we could now remove the dust masks and wipe off the Vicks. Now we could do a thorough search of the house without gagging. I took Bobby to Jim's son's room and told him to look through there for clothing items. "One of the things that you need badly, Bobby, is some hunting boots. Hiking boots would be best." Susan and I searched the walk-in closet for clothing items for her. They both found items that would fit them, including hiking boots.

I decided to search Jim's room more thoroughly now that I could breathe in there. In one of the drawers of the nightstand, I found a small key ring with two keys on it. "Hmm, I wonder if these are the keys to the gun cabinet? I'll check that out when we go downstairs."

Susan found a jewelry box full of expensive jewelry and asked, "What should I do with this?"

I thought about that for a moment and replied, "Let's take it. If we find civilization, we may be able to use it for bartering." We also found various money, both coins and bills.

Then we all went to the spare room that was full of boxes. As we searched through the boxes we discovered that some of the boxes were full of MREs (Meals Ready to Eat). Nice! That would help our food supply. We closed the doors and headed downstairs to search more.

I assigned the kitchen and dining room area to Susan to search, and Bobby the living room. I was going to search the office and check out that gun cabinet. I instructed Susan and Bobby to put everything in the middle of the room that they found to be useful.

We all went about our tasks. Susan found some cleaning items and some snack foods that appeared to still be good.

Bobby found a samurai sword and said, "Hey, check this out!" I went to look at it. It was well made and quite sharp.

I told Bobby to put it in the pile of useful items.

Bobby smiled and was happy that he now had a samurai sword.

But I would have a talk with him about that later. I tried a key in the gun cabinet. Lo and behold, it worked, and I finally got the gun cabinet open. There were two rifles and two handguns in the cabinet, and the bottom drawers were full of ammunition. The first rifle was a Remington BDL bolt action 308 with a 3 to 9 Redfield scope. The second rifle was a Ruger .44 Magnum carbine with iron sights. The first handgun was a 9mm Beretta, and the second one was a .45 ACP 1911 Kimber with laser pointer. Very nice! I also found binoculars, a tactical knife, and a buck 6-inch blade-hunting knife. In the bottom drawers I found five boxes of ammo for each weapon.

Suddenly Bobby said, "Hey, there's an ambulance in the garage!"

I replied, "Yes, I know. I put it there." Susan and Bobby both looked at me curiously. I took a drink from my bottle of water and explained to them where the ambulance came from.

Susan asked, "Does it run?"

I said, "Yes, I drove it here and put it in the garage."

She asked, "Have you tried the emergency radio in it?"

I answered, "No, I haven't done much with it other than drive it here and put it in the garage. Though now that you've brought it up, that sounds like a good idea. Let's try it out." But before we could go into the garage, we heard a vehicle coming down the road.

We went to the front windows and looked out toward the road. I instructed Susan and Bobby to stand back away from the windows so they would not be spotted. The vehicle was the red hillbilly truck with four more hillbillies in it. It stopped in the road between this house and our house. I thought to myself that this was not going to be good. I told Susan and Bobby to squat down and stay out of sight. "If we have to engage them, do not shoot until I do, and follow my lead and instructions precisely."

I waited and watched to see what the hillbillies were going to do. They got out of their truck and start talking. I noticed that two of them had semi-automatic weapons and the other two had shotguns. They were talking and pointing at the old Chevy truck parked in front of my house and seem to be intensely interested in it. All four of them walked in that direction and started looking over my truck. On the front porch of Jim's house there were stacks of firewood along the railing on each side of the entranceway. I told Susan and Bobby that we were going out there and for them to lay low behind the piles of firewood, and I'd go around Jim's car, "Keep your head down and do not make any noise, or fire on them, unless I do." Susan and Bobby looked very frightened but followed my instructions. The hillbillies were not looking in our direction, and their truck was also blocking part of their view, so we went outside.

From behind Jim's car, I stood up and yelled to them, "Hey, what are you doing?"

They turned and spread out. One of them said, "Howdy, partner. Didn't see you there."

I replied, "What do you want?"

"We were just driving around hunting and looking for supplies when we seen this old truck here."

I said, "That's my truck."

He replied, "What do you want for it?"

As he was trying to barter for the truck, I observed two of his buddies trying to flank me. Just then, Bobby knocked a piece of firewood off the stack that he was hiding behind, and his .22 rifle went off. The two hillbillies that were trying to flank me took positions behind trees, bringing their guns to bear in my direction. The two hillbillies by the truck took up defensive positions behind their truck and brought their guns to bear in our direction. The hillbilly closest to Bobby fired his shotgun in Bobby's direction. I ducked down behind Jim's car and fired on the hillbilly who shot at Bobby.

This action, of course, kicked off a firefight. Multiple shotgun blasts were being fired in Bobby's direction, but they hadn't spotted Susan yet. I was taking rifle fire from the two hillbillies behind the truck, and the fourth one was still trying to flank me. I ducked down behind the car and saw the fourth hillbilly crossing the road. He was running in the open; I fired on him, dropping him in his tracks. The hillbilly with the shotgun that was firing at Bobby now had to reload. As he was reloading Susan came from behind the stack of wood and fired rapidly in his direction with the MP5, striking her target. The guy started rolling around on the ground screaming, "I've been shot!"

The two hillbillies behind the truck stopped firing in my direction and looked at their buddy who was screaming. I took advantage of this and moved to the tree line and began firing on the hillbillies by the truck. I yelled to Bobby and Susan to open fire on the ones by the truck. Susan, walking backwards and firing on the hillbillies by the truck, made it to the other end of the porch where Bobby was. Bobby was laying on his belly, firing from around the woodpile on the porch and breaking the windows in the cab of the truck. I rapidly fired on the hillbillies by the truck, keeping them pinned down. After a minute or two, the two hillbillies by the truck hollered, "We surrender! Stop shooting, we surrender!"

I told them to throw out their weapons where I could see them. "Stand up with your hands held high over your head." I told Susan and Bobby to hold their fire. The two hillbillies by the truck complied with my commands. I told them, "Come around to this side of the truck, turn and put your hands on the truck." As they obeyed, I told Susan and Bobby to come out and disarm the wounded one over by the tree. "Susan, you stay on that guy. Keep your weapon pointed at him. If he makes any suspicious movements or looks like he's reaching for a weapon, shoot him! Bobby, come here and hold your weapon on these two."

I frisked the two by the truck and the removed knives, ammo and weapons that I found on them. Bobby said "These are some of the guys that tried to harm us in town." I told him to be quiet. To myself I was thinking the hillbillies happened on us by accident, and I didn't believe they had connected us to being in town. I did not want them to associate us with the deaths of their buddies in the courthouse.

I interrogated them for a few minutes asking; "How many more of you are around here? Where do you live or where is your base camp?" They were not willing to give up any information. I wasn't interested in torturing them to get the information, and I didn't want to have to kill them.

Their buddy that Susan shot had been hit in the leg and the arm, but I believed if we put a bandage on it to stop the bleeding, he would probably live. I made them lie face down on the ground with their fingers locked behind their heads and told them if they moved or tried to get up, I'd shoot them. I instructed Bobby to stand a few feet away from them and keep his weapon trained on them. If they tried to get up, he should shoot them.

I then went to the one who had been wounded and did a quick frisk for weapons, removing a knife and a box of shotgun shells. I checked out his wounds. The bullet wound in his leg was in the upper fleshy part of his leg. The bullet passed straight through and did not hit bone nor an artery. The bullet that struck the hillbilly's arm hit his forearm and broke one of the bones there. But the bullet passed straight through. I took my first-aid kit, put some gauze on the wounds and tied them off with handkerchief. I went back to his two buddies, telling them to get up, get their friend over there, and leave and do not come back. "If I see you on this road again, I'll not hesitate to kill you." Then I told them to get walking.

They protested about having to walk and asked about their other buddy lying dead in the road. They said, "We can't just leave him there dead in the middle of the road."

I said, "You want to take him with you?"

They said, "Walking, how are we going to do that?"

I went down to my house and got two 6 foot long 2 x 4's. I handed the two hillbillies the 2 x 4's and told them to hold them at the ends, facing each other and holding one 2 x 4 in each hand. I said, "Now hold still." I pulled their shirts off over their heads and slid the shirts down over the 2 X 4's. I said, "There now you have a stretcher to carry him on."

We went down and we rolled the body onto the stretcher. I had the two hillbillies pick it up and told them to get moving. As they started slowly walking up the road, leaving a blood trail from their dead comrade, I said, "If you come back here trying to steal from me again, I will not hesitate to kill you all. Now that you're going to have to walk out of here, that'll give you lots of time to think about *not* coming back here."

As the hillbillies were walking up the road, I asked Bobby and Susan if they were okay. Bobby had a wound on his leg where a shotgun pellet passed close to his leg, breaking the skin, but it was not serious. He also had a bruise on his arm where a piece of firewood fell off the stack and hit him. My left arm was grazed by a bullet up by my shoulder, and my shirt was torn. I was bleeding a little bit but was okay. I told Susan and Bobby to go back into Jim's house and start bringing the stuff we found over there to our house. I was going to cautiously walk up the road to the intersection and make sure the hillbillies kept on going in the town's direction. I caught up to the hillbillies and when they got to the intersection of Crown Mountain Road, they turned right, downhill toward town. I left them and returned to Susan and Bobby.

When I got back to the house, the front door was not locked, and I just walked in. I told them, "You guys did good today, but we were lucky. Susan, you surprised them with your assault, but it was somewhat reckless."

Bobby said, "I'm sorry for knocking over the wood and my gun going off."

I said, "It's okay, but that's why you need to keep the safety on until you're ready to fire."

He said, "I'll be more careful next time."

I instructed Susan, "Next time, don't stand up to fire at your enemy like that. You're exposed and could've been killed. Stay down behind the cover and fire from there. The woodpile would have kept you better protected. But you guys both did well in your first combat encounter." I hesitated, then, "One more thing. The door was unlocked when I came back. Always remember to lock it. That way no one can sneak in on you."

Susan said, "We're sorry."

I said, "It's okay. You'll get used to the routine the more often we do it." I had to be patient with them. I was angry at their carelessness, but it wouldn't help to yell. They would learn.

Bobby said, "Yeah, we kicked their asses! We taught them hillbillies not to mess with us."

I said, "We can't get cocky. We surprised them this time, but we'll have to keep on guard in case any of them come back around here. We won't be able to surprise them again. Now, back to our original project."

"We need to go out there and do something with that truck, and I see you guys already gathered up their weapons. Let's take a look at those and see what they had." Now we had two Ruger Mini 14's and two Remington pump shotguns. "The Ruger Mini 14's will make good weapons for you two." I handed one to Bobby and one to Susan. They looked them over and unloaded them and reloaded them again, and then they stood them in the corner.

Bobby said, "I'm hungry."

I said, "Okay, let me take care of that truck out there first and then we'll get something to eat. Susan, do you know how to drive a standard shift?"

She replied, "No, I don't. I've only driven an automatic."

I said, "Okay. Well, let's go out and look over their truck anyhow."

The hillbillies' truck was an automatic, so Susan would be able to drive it.

I said, "I'll drive the Chevy truck, and you, Susan, drive the hillbillies' truck and follow me. We'll take it down to the officer's house at the end of the road and park it there, out of sight."

Susan followed me in the hillbilly truck, and we drove it out around back of the officer's house and parked it there where no one would see it easily. We found another couple of boxes of ammo for the Mini 14s (2 boxes of 20 rounds each) and shotguns shells (00 Buckshot, 10 rounds) in the glove box. We took the keys and ammo, got in my truck, and then we went back to the house for some lunch.

As we were eating our lunch, I told them, "Those guys will be back again, with reinforcements, at some point. We'll need to be ready for that."

Bobby said, "If my gun had not accidentally gone off, we might not have been in that firefight."

I said, "I think they figured out that we were the ones who killed the other four hillbillies in town. So, I'm sure their intentions were not good ones. Sooner or later, we would've ended up in a firefight with them guys anyway. We were just lucky that we caught them off guard this time."

Susan said the clothes that she got from Jim's house smelled really bad, and she couldn't wear them. They would need to be washed.

I said, "Yeah, I figured that, and I think I have an idea of how we can wash them. Bobby, come with me and give me a hand." To Susan, "We will be right back."

We grabbed our weapons and gear and went over to Jim's house. Behind his house, we got two more of the plastic drums and dragged them back to my house and took them down to the backyard. I took the tactical knife and cut the barrels in half. Then I set them up and grabbed a couple of pails, giving one to Bobby. "Now we need to get some water out of the rain barrels and dump it into these half barrels."

I got Susan, and she brought the clothes from Jim's house. I told her that one of the barrels we would fill with soapy water and the other one, rinse water. Then all three of us went about the task of washing the clothes. We put up a clothesline and hung everything out to dry. Bobby and I went back over to Jim's house to get the guns, ammo, and other stuff out of the gun cabinet and brought them back over to our house. We spent the rest of the day sorting through the stuff, putting the supplies in the supply room.

Bobby and Susan were trying on clothes and getting their wardrobe in order. Bobby came out of the bedroom wearing some of the clothes that he got from Jim's house. Sideways on his head, he had a camouflage ball cap. He also wore a white T-shirt with a picture of a girl in a bikini on it. The waistband of his blue jeans was halfway down to his knees, and his underwear was sticking up out of them. On his feet were hiking boots.

Bobby said, "These clothes are pretty cool. Look at me!"

Susan and I looked at each other. Susan just smiled and shook her head but said nothing. I said, "Bobby, yeah, you look real cool, but you're not going to high school today, sorry. It's a new time in our existence. Dressing cool is not always the best way to dress in the survival situation that we're living in now."

"Your hat needs to be on straight. Then the brim can shield your eyes from the sun light, and you'll be able to see dangers better. Your pants need to be pulled up to your waist and held up with a belt so that they don't fall down in case you have to run away from one of those zombie dogs. If your pants fall down to your knees, you're going to fall on your face and get eaten alive. So, for your safety and ours, please dress appropriately."

With a sad look on his face, he looked down at his clothes. Then he went back into the bedroom to change. This time he came back out with his hat on straight, a dark colored T-shirt, camo pants belted at the waist, and he was wearing the knife, Maglite, and ammo pack.

Bobby said, "How is this?"

I told him, "Very good. You look like you're ready to kick some ass now, Bobby."

Bobby smiled and agreed, "Yes I am!"

That evening after dinner, I took Susan and Bobby with me and showed them how to set up the perimeter alarms around the house. Then we came back inside and played cards for a bit by lantern light. Then we got ready for bed with our flashlights and firearms within reach. All of us were thinking: "Will the zombie dogs try to attack us again tonight?"

Night Six/Day Seven.

Sure enough, about 2 AM, the perimeter alarms went off, alerting us to the fact that someone or something is outside the house.

Bobby said apprehensively, "The zombie dogs are back."

I told him to be quiet, listen, and not turn on the lights yet.

We heard barking, growling, bumping noises, and movement all around the house. Susan and Bobby were sitting close to me, intently listening. I could tell they were frightened.

I told them, "Okay, here's the plan. We have the back porch set up as a defensive position now. We will use red lights only until we get into position. Susan, you go to the south end of the porch with the MP5. Bobby, you'll take the middle of the porch, overlooking the backyard with the Ruger Mini 14. Take the second clip out of the other Mini so that you're able to reload. I'll take the north end with the AR15. We'll leave the back door of the house open so that we can retreat into the house if we have to. Once in position, we'll turn on our lights. Let's pick our targets and take out as many of them as possible. If you have to reload, holler 'reloading,' so that someone is able to cover you as you reload. Grab your gear. Let's do this! We'll leave backup weapons just inside the back door where we can easily retreat and grab them. It's going to be OK, guys."

We opened the back door and stepped out on the porch, assuming our assigned positions. We could hear the zombie dogs moving around and knew they were close and that there were a lot of them. I said, "Now! Give them hell!" We turned on our lights, searching for targets. Zombie dog targets were not hard to find. They were close by and moving around. We opened fire on them from our three positions. As the battle started, there was a lot of barking and yipping from the zombie dogs. They quickly moved out of the range of our lights into the woods, barking and howling, but they did not leave. A group of four or five charged south to where Susan was. She screamed and opened fire on the group of dogs. Bobby and I both looked in her direction. Susan's gunfire quickly drove them back. They disappeared back into the woods as quickly as they came. Bobby and I were both still looking in Susan's direction to see what was going on when I heard a crash behind me. I made the mistake of not keeping my eyes on the perimeter zone that I was supposed to be covering! The zombie dogs charged my end of the porch, breaking down the door just as I turned around. I turned and fired quickly in their direction, but they were already on the porch. One of them hit me and knocked the AR15 from my hands. I yelled for assistance from Bobby and Susan. I was flat on my back on the porch floor with a zombie dog right at my feet. I saw those evil eyes, snapping jaws and ivory colored teeth ready to tear me apart. I quickly reached for my 9mm handgun. Before I could get my handgun clear of the holster, Bobby and Susan were already firing in my direction, killing the zombie dog at my feet and firing into the group that was trying to come through the North gate. I fired a few rounds with my handgun into the pack of zombie dogs at the gate. All the gunfire in this direction drove the pack back away from the North end of the porch. Turning onto my belly, I grabbed my AR15 and moved back toward the back door of our house. There I was able to take a prone position and fire at the approaching zombie dogs at the north end of the porch. The zombie dogs were making another run at the South end. Susan was hard-pressed to keep them at bay. Bobby, covering the middle and being our backup, was confused on which direction he should be firing.

I yelled, "Into the house!" I followed behind them, closing the gate and the glass doors. After securing the doors, we grabbed our backup weapons and turned the table up on end and against the glass doors. Then we assumed defensive positions in the middle of the house, watching and listening in all directions. We heard the zombie dogs moving around outside the house but none came onto the porch or attempted to come in to the house through any windows or doors. Then all went silent. We waited about three minutes, wide-eyed and alert. Nothing. I say, "Well, I think they left."

We went to the windows, looked outside, and listened. Still nothing. I moved the table away from the back door and cautiously opened up the back door and the gate. I shone my light in both directions out onto the porch, seeing nothing. I stepped out, shining the light into the backyard and around the north and south ends. One dead zombie dog lay on the porch, and I saw a couple other zombie dog bodies but no noise or movement. The north door was broken and could not be repaired easily right now, so I went back in the house, securing the gate and the sliding glass door as I went inside.

We sat and talked for a few minutes, letting our adrenaline calm down. I told Susan and Bobby, "Good job, and thanks for saving my ass!"

Susan said, "You're welcome, but it's not all us. Even though we were scared as hell, when the shit hit the fan, your training kicked in, and we instinctively knew what to do and just did it, without even thinking."

Bobby said, "Yeah, I was even able to reload without any problems".

I said, "A good job, both of you. Now we need to make sure our weapons have full magazines and go back to bed and try to get some sleep. If the trend continues, they probably won't be back again tonight."

There were no more zombie dogs or disturbances; we slept until 7 AM.

Day Seven.

We put on our shoes and went out to the kitchen, looking around at the aftermath from the events of the night.

"Well, we need to get the kitchen back in order. I'll put on some water for our breakfast. Bobby, you start checking our weapons and ammunition and make sure everything loaded out 'to the max.' Susan, you can go and pick us out something for breakfast and make our coffee. I'm going outside to the check the damage to the perimeter."

I went out on the back porch and started looking things over. The north door and gate were damaged so badly that they would have to be replaced. One dead zombie dog lay by the doorway, three were out on the north end of the house, three dead at the south end, and two or three more in the backyard. The clothesline was on the ground, and all the clothes we washed were scattered around the backyard. I shook my head at all the events and went back into the house to have breakfast with Susan and Bobby.

I told Susan and Bobby that we were going to have to repair the door on the porch and do something with the dead zombie dog bodies. We would have to re-wash all the clothes and fix the clothesline.

Susan said, "All the work that we did yesterday and now we gotta do it all over again?"

I said, "Yeah, two steps forward, one back."

Bobby said, "What are we going to do with the dead zombie dogs?"

I replied, "I'm not sure, we're running out of space to bury them, and It's turning out to be a lot of work."

We sat in silence for a few minutes. Bobby said, "All the guns are loaded and ready to go again when we need them."

I said, "Good. Thank you, Bobby."

I sat there drinking my coffee; no one was talking. I watched Susan drink her coffee, standing by the back door looking out into the backyard.

In this silence, sitting there drinking my coffee and looking around, the reality of everything that had happened in the last few days flooded my mind. I got up and walked out onto the back porch, putting my hands on the railing and looking down into the backyard. I saw the two crosses of my wife's and son's graves. This was first chance that I had to think about them, and I wondered how they would have handled all of this. They had both been out of touch with current events and would have had a hard time connecting the dots and seeing the warning signs of the nightmare that I was now living. I'm not sure how they would have handled it, but I knew they would have been looking to me for guidance, support and protection. I believed they would have quickly adapted and been a lot like Susan and Bobby. Suddenly, I was overcome with the emotion of missing them, and I started crying as I was looking out at their graves.

Susan saw my emotions and came out and put her arm around me. She said, "I know you miss them. I miss my husband and daughter too. But now you have me and Bobby, and we have you, and together we will survive and take care of each other." Her voice was soft and soothing.

Bobby was standing behind us, watching and listening. He walked over to the dead zombie dog on the porch and started kicking it, saying, "Take that you dirty bastard! Come back here and screw with us again and I'll kill you all!"

Susan and I went over and pulled him away from the zombie dog body. I said, "Bobby, it will be all right. You have us and we have you. You did a good job last night."

Bobby turned around gave me a big hug and said, "Those damn monsters got my dad and my sister. I will not let them kill you too!"

I hugged Bobby back and I said, "I know you won't, and we will protect each other and kill any of the monsters that try to harm any of us."

I thought to myself that things were getting too emotional, which could be good to a point, but we needed to get our minds back on survival if we were going to survive.

I said, "Well boys and girls, I guess it's time we get to work and clean up this mess."

I said to Susan and Bobby, "I think I know what we'll do with the zombie dog bodies. We'll load them in the back of the truck and take them down to the end of the road. Across the field down there is a steep embankment. It's a long way from here and we can just throw the bodies in there for now. Bobby, you go get the wheelbarrow, and we'll start loading the bodies into the truck. Susan, you can start picking up the clothes that need to be rewashed, and we'll be back to help you shortly. Remember to stay armed and stay alert!"

We each went about our tasks. Susan looked a bit worried about being left alone, but I believed she'd be okay. We'd only be gone a few minutes.

It was a gruesome task, but we loaded all the zombie dogs into the back of the pickup truck. Then Bobby and I drove down to the end of the road and across the field to dump the bodies into the ravine. Back at the house, we went down to help Susan with the laundry.

Susan said, "I was a bit worried being here, all by myself. I kept looking around in the woods, so I did not get much done yet."

I said, "That's okay. We're all here together now and will get this job done quickly."

With the laundry completed, we walked back up to the house. I checked the mattress from my bed that we had left out on the back of my Toyota truck. The mattress seemed to be dry and okay. We could take it back into the house and set the bed back up. Bobby and I grabbed the mattress, brought it into the house and started setting the bed up. Susan got some clean linen from the closet and started making the bed. I said, "Come on, Bobby, we'll put on some water and start fixing lunch."

As we were eating our Spaghetti-Os Bobby said, "I would love a Big Mac and fries about now!" Susan and I laughed.

I said, "Yeah, it would be nice to have some normal food for a change. We'll have to go do some exploring and food-gathering soon, and maybe we can find something better to add to our food supply. But I think we need to go back and try that emergency radio in the ambulance like you suggested, Susan. Maybe we can pick up some communications on there or hear something about the state of the country and what's being done to help people and put things back together. I believe it's going to be a long time before things are normal again. But we need to keep going and keep hoping for a normal life."

I went to our weapon and ammo supplies. I picked up the 9mm Beretta and a holster. I still had two clips from my old Beretta, and I handed these to Susan. I said, "A handgun is a good backup weapon, and after last night, I see the importance of having a handgun for both of you. So Susan, you take the 9mm Beretta and keep the MP5 as your primary weapon. Both the Beretta and MP5 use the same ammo, so you only need to carry one type. This will be convenient and easy for you. Bobby, the Mini 14 seems to be working good for you, so that'll be your primary weapon. We only have two clips for it, so that'll have to do. Here, you take the 9mm Browning for your backup weapon."

With a big smile on his face, Bobby took the 9mm Browning and strapped it on. I said, "I'll use the .45 from now on for my backup weapon. We have plenty of 9mm and 5.56 NATO rounds for all our weapons."

"Okay, grab your packs! Let's go next door and check out that ambulance and its electronics and see how much of it still works." We went next door to Jim's house, opened up the door to the garage, got in the ambulance and started it up. Bobby and Susan were in the front seat of the ambulance with me. The engine roared to life and I drove the ambulance out of the garage and into the driveway.

Bobby said, "Wow, there's a lot of electronic stuff in here!"

I said "Yes, there is Bobby, and we'll check it out one thing at a time until we figure out how it all works."

The radio had a lot of frequency selections and channels. I've never spent any time inside of an ambulance, but it looked like it had a lot more stuff than you would find in an everyday ambulance. "Okay, let's turn it on and see if it works."

I found the power switch and clicked it on. The display lit up. Okay, that looked promising. I found a tuner dial and started turning slowly through the frequencies and channels, but all I was getting was static.

I said, "Okay, here's a button that says WB. I hope that stands for wave bands, and maybe that's short wave bands?"

I tried it and some frequency numbers came across the display. I then pushed the scan button. The 'scan all frequencies' worked, and the frequency numbers on the display started cycling through all the frequencies. Then it stopped on frequency 2325 KHz, and a voice came out of the speakers. We all looked at each other with surprise and anticipation of what we might hear.

The radio voice said, "......community building starts here in Savannah at Faith Christian Church, Savannah, Georgia. Food, water, medical and other supplies are available at our community. Contact us at frequency 2485 KHz. We can help you. We are looking forward to hearing from you. This is PBS Faith Christian Church, Savannah, Georgia at 2325 KHz. We will broadcast this frequency three times a day: 7 AM, noon and 7 PM. This broadcast will repeat for one hour. Then, due to our limited amount of power, will go off the air until the next scheduled time. PBS 2325 kHz." Then the message repeated again. We listened to it a few more times before turning it off.

We looked at each other incredulously. Susan said, "Yahoo! We found more people."

I said, "Yeah, but Savannah is a long ways from here and as of right now, we have no way to contact them."

Susan said, "You think we need to go there?"

Bobby said, "I've never been to Savannah."

I said, "Well, I guess it's worth checking out, but we are going to have to gather a lot of supplies and do a lot of work before we head out on a trip like that. Before all this crap took place, on a normal day, it would take about four or five hours to get to Savannah. Under our current conditions, I believe it'll take us a lot longer. You know, we just can't pull into a local gas station and get gas or stop off at a fast food joint for lunch. And I'm also sure that between here and Savannah we're likely to run into some other bad guys like those hillbillies that are here in Dahlonega. I know we haven't seen or had any problems with the zombie dogs during the daylight hours, but we only know about some of the dangers and problems right here in the Dahlonega area. I believe it would be best for us to search out some of the closer towns and cities first before we try a long trip like going to Savannah. We'll also have to see if we can find some way to communicate with the people there before we start out on a long trip like that."

I said, "Any thoughts, concerns, or suggestions other than what I've just mentioned?"

Susan said, "To find other people and a community would be nice."

Bobby said, "I like it here with you guys, but it would be nice to have some other guys my age to play some video games with."

Susan and I both laughed.

I said, "Well Bobby, I'm not sure they'll have any video games, but a community like that is a start to getting back to normal. I think we'll just put this ambulance back in the garage for now and make some plans to go on a scavenger hunt for supplies."

Susan said, "There's a mic here on the radio. Do you think it'll work to talk to the people in Savannah?"

I replied, "I don't know. Let's try."

I tuned in frequency 2485 kHz, picked up the mic, keyed it and said, "Hello, can anyone hear me?"

We waited but heard nothing but static. I tried again a few more times, but all we got back was static.

I said, "Well, I guess either this mic doesn't work, or we don't have enough power to reach them. We can hear them but they cannot hear us. With this radio we have to be a lot closer, I believe."

Susan said, "Are you saying that we'll have to drive the ambulance to Savannah?"

Bobby said, "Yeah, we can turn on the siren and make it there a lot faster."

I laughed at Bobby and said, "The siren isn't going to make it go any faster and will only alert everyone and everything to our presence. That would not be a good thing. This ambulance is valuable. I'm sure there are a lot of bad guys out there that would want to take this ambulance away from us. Susan, I don't believe we'll be driving the ambulance to Savannah. It would be quite a gas hog, and a target for every group of bad guys between here and Savannah."

Susan replied, "Then how would you be able to use the radio to contact the people in Savannah once we get close enough?"

I said, "Well, one option is that I could remove this radio and install it in the Chevy truck. However, before I do that I'd like to see if we can find a short wave radio or the components to put together to build one powerful enough to transmit from here and contact the people in Savannah before we even start out on that trip."

Susan said, "You know how to do that?"

I said, "Well, I used to work as an industrial electrician and know a lot about electronics. I believe I can fix up a radio and transmitter if I can find the right components. But the biggest problem is going to be finding components that were not damaged by the EMP. My solar panel, which powers the fence charger that I hook onto the vehicle at night, is still working, so apparently the EMP did not damage the solar panel itself. So, if we can get some more solar panels, I can put them together to charge more batteries. Then we'll need an inverter to change the DC voltage battery power to AC voltage, and that way we'll be able to power some other equipment. Let's go back to the house, start putting our plans together and see what we can come up with."

We sat down at the kitchen table to discuss our options, problems and solutions.

I said, "We could survive here for a long time. I'm sure we would be able to find enough food and water in this area to sustain us for an extended period of time, maybe two or more years. However, we have two major problems to overcome in order to do that."

"The danger of the zombie dogs attacking us every night is the first. Sooner or later, they're going to get lucky and break in here and harm one of us. My first encounter with the zombie dogs was in the officer's house at the end of the road, and I found puppies there. That means they are breeding. So no matter how many we kill, there will be more to take their place. We might be able to find their den and kill off one pack, but there's nothing to say that another pack won't move in to take over their territory and threaten us just the same."

"The hillbillies that we've seen are an even bigger problem. There are only three of us, and I'm sure there are a lot more than three or four hillbillies out there. We've already made enemies of them. So eventually, they're going to decide to launch a full attack on us. I'm sure we'll be outnumbered and outgunned when that happens, and it is not a question of 'if,' it is a question of 'when.'"

"So, planning to stay here for a long period may not be our best option. However, there are many unknowns: when we start traveling to some place farther away, like Savannah, a trip like that could be more dangerous than staying here and facing the hillbillies and the zombie dogs. Though, on the road we're going to run into more groups of bad guys that may be a lot worse than the hillbillies. Plus, if the zombie dogs are here, I'm sure there are more of them between here and Savannah, as well."

"If we travel to Savannah, we'll have to use the secondary roads. I'm sure all of the highways are blocked with disabled vehicles and may be impassable in certain areas. We'll also want to avoid large towns and cities. Due to the disabled vehicles and whatever other damage to the roadways in the city there are, travel will be very difficult. Moreover, in cities and large towns, the chances of encountering armed gangs are a lot higher than traveling the country roads. On the country roads, we may encounter downed trees, power poles and some disabled vehicles, which with a little work we should be able to clear. Everything that we need and want we're going to have to bring with us. We're not going to be able to bring everything that we have here, and the hillbillies will scavenge anything left behind, so we'll have to consider it lost. Some things we may be able to hide. If we're lucky, the hillbillies won't find them. If we return at some later date, we might have them, but don't plan on that. So, do we go or stay?"

Susan and Bobby were both looking at me, and I could see that they were just as undecided as I was.

Susan asked, "Do you think we could make it to Savannah in one day before dark?"

I said, "Possible, but unlikely under the current circumstances. It's over 300 miles from here to Savannah. We'll be traveling on back roads of unknown condition, encountering unknown hazards; both man-made and natural obstacles will occur which we'll have to overcome or clear. I'm guessing it to be about a 10 to 12 hour trip, which means we'll be sleeping out at least one night. I believe traveling after dark would be too dangerous."

Susan said, "Well, I think camping out overnight would be dangerous, also."

Bobby said, "Yeah, there's no way to keep those zombie dogs away if we only have a tent to sleep in."

I said, "Yes, I agree with both of you, so that means we'll have to secure an indoor place to stay for the night. We'll also have to make sure that the truck and all of our supplies are out of sight when we're not driving it. The whole trip is going to be a real challenge, so we're going to need to practice and hone our combat and survival skills. That's why I believe going on scavenger hunts to some closer towns will be good practice for when we have everything ready for the long trip to Savannah."

Susan asked, "So, what town do we go to first on our scavenger hunt?"

I answered, "Dahlonega."

Susan said, "There isn't much left there. The hillbillies have scavenged everything and looted all the stores and shops of anything useful. Plus, I'm sure we'll run into more hillbillies that we'll have to deal with."

I answered, "Yes, I'm sure the hillbillies have looted most of the town. But I've been living here for five or six years and I've met some of the hillbillies when I went deer hunting up in the mountains. I've also encountered them and their families at town events like the Gold Rush Festival, the fair and other events like that. If you want some good moonshine, marijuana, a good hunting dog or your car fixed, the hillbillies are the guys to talk to. But, when it comes to high tech stuff like solar power, video games, computers and other electronic things, the hillbillies don't know much about that stuff. So, when they were looting the town, I'm counting on them having overlooked a lot of useful stuff. Stuff that we need and can use. In the first 72 hours after a disaster is when most stores are looted, and most things are either stolen or destroyed. In addition, people in a panic don't think in realistic survival terms, so many useful things may be missed and left behind. If we search carefully, we can take advantage of that."

"Most high-end electronics come packaged with static guard and other shielding, protecting it for shipping. Therefore, we need to find storerooms with unopened packages of the electronic components that we'll need. We'll be looking for an inverter DC voltage to AC voltage, solar panels 4x4 feet or smaller, and wire 2/0, like what's used for battery jumper cables and other electrical stuff. I'll give you guys a list. I also want to find an electric fuel pump and 12V DC rechargeable batteries that are used in emergency lighting equipment. These are small dry cell batteries that are easily transported and will operate small electrical devices for short periods of time. We'll also be looking for two-way radios, ham radios, or short wave radio equipment still in its original packaging. Hopefully the packaging protected it from the EMP. And, of course, we'll always be on the lookout for food supplies. We'll need five 5-gallon gas cans, two 6-quart metal pans from an automotive department, and a large metal funnel. This we'll use to drain oil or antifreeze from abandoned vehicles. We may need it, and tire repair kits are useful if we get a flat on our trip."

"It's a bit late in the day today to go into town, and we need to fix up the doors on the back porch that the zombie dog broke last night. There's some lumber and household repair items down at the officer's house. We can take the truck down there and get the materials to fix the door with. Also, in the shed out back, there were some gas cans and lawn equipment. Maybe we can use some of that. We'll also check out the garage at the officer's house and Jim's house to put together some tools to take with us on our trip: bolt cutters, a crowbar and basic mechanic hand tools."

"Okay, guys, let's gear up and start gathering up some supplies and get ready for night. Susan, I believe your clothes on the line are dry. You can go gather those and Bobby and I will go next door to Jim's house and get some stuff from over there. Meet you back here in a few minutes."

At Jim's house, Bobby and I went into the garage and started putting together a toolbox of various tools that we needed for the trip. I also told Bobby that we would go into the back of the ambulance and gather some first-aid supplies and put together some small first aid kits for our survival packs. We went back to the house and picked up Susan, secured the house, and headed for the officer's house. There we gathered up the supplies to repair the porch door and found one 5-gallon gas can. We then headed back to the house and repaired the porch door.

"Okay, Susan and Bobby. I'm going to have you guys set up the perimeter alarms and show me that you know how to do it." They successfully set up the perimeter alarms and we went back in the house to have dinner. As it started to get dark, we turned on the lanterns to play some cards and talk. I said to Susan and Bobby, "On our scavenger hunts we'll have to keep an eye out for flashlight batteries and see if we can find a charger and some rechargeable ones. I think with some solar panels I can get the charges to work. That way we can recharge batteries and will not have to keep scavenging for them. I'm sure batteries are going be in short supply and high demand."

"On our scavenger hunts inside the buildings, stores or shops, we'll have to stick together, staying in sight of each other. As one of us does the searching through boxes or shelves, we'll have to post a watch to keep an eye out for any dangers like the hillbillies, zombie dogs or any unexpected problems that we might run into. We'll always have to be alert and pay attention to our surroundings."

Night Seven.

After we finished our card game, we started getting ready for bed. We strategically placed our weapons around the house and got into our beds.

I said, "Susan, do you and Bobby want to use the big bed? It's all together and ready now."

Susan and Bobby looked at each other for a moment. Then Susan replied, "No, we feel safer sleeping out here on the cots in the living room with you."

Bobby said, "What you think about posting a watch at night here?"

I said, "I don't think we need to do that; we have the perimeter alarms, which have been doing a good job of waking us up if anything comes around. If we set a watch schedule, I think that would leave us tired for the next day's adventure."

Susan said, "Yes, staying up half the night by myself and looking out windows would scare me to death, or I would get bored and fall asleep."

I nodded. "If we end up having to camp out overnight on any of our trips, we'll have to set up a watch schedule because we'll not be able to depend on perimeter alarms. We will cross that bridge when we come to it. Let's try to get some shut-eye now; we have a long day ahead of us tomorrow."

At about 1 AM we were awakened by loud howling and barking. Bobby and Susan got up from their beds, came over, and sat on the couch with me.

Bobby whispered, "Them damned zombie dogs are back again. Are we going to give them hell?"

I whispered back, "They haven't set off the perimeter alarms, so they are not close to the house. Let's just wait and see what they do."

After five or ten minutes the howling and barking stopped. The perimeter alarms never went off.

Susan said, "I think they left."

Bobby said, "Yeah, I think they've learned not to screw with us anymore."

I said, "Well, I'm not sure why they left, but it seems like they did. That's better for us, not having to fight them. Let's try to go back to sleep now."

Bobby and Susan went back to their cots, and we all settled in to go back to sleep. We drifted back to sleep and were not awakened again until daylight came shining in through the windows.

Scavenger Hunt Day One

We ate breakfast and started preparing our gear for our scavenger hunt into town. I told Susan and Bobby, "We could be in town all day today, so we'll have to add some extra items to our packs. There's a small first-aid kit for each of you. We'll need to take two bottles of water, one 12 ounce Gatorade each, flashlights, extra ammo, and we'll need to bring some tools in case we need to break into some buildings: screwdrivers, a hammer, wire cutters, and a crowbar. We can probably find some boxes or maybe a market cart somewhere to put stuff in to bring back to the truck. We'll park the truck and go on foot for most of our search. Okay, let's load up and move out."

We hopped in the truck and headed off on our first day of scavenger hunting. I decided we would go to the water tower first and survey the town with binoculars from up on the hill before we actually went down there. That might give us an idea if there were any hillbillies wandering around that we would have to look out for.

We drove up to the water tower on Crown Mountain and parked the truck. I instructed Susan and Bobby to stay low as we approached the edge of the hill overlooking the town. I told them that we didn't want to silhouette ourselves to anyone down in the town who might be looking in this direction. We lay on our bellies and looked over the town.

Bobby said, "Look over there to the right. I think I saw something moving."

I took out my binoculars and surveyed the area that Bobby indicated. Sure enough, there were three hillbillies walking together up one of the side streets.

Then Susan said, "There! To the left."

I focused the binoculars on the left side of Main Street and spotted three more hillbillies walking between the buildings.

We stayed there and watched for another 30 minutes or so.

I said, "It appears that the hillbillies are patrolling the streets. Why or for what I don't know. We'll have to do our best to avoid them and stay alert as we search for supplies."

Bobby said, "There's hillbillies all over the place down there! Are we really still going down there?"

I said, "Yes, we need supplies, and we need to practice our urban building-to-building tactics. You'll learn how to avoid danger and how to deal with enemies if we're spotted. We'll probably end up doing quite a bit of this kind of stuff on our way to Savannah and in the smaller towns that we come to. Okay, back to the truck and let's do this."

On the drive down the mountain toward town, I saw that Susan and Bobby were a bit nervous. I said, "Try to relax and stay calm. Follow my lead and remember how we trained, and you'll be okay. With our skills and some luck, the hillbillies will not spot us and we can accomplish our mission and be out of there without them even knowing we were there."

Susan replied, "I hope you're right."

Turning up the main road into town I saw something on the side of the road and slowed down to see what it was. Bobby was sitting by the passenger's door and pointing. I asked him, "Bobby, what is that?"

Bobby replied, "That looks like the stretcher that you made for the hillbillies out of their shirts."

I said, "Hmm, maybe as they were walking back to town some of their friends spotted them and gave them a ride from here."

Susan said, "Maybe."

Bobby said, "I'm not sure about that. Look up ahead."

About 100 yards or so up the road, something was laying on the side of the road. I slowly drove up to inspect it. No need to get out and look at it to see what it was. It was the bodies of the hillbillies that we had the shoot-out with, or what was left of them.

I said, "It looks like they didn't make it into town before dark and were attacked by the zombie dogs. Because their bodies are still here like this, it's my guess that the other hillbillies haven't found them yet. That may be what they're patrolling the town for: looking for their lost buddies. The zombie dogs did us a favor."

Bobby said, "Yeah, killing those scumbag hillbillies. Good job, zombie dogs."

I said, "What I meant by them doing us a favor was that now we're not going to get the blame for killing them. The zombie dogs will be blamed for killing them. That explains why twenty hillbillies didn't show up on our doorstep the next day, ready to kill us."

Susan asked, "Because they don't know that we had anything to do with it?"

I said, "That's right."

We continued into town and parked the truck in the same car wash where I parked it before.

We got out of the truck and I said, "Let's pull this plastic curtain across the front of the entranceway of the car wash. That'll make it harder for anyone to spot our truck. Two blocks up the street, there's a RadioShack and a solar power supply center. We'll check those two stores out first. Right across the street from here is a NAPA Auto Parts. We'll go there last."

We went to the RadioShack first. The glass front door was broken and the store had been ransacked. Bobby looked around and said, "I don't think there's anything useful left here. What hasn't already been taken is broken."

I said, "We want the stuff in the back storage room. That's where we'll be looking for things like shipping packages that haven't been put out on the shelf for sale yet. Susan, do you want to stand guard on this one?"

Susan replied, "You're not going to leave me alone, are you?"

I said, "No, all you need to do is stand here by the counter, out of sight from the windows, and keep a lookout for any hillbillies coming this way. If you see them, step into the back and signal us with a low whistle. Bobby and I are going into the back to search through the boxes in the storage area."

Susan took her position, and Bobby and I went into the back storage area and started searching through everything.

In the front of the store, the sunlight coming through the front windows allowed us to see the items in the store without much trouble. However, in the back storage area there was no light. It was completely dark, and we had to use our headlamps to see. There were boxes, both opened and unopened, scattered everywhere. Other miscellaneous items, broken and unbroken, littered the floor. Searching through this jumble was quite a challenge. We had to be careful to not fall, get cut, or hurt on broken glass or metal. But we eventually found some of the things we needed.

We started putting some electrical supplies into empty boxes: wire nuts, wire, solder, and a butane-soldering torch. We also got lucky and found a ham radio transmitter and receiver, brand-new in a factory-packed box!

I said, "See, Bobby, this is exactly what we're looking for."

I found an antenna to go with it and we headed out of the store. Bobby found a battery charger kit with batteries in it (AAA, AA, C, D, and 9 volt).

I said, "Come along Susan, we'll take the stuff to the truck so that we don't have to carry it around with us. We'll go to the solar energy store next." It was only two blocks back to the truck, so it was no big deal to make trips back to the truck with our supplies.

After putting the electrical stuff in our truck, we headed for the solar energy store. On the way up the street, we spotted two hillbillies coming down the street in our direction.

I said, "Quickly, in here!"

We ducked into a real estate office, hoping the hillbillies hadn't spotted us. Inside the real estate office there was the main greeting room with one large office on the left side and three smaller offices on the right. I told Susan and Bobby to go into the offices on the right side, close the doors, and hide in there. I would hide in the office on the left side. I went into the larger office and closed the door. Then we waited.

I heard the bell over the front door jingle as someone entered the building. I decided that they must have spotted us. I listened and I heard the hillbillies talking. One of them said, "I know they came in here. I seen them."

The other one said, "Look in those rooms over there. I'll look in this one."

I stood to the side of the door, waiting for it to open. The door swung open slowly. The hillbilly was holding on to the door handle, walking into the room and pushing the door open as he entered the room. Big mistake on his part. I struck him quickly in the face with the butt of my AR15. Then I swung the butt end of my AR15 downward, striking the hillbilly's wrist, knocking his weapon free from his grasp. I stepped forward, bringing my knee up hard into his midsection, knocking the wind out of him. The hillbilly doubled over, grabbing his midsection and gasping for breath. I then brought the AR15 down hard on the back of his neck, dropping him to the floor. Then I brought the rifle to bear on the other hillbilly, who was opening the door of the second office on the other side where Susan and Bobby were.

I yelled to him, "Hold it right there!"

He turned in my direction and saw the weapon I had pointed at him. He said, "Whoa, where did you come from?"

I said, "Drop your weapon and hands up!"

He thought about this for a moment. Then Bobby came out of the office the hillbilly had been about to enter, and Susan came out of the other office. Both were holding their weapons on him.

Susan said, "Drop it, mister."

Seeing that he was outnumbered and outgunned, the hillbilly complied, dropping his weapon and putting his hands up.

I said, "Face the wall, put your hands behind your head, interlocking your fingers. NOW!"

After a second's hesitation, he complied. I then reached down, pulling the other hillbilly to his feet and pushing him against the wall.

I said to Susan and Bobby, "One of you keep your gun on him, the other one frisk him for weapons. I got this one."

After frisking them, we lay their weapons on the desk in the greeting room. I put two chairs against the wall and made the men sit in them.

I sat on the edge of the secretary's desk and said to them, "We do not want any trouble. We're only looking for a few supplies, and then we will be on our way. We're sorry to have to have met you this way, but these days you can't be too careful."

The bigger one spoke up. "We weren't making no trouble. We just seen some people go into this building and was wondering who you were and why you was here."

I said, "Who we are is not important. Why we are here is: we need a few supplies and then we'll be moving on."

The other one spoke up and said, "Poppa is not going to be happy about this."

I said, "Your father doesn't need to worry; we're not going to harm you."

The big one said, "Poppa isn't our father. He's our clan elder and this is his town."

The smaller one said, "No one takes anything from this town without Poppa's permission."

The big one said, "and Poppa doesn't give permission to outsiders."

I said, "Poppa is just going to have to get over it. We don't have time to negotiate or barter with him."

The smaller one leaned toward his partner, "All them big words. You know what he's talking 'bout?"

The bigger one said, "Yeah, he doesn't want to make a deal with Poppa. He's just gonna take what he wants without permission."

The smaller one's eyes got big. "Oh boy, Poppa is not going to be happy."

I said, "Okay you two, get up and get in there." I pointed with my rifle to the restroom.

The smaller one protested, "Hey, that's the shitter, and I don't need to go right now!"

I said, "Shut up and get in there! Maybe you'll have to go before you get out."

After they were in the small room, I took a chair and wedged it under the door handle to block the door shut so they couldn't get out.

I said, loud enough for the hillbillies to hear me, "Bobby, you stay here and make sure those guys don't get out of there. If they give you any crap, just shoot them right through the door."

Bobby looked at me, horrified.

I whispered in Bobby's ear, "I'm not really going to leave you here to watch them; I just want them to think that." Bobby nodded his head and started to speak, but I put my finger to his lips, signaling him to keep quiet. I then motioned to Susan and Bobby to follow me out of the real estate office.

We went up the street to the solar energy store. I told Susan, "Stand guard here by the window and keep an eye on that real estate office. But you'll also need to look up and down the street for any more of the hillbillies. Bobby and I need to search around here for some solar panels and an inverter."

Solar panel kits were not difficult to find, but we had to open fifty boxes before we found an inverter. Then we left the solar energy store and went back to the truck. Stopping by the real estate office on the way, I went in and knocked on the bathroom door. "I hope you guys are comfortable, but don't worry we'll be done soon and let you out, so you can go home to Poppa."

The reply was "Yeah, yeah, yeah just go away and leave us be."

"Oh, I'm not ready to leave you alone just yet. Bobby is out here and he's got an itchy trigger finger. He'll keep an eye on you for a bit longer."

Then I went back outside with Susan and Bobby. Now to the auto parts store. Then we could be done and get out of here.

Inside the NAPA, I had Bobby stand watch and Susan helped me search this time. The store wasn't ransacked as badly as the others had been. Things were thrown about, but it looked like most of the items were still in the store. I guessed that people weren't too interested in looting an auto parts store. I easily found a 12V DC fuel pump, oil pan and other items. Then I spotted some emergency lighting on the wall. I found a ladder, climbed up to the emergency lighting, and removed it from the wall, handing it down to Susan. After removing two of these, we left and headed for the truck. Just as we were turning down the road out of town, three hillbillies came around the corner near the real estate office. We heard them yelling, "Stop!"

I just kept driving. Then they started shooting in our direction, and I floored the truck and headed home.

On the way up Crown Mountain Road I said, "We better go on up to the water tower and look back into town to see what the hillbillies are up to now just in case they decide to get a group together and try to find us."

At the water tower we went to the edge of the hill and took out the binoculars and looked back into town.

We saw several hillbillies standing in the middle of a street, talking. Then a pickup truck and a Jeep came up to the main street from one of the side streets and stopped. They picked up the eight hillbillies standing in the road and drove off down one of the side streets. As I watched through the binoculars, I noticed they only used the side streets to drive around town. I made a mental note that they kept the main streets in town blocked in and congested, but they had cleared the side streets. A smart tactic. This would keep anyone who happened to come up on the town from being able to drive around very easily. That would give the hillbillies an advantage and time to intercept any intruders. I said to Susan and Bobby, "It doesn't look like the hillbillies are going to follow us, so we can go on to the house now."

As were unloading the stuff and bringing it into the house, Susan said, "Summer's here. It's getting really hot now. I wish we had some air-conditioning. I'm all sweaty; I need a shower really bad."

I said, "Well Susan, I think I can help you out with a shower."

She looked at me and said, "What are you going to do, pour buckets of water on me?"

I said, "Close, but not quite. Come with me out here on the back porch."

I showed Susan and Bobby the 'MacGyver' shower system that I made.

Bobby said, "Cool! Neat idea!"

Susan made a face. "That might work out okay. But, I don't think I'll feel very comfortable showering exposed in the backyard."

I said, "Bobby and I will stay up here on the back porch with our weapons and keep a lookout for any dangers that might be coming around as you shower, and you guys can do the same thing for me."

Susan thought for a moment. "If it's okay with you, I would rather have you in the backyard with me and let Bobby stand watch up there on the porch."

I just looked at her without answering right away. Susan smiled and said, "Under these conditions, modesty kinda goes out the window."

I said, "Okay, I guess that'll work out better." I grinned. "Anyhow it would be kinda hard to see danger coming or to fire a gun with soap in your eyes."

Susan laughed and said, "Yeah, could you picture us running around naked all covered with soap trying to fend off an attack by the zombie dogs or the hillbillies?" We both started laughing.

I said, "Okay, shower up, but we have to conserve water. We only have three quarters of a barrel. So just get wet, soap up, and wash it off. We'll wash our hair in the sink. I think we'll use less water that way. The person standing guard up on the porch will take this pole and push the water valve shut at the bottom of the barrel if it doesn't close off. Okay, who's first?"

Susan said, "I brought it up, so I guess I'll go first." Susan got some clean clothes together, and I got a chair. We could put the clothes on that instead of putting clean clothes on the ground. Before going down there, I went into the basement and brought out a piece of plywood to put on the ground under the showerhead. We could stand on that when taking a shower so we didn't have to stand in the dirt. Susan started taking her clothes off to get into the shower. I turned my back to her.

Susan said, "You're not going to be much of a lookout or bodyguard if you are afraid to look in my direction just because I am nude."

I turned around and started observing the perimeter around the backyard. Susan got in the shower and started washing up. I couldn't help looking in her direction. Susan was a petite, attractive woman. With all the work and exercise that we had been getting, her body had firmed up nicely. Susan saw me looking at her and smiled. She turned her back to me, bent over, and started washing her feet. I got the impression that she was teasing me. She finished washing and then started getting dressed.

Susan said, "Now, it was not all that bad was it?"

A bit embarrassed, I said, "Well, I have to admit, I think I spent more time watching you than I did the perimeter."

Susan smiled and said, "Okay, now it's your turn, and I get to watch you."

I said, "Okay," and blushed a bit.

Susan said, "I brought your clothes down with mine."

I smiled and said, "How thoughtful." Then I took my turn. The sun had warmed the water. It really wasn't all that cold, and it felt good. But I think I really needed a cold shower at this point.

Then we went upstairs and told Bobby it was his turn to shower. Bobby looked kind of horrified at being told to shower naked in front of us.

Susan said, "Bobby, you can go down there and shower and we'll stay up here, so as not to embarrass you too badly."

Bobby gave a sigh of relief. "Okay, I guess that'll work."

He took his clothes and he went down to shower. As he was showering, Susan heated a pan of water to wash her hair.

Susan said, "We may have to shower using cold water, but we don't have to wash our hair in cold water."

I agreed, "Yes, that's a good idea. The warmer water is better for cleaning our hair than cold water would be."

"Yeah, trying to wash soap out of our hair with cold water would be difficult," she said.

"We have lots of propane, so heating water to wash with is not a problem."

After we all washed up and were clean and smelling good, we sat down to have something to eat. Our meal was some spaghetti sauce and some pasta, but we had no meat to put in it. But Bobby and Susan decided that some real spaghetti, even without the meat, was still better than eating Spaghetti-Os from a can.

After dinner, I looked over the supplies that we got from town, checking out the electrical stuff, the solar panels, the inverter, and stuff like that.

Susan asked, "Do you think you're going to be able to get that to work?"

I replied, "I'm not sure, but I'll give it a shot tomorrow. It's too late tonight to start messing with it."

Bobby agreed, "Yeah, it's going to be getting dark soon. We need to get our perimeter alarm set in case those damn zombie dogs come back tonight."

I said, "Yes, you're right, Bobby. Let's go set those alarms." Then, "Susan, you can check our weapons and get our beds ready. I think we all need some rest, and we'll not be staying up after dark to play cards tonight."

Susan said, "Yes, early to bed, early to rise."

After setting the perimeter alarms, Bobby and I went back into the house to get ready for bed. I walked into the living room. The cots were still folded up and standing in the corner. There was a lantern on the coffee table and bedding on the couch. Susan was in the bedroom with a lantern on the nightstand.

I looked at Susan and asked, "You decided to use the bed tonight?"

Susan said, "Yes, those cots are not very comfortable. But the bed is for us, and Bobby will be sleeping out on the couch tonight."

Bobby looked at me and said, "Yeah, those cots are not very comfortable. I'll sleep on the couch. I'll be okay. You guys are only in the next room."

Susan took me by the hand and lead me into the bedroom. She closed the door and stripped down to her underwear. She got into the bed and asked, "Are you coming?" I was a bit surprised, but I joined her in the bed and turned out the light.

She said, "I hope this isn't too uncomfortable for you. I just think we need to unwind. We're going to be together for a long time it seems, and we're both adults. I think the time is right."

I give her a kiss and said, "Nom it isn't uncomfortable. It's very comfortable! But, I have to admit, I am a bit surprised, in a good way."

Susan said, "Just a minute." She got out of bed, went to the bedroom door, and looked out at Bobby. Then she closed the door and came back to bed.

She said, "Bobby's exhausted. He's already out cold."

Then she wrapped her arms around me and gave me a long kiss. I returned her kisses and affection. The lovemaking was very refreshing and a needed distraction from our daily struggles.

Preparations day one

After the intimate evening, we fell right to sleep. The next thing I knew, I heard a knocking noise and someone speaking. I immediately became alert and listened intently.

There was knocking on our bedroom door. "Are you guys getting up? I'm hungry."

I smiled to myself – it was only Bobby waking us up. It was daylight and I looked at my watch. It was 8 AM! I looked over at Susan who was also awake. "Wow, I guess we slept well last night, and I think Bobby is looking for some breakfast."

Susan smiled, saying, "I guess we needed that. Yes, Bobby we hear you, we'll be out in a minute to fix breakfast. Hold your horses!"

We got dressed and went to fix breakfast. As were sitting at the kitchen table drinking our coffee and eating our breakfast, Bobby looked at me and said, "You know I miss my dad, but I think you would be a great dad to me, also."

I smiled and gave him a hug. "I would be proud to have you as a son also, and you can even start calling me 'dad' if you want to."

Susan looked at us both with a huge smile on her face. She came over and we all had a group hug. "Now we're one big happy family."

Bobby mentioned, "The zombie dogs didn't attack last night."

I said, "Well, I guess they didn't come around, or we just didn't hear them."

Bobby said, "I'm glad they weren't here; I was really tired and needed to sleep."

I stood and looked out the back door. It was raining outside. One of those steady, all day type of rains. I said, "WIth all this rain, it should fill up our water barrels, and we'll have plenty more water for showers."

Susan said, "Oh, are you looking forward to another shower show?"

I said, "Well, I did enjoy the last one, but actually, I was only stating a fact. I don't think we'll be doing much outside today, so we'll just stay in here and work on this solar panel project."

Bobby said, "Don't we need sunlight to make the solar panels work?"

I said, "Yes, but even though it's raining, there's still enough sunshine to make the panels work, maybe not at 100%, but they'll still work as long as the EMP hasn't damaged them."

So with Bobby and Susan's help, I got to work at building a solar powered generator. I said, "We have some batteries in the cars around here. We can get those and put them in one of these plastic totes. Four 12-volt car batteries ought to do the trick. Bobby, I have a handcart in the storeroom. Will you get that for me? We're going to need two more totes all with covers. I think there are some in the closet in the bedroom. We'll just empty the clothes out of them."

I started wiring up the charge controller and the inverter. Then I assembled the solar panels and took them out onto the back porch. I angled the panels to collect the most sunlight. I completed the wiring for the charge controller and the inverter. Then, I cut holes in the side of the tote with the inverter in it and added in two receptacles.

I said to Susan and Bobby, "Now all we need are some batteries. I have some raincoats for us, and we can go out and take the batteries out of my wife's car and my Toyota truck."

We got two batteries out of the vehicles and brought them into the house. I put the two batteries in one of the totes, completing the wiring from the batteries over to the charge controller and inverter. Then I strung the rest of the wire out onto the back porch and wired everything to the solar panels. The indicator lights on the charge controller and the inverter all came on!

I said to Susan and Bobby, "See those lights? That means it should be working."

I then took my multimeter and tested the voltages of the batteries. 14.4 V. Good, the batteries were charging! I then checked the output voltage from the inverter - 118 V.

I said, "Okay Bobby, get that table lamp from the living room, and bring it over here."

I plugged in the lamp, flipped the switch, and we had light.

Susan and Bobby both at once said, "It works!"

I said, "Yup, looks like we're in business. After it stops raining, I want to take the battery out of Jim's car. And the old battery that was in the Chevy truck is down at the officer's house. I want to get that one, also. With four batteries, the output of this solar generator should be somewhere around 1000 W. That'll be enough to run some small appliances. I want to charge up the batteries for the power tools so we can build a few things that we need, and make some modifications to the bed of the Chevy truck for our trip to Savannah. After we get the other two batteries and let them get fully charged, we'll hopefully have enough power to run the transmitter for the ham radio. That should have enough power to contact the outside, maybe even as far as Savannah."

It rained all day long. We spent our time that day trying out small electrical devices with the solar generator to see which ones still worked and which ones had been damaged by the EMP.

Bobby said, "I wish I had my Xbox now. With this generator, I would be able to play some video games."

I said, "Well Bobby, I am sorry to tell you this, but I think all of the gaming systems were damaged by the EMP and even if they were not damaged, we would still have to find a working TV or monitor."

Bobby was dejected, "Just my luck; no more video games."

I said, "You shouldn't be too upset. You have other fun things to do."

Bobby said, "What fun things are there to do for teenagers like me now?"

"You're living a real-life video game, shooting zombie dogs and running from wild hillbillies, all of them wanting to kill you."

Bobby shook his head, "That's really not a lot of fun. It scares the shit out of me!"

I said, "Yeah, I know, I'm just joking with you. Maybe we'll be able to find some fun stuff for you, like video games or something else that still works when we get to Savannah."

Bobby said, "That'd be great!"

We plugged the battery chargers into a power strip which was plugged into the generator. After we got them all charging, we went about the task of cleaning all the guns.

With that done, I said, "Let's gear up and go get the batteries out of those vehicles. Down at the officers house I want to get some materials to build racks on this handcart. If I can do that, I can make this generator portable. We'll go across the street to Jim's house first. Susan, as Bobby and I are taking the battery out of Jim's car, I would like you to go into the back of the ambulance to gather as many of the medical supplies and medicine as you can fit into one of the big medical bags. I want to take them with us. We're going to have to leave the ambulance here, and I'm sure after we're gone, the hillbillies will find it and confiscate the ambulance and all of the supplies."

"Speaking of the ambulance, I have an idea. I believe it has a large battery compartment to run all the electronics aboard. I think we can use those batteries for the solar-powered generator. I also want to take the radio out of there and see if I can install it in our truck. We should get started on stripping the ambulance of all the useful supplies and materials that we'll need."

Getting everything useful out the ambulance took us all morning. The vehicle had four heavy-duty 12V batteries. I wired them together in the bottom plastic tote for the generator. I assembled the totes onto the handcart and took it out onto the back porch. We then took the solar panels and laid them on top of the Toyota truck, where they could gather the most sunlight. Then we ran the wires back to the porch and hooked them into the generator so the solar panels could charge the batteries. It was still raining, so we stayed in the house and worked out our plans to modify the Chevy truck for longer trips. It had to hold all of our gear and supplies.

After lunch, we started working on setting up the ham radio. We attached the antenna to the side of the house and ran the wires into the house. We would have to let the batteries charge for a few hours before trying to hook the ham radio to the generator, because I believed it would take a lot of power to operate the transmitter.

We planned and organized our supplies for the long trip to Savannah. We were not going to be able to take everything we had, so we gathered the stuff that we couldn't take with us and stashed it in the basement. Maybe we'd come back at a future date.

In the late afternoon it stopped raining, so we went to work at modifying the Chevy truck with the parts that we stripped off the ambulance. We replaced the Chevy generator with the one from the ambulance for a higher amp output. We took the white lights from the ambulance and installed them on the Chevy truck for spotlights. We took the dashboard apart in the Chevy truck and installed the emergency radio from the ambulance. We took my gun safe and put it in the bed of the Chevy truck, laying it down up near the cab and bolting it to truck bed. We took some lumber from Jim's house and the officer's house and built racks on the bed of the Chevy. We made the racks high, with framework that would support a tarp over the top. The top was high enough so we could stand up in the bed of the truck. The framework over the top would be able to support the solar panels for the solar generator. We took the electric fuel pump we got from the auto parts store along with a battery and pumped the gas out of the ambulance into our gas cans. We then made racks for the gas cans on the back of the Chevy truck bed. This took us into the evening. With the sunlight fading, we didn't have time to complete all of the modifications. Bobby and I set the perimeter alarms and then went into the house to get cleaned up for dinner. After dinner, we started reading over the instructions on how to hook up and use the ham radio.

Savanna, GA. Pre-trip night one.

After reading over the user manuals that came with the ham radio equipment, we decided it was too complicated to work on it that night, so we decided to just go to bed. We checked our weapons and ammo, placing them strategically about the house. Bobby made up his bed on the couch and settled in for the night. Susan and I went to the master bedroom, placing our weapons and flashlights on the nightstand and settled ourselves into bed.

During the night, we were awakened by loud noises. Our perimeter alarms had been activated, and there was loud barking and howling. We sat up in bed, instantly alert. We got dressed and armed as quickly as possible. Then we all met in the kitchen, armed and ready, red lights on low.

Bobby said, "I guess those zombie dogs are not going to give us two nights' sleep in a row."

Susan said, "It sounds like there's a lot of them out there tonight."

Bobby nodded, "I guess they're not too smart. We kicked their asses last time, and now they're back for more."

I said, "Bobby, never underestimate your enemy, and always be ready for the unexpected."

Susan asked, "Are we going out there to fight them?"

I said, "We could take a defensive position and just wait inside the house, but if they are intent on attacking us, they'll find a way in here, and we'll be fighting them in close quarters inside the house. I think it's better to opt for an offensive posture, attacking them. Hopefully this will teach them that if they come close to our territory, we'll fight back with deadly force. We'll also do the same as before, keeping the back door open in case we need to fall back. Okay, you know the drill. Let's get to it, and give them hell!"

Out the back door we went. Susan took the south end of the porch, and Bobby took the middle, covering the backyard. I took the north end of the porch. On a three count, we switched on our white lights and opened fire on the large number of zombie dogs.

Susan yelled, "Reloading!"

I looked in her direction, noticing that Bobby had turned to cover her and at that exact moment, the zombie dogs crashed through the north gate, attacking me. I turned back to engage the charge of zombie dogs at the north end of the porch. Bobby heard the crash and turned to assist me with the charge. There was a crash and a scream from the south end of the porch. Another group of zombie dogs had crashed through the south gate, attacking Susan.

I yelled to Bobby, "Go assist your mother! I have this end!"

One of the zombie dogs that crashed through the south gate had knocked Susan to the ground and was viciously trying to bite through her defenses. She was holding the creature at bay by holding the MP5 crosswise in both hands as a barrier to keep the creature from biting her in the face. Bobby let out a war cry, drawing the samurai sword, which he had attached to his belt, and cleanly sliced off the head of the zombie dog that was attacking his mother. Susan drew the 9mm Beretta and started firing into the group of zombie dogs that were trying to get through the gate at the south end of the porch. A zombie dog landed on my end of the porch, leaping for my throat before I could get a bead on him and fire. I quickly slammed my rifle into the side of the dog, knocking it to the ground. I then recovered the hold on my weapon and fired three shots into its body, killing it. With more dogs charging, I fell back toward Bobby and Susan. They were falling back toward my position, holding off the creatures' charge with their handguns. We all retreated through the back doors into the house. Closing the gate and securing the back doors, we flipped the kitchen table up, taking our defensive positions in the middle of the house.

Through the glass doors, we saw several zombie dogs on the back porch. I told Susan and Bobby to not shoot through the glass doors. "Hold your fire. If the zombie dogs should break the glass then we will fire."

We watched and waited for several minutes. Then, as a group of zombie dogs was walking past the glass doors, they stopped. There was a large one in this group. Its color was a dark red and he was twice the size of the others. He looked straight at us, showing his teeth. He gave two short barks and moved off, out of sight. After a few more minutes of barking and howling, it got quiet and we assumed they left.

Bobby said, "Holy shit, I thought we were dead!"

Susan said, "I would've been dead Bobby, but you saved my ass. Thank you, honey!" She kissed him on the cheek.

Bobby said, "I was scared as hell, but I was not going to let those monsters kill you, Mom."

I asked, "Was anyone bitten or injured?"

Susan said, "I'm okay, not even a scratch, thanks to Bobby."

Bobby said, "I'm good. Only zombie dog blood on me. But I think I need to change my shorts."

I said, "That was a very aggressive attack that they made on us tonight. For a few minutes there, I thought we were all goners. But you two did very well in defending yourselves. Nice work with the sword, by the way, Bobby."

Bobby grinned. "Oh, you saw that?"

I nodded, "Yes, I saw that. I wouldn't recommend carrying a samurai sword all the time, but it worked for you tonight."

After several more minutes without hearing any noises from the zombie dogs, we went and checked all of the windows. Seeing no sign of them and hearing no sounds, we decided that they had left for the night. We sat and talked softly, trying to calm down for a bit. Then we checked our weapons and decided to go back to bed.

Chapter 6

Ham radio.

The zombie dogs did not come back again that night. We got up around 7 AM. I said, "Bobby, lets gear up, go outside, and check out the perimeter."

Susan said, "I'll get coffee and breakfast started."

Bobby and I went out the back door onto the porch where we found seven zombie dog bodies, including the one without a head.

Bobby said, "It looks like we killed seven of them, and I'm sure we wounded a few more. Where do they keep coming from? We kill a few of them every time they attack us, but they keep coming back with more than the last time."

I asked him, "Remember that big red one?"

Bobby said, "Yes, I'll never forget the way he looked at us."

I said, "He's the alpha dog, the leader of the pack. I think he's calling in more zombie dogs from around the area to increase the size of his pack and territory. Because we kill a few of them each time, they attacked us. Because they haven't been able to break through our defenses and harm us, that makes us a threat. I think that's why he keeps coming back, hoping for a victory… to kill us or drive us away."

Bobby's brow wrinkled, "But we're getting ready to go away; were going to Savannah soon, right?"

I said, "Yes, but the zombie dogs don't know we're leaving, so as long as we are here, we are a threat, and they'll keep attacking us."

Susan called from the door, "Breakfast and coffee are ready."

We went inside and sat down at the table. I told Susan about what we found outside and about the alpha dog and his pack of zombie dogs. I also said that we needed to repair the north and south gates.

Susan said, "How soon before we are going to be able to leave?"

"Well, it's going to take a few days to get all the modifications to the truck done, learn how to use the ham radio, and map out a route to Savannah. Plus, we need to hide any supplies that are left here that we cannot take with us. I also want to do some training for the tactics that we'll use on the road if we should encounter any problems. So a rough guess would be in about three or four days."

Bobby said, "Are we going to have enough ammo and be able to defend ourselves against the zombie dogs for that long?"

I said, "Yes, I think so. We haven't used up that much ammunition, and I'll reload some more tonight. The first thing we need to do is take care of the zombie dog bodies. We'll do the same as we did before: load them in the back of the truck and take them down to the ravine. Bobby and I will take care of the zombie dog bodies and get the materials needed to repair the porch. Susan, I need you to gather up the spent brass from our firefight with the zombie dogs last night and prep them for reloading later. Then we'll repair the north and south gates on the back porch. After that, we'll see if we can get anything on the ham radio."

We set about the tasks of disposing of the bodies. On the way back, we picked up some lumber supplies from the officer's house. After repairing the gates, we sat down for lunch and went over the manual on how to operate the ham radio.

I got my equipment and tools out. I tested the solar generator and the batteries seemed to be at full charge now; the output was at 100%. Then I went about the task of hooking up the ham radio. I started the process of tuning through the different frequencies.

Into the 4000 frequency range, we started hearing voices. As I adjusted the dials, it became clear.

"Voice of America Radio on the aircraft carrier USS Ronald Reagan is off the coast of Carolina along with the Atlantic Fleet. From here, the government of the United States of America will be launching missions to stabilize the populace, reestablish communications, reestablish electrical power, and distribute food and medical supplies, starting with Charleston and Charlotte, then branching out to surrounding areas from there. Due to the epidemic outbreak of canine flu, all citizens are being advised not to travel. Help will come to you. Remain at your current location and stay tuned to this frequency for more news and updates."

"Voice of America Radio news April 10, 2020; multiple forces of North Korea, Iran, ISIS and Al Qaeda have attacked the United States. US forces abroad are currently engaged with our enemies, striking devastating blows every day. US naval assets from abroad that are not directly needed in the fighting are being brought back to the US to assist in the recovery of our great nation, the United States of America. Air Force One, with the president and staff on board, has crashed, and is now missing. Air Force Two, with the vice president aboard, is also missing. Acting president is Secretary of State John Hagar, aboard the aircraft carrier USS Ronald Reagan. Peacekeeping forces from Russia and China have been placed at various locations across the country to help bring peace and stability to regions of extreme violence. These forces are under the command of the United Nations. British forces are assisting and are in control of the New England states. Australian and US forces are in control and bringing stability to the West Coast states. Texas, Oklahoma, and New Mexico have gone rogue from the United States, and all citizens are advised to stay clear of that territory. Food and medical supplies will be airdropped into populated areas starting in the next few days. This broadcast will repeat 24/7. New information will be added as it becomes available."

The message then started to repeat.

Susan said, "Wow, that's great. Help is on its way."

Bobby asked, "Does this mean we're not going to Savannah?"

"I don't really know yet Bobby," I replied. "This is some good information, and more than we've ever had. But I don't see how it really helps us directly anytime soon."

Susan said, "They said they were going to have airdrops of food and medicine in a few days."

I shook my head, "Yeah, maybe in *populated areas*. This is not one of them. If we stay here and wait for them to get to us, then we'll either run out of food or ammunition. Then the zombie dogs will have us for their dinner. Just sitting here waiting is not a practical option. But it's going to be a few days before we're ready to move out anyhow, so in the meantime we'll keep checking back to this frequency for any more updates. I'll also keep scanning the channels for any other news or communications from the outside world."

We continued our preparations and training for the trip to Savannah. Three days and nights went by without any notable events.

Road Trip. 4/14/20

After breakfast each day I would go through the frequencies on the ham radio. I hadn't picked up any communications from Savannah and hadn't gotten any answers from any of my transmissions, either. I'd have to continue trying to transmit on some more channels. If I didn't hear anything, I'd give up trying to contact anyone from here. We'd be taking the ham radio and the solar powered generator with us, so we could try again when we got closer to more densely populated areas.

At least that one transmission had given us some information that was helpful. We now knew that it was April. This was important because we now knew it was tornado season, and that's one more dangerous obstacle we had to be aware of. We didn't have Doppler radar or weather reports to keep us informed about severe weather, so we're going to have to keep our eye on the sky and hope that we don't run into any tornadoes between here and Savannah. Our preparations were almost complete. We should be able to head out first thing in the morning.

When Bobby found out, he was excited. "Yahoo! I'm really looking forward to this trip!"

Susan said, "The zombie dogs haven't bothered us in the last few nights, so we are due for an attack. I want to get out of here before they come back."

"Bobby, be careful what you wish for," I cautioned. "This is going to be a long, difficult, dangerous trip."

Susan asked, "Do you think we're ready?"

Bobby was practically hopping. "I'm ready! I've got my samurai sword!"

I said, "We've been training hard and I think we're ready, but I'm not sure how much use Bobby's samurai sword is going to be."

Susan shrugged, "It makes him happy to have it, and bringing along one more weapon isn't going to hurt."

I said, "Oh, I agree, and it may come be useful for nothing more than for cutting some brush or firewood."

Bobby said, "No cutting brush or wood with my samurai sword! It's only for cutting the heads off zombie dogs."

I said, "Okay, well it's time to check our perimeter and set about getting our chores done."

After completing our morning chores, I told them, "Today I want you guys to train with some of the other weapons that you haven't fired yet. I haven't trained you in the use of a 12 gauge shotgun or a high-powered rifle. Both of these weapons have substantially more recoil than the other weapons you are used to. At some point, you're going to have to use the more powerful weapons, so it's time that you get used to the recoil."

Bobby said, "Cool! I'll really be able to kick some ass on those zombie dogs with a shotgun!"

"After firing a few heavy rounds, you might not be so enthusiastic about using a 12 gauge as your primary weapon."

Susan was apprehensive. "Is the recoil really that bad?"

I encouraged her, "I think you guys will be able to handle

it okay now, and a shotgun makes a great backup weapon for an emergency. You both need to know how to use it. The 308 Remington bolt action with the scope is great for hunting and distance shooting."

Bobby said, "That's also a sniper rifle, right?"

He *has* been listening, I thought to myself. "Yes, using it as a sniper rifle is most likely the primary reason to bring it with us, and you both will need to know how to use it proficiently, too."

I'd been putting off teaching Bobby and Susan how to use the 12 gauge shotgun, because I didn't want them to get recoil shy. Susan was very petite and only weighed about 110 pounds. Bobby had a slim build and only weighed about 140 pounds. Neither one of them had fired a weapon with much recoil, but they both needed to know how to use them so they knew what to expect.

We took the 12 gauge Ithaca pump and the 308 Remington bolt action out back to do some target practice. I said, "I'm going to start you guys out with a 308."

I showed them how to hold the weapon standing, sitting, and lying prone. "Okay Bobby," I said, "You're up first. Take a sitting position and fire three rounds at the bull's-eye."

Bobby fired his first shot, worked the bolt, and fired the other two shots. After clearing the action he stood up and said, "That was cool; it didn't kick that bad at all."

I nodded approvingly. "It looks like you did pretty good. You've got about a 1 inch group down there and you handled the 308 well."

Bobby stood there, grinning from ear to ear, and handed the 308 to his mother saying, "You're next."

Susan took a sitting position with the 308 and carefully took aim. After a few seconds, she fired the first round. She wobbled a little bit and said, "That wasn't so bad."

"Fire two more shots," I said. She worked the bolt and fired two more shots at the target. Then she cleared the weapon, stood up, and handed the Remington to me.

She said, "I like my MP5 much better, but if I have to, I believe I can handle this one, too."

I agreed, "Yes, the MP5 is a much better weapon for you, but you are right, you did great. Okay Bobby, now we are going to go to the 12 gauge shotgun."

I set up three cans downrange about one foot apart. "I want you to blast each one."

I handed Bobby three 12 gauge birdshot target rounds. Bobby loaded the three rounds into the tubular magazine and pumped the action, chambering the first round.

He started to sit and I said, "No Bobby, we're going to shoot this weapon from a standing position, which will be the most common position we'll be using a shotgun from."

Bobby stood straight, tucked the stock in close and tight to his shoulder and fired the first round. The recoil bumped him pretty good, but he hit the can and kept his balance.

Bobby was delighted. "Wow, I annihilated that can!"

Bobby then pumped the action and blasted the other two cans. He cleared the weapon and handed the shotgun to me. He rolled his arm around and held his shoulder saying, "I could feel that recoil."

I said, "It has a bit more than the mini 14, right?"

Bobby said, "Yes, and more than the 308, also."

He turned to his mom and said, "It has some recoil, but it's really not all that bad. I'm sure you can handle it."

Susan grimaced. "Okay, I guess I'll give it a try now."

I handed Susan three birdshot rounds. Susan loaded the weapon, chambered a round, and took aim at the first can. After a few seconds, she fired. The recoil pushed her back onto one foot and she almost dropped the shotgun. But she kept control of the weapon and gave me a look that said, *should I continue?*

I told her, "Go ahead, blast the other two cans."

She chambered another round and fired at the second can, this time leaning into the weapon a little more. She was able to absorb the recoil and kept control of the weapon. She then chambered the last round and fired at the last can. After clearing the weapon, she handed the shotgun back to me.

I said, "They were only target rounds, you're going to have to get used to using the heavier buckshot and slugs."

I set up a 5-gallon pail at about 30 yards out. I handed the shotgun to Bobby and one round of buckshot.

Bobby looked at it and said, "Only one round?"

"Yes," I said, "because I don't have very many rounds of buckshot."

Bobby chambered the round of buckshot and took a bead on the pail. When he pulled the trigger, the recoil rocked him backwards pretty good. The pail went flipping off down into the woods.

Bobby said, "Wow, now that's some real power."

I said, "Well Bobby, it looks like you handled that one well."

Susan said, "I guess I'm next."

Bobby handed the shotgun to Susan, and I gave her one round of buckshot. She chambered the round and looked at me, a little bit worried.

I said, "Go ahead, you'll be okay."

Susan took a bead on the pail and fired. The recoil pushed her backwards about two steps, but I caught her before she fell. Keeping the shotgun pointed straight up like I had taught her, she turned and faced me. "I hope I never have to use this weapon!" She handed me the shotgun and stepped off to the side, rubbing her shoulder and arm.

I said, "Sorry Susan, but you had to know what to expect in case you ever have to use this weapon."

"Yes I know, it's okay. My shoulder will be sore for a day or two, but I'm okay."

I turned to Bobby. "Do you want to try a slug?"

Bobby said, "Yeah, I'll give it a shot."

I handed Bobby the shotgun and a slug. I set up a 6-inch piece of firewood as a target. Bobby chambered the round and took aim. He pulled the trigger and the it tipped over, wood splinters flying. The recoil pushed Bobby back about one step, but he kept control of his balance and the weapon.

Bobby said, "I hit it, and look at the damage I did!"

Bobby cleared the weapon and handed the shotgun back to me. I took the shotgun and smiled when he rubbed his shoulder.

"How's your shoulder, Bobby?"

Bobby said, "I really felt that one, but I'll be okay."

I told Bobby to go down and set up five cans about one foot apart.

When he returned from setting up the cans, Susan asked, "Do we have to shoot the shotgun anymore?"

I said, "No, I just wanted to show you how a shotgun works. I'll be doing the shooting."

Susan said, "Thank God! I'm not sure my shoulder could take much more of that."

Bobby was eager. "I'm ready for more training!"

I said, "No, not today. I'm going to let your shoulders rest up. We're going to need to be in tip top shape for tomorrow."

I loaded five rounds into the shotgun. Without warning, I quickly shouldered the shotgun, taking aim at the first can and rapidly fired, blasting all five cans.

Bobby said, "Wow, that was some fast shooting!"

"As you get used to using a pump shotgun, you can fire accurately and rapidly at both still and moving targets. I think this is enough training for today. Let's go up to the house to see what we can get on the ham radio."

We sat down at the ham radio and started going through the frequencies. We'd done this every morning and every evening for the past three days without being able to make any contact or get any new news updates.

As I was transmitting on frequency 2245, I said, "This is Dahlonega, Georgia transmitting on frequency 2245. Is there anyone out there? Can anyone hear me?"

I waited two minutes and repeated my message. This time I got a reply! "*Yes, I hear you neighbor.*" We looked at each other in total surprise. We got an answer!

I keyed the mic and said, "Hello, this is Mark, and your name is…?"

The reply came back, *"Hello. I'm Sam."*

"Glad to hear your voice, Sam! Where are you located?"

The reply came back, *"Good to hear you also, Mark."*

I waited a few more seconds but he said nothing more. I repeated, "Sam, we are in Dahlonega, Georgia. Where are you?"

"It's not safe to give out your exact location," he cautioned. *"I am close by, neighbor."*

I replied, "Thanks for the warning, Sam. Did you hear the broadcast from the Ronald Reagan?"

"Yes, that line of bullshit has been going on for weeks now."

I said, "So you don't believe this broadcast, Voice of America?"

"Some of that information is true, but not all of it."

Interesting, I thought. "Do you have more accurate, up-to-date information?"

Sam ignored my question. *"Mark, how is it that you have a radio and communications?"*

So he was worried who he was talking to. "We confiscated some supplies from the storerooms of electronic and automotive stores to build this radio," I told him.

Sam replied, *"Good thinking. You said we; how many are you?"*

"Three of us here, but there are groups of hostiles, locals controlling the town."

Sam agreed. *"Yes, I'm well aware of the hostiles, both human and animal."*

"We've had problems with wild animals attacking us at night."

"Uh huh, the dogs only come out at night," he said, *"and the vicious bastards are smart! You'll have to look out for them, so be careful."*

I decided to tell him, "We are getting ready for a road trip soon but unsure of all the dangers and conditions that we might run into. Any info that you could give us would be extremely helpful."

There was a short pause. *"You have transportation?"* he asked.

"Yes, we have equipped and modified a late-model pickup truck. Do you have transportation?"

"Nice, lucky you. But do not broadcast too much information like that. Yes, I have transportation. I also have information for you that I

cannot give you over public band frequencies. I'm going to trust you and offer you an in-person meeting, if you are interested."

I was curious. "How many people are there with you?"

"I'll only answer in a personal meeting if you're interested."

"Okay how far away are you?"

"I'm not very far away. Head down Highway 60 going into Gainesville. I'll meet you along that route. You'll know me because I'm sure no one else on a motorcycle will be out there".

"When do you want to meet?", I asked.

"The sooner the better."

I offered, "This afternoon okay?"

"Perfect. Remember, look for the guy on the motorcycle."

"Got it, see you this afternoon…out."

Susan let out her breath. "We really got to talk to someone."

Bobby thought out loud, "I wonder if he has any other teenagers living with him?"

"I'm not really sure if we can trust him," I cautioned, "but we have to trust someone, and we might as well start with this guy. We'll strip down the truck and gear it up for a short day trip. We'll meet this guy and then come back here later tonight."

Bobby was worried. "Before dark, I hope."

I said, "Yes, we'll tell the guy we have to be back home before dark. He's already aware of the zombie dogs, so I'm sure that won't be a problem."

"He seems to be very secretive and not very forth coming with information," said Susan.

"After everything that's happened, most people are going to be scared and suspicious. I'm sure there's a lot of people out there who are willing to kill for anything of value that they can get their hands on."

"We'll take the racks off the truck and take the gas cans down to the basement. The gun safe is already mounted in the truck so that'll have to stay there. We'll take some extra water and food supplies along with first aid kits, a tool bag, and the extra ammo. Susan, I'm going to have you take the Ruger .44 Magnum carbine this time. We only have the one 10-round magazine for it. Out on the road you're going to need a weapon that has a little more range and power. The MP5 is only good for close combat out to a maximum of 50 yards. The .44 carbine is effective out to 100 yards. Because you only have one clip for it, we'll also take the 30-30 lever action as your backup weapon. If we should get into a firefight, don't try to reload the clip for the .44 carbine. Just put it down and pick up the 30-30."

Susan asked, "Why not just take the 30-30?"

I said, "You haven't used the 30-30 lever action in a fast shooting scenario yet. I'm worried that if you didn't completely work the lever to the full stroke when chambering a round under stress, it would jam on you and then you'll have no weapon. Using the .44 carbine first, by the time you need the 30-30, the initial panic of the situation should be past you."

Susan nodded, "Okay, I get it. Things could start out as a surprise and then our training would kick in, and I'd have better control over what I'd be doing right?"

My head bobbed, "Yes, Susan, you got it."

Bobby said, "Can I bring this samurai sword?"

I shook my head, "I think the sword would be too long and bulky to take in the truck. This time, anyhow."

Bobby put his head down and said, "Okay."

Chapter 7

Sam Jay.

We went out to the truck, and I told Bobby to ride in the truck bed standing up and overlooking the cab. "Have your mini 14 in your hands. We'll keep the back window of the truck open so we can talk to each other. You'll be able to see the sides of the road and up ahead better than we will inside the cab. You're going to be our look out. If you should see anything suspicious, people or animal, knock on the roof and give us a direction to look. Use the hands-of-a-clock directions system. 12 o'clock straight ahead of us, 9 o'clock straight to the left, 3 o'clock straight to the right. Do you understand what I'm saying?"

Bobby said, "Yup, I got it."

We went up to Crown Mountain Road and turned left, downhill. Once we reached Route 60, we turned left, heading east toward Gainesville. We were driving slow, about 35 miles an hour. There was a lot of debris on the road now, tree branches and the occasional abandoned vehicle, all obstacles we had to maneuver around. The weather was nice, a sunny day with the temperature around 80 and a light breeze. The Chestatee River looked cool and inviting. I thought, "I'd like to be down there doing some trout fishing. I doubt that I'll be doing any fishing anytime soon. All of my time is being spent surviving."

As we approached the intersection of Route 60 and 400, Bobby knocked on the roof and said he saw a motorcycle in the middle of the road. We approached the motorcycle slowly. I noticed that it was a late-model Yamaha 360 dirt bike. The EMP shouldn't have affected this motorcycle, so it shouldn't be abandoned in the road like this.

We stopped and looked around from inside the truck. I told Susan to get out of the truck on her side and cover me. I told Bobby to stay put and alert. I walked up to the motorcycle to investigate it more closely. I put my hand down near the exhaust pipe. It was still warm.

I looked around and hollered, "Sam, are you here?"

A man's voice came from the trees on the side of the road. "State your business."

I said, "I am Mark looking to meet up with Sam. Are you Sam?"

A man stepped out of the woods, carrying an AK-47. He was dressed in the older style camouflage fatigues, wearing camo sneakers and a black helmet with a silver spike on top.

He said, "Yes, I am Sam," and approached us.

When Sam got close enough he put out his hand for a handshake and said, "Glad to make your acquaintance." I shook his hand, introducing myself, Bobby and Susan.

Sam said, "It's not safe to be out here in the open for very long. Follow me and we'll go to my compound."

I started to ask him where and how many people were there but Sam cut me off saying, "No time to talk here. I'll answer all your questions when we get to my compound. Follow me."

Sam jumped on the Yamaha, kicked it over, and started driving south on 400. We got in the truck and followed.

A few miles south on 400, Sam made a left turn onto a side road. We continued following him down three or four other side roads until we came to a dead end with a steel gate and a 10 foot high chain link fence. On the other side of the fence was a two-story log house with a large front yard.

Sam stopped the motorcycle, got off to open the gate, and then motioned us in. We saw no other people around, and it didn't look like an ambush, so with caution I drove through the gate. I stopped and waited for Sam. He pushed his motorcycle through the gate, then closed it and locked it.

"Follow me," he said. We followed Sam up to the log house. He said, "Park your truck over there," indicating a carport. I did as he asked. Sam came over to us and said, "Let's go inside and have a drink. We can talk in there."

Sam unlocked the front door and invited us inside. Once we were all in, he closed and locked the door, which included setting a 2 x 4 in heavy brackets across the middle of the door. He lead us through a living room into a dining area. The inside of the house was a bit dark and it took a few seconds for our eyes to adjust. It was a normal-looking home, neat and clean. The furniture and decorations all looked to be upscale. The temperature was cool and comfortable.

Sam told us to be seated at a large dining room table. Then he offered us drinks. "I have cold drinks: beer, soda, water, whatever you want."

Bobby's mouth fell open. "You have cold Pepsi?"

Sam said, "I sure do, young man."

Grinning from ear to ear, Bobby said, "I'll have a Pepsi."

Susan and I looked at each other and I said, "A cold beer sounds good to me."

Susan said, "I'll have a Pepsi, thank you."

Sam went into another room and a few seconds later brought out our drinks. The drinks were cold, just as Sam had promised.

Bobby said, "Thank you Sam. I've been dying for a Pepsi."

Susan and I also thanked Sam for the drinks.

Of course our first question was, "Sam, how is it you have cold drinks?"

Sam smiled, "I'll show you later. First, let's get to know each other a little bit."

At first Sam was all questions; how we all came to be together, what we did before everything happened, how we survived the last few weeks, have we made any contact with anyone else from the outside world, and what our plans and goals were.

After answering all of Sam's questions, I said, "Okay Sam, now it's your turn to answer some of *our* questions."

Sam told us that he was a retired Army Ranger: E9 Sergeant Major. He did two tours of duty in Iraq and two tours in Afghanistan. He had been retired now for three years and living here in this home as a survivalist. He used his savings and retirement money to buy this property and build the compound. He was divorced three times over with no children. He said, "No offense Susan, but modern-day women want to live a modern-day life, pampered by all the modern conveniences which are now gone."

Sam had not gotten the sickness and had stayed in contact with his military buddies throughout the catastrophe. He said, "Let me bring you up-to-date on what's happening here in our country and around the world, or at least as much of it as I know."

"Public **R**elations policies (PR), political correctness, their political careers, and power and greed have blinded our dumbass government. So even after being warned about potential threats, they were too worried about the PR backlash of taking any action before it became too late. Most of the rioting was over racial tensions instigated by a few idiots who were making millions of dollars from the blood and sweat of those people caught up in the racial tensions."

"As the protests and civil unrest increased across the country, Russia and China devised a plan to infiltrate and conquer the United States without ever having to go to war. They sent thousands of college students here on student visas with skills to keep the protests and violence going so that eventually Russia and China would be asked to come to the aid of the US with peacekeeper troops backed by the United Nations. By the way, some of those troops are still here, and I'll tell you more about that later. Russia also sent scientists and engineers to NASA to work on the special deep space exploration projects. They are the ones who built and fired the EMPs. Of course, our dumbass government has blamed North Korea for the EMPs. Being non-nuclear and high tech, the EMP design was overlooked by our scientists because the ones who knew what to look for were kicked out of the NASA program for various PR problems. I'm sure they were framed or set up by the Russians to get them out of the way. But there was one thing the Russians and Chinese did not count on: ISIS and Al Qaeda had a lot of sleeper cells in this country. They came here under the same education visa programs, just like the Russians and Chinese. The terrorist sleeper cells either brought or acquired chemical and biological weapons here which they put into suicide bombs to be detonated all over the country. Every metropolitan city and every college town was hit with these chemical or biological weapons. I believe they got the biological ingredients from medical labs where they were attending college. With all of the violence and protesting going on, security lapses made it possible to steal the biological and chemical ingredients for the suicide bombs that they used."

"The Russian and Chinese 'peacekeepers' are still trying to complete their mission and doing a damn good job of it. Those left in our government are still just as blind and dumb as ever. You heard the message from Voice of America. Those dumbasses still think the United Nations, Russia, and China are here to help. That's bullshit! Fuck those assholes in the blue hats! If I get a chance to fill any of them full of hot lead, they'll be dead meat, and I'll feed them to the wild dogs."

"There's a unit of Russian soldiers in Gainesville. They have a lot of US citizens held there in the so-called FEMA camps which are really concentration camps. I've gotten close enough to see them with my own eyes. The Russian unit that is there is well equipped, and it would take a large force to retake control of Gainesville. I do not believe the Russians nor the Chinese have control of any of the metropolitan cities, only smaller cities in urban areas. But they do have units mixed in with US forces in some metropolitan areas like Atlanta, Charleston, and Savannah. That I know of for sure."

I said, "Yes, I was getting some radio messages from Savannah, but they have stopped now."

Sam agreed, "Yes, that was one of my old military buddies. He was starting up a relief camp, but he was overrun and shut down by Chinese and Homeland Security forces. He's now retreated to a secluded compound outside of the Savannah area."

"Have you heard from him recently?"

"Yeah, we make contact once a week. He has a small force of fighters there, building up a resistance. But they are outgunned and outnumbered. The acting US government sees them as hostile rebels, making their cause more difficult. They're talking about making their way to the territory of Texas and teaming up with the Texas Rangers and forces there. By the way, the Texas government is the only one that seems to have a lick of sense. They see what's really going on. But they are too small in numbers and equipment to launch a full-scale attack against the real problems in the rest of the country. That is why they have closed their borders to everyone and taken defensive measures to protect themselves. George, my buddy in Savannah, and I believe that if we could make it there, Texas would welcome the extra manpower. Then again, they just might shoot us on the spot."

"Do you know anything about what's happening in the rest of the world?" I asked.

Sam said, "We nuked the hell out of the Middle East and North Korea. South Korea is a real mess."

"Isn't China upset about us nuking North Korea?"

Sam shrugged. "The Chinese consider the loss of North Korea collateral damage in their larger plan to divide the US with Russia. For the Chinese, it has been a way to get rid of that pain-in-the-ass dictator in North Korea without a lot of global political fallout from the United Nations."

"We do have some other countries on our side: Great Britain, Israel, Australia, South Africa and the Philippines. Most of the other countries in Europe, Asia and Africa are staying out of the conflict as much as possible. They are all battling and worrying about the spread of the canine flu, which by the way, is what mutated the domestic dogs and any other canine species."

I asked, "Is that from the biological weapons that Isis and Al Qaeda used?"

"Not exactly," Sam said, "but the combination of biological ingredients that they used in their suicide bombs mixed and mutated, killing large numbers of the human population and mutating the canine species that didn't die from the disease. The best I can tell is that it's a blood-borne disease spread by the saliva of infected people or animals. Most of the humans who have lived through the initial attack of the disease now have a degree of immunity to the canine flu. But I would still advise caution when dealing with any dead bodies, human or canine."

"What about Canada and Mexico?" I asked.

Sam answered, "Canada and Mexico have closed their borders and are dealing with keeping out an influx of refugees from the US; they also have suffered some effects from the EMPs."

I shook my head, "Isn't that ironic? Before all this shit took place, we were battling an influx of immigrants from Mexico. Now the shoe is on the other foot, and they're not liking it very much."

Sam said, "That's about all I have on news. I think you're up to date on everything that I know. Let's get down to business: the main reason I invited you here. I want to strike a blow to those Russian bastards in Gainesville. I know we cannot retake Gainesville and release the prisoners in the concentration camp, but I picked up some Russian chatter on the radio. They are planning a raid into Dahlonega. I have a plan that I need your help with. You want to kick some Russian ass?"

I leaned in, "What's your plan?"

Sam said, "The Russians will send one or two platoons into Dahlonega to check out the resources and any resistance that might be there. I'm thinking that they'll run into the locals, who as you know, are an aggressive bunch of hillbillies. The hillbillies have set up a watch on the main road coming into town, probably looking for you, Mark. But they'll see the Russians coming too. As you know they already have defenses set up in the town. This will slow the Russians down, forcing them to take a defensive posture. That's where we come in and hit them from behind. Basically, the Russians will be surrounded, and with any luck, we can take them all out. This will also put us in good favor with the hillbillies."

"Being on their good side will help us navigate the other small mountain towns which we'll have to pass through in order to get around Gainesville. Then we can continue on down to Savannah to meet up with my buddy, George. What do you think, are you in?"

I said, "It was our plan to go to Savannah. Without the new information that you've given us, I doubt that we would've made it without being killed or captured by the Russians. So I guess we owe you our lives." I turned to Susan and Bobby. "What do you say?"

Bobby said, "Yeah, I'm all for it. Let's kick some Russian ass!"

Susan said, "I'm a little bit worried about this plan. What if the hillbillies decide to attack us and take our equipment?"

"I believe and hope that the hillbillies will be grateful for our assistance," I said, "and we'll be able to make peace with Poppa, their leader. But what worries me the most is that the Russians are real soldiers with automatic weapons and military equipment. This means they'll have body armor, communications, and be well-versed in military combat tactics. So we'll be outnumbered and outgunned."

Sam said, "My plan doesn't involve a full contact assault on the Russian unit. I believe that we can hit them from the rear, catching them by surprise and taking out their heavier weapons. That will give the hillbillies a better chance for a frontal attack."

I said, "So you're counting on the hillbillies launching an effective head-on attack, taking advantage of the confusion in the ranks because of our attacks at the rear of the Russian position."

Sam nodded, "Yes, that's about it. Unless you have a better plan."

I thought for a moment. "We do have an advantage. We know the landscape and the territory, and so do the hillbillies. If we can keep the Russians on the defensive from two sides, this just might work."

Sam said, "Great! It's a go, then. The weapons you have now, are they the best you got?"

"Pretty much," I said. "We have plenty of ammo, but Susan only has one clip for that carbine and Bobby only has two for the mini 14. I have four for this AR15, so I'm okay. We also have some shotguns and two scoped rifles. We're a bit short on Buckshot or slugs for the shotguns, though."

Sam said, "I have a pretty good stock of weapons and ammo that I've been collecting over the years. Let's go to my armory and see what we can put together."

Sam had quite the collection in his armory. We were all able to get outfitted with some light body armor. Susan got three more clips for the Ruger carbine. Bobby traded in the mini 14 for an AR15 with five extra magazines and tactical sights. I picked up a couple of extra magazines for my AR15, and Sam gave us 100 rounds of 00 buckshot and slugs. Sam also had ear piece communication radios for each of us. He showed us his modified late-model Ford F150 pickup truck that had a 30 caliber gun turret mounted in the bed.

I asked Sam, "Do you know when the Russians are planning their mission into Dahlonega?"

Sam answered, "I don't know the exact day or time, but I have a radio in my truck to monitor their chatter. I also understand a little bit of Russian. I park my truck out of sight behind the minimart at the intersection of 400 and 60. I've been camping out there every day from dawn to dusk, keeping an eye out for them Russian bastards. You keep your radio on, and when I see them go through, I'll call you and then head up to your place the back way."

I said, "If we put Susan and Bobby up by the water tower with sniper rifles, they'll have a clear shot at the main street leading into town. Then we come in low and behind the Russians."

Sam agreed, "Sounds good, but no one starts shooting before the hillbillies and the Russians are engaged. We need to surprise both the Russians and the hillbillies in order to achieve the results we're looking for."

I said, "Okay, I think we've got it. Sam, you were going to tell us about your little compound here and how it is that you have cold drinks and air-conditioning."

Sam smiled, "Oh, that's quite simple, actually. Over here." He took us to another part of the basement. "I have circulating pumps that pump cold well water through cooling coils that cool the house. The pumps don't use much power and the water from the wells stays at about 40°. My solar panels provide enough power to operate most everything in my house, including the refrigerator. By the way, I had to replace over half of those panels after the EMP. Good thing I had extras on hand."

Susan asked, "Won't you be regretting leaving this place to go on a dangerous trip with strangers to Savannah?"

Sam nodded, "In some ways, yes. But basically, I've been cooped up in this compound for the last three years. I'd love to get out of here for adventure, excitement, killing Russian bastards, and maybe even some Chinks. I'm kinda looking forward to it."

Bobby said, "Are we really going to have to fight the Chinese too?"

I answered, "Bobby, we will avoid fighting or killing anyone, if at all possible. But if we have to fight, we'll be going all out and not pulling any punches. It's all about survival."

Susan said, "The more fighting and killing we can avoid the better."

I turned to Sam. "It's getting late, and thank you for everything, but we need to be heading back to our place before dark comes."

Sam said, "You're welcome. I don't get much company. Will you stay for dinner? I'll be cooking steak and potatoes."

Bobby practically drooled. "Oh man, real food."

Susan said, "That does sound good, but I'm not sure we have time." She looked at me.

I said, "It does sound good." Then looking at my watch, I said, "Okay Sam, we're here for dinner, you convinced us."

Sam slapped his hands together. "Great! Upstairs to the kitchen, everyone. If you guys want to eat then you have to help cook it."

After a dinner of steak and potatoes at Sam's house, we drove back home, arriving there just before dark, without incident. We drove back up Golden Avenue, the back way to our house, to make sure it was clear for Sam. No major obstacles in the road to prevent him from getting to our place.

We unloaded the gear and supplies that we got from Sam.

Bobby and I went outside to set the perimeter alarms and make sure everything was secure. All looked okay, just as we had left it. When we went inside the house, Susan was heating up water for coffee.

I said, "Good thinking, Susan. We're going to need to stay up a little bit to make preparations for our attack on the Russians. We don't know what day they are planning to come into Dahlonega; it could be tomorrow or it could be three or four days from now, but we need to be ready when they do."

Susan said, "Our weapons and gear are already set to go. What else do we need?"

"We have to get our packs loaded up for a bug out and attack scenario. That means extra water, snacks, and all the extra ammo that we can carry. I also want to put together a special surprise package for those Russians."

Bobby perked up. "What kind of a surprise package are you putting together?"

"Bobby, go to the bedroom closet and get those two cans of tennis balls and bring them out here to the kitchen. Susan, get me all the rolls of electrical tape that we have left."

As they did this, I got three cans of black powder and a roll of cannon fuse.

I say to them both, "We're going to make some homemade hand grenades."

I made one, showing them how to assemble everything. We had enough materials to make nine black powder hand grenades.

Bobby was excited. "With hand grenades, we'll kick those Russian bastards' asses!"

Susan asked, "Will they really work?"

"They are not as strong as modern hand grenades but they should do the trick to 'put a hurt on them.' They can be quite dangerous, so Sam and I will be the only ones using them in this battle."

Bobby wasn't happy. "Dang, I wanted to blow up some Russians!"

Susan frowned. "Bobby, you're becoming a real warmonger."

I was firm. "This is no game. We are going up against real, trained soldiers. They are battle hardened and know combat tactics better than we do. We'll be outnumbered and outgunned. They have automatic weapons and could possibly call in reinforcements or air support. In either case, we'll be lucky to get out of there in one piece. This whole plan hinges on the hillbillies being able to put up a strong enough fight to take the Russians out quickly. We are just going to help the hillbillies so that they are able to overrun the Russians before they can call in any reinforcements. If the hillbillies retreat, we will retreat. If the Russians get any type of help, we will retreat. If any of that should happen, and we need to retreat, do not wait for Sam and I to pick you up with the truck. You pack up and head to the house through the woods, staying off the roads and out of sight. Sam and I will meet you at the house as soon as we're able. If we go into retreat mode, that means radio silence. The earpiece radios that Sam gave us could be tracked by the Russians, so be sure to turn them off. I need you to promise me: no heroics! Stay undercover and do not expose yourself. The Russians are professional soldiers, remember that!"

Susan and Bobby both promised to be careful and follow the orders and tactics that we outlined.

I said, "Okay, time to hit the sack and get some rest. We have to be up early in the morning, with one of us standing by the radio at all times until we hear from Sam."

We placed our weapons within easy reach and went to bed.

Night one before the attack on the Russians.

Susan and I got into bed and turned the lights out. She rolled over and put her arm around me. She said, "I'm not very pleased about helping the hillbillies or making any kind of peace agreement with them. They're dangerous, cruel sons of bitches."

I agreed. "You're right about the hillbillies. They wanted to kill us and take our supplies. However, they are Americans - born here and lived here for generations. They might not be the nicest people around, but they're still Americans trying to survive, the same as we are. The Russians want to conquer us and enslave us. So, it is to our advantage if all Americans, hillbillies included, band together and fight back to send the Russians and the Chinese back to their countries with their tails between their legs. I believe Poppa and the hillbilly clans will see it the same way."

Susan gave me a kiss and said good night.

Later on in the night we were awakened and by the perimeter alarms, and lots of barking and howling. We grabbed our gear and met in the kitchen.

Bobby said, "Those damned zombie dogs are back again! Time to try out this AR15 and kick their ass."

I said, "No, Bobby! They are just trying to call us out. We go out there to fight them and they'll drive us back into the house as they have done before. This time we'll just take a defensive position here in the house and see what they do."

The zombie dogs howled and barked. Then they crashed into the gates on the back porch and ran past the sliding glass backdoors, barking and howling for about 30 minutes. When we did not go outside to engage them, they became quiet, walking around the perimeter of the house. Finally, they left.

Susan said, "I think you're right. I think they wanted to fight."

Bobby said, "Dang, I wanted to try out this AR15 on them."

I said, "Yes, I think they wanted to fight. They wanted to draw us outside, and then I'm sure they had some kind of a plan to overrun us. But when we didn't go outside to engage them, they became confused and didn't know how to precede, so they just left. But I'm sure as long as we stay here they'll keep making attempts to kill us or drive us away."

Susan smile was grim, "Once we head for Savannah, they can have this place!"

"Once we're gone it won't take them long to figure out that we're no longer here. Then I'm sure they'll lose interest in this place. They'll consider it a victory."

Bobby asked, "But what if we should come back here?"

"I don't believe we'll be coming back here anytime soon," I said, "and if we do, it will be when this territory is under the control of real American citizens. Together, the citizens of the United States of America have the will, the strength, and motivation to drive all foreign threats from our land - Russian, Chinese and even the zombie dogs. Okay guys, let's go back to bed and get some sleep. Sunrise comes early."

Day one attack on the Russians.

We got up around 6 AM. The first thing I did was turn on the short wave radio to start listening for Sam's warning about the Russians. Susan started breakfast while Bobby and I went outside to survey the perimeter and see if the zombie dogs had done any damage. We found some damage to the gates and some of the perimeter alarms. We went back inside for breakfast after fixing them.

Our breakfast was pancakes made with powdered milk, along with powdered scrambled eggs. Yummy. We had no butter, so maple syrup was the only treat we had to put on our pancakes. We spent the rest of the day doing odds and ends around the house. I found a bipod which I mounted on the 308 Remington. I instructed Bobby and Susan on bullet trajectories and went over other battle tactics.

We had plenty of water and didn't know when we were going to have the opportunity to take any more showers, so we all decided that having a shower was a good idea. It was a hot day, so taking a shower felt good. We were all getting used to the inconveniences and were not so shy about taking showers outside where we could see each other.

Evening came and there was still no word from Sam about the Russians. We went to bed that night, prepared as always for the zombie dogs return, but all was quiet. We got a full night's sleep.

Day two attack on the Russians.

The day started off about the same as the day before. But at about 2 o'clock in the afternoon, Sam came on the radio.

"Alert one, alert one, Russian chopper traveling to your location. Stay out of sight. Radio silence, starting now."

Shortly after Sam's radio transmission, we heard the chopper coming up the valley toward Dahlonega.

Susan was scared. "A Russian helicopter coming this way! My God, there's no way we can fight against that!"

Bobby asked, "Do we have anything that'll take a chopper down?"

I said, "With a real lucky shot from my high-powered deer rifle, maybe we could take it down. I'm hoping that if we stay out of sight, we won't have to engage it."

Susan's eyes were big. "So what do we do, just sit here in the house and do nothing?"

I nodded. "After it passes our location, we'll hike up the road to the water tower. We'll leave the truck here so as not to attract any attention and just go up there on foot. Get your gear, we'll go in a few minutes."

Bobby asked, "Can we bring the sniper rifle?"

I said, "No Bobby, leave the 308 Remington here and just bring your AR15. You and your mom are going to be my backup with your rifles. I'm bringing the 35 Whelen. It's the only weapon we have that stands a chance of taking down a chopper."

Susan asked, "You're not really going to try to shoot that thing down are you?"

I said, "I'm not going to engage that chopper unless we're spotted and have no choice. I just want to go and see what they're up to. Okay, let's go. Keep out of the center of the road and stay close to the woods."

It took us about 45 minutes to get up to the water tower. We were all hot and sweaty from the fast jog of 3 miles up to the water tower. When we got there, we took cover and observed the helicopter making a low circle up near the Walmart store on the north end of town. After two circles, the chopper started back south again toward Gainesville, flying near our position. We ducked into the trees before the chopper got close and continued to observe its course. Once the chopper was out of sight, we hiked back down to the house.

Back at the house, Susan said, "I'm glad to be back here; that was scary!"

Bobby said, "What are we going to do if that helicopter comes back at the same time the Russians go into Dahlonega?"

I said, "That helicopter does put a new perspective on our plans. I'll give it a few minutes and if we don't hear from Sam, radio silence are not, I'll try to contact him."

We all sat around the radio patiently waiting to hear from Sam. After about an hour, I reached for the radio. Just as I was picking up the mic, we heard a motor coming down the road outside. We grabbed our weapons and looked out the window. It was Sam coming down the road on the old Yamaha. We went out to greet him.

Sam saw us and drove his motorcycle in our yard. Sam got off the motorcycle and said, "Hey neighbors. I guess you saw the Russian chopper."

I said, "Yes, we saw it and ran up to the water tower to see what it was up to. The chopper just circled the town a couple of times, made a couple loops around by the Walmart, and then flew off back toward Gainesville."

Sam said, "I saw it go back toward Gainesville. That's when I figured it was safe to run up here and check on you all. Now that I see y'all are okay, I feel a lot better."

Susan said, "Thanks for coming to check on us, Sam."

"You're welcome. I think that was a scouting mission, looking for any type of resistance that the ground forces might run into before they send them here. I think it's a pretty good bet that the ground unit will be making a move on Dahlonega tomorrow."

I said, "That helicopter kind of throws a wrench into our plans, doesn't it?"

Sam said, "I suspected that they had some type of air support to back them up. I know the US government and the United Nations did not allow any of the peacekeeping forces to bring any heavy equipment or weaponry onto US soil. That included fighter jets, combat helicopters, tanks, and artillery. They do have jeeps, trucks and armored personnel carriers. Now, we also know that they have transport helicopters like the one we just saw today. That type of helicopter is an older one which was probably hardened against EMP. A transport helicopter designed to transport troops and equipment is big and slow and uses a lot of fuel. That's probably why they didn't hang around very long before going back to Gainesville. I guess their fuel supplies are limited in this area like all the rest of us."

I said, "Okay, that is all well and good, but the fact is the Russians still have a helicopter for air support and there's not much we can do about it."

"I knew about the helicopter, and I wouldn't be asking you guys to join me in this endeavor without having a few tricks up my sleeve," Sam said. "After the shit really started hitting the fan around here, when half the population was dying or sick and Homeland Security pulled out of Dahlonega and moved to Gainesville, I put on my hazmat suit to protect myself from the disease, hopped on my old bike here, and went up to the Ranger camp and appropriated a few choice items. Where do you think I got the belt fed 30 caliber mounted on the back of my Ford truck from? Also half of the weapons in my armory."

Susan said, "So you have a weapon that'll take out that helicopter?"

Sam nodded, "Yes honey, I believe I do. I have four Lars shoulder-fire rockets. These babies are heat seekers and will take out low-flying aircraft or armored vehicles. I just wish I had more of them."

Bobby said, "We made some special packages to deliver to them Russian bastards, too. Black powder hand grenades."

Sam was impressed. "I'll be damned! Hand grenades are one item that I'm lacking. Someone already heisted all the hand grenades from the armory at the Ranger camp before I got there. Had to be some of the soldiers because the armory was still locked up, and I had to break in."

I said, "We only have nine black powder hand grenades. They are not as powerful as modern-day hand grenades, but they should do the trick when we need them."

Sam said, "I'll use my old Yamaha here to run down to my place and get you guys two of those Lars rockets, just in case I don't get a chance to drop them off to you before the Russians strike tomorrow."

I agreed, "That'll be great, Sam."

Bobby had a sheepish grin on his face. "Seeing how you are coming back here today, could you bring us a couple of cold Pepsi?"

Sam laughed and said, "Sure thing, cold Pepsi coming up. I better get going now. I'll be back in about an hour with the rockets. See y'all later."

After he left, Susan said, "That Sam! He sure is a character! When it comes to weapons and survival, Sam is a guy we want on our side."

Just about one hour later, Sam came by on his Yamaha and handed us two Lars rockets, a six-pack of Pepsi, and a six-pack of Bud Light, all cold! He said, "Later, neighbors!" and buzzed off on his dirt bike.

We went in the house to enjoy our drinks and to read the instructions on how to use the rockets.

"I'm going to leave one of the rockets with you two at the water tower. The other one I'll take with me. If that helicopter shows up and becomes a problem, between all of us and Sam, we should be able to take it out."

Through dinner and into the evening we continued to chat about possibilities in the upcoming conflict with the Russians. Then we set our perimeter alarms and went to bed. The zombie dogs did not make an appearance that night. We awoke at 5:30 AM, before sunrise.

The Russian attack on Dahlonega.

Susan got breakfast started, Bobby went outside and checked the perimeter, and I fired up the ham radio, listening for Sam's call. Just as were sitting down to eat our breakfast, Sam's voice came over the radio.

"Alert one! Alert one! The Russians just passed my position heading for Dahlonega. Going silent. On my way to meet you."

I looked at them. "Okay boys and girls, lock and load. Gear up and let's roll!"

Gulping down our coffee and grabbing our gear, we rushed out to the truck. I dropped Susan and Bobby off at the water tower. She gave me a kiss and told me to be careful. Bobby gave me a hug and said, "I've got your six, dad." I hugged and kissed them, and I told them to remember what I said about retreating. Susan said, "We remember."

I got in the truck and drove down Crown Mountain Road to meet up with Sam. He stepped out of the woods when he saw me coming. He hopped in the truck and said, "We don't want to drive up too close. We'll go in the last half-mile on foot."

As Sam and I approached the town, we heard sporadic gunfire.

Sam said, "The hillbillies must have engaged the Russians. Time for us to move in and get busy."

Silently, we moved from cover to cover in the direction of the gunfire. I was thinking to myself that I must be nuts to run toward gunfire. On any normal day and time, most smart humans would be running away.

We got within sight of the Russian unit. They had three vehicles and two transport trucks parked in a V formation, pointing up Main Street. A Jeep was parked in the middle of the V with a heavy machine gun mounted on it. The Russians had automatic weapons, but the hillbillies were mounting a good counterattack. They were keeping the Russians pinned down in one spot. The hillbillies were alternating their attack positions. First, a group from the left side of the street would appear and fire from behind buildings or cars. Once they started taking heavy fire, they ducked down an alley out of sight. Then the next group of hillbillies on the other side of the street would appear and fire on the Russians, forcing the Russians to reposition.

We just watched and waited for a moment. Just then the Russians fired rocket-propelled grenades to both sides of the street, at the same time laying down cover fire with automatic weapons. Two six-man squads of Russians broke off from the main unit, one going left and one going right, in an attempt to flank the hillbillies. The heavy machine gun on the Jeep and the grenade launchers were major obstacles preventing the hillbillies from advancing on the Russian position.

Sam signaled that we needed to take out the heavy machine gun and then alert the hillbillies about the two squads who were trying to flank them.

I nodded and turned on the radio. "Susan and Bobby, do your best to take out that machine-gun that's mounted on the jeep."

Susan replied, "We're on it!"

Two seconds later the soldier operating the heavy machine gun collapsed. While the Russians repositioned to get another soldier on the heavy machine gun, Sam and I split up and went after the two squads that were flanking the hillbillies.

I went after the far left group and Sam went after the right-hand group. I caught up to my group and spotted them sneaking along the far side of some buildings. I took up a position behind a stonewall and fired on them with the AR15, dropping one of them. The others took up defensive positions and returned fire in my direction. "Oh shit," I thought, "I opened a hornet's nest now."

I heard bullets zipping by me and ricocheting off the stonewall. A lot of automatic gunfire had been trained on my position. I was pinned down and too scared to stick my head up to fire back. All I could do was clutch my weapon and hope they didn't rush my position.

Bobby and Susan had been observing the whole event from their position. Bobby took out the first and second heavy machine gun operators. So far, the Russians weren't aware that Bobby and Susan were sniping behind their position. While the heavy machine gun had been down, the hillbillies had managed to make some headway and they had advanced on the Russians. The hillbillies had set afire to a truck tire full of diesel fuel. They rolled it down the street toward the Russians' position. This further hampered the Russians' attack and their ability to keep an accurate track of where the hillbillies were shooting.

Sam caught up to the Russian squad that he was trailing and engaged them. He was in a good position behind some road barriers and was able to move around from one barrier to the other and fire at the Russians from spaces between the barriers. This kept the Russians occupied long enough for the hillbillies to notice they were being flanked. A group of hillbillies moved in on the Russian squad that Sam was having the firefight with and annihilated them. Sam stuck his head up from behind the road barriers, waving his hand and yelling "Thank you, friends."

The hillbillies, not recognizing Sam as a friend, opened fire on his position. Sam ducked down behind the road barriers but did not return fire.

All of a sudden, I heard a lot of Russian voices and more gunfire, but no bullets were coming in my direction any longer. Because the Russians had fired on my position, the noise alerted the hillbillies on this side of the street that they were being flanked. The hillbillies moved in and engaged the squad of Russians that had been shooting at me. This gave me an opportunity to come out of my hiding place and fire on the Russians. Taking fire from two directions, the Russian squad was quickly eliminated. I waved to the hillbillies, stood up, and tipped my hat to them. They didn't fire on me, approach my position, or in any way try to make contact with me. They just faded back in between the buildings to continue engaging the main group of Russians on Main Street.

I worked my way back down, flanking the main Russian unit until I found a good position and began firing on them. I saw three Russians off to one side. Two had AK-47s and were laying down cover fire on the opposite side of the street. The third had an RPG, ready to fire on the hillbillies position on the far side of the street. I did not have a clear shot at the Russian with the RPG. I pulled a BIC lighter from my pocket and one of the black powder hand grenades. I lit the fuse on the grenade and threw it as hard as I could in the direction of the three Russians. The grenade hit the ground short of their position, bounced, and rolled right to them. This startled the Russian soldier with the RPG. He stopped and looked down at it with a curious expression. Just then the grenade exploded, knocking all three soldiers over. The RPG fired in the direction of the main Russian unit, striking the closest transport truck. There was a loud explosion and most of the Russian unit was taken out: either killed or knocked unconscious. The hillbillies took advantage of this situation and charged the Russians in full force. About forty hillbillies, men, women, and young boys, all armed with deer rifles and hunting knives, converged on the Russians. I kind of felt sorry for the Russians. Not really.

The battle was over and I started making my way back to where we left the truck. I keyed my radio to contact Sam.

"Alert two, alert two, what's your status?"

There was no reply. I repeated, "Alert two, alert two, status report." Still no reply.

Now I was worried, so I tried to contact Bobby and Susan. I keyed my radio, "Alert three, alert three, status report."

The voice came back, *"Alert three all safe and well."*

"Thank God," I said to myself. Again I keyed my radio, "Alert three, do you know the status of alert two?"

Susan's voice came back, *"Alert two's position has been overrun by the hillbilly forces, status unknown."*

I keyed up, "Alert three, stay put and stay vigilant. Going dark for the next 45 minutes."

I worked my way around the Russian position to where I had last seen Sam. As I was doing so, I saw that the hillbillies had captured five Russian soldiers and Sam. They had everyone's hands tied behind their backs, and the hillbillies were marching them north toward the old Walmart store. I followed at a safe distance, keeping to cover, hoping that the hillbillies would not spot me.

They went into the Walmart parking lot. The outer perimeter of the lot was blocked off with all kinds of vehicles: trucks, cars, buses and even a tractor-trailer. Inside this parameter were tents, teepees, and campers of all shapes and sizes. There was a big wooden platform at the front of the store. There were a few guards posted around the perimeter. The guards were intent on watching the parade of prisoners being marched across the parking lot, so I was able to sneak up to the vehicles at the perimeter and get inside one of them. From there I could observe what was going on.

The hillbillies brought the prisoners up in front of the wooden platform and then forced the prisoners to their knees, facing it. There were over forty hillbillies that I could see from my position, and I could see no way to make a rescue attempt for Sam, so I continued observing. Twelve more hillbillies came out of the Walmart store and walked up onto the platform. The middle one was an old man, rather large and wearing a coonskin cap. I decided this must be Poppa. I was too far away to hear what was being said, but there was a lot of chatter and arguing. Then I heard the rotor blades of a helicopter coming. 'Oh shit, this isn't going to be good.' I thought. I looked to the south and saw a helicopter coming straight into town. All the hillbillies heard and saw it. They were pointing and running around, apparently trying to find cover positions from which to attack the helicopter. One hillbilly ran over and knocked all the prisoners down with the butt of his rifle so that they were lying face down. Then he dropped to his belly and slid beneath the platform with his weapon trained on the prisoners. The twelve hillbillies who were on the platform grabbed nearby weapons and joined their brothers to engage the helicopter. The only weapons that I saw in the hands of the hillbillies were deer rifles and shotguns. Even the mini 14 was only a glorified deer rifle, no match for a helicopter equipped with heavy machine guns. The helicopter was a big, heavy transport helicopter. It would take a lot to knock it out of the sky.

The only hope of defeating this chopper was the rocket I had. Even then, I was going to have to get a really good shot to take it down with only one rocket. I readied the rocket and waited for an opportunity. The chopper flew over the burning Russian vehicles.

Then, flying in a small circle, it maneuvered and headed right toward the Walmart, the hillbillies, and me. When the helicopter got within range, the hillbillies opened fire on it. The helicopter climbed to put some distance between it and the hillbillies firing on it. As the helicopter turned broadside to us, the machine gunner on the side opened up on the hillbillies, laying down a spray of deadly, high caliber bullets. One hillbilly started screaming, yelling, and running in all different directions. As the helicopter maneuvered around for another strafing run with the heavy machine gun, I saw my window of opportunity. The helicopter was close to my position and was turning to bring the other machine gun to bear on the hillbillies. I stepped out of the vehicle I had been hiding in, took aim with the rocket launcher, and fired at the helicopter. I was aiming for the engine area, but the rocket struck the cockpit, filling the helicopter with fire and smoke. As the chopper spiraled to earth, the two machine gunners bailed out, hitting the ground hard.

I was mesmerized, watching the helicopter crash to the ground, and didn't notice five hillbillies converging on my position. I heard, "Hey you! Hold it right there! Drop your weapons and put your hands up."

I turned to face them and saw that they were too close to me, and they were armed. I had no choice but to comply with their demands. They took my weapons and roughly brought me over to where the other prisoners were.

I looked at Sam and said, "I guess now we both get to meet Poppa."

The twelve hillbillies that had been on the platform before climbed back up, but there were only ten of them now. The hillbilly that was under the platform came out and yanked the other prisoners, including Sam, to their feet. We all stood there facing Poppa and the elders of his clan, waiting to hear our fate.

Poppa pointed his finger at me and said, "Who are you? Why are you here?"

I said, "My name is Mark and I have lived here in Dahlonega for close to five years now. I've been hunting and fishing in these mountains for years. I've met some of your people and they may recognize me. My friend here," pointing at Sam, "and I saw the Russians coming into town and thought you might need some help."

Poppa crooked his finger at me. "Come here, Mark." I joined him on the platform, and he turned me to face the crowd. "Anyone here recognize this man?"

Two hillbillies stepped forward and one said, "We do. He's the one that locked us in the john at the real estate office."

Poppa's eyes narrowed. He looked at me and said, "You are the one who's been stealing property from this town, *my* town, without permission?"

Not to be intimidated, I replied, "I was not aware that anyone still living claimed ownership to anything left here that had not already been looted."

Just then a woman spoke up. "I recognize this man. He hunts on our property every year and has not bothered a single plant or our still. As far as I recollect, he has not reported them to any government men."

A few others spoke up, confirming the woman's words.

Poppa nodded his head and thought for a moment. "Thank you for your assistance in fighting these Russian bastards, especially blowing the shit out of that helicopter. Your debt for taking items from my town without permission has been paid. You are free to leave. If you need anything or come back to this town, come here first, for permission."

I said, "What about my friend Sam, here. Is he free to leave also?"

Poppa looked at him and said, "Yes, the same goes for him. Take him with you."

I said, "Poppa, we have one more favor to ask of you."

Poppa gave me an angry look. "You're pushing your luck today, aren't you? What's this favor you're asking?"

I said, "We have friends and relatives in Savannah. We would like to try to reach them, but we cannot go through Gainesville because the Russians control it. We need to go around Gainesville, through the mountain farm towns of Claremont and that area. It's my understanding that you are well known and well respected by the other mountain families. A letter from you to give us safe passage through the mountain towns would be a big help."

Poppa was flattered and puffed out his chest. "Yes, the other families know who I am. Seeing as how you're leaving this area for Savannah, I doubt that you'll be coming back here anytime soon, if ever. I'll give you a note of safe passage."

He turned to one of the other hillbillies. "Give me some notepaper and a pen."

The hillbilly went into the Walmart and returned a few minutes later with a sticky note pad and a pen. Poppa looked at him and shook his head. He scribbled something on the pad and handed it to me. I looked at what was written on the pad. It said:

Good folks
Poppa–Dahlonega

I looked at him and then back at the note. I guessed that that would do the job. The hillbillies then handed us our weapons and gear, minus the rocket launcher that Sam had. They then escorted us to the main road out of town and told us to get walking. They didn't remove our earpiece radios, so once we were clear of the town and the hillbillies, I keyed the radio. "Alert three, alert three, status report."

Immediately Susan replied, "Thank God! We've been scared to death waiting to hear from you. We saw the helicopter crash and everything."

I answered, "Alert three, return to base one. We'll meet you there. Keep the chatter to a minimum."

Sam agreed. "Good idea not to be talking much on radio waves. Those Russians are going to want to know what happened to their helicopter and the unit of soldiers they sent to Dahlonega.

We don't want to be out in the open, caught with our pants down. We need to get somewhere, lay low for a few days, and let this blow over a bit. I recommend you guys all come to my compound, and we can prepare everything there for our trip to Savannah. I'll even introduce you to George, on the radio of course."

We made it to the truck, picked up Sam's motorcycle, and headed to my place to meet Susan and Bobby. At the house, when I got out of the truck, Susan came running out and jumped in my arms, kissing my face all over, crying and saying, "I thought you were dead, I thought you were dead."

Bobby gave me a big hug and said, "I knew you guys would kick ass and get out of there okay." He went over and gave Sam a big hug also. We all went inside to have something to eat, drink a couple beers, and burn off some adrenaline by praising each other and talking of our deeds. We kicked ass against the Russians and made peace with the hillbillies. Mission accomplished.

Sam's Compound. The Jay Estate.

With Sam's help, we packed up all of the supplies and gear from my house that we had room for on my truck and in the utility trailer from the officer's house. Everything we had we moved to Sam's house and compound. At the new compound, we had all the comforts of home: running water, real food, and protection from the zombie dogs, due to his perimeter fencing. We stayed there for six weeks. We continued to monitor the radio transmissions from the USS Ronald Reagan and from the Russians in Gainesville.

We made contact with George in Savannah, and he updated us on the situation there. The Chinese and Homeland Security forces controlled downtown Savannah and Hunter airbase. A street gang calling themselves the Bloods, made up of Black Americans and Mexicans, controlled most of the surrounding area of Savannah, including Pooler and Hilton Head, South Carolina. Richmond Hill down to Midway and Fort Stewart was held by the

3rd Infantry and the GGF (God, Guns and Freedom). George was part of that group.

George told us that the GGF had tried to make an alliance with the Bloods to push the Chinese out and retake Savannah. However, the GGF, being a Christian group of freedom fighters, just could not come to an alliance agreement with the Bloods. The Bloods were a group of gangbangers and drug dealers that were enjoying their lawless behavior of drugs and murder.

The Chinese force, being under constant threat of the Bloods, had not been able to expand their control of the area. Neither the Chinese nor the Bloods had been able to gain an upper hand because they were evenly matched. The GGF had stayed away from the fight for Savannah as much as possible.

The GGF had been taking in refugees and building a force of freedom fighters to retake control of the United States of America, starting with the Southeast. But by having spent so much of their resources in feeding and caring for the refugees, they had not been able to mount a force strong enough to take on the Chinese and the Bloods.

The US forces that were home-based on the USS Ronald Reagan had taken control of Charleston and Charlotte. Those forces still believed the Chinese and Russians were there to help and were blind to their real mission: dividing the US between themselves.

The Chinese had taken over full control of California and most of the West Coast west of the Rockies. The Russians had taken full control of Alaska and most of western Canada. General Henry van Horn of the British Army, along with American forces, were in control of the northeastern United States, from Maine to Pennsylvania. Mexico had been engaged in fierce fighting on the Texas border, trying to take control of the Texas territory.

Chapter 8

Pigeon, Pennsylvania.

Outside the general store they saw a 1924 Ford model T pickup truck, two saddled horses with the reins tied to the bicycle parking rack, and three bicycles. They went inside the store to see if there was anyone else around. There they saw four people sitting at a table by the deli. All the people in the store turned and stared at them, including the storekeeper behind the counter.

A woman stood up and said, "It's about time the government sent some help here, but I'm a bit surprised to see the Air Force."

Lt. Col. Mullen said, "The government didn't send us here, and we're not exactly here to help. Our plane crashed a few miles north of here, and we're actually the ones looking for help."

The woman said, "Well, I'm Elizabeth Brock, the mayor of Pigeon, Pennsylvania. Six days ago, the power went out along with the phones, including cell phone service and most of our cars. The only transportation we have is my old model T truck, a few horses, and bicycles. So I don't know how we're going to be of much help to you."

Lt. Col. Mullen introduced his group. Liz introduced townspeople in the store. "The storekeeper is Pete Lockrow, the two locals are Dan and Sandy Hicks, and the other two are Tom and Jenny Maxwell from Rochester, New York. Tom and Jenny were stranded here when their car died a couple of miles up the road, and they rode their bicycles here."

Lt. Col. Mullen said, "I see there's a lodge here. Are there any rooms available?"

Pete answered, "I only have two rooms available at the moment. Sorry, no lights or running water. I can only provide you with sleeping quarters."

Agent Forster said, "To sleep in a real bed beats the hell out of sleeping on the hard cold ground! We'll take it."

Lt. Col. Mullen said, "I'll see to it that the government reimburses you, and we thank you for your hospitality."

Dan asked, "What kind of a plane were you flying? Did your mission have anything to do with this power outage?"

Lt. Col. Mullen said, "We were only flying a routine transport mission when our plane lost power and crashed into the forest. That's all we know. We were hoping to get more information about what's going on from you."

Liz shook her head. "We're a bit secluded here. I really haven't gotten any information about the electricity being out, or what's going on in the rest of the country. Even on the battery operated radios that do work, we are only getting static. We have not seen any police, Homeland Security, or Red Cross people."

Lt. Col. Mullen asked, "Is there anyone around here who has a short wave radio?"

Sandy smiled wryly, "The best we can do is carrier pigeons. But they only fly to locations which they've come from. We sent two out a couple days ago, one to Philadelphia and one to Rochester. But neither has come back yet."

Pete said, "Hey, what about crazy Frank Paretsky? You think he'd have a short wave radio?"

Dan answered, "Maybe. But that crazy bastard would shoot you before he let you use his radio."

Liz said, "Maybe I can go up there and talk to him without getting shot. But that'll have to wait until tomorrow. I have a lot to do today."

Ted said, "We could use some rest anyhow before we do much traveling."

Rebecca said, "I would like to just lie down on a nice, soft bed."

Lt. Col. Mullen said, "Pete, I guess we'll take those rooms and rest up for a bit."

Pete took the group to their motel rooms. He said, "Both rooms are equipped with two twin beds, like all the rest of our guest rooms. If you want to get cozy you can push the two beds together. There are two buckets of water in each bathroom for you to clean up with. Please do not use the toilets in the rooms. There are porta-potties at the each end of the lodge. Out behind the buildings are rain barrels of water. If you should need any more, check with me first because we need to conserve water. If you need light in the rooms, there are some candles in jars, but be careful with them. We don't need any fires. Due to the loss of electricity, we've been cooking up all the meat in the freezers and having a town wide barbecue every afternoon. If you're willing to help with the preparations and the cleanup, you'll be welcome to join us."

He handed Lt. Col. Mullen the keys and walked back to the store.

Lt. Col. Mullen said, "That sounds good. We'll help in any way we can. That includes you, Forster."

Agent Forster was already thinking ahead. "This could be interesting. Who are you bunking with Williams?"

Lt. Col. Mullen looked at her and said, "It's up to you, Sgt. Williams, but as you know, I'm married and loyal to my wife, so I believe you would be safer in my room."

Sgt. Williams quickly agreed, "Yes, I believe I'm safer with your officer ethics than I would be with either of those two buffoons."

After the group settled into the rooms, they washed up, changed their clothes and met back outside.

Agent Forster said to Lt. Col. Mullen, "What are we going to do about the TACCOM briefcase? I don't want to leave it in the room unguarded."

Mullen replied, "We'll have to just put it under the bed for now and lock the room. I'll ask Pete or the mayor if there are any safes or vaults in town where we could lock up sensitive items."

Later, the group noticed the activity picking up behind the motel. They went out back to assist the town people in preparing the barbecue. At first the townspeople were suspicious of the newcomers and not very talkative, but Sgt. Williams and Ted Adams were able to strike up conversations, getting some of the townspeople to open up and be more friendly. Pete, the storekeeper, found that agent Forster was a good chef at the barbecue pit and kept him busy cooking. Lt. Col. Mullen engaged Mayor Liz in conversation about their current situation. She told him that water, fruit, vegetables, medicine, and working vehicles were in short supply. No one had any communication with the outside world. Their only chance of making contact with someone outside of Pigeon lay in the hands of crazy Frank Paretsky who might have a ham radio. Liz said she'd need to go up there alone and talk to him first before bringing anyone else along.

That evening, after the food and trash was picked up from the barbecue. Lt. Col. Mullen and agent Forster were sitting at picnic tables out back, drinking beer and talking with Pete the storekeeper. Todd and Sgt. Williams were playing with some of the children and their dogs. Just then, they heard a vehicle coming up the road and saw headlights. A late-model Ford F150 careened into the parking lot, plowing into the store sign. The driver's door opened and a man stumbled out yelling, "Help us! Someone, please help us!" and then he collapsed on the ground.

Everyone got up from their tables and rushed to the parking lot to assess the situation and see if they could help. Pete grabbed a kerosene lantern off the table and brought it with him. As they approached, they saw the man lying on the ground, severely injured. Lt. Col. Mullen and Sgt. Williams shone their flashlights on the man. It was immediately obvious that the injuries were not from the minor accident of hitting the store sign. The man's clothes were ripped and torn, barely remaining on his body. He was still alive, but bleeding badly.

The man, barely able to speak, pointed to the truck and said, "My daughter, help my daughter. Please."

Agent Forster shone his light into the back of the truck. There they found a young girl of about 12 years old. She was wearing a dress that was covered in blood, and she was holding her arm. Her arm and right leg had serious injuries. The flesh had been ripped away, exposing the bone. The girl was still alive, but barely conscious. Agent Forster turned away and started puking.

Mayor Liz took charge. "Pete, get some blankets and load them in the back of my truck. I'll take them to Doc Benson."

As Pete and Todd were loading them into the back of the mayor's truck, Lt. Col. Mullen and Agent Forster examined the damage to the man's truck.

Rebecca Williams got in the back of Mayor Liz's truck with the man and his daughter. Todd Adams got into the passenger seat of the Mayor's truck.

Lt. Col. Mullen said to Mayor Liz, "Their truck isn't badly damaged. I believe it's still drivable, so agent Forster and I will follow you to Doc Benson's."

Sandy Hicks, who had been standing to one side, turned to her husband. "Oh my God, Dan! We need to get the kids on the horses and get them out of here and away from this."

As they were driving away, Tom noticed that the dogs out in the parking lot were licking the blood off the pavement. He said, "Jenny, find a bucket and get this blood cleaned up!"

Jenny just put her head in her hands and pleaded, "Tom, we need to get away from this place as soon as possible. I cannot take any more of this. It's bad enough that they're killing animals and eating their flesh. Now we have humans bleeding all over the place, too."

Tom said, "Maybe tomorrow we can load some supplies on our bicycle packs and ride out of here."

Jenny brightened, "Oh, please Tom, that would be so good to get away from here. Everyone has guns and is killing animals to eat them. I just don't know how much more of this I can take."

Mayor Liz turned the truck into a driveway. She was blowing the horn as they drove up to the farmhouse. A man holding a shotgun came outside.

Mayor Liz got out of her truck and shouted to the man. "Doc! We have two severely injured people here. We need your help."

The man put down his shotgun and came over to the mayor's truck. Looking at the man and the young girl, he said, "Bring them into the barn where I can get a better look at them."

Inside the barn Doc Benson started lighting some kerosene lanterns. There was a gurney and a large table in the middle of the room. Medicine cabinets and medical devices were all around the room. They put the girl on the table and the man on the gurney.

Todd looked at Doc Benson in amazement. "You practice medicine out of your barn?"

Doc Benson looked back. "Yes, of course. I am a veterinarian and horse farrier."

Todd's jaw dropped. "A veterinarian? A horse doctor!"

Mayor Liz said, "Yes, a veterinarian. He's the only doctor we have."

Doc Benson quickly assessed them. "This man's injuries are too severe. I don't believe there's anything I can do for him."

The man whispered, "Don't worry about me, save my daughter. Please!"

Doc Benson patted his arm. "Don't worry, I'll do the best I can for her. Giving the man a shot of morphine, he said, "This will help you with the pain." Then he turned to work on the young girl.

Lt. Col. Mullen leaned over the man. "What happened to you?"

The man said, "My wife and daughter and I escaped Pittsburgh on our way north into the country, looking for a safe place with food, shelter and water. We were camped a few miles south of here. Suddenly we were attacked by a pack of wild dogs. Those dogs were not normal; they were large and vicious. They grabbed my daughter by the leg and dragged her right out of our tent! When my wife and I tried to rescue her, beating the dogs with a baseball bat, the dogs turned on us and killed my wife. They tore her to pieces while she was still alive, right in front of my eyes!"

The man started crying and couldn't continue for a few moments. "There was nothing I could do. I grabbed my daughter, putting her in the back of my truck. Before I could get in, the dogs pulled me to the ground, tearing at my flesh. I don't know how, but I managed to get away from them and get into the truck and drive away. I saw some lights at your place and pulled in there for help." The man started coughing and weeping.

Lt. Col. Mullen said, "Why did you say 'escape Pittsburgh?' What has happened in Pittsburgh?"

The man said, "Sickness, death, and gangs of people gone mad. Stay far, far away from Pittsburgh if you want to live!" Suddenly, the man went into convulsions and died. The group all looked at each other, wide-eyed with expressions of shock.

Doc Benson said, "I'm not a surgeon used to working on humans. But in order to save this girl's life, we are going to have to amputate her left forearm and lower right leg. Too much tissue damage. There's no way to save it. And I say 'we' because I'm going to need help. Any volunteers?"

Agent Forster shook his head adamantly, "Sorry, not me. I'm already getting sick. I have to go outside."

Mayor Liz said, "I'm no nurse, but if you tell me what to do, I'll help."

Sgt. Williams said, "I have some field medic training. I'll help too."

Lt. Col. Mullen said, "My stomach is a bit stronger than Forster's, but I'm sure I wouldn't be able to handle that. Thank you, Williams, and good luck to you all. I'll be outside."

Todd said, "If there's something I can do without having to watch, I'll help."

Doc Benson waved his hand dismissively. "You go outside with the other weaklings. The ladies and I should be able to handle this."

The guys went outside to let Doc Benson and the women work to try to save the young girl's life. Once outside, they noticed steam coming from the man's truck and liquid leaking out onto the ground.

Agent Forster said, "I guess that crash into the store sign broke the radiator, and now that truck is a true Ford: found on road dead."

Todd said, "I'm sure the mayor will give us a ride back to the motel."

Lt. Col. Mullen looked down at all the blood. "This uniform is ruined. I only have the fatigues and coveralls that I wore from the plane crash."

Todd said, "We all could use some clean clothes. Maybe Pete or the mayor know where we can get some."

After a couple of hours, Mayor Liz and Sgt. Williams emerged from the barn. The mayor said, "It's done, and Doc Benson will stay with her for the rest of the night. We can check back with him tomorrow afternoon."

Sgt. Williams took a garbage bag with the girls amputated limbs around the corner and put them in a garbage can. She said, "I need to get cleaned up and get a clean change of clothes."

Lt. Col. Mullen said, "We were just discussing clothing. Liz, is there any place in town where we can get clean clothing?"

Mayor Liz said, "There's a thrift shop at the church. I'm sure we can find some clothes there that'll fit you. If you can get by tonight, I'll take you there tomorrow."

Agent Forster said, "Mayor, that truck over there has a busted radiator. So we would appreciate it if you could give us a ride back to the motel."

Mayor Liz nodded. "I sure can, if you don't mind riding in the back. I think we all need to get cleaned up and get some rest."

As they climbed into the back of the mayor's truck, Todd couldn't resist saying, "Forster, the mayor's nice enough to give us a ride, so no puking in the back of her truck."

Agent Forster scowled. "Screw you, NBC news."

Day two in Pigeon, Pennsylvania.

In the morning the group got up and walked over to the general store where the smell of fresh coffee greeted them.

Pete was in good spirits. "Good morning, soldiers. I'm sure you could use a fresh hot cup of coffee."

He pointed to a table that held a Coleman stove and two metal percolator coffee pots. The group was delighted at this sight. As they were drinking their coffee, the mayor and some other town people showed up with bacon and eggs. As they were all eating breakfast, their conversation consisted of speculations about the events of the night before. Everyone was worried about the attack on the man and young girl. But what was causing the most chatter were the conditions that the man had described in Pittsburgh. After breakfast, the mayor took the group to the church thrift shop to find clean clothing. Afterward, they anxiously drove to Doc Benson's farm to check on the condition of the young girl.

As they approached Doc Benson's farmhouse, they saw the doc outside his barn, cleaning up trash. He told them that it appeared that wild animals got into his trash cans and ran off with the amputee limbs. He reported that the girl passed away early in the morning.

Doc Benson was perplexed. "I was sure that the surgery was a success, and that she would pull through. I'm no expert, but I don't believe she died from her injuries, or the surgery. I'm sure there were some other complications, but without lab tests, I cannot be positive."

Everyone was sad to hear the news of the girl's death. They took the bodies to a nearby graveyard and buried them, performing a small memorial service.

The mayor dropped the group off at the motel and said, "I'll be back later, around dinnertime. I'm taking Doc Benson around to check on some of his patients. Being the only doctor in these parts, he has both human and animal patients to attend to daily. We get food and gasoline in payment these days. I'll also stop by and see if I can talk some sense into crazy Frank. I'll see you later unless Frank shoots us for trespassing."

Later that afternoon, as they were preparing the usual barbecue dinner outside the general store, the mayor and Doc Benson returned. Liz said, "As I was taking Doc Benson around to his patients today, we were getting some disturbing news. A number of people in the southern part of the county have been getting seriously ill. Along with that, there's been a number of attacks on farm animals by wild dogs. Crazy Frank has himself barricaded in his compound and won't come out to talk to us. He said that if we came back, or if any military people came around his property, he would not hesitate to shoot on sight. I tacked a note to one of the posts outside his barrier fence telling him about incident with the man and young girl the other night. Hopefully he'll come out and read that note and either leave us a note in return or become more cooperative tomorrow."

As they were sitting at the picnic tables, eating their dinner, Doc Benson leaned over and looked closely at Lt. Col. Mullen. "You look a bit peaked. How are you feeling?"

Lt. Col. Mullen wiped the sweat from his brow. "I feel weak and a bit overheated. I think I'll just go to my room and lie down, if that's okay with everyone."

Doc Benson said, "I'll come with you and check you out when we get to your room."

Agent Forster said, "I'm not doing so well myself, doc. I'll come along too."

A short while later, Doc Benson came back out to the barbecue area and announced that the Lt. Col. and the FBI agent seemed to be getting ill. "Not much I can do for them. We need a real doctor. I told them to drink lots of liquids and stay in their rooms. I will check on them in the morning. How are the rest of you doing. Is anyone else feeling sick?"

Rebecca said, "I'm feeling okay. I'll get my stuff from Lt. Col. Mullen's room and move into Todd's room for now. Don't look so happy, Todd." She held up her tactical knife. "If you don't behave yourself, I'll cut your balls off."

Pete said to Doc Benson, "Maybe you could talk some sense into them out-of-towners, Todd and Jenny Maxwell. You know, they're city people. They don't like our way of life here, even before the power went out. They're packing up and riding for Rochester on their bicycles. I tried to convince them to stay here, telling them that it wasn't safe to travel long distances on a bicycle. They would not listen to me. I tried to give them some beef jerky for the trip and Jenny screamed at me 'get that dead animal meat away from me.' When I tried to loan Tom a .22 for protection, he said he didn't believe in killing anything and would not take it."

Doc Benson shook his head. "Some people, when they get their mind set on something, there's no changing it, even if it's going to get them killed."

The next day Lt. Col. Mullen and agent Forster were even sicker, and there were large numbers of other people in the town of Pigeon reporting that they were feeling ill as well. There were increased reports of wild dog attacks on livestock and people. The sickness and wild dog attacks increased over the next several days. After being advised to stay put in town, Tom and Jenny Maxwell, ignoring the advice of everyone, rode off on their bicycles, heading north on Route 66. Doc Benson and the mayor became increasingly concerned as they saw their friends and neighbors falling ill and dying, one after the other. Pete had been expressing his concerns about the wild dog attacks on livestock. The town's food supply depended on the livestock, and with the wild dogs attacking and killing them, it was threatening the survival of the people.

Canine Flu in Pigeon, Pennsylvania.

Lt. Col. Mullen and agent Forster had lapsed into a comatose state. Doc Benson had them on IV saline solution, along with over half of the town. Sandy and Dan Hicks died two days later. Over a hundred townspeople had died. Pete was no longer having town barbecues at his general store. Everyone was staying home and trying to avoid contact with other people. Fear of catching this mysterious illness was paralyzing the town. Todd Adams and Rebecca Williams had been making rounds with Doc Benson to assist in the care of the residents. Wild dogs had killed three people and half the livestock in the town of Pigeon. Everyone that was not sick was armed and never ventured outside without a weapon. Up to this point no one had seen or killed any of the wild dogs. But the attacks continued and everyone was on edge.

That evening in the general store, Todd, Rebecca, and Pete were discussing the current conditions of the people in Pigeon when Rebecca excused herself to one of the outside porta-potties. A short time later Todd and Pete heard a scream and two gunshots, followed by fierce barking and growling from outside.

Todd snatched the lantern and ran outside. Pete grabbed his old side-by-side double barrel 12 gauge Stevens and followed Todd out the door. There they saw six dog-like creatures attacking the porta-potty with Sgt. Rebecca Williams inside. Pete put the old double barrel to his shoulder and took aim at the creatures, giving them both barrels of 00 buckshot. He dropped one of them and wounded another. Todd held the lantern in one hand and drew his 9mm Beretta with the other, firing at the group of creatures, driving them off.

Todd ran to the porta-potty yelling, "Rebecca, are you okay?"

Sgt. Rebecca Williams came stumbling out, looking frightened. She ran to Todd, putting her arms around him and embracing him in a big hug. She was shaking and crying.

Rebecca said, "Thank God you came out here right away! When I opened the door of the potty, I heard a growl and saw those evil eyes and snapping jaws coming right at me. I thought I was dead. I drew my M9 and fired two shots, then slammed the door closed. Those creatures started smashing into the sides, trying to break in here to tear me apart like that little girl. Thank you, thank you so much, both of you."

Pete was standing over one of the creatures, staring at it. "I got one of them over here. Did you ever see anything like this?"

Todd joined him. "It appears to be a dog of some type. The body shape is kind of like the hyenas I've seen in Africa."

Pete exclaimed, "Look at the claws on that thing! It has larger claws than the black bear I shot last fall."

Rebecca was still shaking. She looked around her. "Let's go back inside before they come back."

Todd agreed. "Yes, it's probably not safe out here. We better go inside."

Pete said, "Tomorrow, before we buried that thing, I want to show it to Doc Benson and Mayor Liz."

Inside the store, Rebecca declared, "I'm never going outside after dark again!"

Todd said, "We have to go outside to go back to our room."

Rebecca was adamant. "I'll sleep right here on the floor if I have to; I'm not going back out there again tonight."

Pete said, "I have a spare room upstairs in my apartment. You guys are welcome to sleep there, but there is only one full-size bed in that room."

Rebecca said, "Thank you Pete, that'll be fine," and she started following Pete to the stairs leading to the second floor. She looked back at Todd standing there holding the lantern, looking like a lost puppy dog. She asked, "Are you coming or are you just gonna stand there all night?"

He broke into a big smile and followed them upstairs. Pete showed them their room and went off to his own.

The bedroom was furnished in a colonial decor, with dresser, nightstand, two chairs, and a full-size bed covered with a white comforter. Todd set the lantern down on the dresser and stood there, looking around the room. Rebecca sat in one of the chairs, taking off her boots. She calmly stripped down to her panties and t-shirt. Pulling back the covers on the bed, she said to Todd, "Are you coming to bed, or are you just going to stand there with your mouth open all night?"

Todd was speechless, but took her invitation, stripping down to his underwear and t-shirt. He got in the bed beside Rebecca.

Then he remembered, "Oh, I need to turn the lantern out."

Rebecca grabbed his arm. "No, leave it on! I don't want to be in the dark." She rolled toward him, putting her arms around him and said, "I don't want to be alone, either. I need to be in a man's arms tonight."

Next Day After Porta-Potty Attack.

The next morning at 8 AM, Pete was fixing coffee in the general store when Mayor Liz and Doc Benson arrived. Doc Benson went to check on Lt. Col. Mullen and agent Forster while Mayor Liz went into the store to have coffee with Pete.

"Good morning Pete. That coffee sure smells good."

Pete replied, "Morning, Liz. Pour yourself a cup. Where's the doc?"

"He went to check on Mullen and Forster."

Pete said, "We had a bit of excitement around here last night."

Mayor Liz's eyebrows went up. "Oh? What happened, is everyone okay?"

Pete said, "Yeah, everyone's okay, but when the doc gets here, I have something to show you."

Todd and Rebecca came down the stairs together. "Good morning. Pete, that coffee smells really good."

Pete had a big smile on his face. "Good morning. Did you two sleep well?"

The mayor looked at them with a curious expression. "Good morning Tom. Good morning Rebecca."

Just then, Doc Benson walked into the store. "Good morning everyone. I have some good news. The Lt. Col. and Forster are awake and feeling better. I removed the IVs and would like to bring them some chicken broth, if you have any Pete."

Pete said, "That's good news! I'll heat up some chicken bouillon." He reached to put a pan of water on the camp stove.

Todd and Rebecca agreed. "That is good news. Are they talking? Can we go see them?"

Doc Benson held up his hands. "Let me get them cleaned up and get some of that bouillon into them before we all rush in there."

Mayor Liz said, "Pete, you were going to fill us in on that incident you were talking about."

Pete, Todd, and Rebecca told Mayor Liz and Dr. Benson about the wild dog attack on Rebecca last night. Then Pete took them outside to show them the body of the wild dog that he killed.

Pete jaw dropped. "Wow! That thing didn't look like that when we left it last night!"

Doc Benson knelt next to the creature. "This thing looks like it's been laying out in the sun, dead for three days, not just overnight."

Mayor Liz was holding her nose. "What would cause a creature to rot so quickly?"

Rebecca wasn't getting too close. "Looking at that thing gives me cold chills, even though it's dead."

Todd said, "The way the skin is all bubbled up, I think the sun is what caused it to deteriorate this badly so quickly."

Doc Benson agreed, "I think you're right. I would venture a guess that these creatures are highly sensitive to sunlight. That would explain why we haven't seen or heard of any attacks during the daytime. I think we need to get this thing buried as soon as possible."

Todd said, "Doc, you're saying that these things are zombie dogs?"

Doc Benson shrugged. "I don't know much about zombies, but they are nocturnal creatures."

Rebecca said, "Zombie dogs are a good name for them. I saw them up close, face-to-face, and they are definitely evil."

Mayor Liz said, "Okay then, as mayor of the town of Pigeon, I declare that these creatures are zombie dogs. Until we find out more, that's as good a name as any."

Todd and Pete took the body of the wild dog down to the edge of the woods and buried it. Doc Benson, Mayor Liz, and Rebecca brought the chicken broth to Lt. Col. Mullen and agent Forster. The group then brought Lt. Col. Mullen and agent Forster up to date on the current events. Mayor Liz and Doc Benson then left to make the rounds, checking on the other residents of Pigeon.

Later that evening, Mayor Liz and Doc Benson returned to the general store. They told the group that some of the other residents were starting to recover like the Lt. Col. and Forster. But the zombie dogs had been taking a heavy toll on the livestock in the meantime. Mayor Liz told them that it was also getting harder to find gasoline for her old truck to take Doc Benson around to the sick residents. Pete said he thought he had an old hand pump that they could use to get gasoline from the underground tanks out in the parking lot. They made plans to work on that project the next day. Lt. Col. Mullen and agent Forster seemed to be making a rapid recovery.

Zombie Dogs Night 2

That night, Lt. Col. Mullen and agent Forster continued to share the end room of the motel. Todd Adams and Technical Sergeant Rebecca Williams shared the room next to them. Pete Lockrow went to bed in his apartment over the store.

Somewhere around midnight, Todd and Rebecca were asleep in each other's arms when they heard loud barking, howling, and the crash of glass breaking. Shouts and gunfire were coming from Lt. Col. Mullen and Forster's room.

Lt. Col. Mullen and agent Forster had been awakened by loud barking and howling. Lt. Col. Mullen sat up in bed and lit the candle on the nightstand. Agent Forster grabbed his SIG M11 .45 auto and asked, "What the hell is going on?"

Just then, a zombie dog came crashing through the window into the room and landed next to Lt. Col. Mullen's bed. Agent Forster quickly rolled out of his bed, laying across Lt. Col. Mullen's bed, and fired three quick shots into the zombie dog, killing it. Lt. Col. Mullen grabbed his 9mm Glock 19 and jumped out of the bed. Both men moved to the far end of the room, ready to defend themselves should any more zombie dogs come through the window.

In the next room, Todd banged on the wall, yelling, "Are you two okay?"

Lt. Col. Mullen yelled back, "We're under attack by zombie dogs. We got one, and right now I don't see any more."

Without thinking to get dressed, Todd grabbed the Remington model 870 shotgun and rushed out the door to assist Lt. Col. Mullen. Rebecca, having no time to do otherwise, grabbed her M-16 and followed Todd out of the room. Using the flashlights mounted on the end of their weapons, they quickly realized the severity of the situation.

"Oh, shit!" said Todd. A dozen or more zombie dogs rushed at them. Rebecca shouted, "Don't just stand there! Start shooting!"

Todd and Rebecca, both in their underwear, opened fire on the zombie dogs. Lt. Col. Mullen and agent Forster, hearing the commotion, grabbed their rifles and went outside to assist. Hearing the commotion and the gunshots, Pete threw on his clothes and grabbed a lantern and his old Stevens double-barreled shotgun. He ran down the stairs and out the front door.

In the lantern light he saw Lt. Col. Mullen, with only his pants on, holding a FN SCAR-L military rifle, Agent Forster in boxer shorts, holding an M4 carbine, Todd Adams in a T-shirt and briefs, holding a Remington pump 12 gauge, and Rebecca Williams in a T-shirt and panties, holding an M-16. There were several dead zombie dogs in the parking lot; the others had apparently been driven off by the attack of the scantily clad Air Force soldiers.

"Holy shit!" said Pete. "This is not a sight I would expect to see every day! Is everyone okay?"

The Air Force group, looking a bit embarrassed, replied that they were okay and gave a few details of the events that took place.

Pete said, "I think you guys need to get some clothes on, and we'll all spend the rest of the night in the store where we're better protected in case of any more attacks."

Agent Forster shined his flashlight on Rebecca. "New Air Force combat fatigues?"

Rebecca fired a round in the ground near Forster's feet. "Do you need to go change those shorts, Forster?"

Agent Forster exclaimed, "Shit, you crazy bitch! You almost shot me!"

Lt. Col. Mullen shouted, "Chill out and calm down people! Let's get dressed and meet in the general store. That is an order."

After getting dressed, the group spent the rest of the night in the general store without incident.

Day 5 Town Of Pigeon.

The next morning at the general store, as everyone was having coffee and fixing breakfast, Mayor Liz and Doc Benson arrived. After the morning greetings, the group told Mayor Liz and Doc Benson about the events of the night before.

Agent Forster was smiling. "Williams is the sexiest zombie dog killer, in those pink panties, that I've ever seen."

Todd said, "And she's pretty good about scaring the shit out of special agents in boxer shorts, too."

Agent Forster sneered. "Getting a bit defensive of your new piece of tail, news man?"

Mayor Liz slapped Forster on the back of the head. "No need to be crude, Agent Asshole."

Lt. Col. Mullen pointed his finger at Forster. "Any more rude comments about Sgt. Williams and I'll shoot you myself."

Mayor Liz said, "We had some zombie dog attacks at Doc Benson's farm last night, too. They didn't attack our house, but they killed his two horses, tearing them apart out in the field. We heard it, but decided it was best to keep the lights out and stay in the house."

Lt. Col. Mullen said, "Things are getting a bit dangerous around here. We need to make contact with the outside world and see if we can get some help."

Pete said, "With all the livestock being killed, we're running low on supplies. I have a pretty good supply of canned goods here in the store, but no meat or any way to keep it fresh with the power out."

Mayor Liz said, "I guess we'll have to go up to crazy Frank's and see if we can convince him to talk to us. I'm sure he has a short wave radio or some ideas on what we need to do. He's a crazy old hippie who's been planning for the end of the world for years. Pete, if you can get some gas out of those tanks out there in your yard, we'll drive up to crazy Frank's and see if we can't get shot."

They buried the zombie dog bodies from the attack of the

previous evening. Pete found his hand pump and was able to get some gasoline out of the storage tanks in the parking lot for Mayor Liz's old truck. The group gathered some gear, climbed in the back of Mayor Liz's truck, and drove up to crazy Frank's place.

Crazy Frank's Place.

Doc Benson got in the passenger seat and Mayor Liz drove. Lt. Col. Mullen, agent Forster, Tom Adams, and Sgt. Rebecca Williams were bouncing around in the pickup bed on the long ride up the mountain to crazy Frank's place.

Mayor Liz turned on to a narrow dirt road. After about a mile, they came to a rising gate bar, which was closed. There was a sign on the gate that said 'no trespassing, trespassers beyond this point will be shot on sight.' Mayor Liz stopped the truck and got out.

She said, "We have to go on foot from here. Frank's place is about a half a mile up ahead."

Everyone got out of the truck and started the long walk to Frank's place. The driveway was narrow, with trees hanging over the road and grass growing in the middle.

Agent Forster said, "By the looks of this road, I'm guessing Frank does not get much company."

Doc Benson said, "That's the way he likes it. He's good at encouraging curious people to stay away."

They walked about a hundred yards, and at the crest of the hill, they saw what looked like an old colonial wooden stockade from the early 1800s. The front wall of the stockade was about 100 yards wide, 10 feet high, and was made from large logs that stood upright, with points on the top. There was a wooden gate about 8 feet wide with an observation tower above it. The driveway leading to the gate was blocked from direct approach by concrete road barriers, arranged in a way that would force a vehicle to zigzag around them upon approaching the gate. As the group was walking around one of the barriers, agent Forster caught a trip wire with his foot. There was a flurry of leaves as a loop grasped his ankle. A treetop sprang straight up, hoisting agent Forster into the air, upside down. At the sound of agent Forster's yell, everyone looked around to see him flailing around, upside down, about 3 feet above the ground.

Agent Forster was yelling, "Get me down! Get me the hell down!"

Smiling broadly, Rebecca walked up to him and said, "Gee, Forster, I kinda like you like this," and she gave him a spin.

Agent Forster said, "Lt. Col., keep that crazy bitch away from me and get me down!"

As everyone was laughing at agent Forster's predicament, a man appeared in the observation tower. He shouted at them, "Who the hell are you, and what you want? This is private property. Leave before I start shooting."

Mayor Liz waved her hands, "Hold on Frank! It's me and Doc Benson here."

Frank shouted, "Who else is that you've got with you?"

Mayor Liz pointed to each in turn. "This is Jack Mullen, Rebecca Williams, Ted Adams, and the guy swinging upside down is Greg Forster. They're friends of ours. They've been staying at Pete's store and helping the doc and I care for the town's residents. Things are getting quite desperate, and we need to know if you have a short wave radio."

Frank said, "What I have or don't have is no business of anyone's except mine."

Doc Benson yelled, "Come on Frank, you crazy bastard, people are dying and we need your help!"

Frank peered at the doc. "Is anyone out there sick?"

Doc Benson replied, "No, none of us are sick. But most of the town folk are either dead or dying from the sickness. The few people who have been surviving the sickness are being killed by wild dogs. Now come on, Frank, are you going help us or shoot us?"

Frank said, "I know about them wild dogs. This sickness mutated them and now they're spreading the sickness all across the country. That's why I am holding up here in my stockade and not taking in any visitors. You have to understand, it's only for my own protection."

Doc Benson said, "Well if you stay in there holed up like some old hermit, you're going to die there all alone, and what good is that?"

Frank thought for a second. "Well doc, if you say none of you are sick, I guess I could let you in to use my radio. But I do not want any shit from anyone about my guns or marijuana!"

Mayor Liz said, "We are not ATF and we don't give a damn about your marijuana. We understand that under the current conditions firearm restrictions no longer apply."

Frank decided. "Okay, cut that guy down and come on in."

Rebecca asked formally, "Lt. Col., may I do the honors of extracting special agent Forster from his little problem?" She had a smirk on her face.

Lt. Col. Mullen bowed. "Be my guest."

Sgt. Williams took careful aim with her M-16 and fired two shots into the rope about one foot above agent Forster's foot. Agent Forster hit the ground hard hollering, "Williams, you are a crazy bitch!"

Todd was smiling. "But she's a good shot, Forster."

Frank opened the gate on his stockade, allowing the group to enter.

As they approached the gate, they saw a man standing just inside. He looked to be in his 50s, about 6 feet tall with a slim build, dressed in military camouflage, combat boots, and a tactical vest with the pockets full of extra clips and other items. He had a 1911 Colt .45 in a tactical holster strapped to his thigh. He was holding an AK-47 and was wearing tactical gloves with the fingers cut out. His black hair and beard were streaked with gray, and there was a red bandanna tied around his head.

The inside of the stockade was about 100 square yards with a two-story structure in the middle. This structure was made up of steel shipping containers stacked and welded together. Parked in front of the structure was a VW bus and a World War II Willy's Jeep. Frank invited them inside. Inside the main structure each shipping container was made into a specific room. Along the walls were shelves holding various supplies of food, water, medical, weapons, ammunition, tools, marijuana paraphernalia, and other miscellaneous items. Frank offered them a seat at the kitchen table.

He said, "Well, seeing as how you guys are my guests, I guess I need to offer you a drink. I have water, orange juice, Gatorade in every flavor, Pepsi, Dr. Pepper, ginger ale, Budweiser, Michelob, and a whole wine cellar full of wine. My favorite drink the last few days has been dandelion wine. Made it myself, last year's batch."

Mayor Liz was amused, but said, "The dandelion wine sounds good. We'll all have the dandelion wine."

Lt. Col. Mullen started to say something but Mayor Liz kicked him under the table, signaling him to accept the dandelion wine. Frank got some glasses and poured a glass of dandelion wine for each of them.

Frank said, "I guess you people haven't gotten very much information about what's been going on. Before I loan you the use of my radio, I'll bring you up-to-date on what I know. I've been recording some of the messages I've been receiving on short wave. I've also translated some Morse code messages and some military encrypted messages that I can decipher. I'll play the recorded messages for you first." He brought out a tape recorder and pushed the play button.

"Voice of America Radio on the aircraft carrier USS Ronald Reagan is off the coast of Carolina along with the Atlantic Fleet. From here, the government of the United States of America will be launching missions to stabilize the populace, reestablish communications, reestablish electrical power, and distribute food and medical supplies, starting with Charleston and Charlotte, then branching out to surrounding areas from there. Due to the epidemic outbreak of canine flu, all citizens are being advised not to travel. Help will come to you. Remain at your current location and stay tuned to this frequency for more news and updates."

There was static for a few seconds and then, *"Voice of America Radio news April 10, 2020; multiple forces of North Korea, Iran, ISIS and Al Qaeda have attacked the United States. US forces abroad are currently engaged with our enemies, striking devastating blows every day. US naval assets from abroad that are not directly needed in the fighting are being brought back to the US to assist in the recovery of our great nation, the United States of America. Air Force One, with the president and staff on board, has crashed and is now missing. Air Force Two, with the vice president aboard, is also missing. Acting president is Secretary of State John Hagar, aboard the aircraft carrier USS Ronald Reagan. Peacekeeping forces from Russia and China have been placed at various locations across the country to help bring peace and stability to regions of extreme violence. These forces are under the command of the United Nations. British forces are assisting and are in control of the New England states. Australian and US forces are in control and bringing stability to the West Coast states. Texas, Oklahoma, and New Mexico have gone rogue from the United States, and all citizens are advised to stay clear of that territory. Food and medical supplies will be airdropped into populated areas starting in the next few days. This broadcast will repeat 24/7. New information will be added as it becomes available."*

Mayor Liz murmured, "They're going to have airdrops of food and medicine in a few days."

Lt. Col. Mullen said, "This isn't a populated area. If we stay here and wait for them to get to us, we'll be waiting until we run out of food or ammunition, and then the zombie dogs will have us for dinner."

Mayor Liz said, "So what are you suggesting we do?"

Lt. Col. Mullen turned. "From the look on your face, and what I see around here, I would say you have more information for us, Frank."

Frank said, "Oh yeah, I sure do. I'm just getting started." Taking another swallow of his dandelion wine, Frank said, "I might rattle on a lot, but I don't get much chance to talk to other people face-to-face. Anyhow, here's what I've got: that message has been playing for about a week now and there's more. **P**ublic **R**elations policies, political correctness, and power and greed have blinded our government. They paid no heed to the warnings because they were too worried about their image. Then it became too late."

Todd said, "I've met Secretary of State John Hagar. I've interviewed him a few times for NBC. I always did think he was a real ass. I don't know how he ever got appointed secretary of state."

Frank said, "You work for NBC?"

Todd shrugged. "Well, I was a news reporter for NBC before the shit hit the fan."

Frank shook his finger. "Well, don't mention my name in any of your reports."

Todd said, "I won't. I don't believe I'll be giving any news reports anytime soon."

Doc Benson held out his hand, "Please continue, Frank."

"As the protests and civil unrest increased across the country, Russia and China devised a plan to infiltrate and conquer the United States without ever having to go to war. They sent thousands of college students here on student visas with skills to keep the protests and violence going so that eventually Russia and China could come to the aid of the US with peacekeeper troops backed by the United Nations. Some of those troops are still here, too. Russia also sent scientists and engineers to NASA to work on the special deep space exploration projects. These Russians are the ones who built and fired the EMPs. Our government, however, has blamed North Korea for the EMPs. Being non-nuclear and high tech, the EMP design was overlooked by our scientists because the ones who knew what to look for were previously kicked out of the NASA program. They were probably framed or set up by the Russians to get them out of the way."

Lt. Col. Mullen's eyes narrowed. "Is this all speculation on your part or do you have actual proof?"

Frank nodded, "I intercepted a message from Republican Texas Sen. Thomas Kane to one of the TACAMO planes in the Pacific. He was talking to Rear Adm. Taylor. I have it all on tape. Sen. Kane was in Houston for the deep space launch by NASA. Sen. Kane and Gov. Carry of Texas have two Russian scientists locked up there in Texas with all this information. There's more, let me continue."

"There's one thing the Russians and Chinese did not count on:

ISIS and Al Qaeda. They had a lot of sleeper cells in this country which came here under the same education visa programs as the Russians and Chinese. The terrorist sleeper cells either brought or acquired chemical and biological weapons. They put them into suicide bombs and detonated them all over the country. Every metropolitan city and every college town were hit with these chemical or biological weapons. They probably got the ingredients from the medical labs where they were going to college. With all of the violence and protesting going on, security lapses made it possible to steal these ingredients for the suicide bombs."

"The Russian and Chinese 'peacekeepers' are still trying to complete their mission and doing a damn good job of it. What's left of our government is still just as blind and dumb as ever. You heard the message from Voice of America. They still think the United Nations, Russia, and China are here to help."

Frank continued, "In the small towns that are controlled by either the Russians or the Chinese, American citizens are being put in so-called FEMA camps. These are actually concentration camps. The Russians or Chinese probably do not have control of any of the metro areas, however. Only smaller cities in urban areas would be manageable, but they do have units mixed in with US forces in some metropolitan areas where there are working airports and seaports."

"There are small resistant forces and fighters scattered throughout the country, but they are outgunned and outnumbered. The acting US government sees them as rebels, making their cause more difficult. The Texas government seems to be the only ones that seem to have any sense. But they're too small in numbers to launch a full-scale attack against the real problems in the country. That's why they have closed their borders to the rest of the country and taken defensive measures to protect themselves."

Lt. Col. Mullen said, "Do you know anything about what's happening in the rest of the world?"

Frank said, "Some. We nuked the Middle East and North Korea. South Korea is a real mess. The Chinese consider the loss of North

Korea collateral damage. For them, it's been a way to get rid of the dictator in North Korea without political fallout."

"We do have some other countries on our side: Great Britain, Israel, Australia, South Africa and the Philippines. Most of the other countries in Europe, Asia and Africa are staying out of the conflict. They are all worried about the spread of the canine flu. Most of the humans who have lived through the initial attack of the disease now have a degree of immunity. But I would still advise caution when dealing with any dead bodies, human or canine."

"Here," said Frank, "read this." He handed an article to Mullen. Mullen ran his hands through his hair as he read it. He then looked up and handed the article to Williams. It explained exactly what had been going on: turning man's best friend into man's only natural enemy… forever.

The canine flu is the disease used in a bio weapon by Islamic terrorists, and it has killed millions in the United States and Europe, spreading into a global pandemic. Domestic dogs and other canine species, which consume the infected human flesh or blood of a victim, then mutate, turning the canine into a vicious nocturnal animal known as the zombie dog. The specific disease, which mutated and affected the canine, is now known to be an extreme canine version of EPP (Erythrohepatic Protoporphyria).

Erythropoietic Protoporphyria (EPP) is a rare inherited metabolic disorder characterized by a deficiency of the enzyme ferrochelatase (FECH). Due to abnormally low levels of this enzyme, excessive amounts of protoporphyrin accumulate in the bone marrow, blood plasma, and red blood cells. The major symptom of this disorder is hypersensitivity of the skin to sunlight and some types of artificial light, such as fluorescent lights (photosensitivity). After exposure to light, the skin may become itchy and red. Affected individuals may also experience a burning sensation on their skin. The hands, arms, and face are the most commonly affected areas. Some people with erythropoietic protoporphyria may also have complications related to liver and gallbladder function. Erythropoietic protoporphyria is inherited as an autosomal dominant genetic trait with poor penetrance.

Erythropoietic protoporphyria is one of a group of disorders known as the porphyrias. The porphyrias are all characterized by abnormally high levels of particular chemicals (porphyrins) in the body due to deficiencies of certain enzymes essential to the synthesis of hemoglobin.

The symptoms include:

- *Blisters*
- *Itching*
- *Swelling of the skin*
- *Pain*
- *Hair loss*
- *Darkening and thickening of the skin*
- *Agitation, confusion, and aggression*

Frank continued to tell them that things across the country were on very shaky ground. The loyalties of military forces across the country had been changing hands, and there was no unified command structure between military departments or the government. For now, acting President John Hager had a shaky control over the U.S. Navy in the Atlantic fleet. He had also been in contact with the British, who were trying to bring stability and control to the northeast, and Canada. He has also been able to coordinate some of the military ground forces. His loyal forces include Homeland Security, the US Marine Corps East Coast, the US Air Force and some regular Army units.

At hearing this bit of news, the Looking Glass survivors looked at each other, worried.

"That British general who was in control of the northeastern part of the United States, Maj. Gen. Henry Van Horn seemed to have his shit together more than most of the rest. He had even been able to get some power back on in certain areas. Last I heard, he was getting control of Rochester, New York. He had already gotten good control from Maine to Boston and into upstate New York. From New York City south through New Jersey, Philadelphia, and Washington DC, all the way to Norfolk, Virginia is a total mess. The Chinese, backed up by a few US Marines and naval forces, have taken control of some of the seaports. But the cities themselves are in total chaos."

"Most of all the local police forces have abandoned their duties and are not effective in enforcing local laws. Most of the National Guard units across the country have formed their own organizations and now control and defend their own local cities, towns and territory. Texas, Oklahoma, New Mexico, and now Arizona have their own coalition separate from the United States, and they're involved in some intense fighting with Mexico. The Chinese have taken over and now control California and most of the country west of the Rockies."

"The Pacific Fleet of the U.S. Navy in the Pacific are holed up in Hawaii and Southeast Asia, awaiting orders on how to proceed. The Russians have taken control of Alaska and most of Canada. Russia and China have formed an alliance to take over and divide North America. In our weakened state, President Hagar, under the advice from some military leaders, does not want to attack Russia or China. This is where the disagreements stem from. From the information I have acquired, I see the takeover being plotted and initiated by the Russians and Chinese. The Russians and Cubans have taken control of the Virgin Islands, Bahamas, Puerto Rico, and Florida. Our Air Force and military have annihilated North Korea and most of the Arabian Peninsula with tactical nuclear weapons. Only Israel, Jordan, and parts of other small countries in the northern area of the Arabian Peninsula still exist and support human life. But due to the radioactive fallout in this area, how much longer humans can exist has yet to be seen. There are scattered Russian and Chinese units in control of small cities throughout what is left of the United States."

"U.S. Navy submarines in the Indian Ocean and South Pacific have detonated high altitude nuclear EMP bursts over Russia and China. The only thing preventing an all-out attack from Russia and China on the United States has been President Hagar's communication with their leaders, insisting that this was not a sanctioned attack by the government of the United States. That's the official word. I think the real story is that the EMPs devastated their countries as badly or worse than ours, preventing them from launching a full-scale modern warfare attack here on the United States. This is evident by the lack of invasion forces here."

"The EMPs destroyed most of the world satellites and satellite communication equipment. There are still a few satellites functioning but communications and GPS coordinates are spotty and unreliable. They only function when the working satellites are in the correct position in their orbit to transmit the data. Only older aircraft that did not depend on satellite positioning would be able to fly long distances and arrive at their correct destination."

Lt. Col. Mullen asked, "With your short wave radio, is there any possible way we can contact Texas Gov. Carry or General Van Horn in Rochester?"

Frank nodded. "With the right weather and sun conditions it's possible for me to transmit long distances. The most likely times would be early morning or mid-afternoon, if we're able to contact Texas or General Van Horn at all. The other problem, if they even hear us, is getting them to talk to us."

Lt. Col. Mullen said, "So when would be the best time?"

Frank thought for a second. "Tomorrow afternoon would probably be best. What is it you're thinking of saying to them?"

Lt. Col. Mullen said, "In case the mayor didn't tell you, I am a Lieutenant Colonel in the United States Air Force. Rebecca is actually Technical Sgt. Rebecca Williams, United States Air Force. Tom Adams, as you already know, is or was an NBC news reporter, and Mr. Forster over there is a special agent for the FBI."

At this news, Frank jumped up away from the table, grabbing his AK-47 and pointing it at the group. Angrily he said, "Mayor, what the hell are you doing bringing these government people in the my compound. I should kill you all right now and feed you to the damn zombie dogs!"

The Looking Glass group all laid hands on their sidearms, but did not draw.

Doc Benson stood up, raising his hands. "Now Frank, just calm down. Calm down and get a grip on yourself. No one here is going to harm you or rat you out about anything. We are all on the same side; put the gun down and relax."

Frank began pacing around the room nervously and talking to himself.

Mayor Liz leaned over to Lt. Col. Mullen and suggested, "I think maybe we should leave quietly now."

Dr. Benson was still talking to Frank. "You just calm down and relax. We'll leave now and come back tomorrow after you've had some time to think things over. Smoke a bowl and calm down. We're leaving now."

Frank agreed. "Yeah, that's what I need. I need to smoke a bowl of my good stuff. My good stuff, Thai stick Hawaiian, that'll do the trick."

The group quietly but hastily made a retreat out of the compound and down the road to Mayor Liz's truck. Frank, being paranoid, stealthily followed the group to the truck, just within earshot so he could overhear their conversation.

Mayor Liz was annoyed. "Why did you introduce yourselves that way? I told you how paranoid Frank was. He could've killed us all."

Dr. Benson agreed. "Yes, Lt. Col., that was pretty risky. Frank believes all that government conspiracy crap you read about in the tabloids. He thinks the government is out to get him because he knows too much."

Lt. Col. Mullen said, "If we are going to use his radio to contact government officials like Gov. Carry or General Van Horn, I would have to tell them who I am. Telling Frank now and getting it out, I saw, was a better option than having him shoot us while on the radio with General Van Horn."

Mayor Liz sighed. "Yeah, looking at it with that logic, I guess you are probably right."

Dr. Benson was nodding now. "Yes, if you sprang that news while you were on the radio, I don't think Frank would've been able to restrain himself, and he would've shot us all right there on the spot."

Lt. Col. Mullen said, "I have a bit more news now that we're all airing our laundry. We weren't really flying a routine transport mission when our plane crashed."

The others all looked at each other nervously. He continued, "We were on board one of the nation's most secret aircraft out of Omaha, Nebraska called the Looking Glass. The command onboard the Looking Glass plane is second only to the president and vice president of the United States. The general in command of the Looking Glass, and all the crew except for us, were killed in the crash. The information that Frank told us, if he really has the truth, is extremely important. We need to get this information to the right people in our government and military."

Mayor Liz asked, "You're not planning on giving that acting President Hager that information are you?"

Lt. Col. Mullen shrugged. "I'm sure whatever we say over Frank's radio will be received by everyone within transmitter range, including acting President Hager. I have coded messages that I can transmit which will authenticate who I am. I also have encrypted codes that can only be understood by military personnel with the right code key. If we contact general Van Horn or Gov. Carry, I plan on playing it by ear to get a real understanding of their position in this whole mess. Don't worry, I've been trained in how to interpret the disposition of friendly forces under duress."

Mayor Liz said, "Well, this has been a very interesting day. I believe it's time to go to Pete's store and have a nice relaxing cup of coffee."

At Pete's Store.

The group arrived back at the store and brought Pete up to date on the information and events that took place at crazy Frank's stockade. Mayor Liz and Doc Benson said that it was best that they all stay at Pete's place tonight. After dinner, everyone retired to their rooms. Mayor Liz and Doc Benson stayed in Pete's spare room above the store.

In the middle of the night, the group was awakened by loud noises. Outside there was howling, barking, screams and loud snorts, squeals, neighs, and roars. Everyone got up and rushed to look out the windows into the front parking lot. It was a clear, moonlit night, so they are able to see fairly well.

In the parking lot they saw a horse and rider being attacked by a dozen or more zombie dogs. The rider was trying to fight off the zombie dogs with a bullwhip and doing a pretty good job at it. The horse was rearing, bucking, and kicking at the zombie dogs. As one of the zombie dogs got close, the horse put his head down, grabbed a zombie dog by the back, and threw it into the air. The zombie dog hit the side of the motel. It yipped once and fell to the ground, still and silent. Upon seeing this horrifying event taking place in the parking lot, everyone ran to put on their clothing. They grabbed their weapons and ran out into the parking lot to assist the rider and her horse.

Suddenly, a zombie dog, much larger than the others, jumped the horse from the left side, knocking the rider and the horse to the ground. All the other zombie dogs swarmed in on the horse and rider like a school of piranha, tearing the flesh from them both.

Lt. Col. Mullen and agent Forster came out of the store, firing with their rifles as they moved to defend the woman and her horse. Todd and Rebecca came rushing out of their room, falling in with Lt. Col. Mullen and agent Forster. Mayor Liz and Pete ran outside with their shotguns, firing on the zombie dogs. After killing several of the dogs, including the larger one, they managed to drive the rest of the pack away. Doc Benson rushed over to the woman and the horse. The rest of the group took up defensive positions around Doc Benson as he examined them.

Dr. Benson said, "This is Mary Michaels. We're too late. There's nothing I can do for her or the horse."

Mary's throat had been torn open and flesh ripped from her body in several places. The horse was moving its legs and trying to lift its head. Flesh had been ripped from the horse's legs, exposing some bone. The horse's stomach was also ripped open, spilling its intestines into the parking lot.

Rebecca, seeing the horse suffering and in so much pain, and knowing that there was no hope in saving it, put the barrel of her M-16 near its head and fired, ending the poor animal's suffering.

Everyone was upset that they hadn't been able to save them. They paced around the parking lot, hugging and comforting each other. Eventually everyone calmed down and they were able to make rational decisions on what to do next.

Rebecca asked, "What do we do now? We just cannot leave them here in the parking lot for the zombie dogs to come back and feed on."

Doc Benson suggested, "We can wrap up Mary's body and put her in one of the empty motel rooms. But the horse is too big and heavy for us to move easily."

Pete said, "My tractor is small, but I think it's big enough to move the horse. We can drag it down to the other end of the field and bury it there."

Mayor Liz agreed, "Sounds like a good idea. We'll put Mary's body in the empty room for the night and bury her tomorrow."

Agent Forster said, "Well, let's get to it. We'll be up all night burying that horse, but it needs to be done."

It took several hours to bury the horse and the zombie dog bodies and clean up the parking lot. Afterward, everyone retired to their rooms to clean up and get some sleep.

Orders From General Briggs.

The following day, late in the afternoon, everyone was gathered in Pete's store, discussing about the remaining supplies. They had used up the remaining rainwater for cleaning up the parking lot and were planning on making a trip to acquire some more water.

They heard a vehicle drive into the parking lot and looked out the window. It was a VW bus. Frank Paretsky got out of the bus and started walking toward the store.

Dr. Benson muttered, "I'll be damned! It's crazy Frank."

Todd said, "He's not carrying a rifle, so I guess he's not here to kill us."

Frank walked into the store. Excitedly he said, "Good afternoon everyone. I've got some good news for ya. You guys know a General Briggs from Omaha?"

The survivor group looked at each other and Lt. Col. Mullen said, "Yes, we know General Briggs. How is it that you know him?"

Frank said, "Yesterday, after I smoked up a couple Thai sticks, I started going through the frequencies on my short wave. I picked up a military conversation between General Briggs and a Col. Whitmore from Georgia. Being a bit buzzed, I decided to break into the conversation. They started giving me a bunch of shit about being on a military channel until I mentioned that I had information about the Looking Glass plane. Then they got all kinds of interested and wanted to talk to me. That General Briggs says he knows you, Lt. Col. Mullen. I'm not exactly sure what it means, but he wants me to give you a message. The message is 'code word rabbit.' General Briggs said you'd know what to do with it."

They looked at each other in surprise. Lt. Col. Mullen said, "Agent Forster, I guess it's time to retrieve the box."

Agent Forster got up from the table and went to the motel room, returning a few minutes later with a large, secure briefcase. He handed it over to Lt. Col. Mullen, who began working the combination on the left side of the briefcase. Agent Forster worked the combination on the right side of the briefcase and the latches popped open. The briefcase was full of folders, tapes and plastic cards. Lt. Col. Mullen looked at the plastic cards and picked one out that had the word "rabbit" in large letters written on it. Lt. Col. Mullen took the card, broke it in half, and removed the paper card from inside. Opening the card he read, "Authentication code HOLE: Hotel, Oscar, Lima, Echo."

Sgt. Williams asked, "What does the word HOLE mean?"

Lt. Col. Mullen answered, "Here's the codebook; look it up."

Sgt. Williams went through the codebook looking for the word HOLE. She found the code word and read the following: "Presidential executive order rabbit hole. Order description: by order of the United States government order 2020: executive branch status – MIA; congressional branch compromised, STRATCOM control code word rabbit, authentication code HOLE, Hotel, Oscar, Lima, Echo, order rabbit hole."

Mayor Liz was still confused. "What does that mean?"

Lt. Col. Mullen said, "That means the president and vice president are dead or missing. What's left of our Congress has been compromised and the military are ordered not to take any orders from Congress. STRATCOM is in control of the military. In this case, that means General Briggs."

Frank said, "Wow! This is some heavy shit. I guess you'll be the one to talk to that General Briggs."

Lt. Col. Mullen nodded. "Yes, I need to speak to him as soon as possible."

Frank rose from the table. "Well just don't stand there, load up and follow me up to my place. I should be able to hook you two up later this evening. Let's go! Don't just stand there with your mouth hanging open."

Mayor Liz said, "Lt. Col. Mullen, you and your group can ride with Frank in his Volkswagen bus. Pete, Doc Benson, and I will take care of Mary Michael's body and will meet you later at Frank's place."

The group gathered their gear and everyone took off to complete their tasks.

Out in the bus, Frank said, "Buckle up, everyone."

Looking around, Lt. Col. Mullen said, "I don't see any seatbelts."

Laughing, Frank said, "Oh yeah, I forgot. No seatbelts in this van. Onward soldiers!" Still laughing, he recklessly careened out of the parking lot and sped up the winding mountain road to his stockade.

Hanging on for dear life, agent Forster said, "You are one crazy bastard, Frank!"

Frank said, "Yeah, that's what they told me at the psychiatric center. But I really wasn't crazy. I was just there for the good drugs. This Volkswagen bus has a lot of get up and go. I suped-up the motor and I'm running my own gasoline. I was trying to make moonshine, but it turned out to be too strong. So now I just use it for gasoline. I have to dilute it with kerosene to keep it from burning holes in the pistons. Maybe when things get back to normal I can get a patent for this stuff and become a millionaire."

They all stared at Frank in amazement.

They arrived at the stockade, safe and sound, with only a few bumps and bruises. Once inside, Frank got out the dandelion wine and handed everyone a glass.

"We have a few hours before we can contact General Briggs," Frank said, "so I'll give you the grand tour and tell you all about my little fortress here. The stockade fence is made from 10-inch pine logs, soaked in a preservative to keep them from rotting and spray-painted with a water seal. I wanted to do the whole thing in oak but that was too expensive. Only the door frames and gate are made of oak, now. The main structure, as you can see, is made from shipping containers. Six below ground level, six at ground level and four for the second story, all welded and electrically bonded together. This protected all of my electronics inside from the EMP. This place can even take a direct lightning strike. I added the 10° pitch roof and solar panels. The EMP did some damage to my solar panels, but I had spares. Back here I have three green houses. The first one is full of my high grade marijuana plants. The other two contain vegetables. I don't have the room for livestock, but I did have a few chickens for a while. But then I dropped a blotter square of acid a year ago and the chickens found it. They all freaked out on a bad trip and died. I cooked them up, expecting to get a good high, but nothing. Just normal, country-fried chicken. Since then I've stayed away from chemical drugs and have gone all organic. Inside, all my grains and food are vacuum packed, and I figure I have enough food to last me about 20 years. Don't tell Mayor Liz, but since my chickens died, I've been robbing her henhouse for eggs and the occasional chicken."

Later on that afternoon, after some more entertaining conversation with crazy Frank, Mayor Liz and Doc Benson arrived. Frank took the group upstairs to his radio room and started tweaking the dials to the frequency needed to contact General Briggs.

Frank said, "I have a Vietnamese encryption crystal in my radio that General Briggs is aware of. We'll be transmitting on encryption channel Venus Golf."

Frank tuned into the encrypted channel and the team awaited General Briggs.

After a few minutes of static, a voice came across the speakers of the short wave radio, *"Rabbit hole to Pigeon, acknowledge, rabbit hole to Pigeon, acknowledge."*

Frank keyed the mic, "Pigeon here, rabbit hole. You are acknowledged."

From the speakers, the voice said, *"This is Army General Briggs from STRATCOM, seeking contact with Looking Glass, acknowledge."*

Frank handed the microphone to Lt. Col. Mullen. Mullen keyed the mic and said, "Lt. Col. Mullen from Looking Glass. We hear you STRATCOM. Good to hear from you, General Briggs, over."

"Good to hear you, Lt. Col. Mullen. I need to confirm your ID and status. Do you have the TACCOM case? Over."

Lt. Col. Mullen keyed up, "Affirmative, we have the TACCOM case, two minutes to confirmation, over."

Lt. Col. Mullen and agent Forster opened the TACCOM case. Mullen removed some documents from it. Then he keyed the mic and read from the documents: "Looking Glass, codename: hummingbird one; status: Condor down, Blue Jay control, code word rabbit, confirmation: Hotel, Oscar, Lima, Echo. Acknowledge, rabbit hole."

General Briggs' voice came back, *"Confirmation acknowledged. Blue Jay control confirmed. Sorry about having to drop all of this on you, Lt. Col. Mullen. But under the circumstances, all precautions are necessary. Also, due to the circumstances, I find it appropriate to give you a field promotion to full Colonel. Congratulations, Col. Mullen. I've been in contact with various military forces across the country, unifying our command structure. I have command as 'chief of staff' over the United States military by Republican Sen. Thomas Kane. He's the only congressional representative that can be confirmed as loyal to the United States of America. Col. Mullen, you are under my orders not to give out any restricted information to any other congressional representatives without confirmation from myself, Sen. Kane, or some other confirmed and trusted source. Sen. Kane is also Lieut. General in charge of the Southwest region of the United States. I'm taking personal charge of the Northwestern United States. Col. Whitmore from Fort Stewart, Georgia is in command of the southeastern United States. Rear Adm. James Taylor is in command of the Pacific fleet and is taking control of Alaska and the western territories of the United States from the Rocky Mountains to the coast. Rear Adm. Ted Pickett, commander of the Atlantic Fleet, is being opposed by self-proclaimed President John Hager. Once rear Adm. Pickett gains full control of the Atlantic Fleet, I'll inform you. In the meantime, be suspicious of any orders coming from the USS Ronald Reagan or the Atlantic Fleet. General Henry Van Horn of Great Britain has command of the Northeast and New England states under my authority. I will contact General Van Horn and inform him of your current location and status. Stay put and await contact from General Van Horn. STRATCOM will continue to monitor this channel and all others for updates and status changes. Blue Jay acknowledged and confirmed."*

Col. Mullen keyed the mic and said, "Acknowledged, Blue Jay confirmed. Thank you for the promotion general. Blue Jay out."

Everyone was excited, talking about the conversation with General Briggs and the promotion of Col. Mullen. Frank poured out some more wine for everyone and offered to cook a stir fry for dinner.

After dinner, Frank said, "Col. Mullen, due to my newfound patriotism, I'm willing to offer you the use of my old Willy's Jeep."

Col. Mullen was grateful. "Thank you, Frank. We sure could use some transportation."

Mayor Liz announced, "Well, it's getting late now. I think we better leave so that we can get back to Pete's store before dark."

Taking the Willy's Jeep and Mayor Liz's truck, they all headed to Pete's store.

Awaiting Word From General Van Horn.

A few weeks passed with no word from General Van Horn or General Briggs. There had been a few minor incidents involving the zombie dogs around the town of Pigeon, though. One morning, as the group was having coffee and breakfast at Pete's store, they heard a vehicle approaching. Going outside, they saw a large, older model, yellow moving van pull into the parking lot of Pete's store. An American soldier got out of the driver side and a British soldier got out of the passenger side of the van. The soldiers approached the group, introducing themselves as Cpl. Walker from Fort Drum, and Sgt. Packard, British special forces under the command of General Van Horn.

In a thick, British accent, Sgt. Packard said, "We are looking for Col. Mullen, United States Air Force."

Col. Mullen stepped forward and introduced himself and the rest of the group.

Sgt. Packard said, "We have bottled water and medical supplies for you and the surviving residents of the town of Pigeon. General Van Horn and his company of American and British soldiers will be arriving in a few hours. I suggest getting word to all of the town's residents. They can assemble here and await General Van Horn's arrival."

Mayor Liz and Doc Benson left to inform all the local residents of General Van Horn's arrival at Pete's store.

A few hours later, with about 100 surviving residents gathered in the parking lot of Pete's store, they heard the approach of vehicles and bagpipe music. Coming down the road toward them, they saw a military jeep with the American flag flying on one side and the British flag flying on the other. Following the Jeep was a large group of military soldiers, marching in formation. The Jeep pulled over on the shoulder of the highway as the marching formation continued past and around the store and into the field behind it. The first group of soldiers were carrying the American flag and the colors from their units in upstate New York. The marching band was playing and the soldiers were singing:

Army -

"Over hill, over dale
as we hit the dusty trail
and the army goes rolling along.

In and out, hear them shout
counter march, and right about
and the army goes rolling along.

Then it's Hi! Hi! Hee! in the field artillery
shout out your numbers loud and strong!
For wher-e'er you go, you will always know
that the army goes rolling along!"

Navy-

"Stand navy, out to sea
fight our battle cry;
we'll never change our course
so vicious foe, steer shy-y-y-y
Roll out the TNT, anchors aweigh!
Sail on to victory
and sing their bones to Davy Jones, hooray!"

Marines-

"From the halls of Montezuma,
to the shores of Tripoli;
we fight our country's battles
in the air, on land and sea.
First we fight for rights and freedom
and to keep our honor clean;
we are proud to claim the title
of the United States Marine!"

Coast Guard-

"From north and south and east and west,
the coast guards in the fight
destroying subs and landing troops
the axis feels our might
for we're the first invaders
on every fighting field
afloat, ashore, on men and SPARS,
you'll find the coast guard shield!"

Air Force-

[big dramatic music intro]

"Off we go, into the wild blue yonder
climbing high into the sun!
Here they come, zooming to meet our thunder
At 'em boys, give 'er the gun!
Down we dive, spouting our flame from under
off with one heck of a roar!
We live in fame or go down in flame
Hey! Nothing will stop the U.S. Air Force!"

Then came the British troops with their band playing, and their troops were singing the following:

MEN OF HARLECH...

Tongues of fire on Idris flaring,
news of foe-men near declaring,
to heroic deeds of daring,
call you, Harlech men!

Groans of wounded peasants dying,
wails of wives and children flying,
for the distant succour crying,
call you, Harlech men.

Shall the voice of wailing,
now be unavailing,
You to rouse, who never yet
in battle's hour were failing?

This our answer, crowds down pouring,
swift as winter torren'ts roaring,
not in vain the voice imploring,
calls on Harlech men.

Loud the martial pipes are sounding,
every manly heart is bounding,
as our trusted chief surrounding,
march we, Harlech men.

Short the sleep the foe is taking;
'ere the morrow's morn is breaking,
they shall have a rude awakening,
roused by Harlech men.

Mothers, cease your weeping,
calm may be your sleeping,
You and yours in safety now,
the Harlech men are keeping.

'Ere the sun is high in heaven,
they you fear, by panic riven,
shall, like frightened sheep, be driven,
far, by Harlech men.

There were about 200 American troops and 200 British troops, all marching around the store and into the field out back. Following all of this were several trucks, jeeps and vans.

A stout, tall man in a British uniform got out of the jeep. He stepped out front and walked over to the front of the crowd. His uniform had a lot of ribbons. Some we recognized, but most Americans don't know all the British honors. He wore a red beret and he introduced himself as "General Van Horn of the British Army, here to assist the United States of America under the command of General Richard Briggs."

Turning to the crowd, he said, "To the good people of Pigeon, Pennsylvania, United States of America. I bring food, water, medical supplies and soon electrical power back to the town of Pigeon." There was a loud cheer from the people. "I'll be leaving a small contingent of soldiers here in Pigeon to assist you with your needs to get your lives back to normal. I have a workforce that is now busily repairing power and communication lines to this area. This is a beautiful town. I'm happy to see all the brave people welcoming my visit here. But unfortunately, there is a lot more work to be done. Tomorrow morning my troops and I will be leaving to continue that work, to make all the small towns and cities safe for everyone. The troops are setting up out back to distribute food and medicine to all who have need."

General Van Horn then met with Mayor Liz, getting a list of survivors and the needs of the town. Then he talked with Col.

Mullen and the survivors of the Looking Glass. General Van Horn told Col. Mullen that he and the survivors of the Looking Glass had been ordered to return to upstate New York with him the next day.

The next morning, Col. Mullen and the survivors of the Looking Glass bid farewell to Mayor Liz, Doc Benson, Pete Lockrow, the store owner, and of course, crazy Frank Paretsky.

Chapter 9

At Sam's Compound.

The Russians in Gainesville, Georgia had been battling the hillbillies in Dahlonega. The hillbillies had been keeping control of Dahlonega so far. The Russians had not been able to take over Dahlonega without weakening their control of Gainesville. But we had just discovered that the Russians were going to be getting some reinforcements. This would turn the tide in favor of the Russians, and the hillbillies were sure to lose control of Dahlonega. So we had decided that we would have to do something to stop the Russians, or at least slow them down.

We got a new news update from Voice of America: "*We have now determined that the canine flu has only been killing people with immune deficiencies and other weakened health issues like diabetes, food allergies, HIV, heart disease, etc. The otherwise healthy people who contract the canine flu have a 90% chance of survival. The canine flu has rapidly spread to every continent on the planet, killing millions and changing the lives of everyone forever.*"

"The worldwide panic has changed to an attitude of survival and new alliances. The Chinese and Russians are now aligned with the American forces to regain control of the United States and bring back stability to our great country. More UN forces, mostly Chinese and Russian, will be arriving in the next few weeks to support Homeland Security and American forces throughout the country.

Stay tuned to Voice of America for more updates as they become available."

Sam was angry. "Our dumbass government is just as stupid and blind to what's really happening as always."

I nodded, "Yes, it sure looks that way. We can't just sit here in the luxury of this compound and let all of this happen around us."

Susan asked, "What can we do about it, with only three of us?"

Bobby agreed. "We've been training hard and are a good, kick-ass group, but there are just too many of those Russian bastards for us to take on."

Sam said, "Well, I am getting a bit antsy just hanging around here doing nothing."

I said, "George and the GGF sure could use our help, and we were planning to go to Savannah anyhow."

Sam said, "With the Russians and Chinese getting reinforcements, the hillbillies here in Dahlonega do not stand a chance. With the Chinese in control of Hunter Airbase in Savannah, they can easily fly in all the reinforcements they need. The Bloods and the GGF will be overtaken quickly."

Susan said, "So you're saying that going to Savannah and joining up with George and the GGF is a hopeless endeavor?"

Bobby said, "It sounds to me like our asses are cooked no matter what we do. If we go to Savannah, we'll end up dead or speaking Chinese for the rest of our lives. If we stay here or try to help the hillbillies, we'll end up dead or speaking Russian for the rest of our lives!"

I agreed, "Nothing like being stuck between a rock and a hard place."

Sam said, "I've got some ideas, and I've been getting real tired of sitting here on my ass doing nothing. I have a three-step plan of what we can do."

I was onboard. "Win, lose or draw, we have to do something. What's the plan?"

Sam laid out his idea. "First, we blow up the bridge between Murrysville and Gainesville. That'll slow the Russians down and they won't be able to easily move troops into Dahlonega to attack the hillbillies there."

"Step two, we meet with the hillbillies in Clermont. I have some military walkie-talkies that I can give to the hillbillies there. They in turn can give some to the hillbillies in Dahlonega so that they can work together to battle the Russians."

"Step three, we go meet up with George and the GGF. Then try to convince him to go to Texas and join up with them. I believe Texas is our best bet."

I thought about that. "Sounds like a good plan to me. Susan, Bobby, what you think?"

Bobby said, "I like to blow things up, and I'm ready to kick some ass: Russian, Chinese, zombie dogs or any other bad guys. Let me at 'em!" He drew out his samurai sword and swished it through the air a couple of times, saying dramatically, "Taste the edge of my steel, you dirty bastards!"

We all laughed at Bobby.

Susan wasn't too sure. "That all sounds dangerous and scary to me. But I do agree that just sitting around here is not gonna work out for very long. Sooner or later, the Russians are going to come knocking on our door and then what are we gonna do? I guess I agree, joining up with the Texas Rangers is our best bet for survival as Americans."

Sam said, "Okay, that makes it unanimous. Let's get down to the details of our plans."

Inside the protection of Sam's compound we could train, plan and relax, day or night, without the worry of being attacked by the zombie dogs. Training and planning is what we did for the next two days. Sam had some C4, construction dynamite, and other explosives that he showed us how to use to blow up the Thompson Creek Bridge going into Gainesville.

Thompson Creek Bridge.

Sam said, "Mark and I will be taking the explosives up Thompson Creek after dark. We will be using the three-man inflatable raft with a trolling motor on it for silence and stealth. Taking a raft up to the bridge and rigging the explosives should not be a big problem. If we stay in the middle of the creek until we get close to the bridge, we should have no problems from the zombie dogs. If the zombie dogs should try to swim out to us, they'll be easy targets that we can take out before they get to us. But if that happens, the noise will alert the Russian guards at the bridge to our presence. Therefore, I'm hoping not to have to fight any zombie dogs on the way up there."

Susan said, "What about the guards at the bridge, won't they be watching the creek as well as the road?"

Bobby said, "That's where we come in, mom. We'll snipe the guards from the woods near the bridge, right?"

I shook my head. "No Bobby, if you went up there at night and tried to snipe the guards on the bridge, you would end up fighting off the zombie dogs *and* alerting the guards."

Sam said, "We do need a distraction to keep the guards busy so that they're not watching the river."

I nodded. "I have an idea. We have a lot of old meat in the freezer that we will never be able to eat before it goes bad. Before dark, we can take this meat up and lay it out in the woods near the Thompson Creek Bridge, as close to the Russian guard shack as we can get. Then, after dark, when the zombie dogs come out, they'll smell the meat and be all around by that guard shack. You know how they like to howl and bark? That should be enough to keep the guards inside the shack, watching the woods and not the river."

"It's a long boat ride from here at Jay's Point to the Thompson Creek Bridge," said Sam. "Susan and Bobby will be coming with us, staying anchored off Viewpoint Peninsula, and we'll take the raft from there to the bridge. They'll keep the bass boat around on the other side of the peninsula, out of sight of the guards at the bridge. Susan and Bobby will be our backup. If we get in trouble, they can rush in with the bass boat."

Bobby was excited. "Do I get to drive the bass boat?"

I said, "Maybe you can drive on the way back, but as a backup, you are the best shot, so Susan will be driving the bass boat for backup operation."

Susan said, "I don't have a lot of experience driving a bass boat."

Sam assured her, "It's easy, and on our way to the bridge, you'll be driving and I'll be giving you instructions and directions."

That afternoon we went up to Route 60, down through Murrysville and parked the truck a couple of miles from the Thompson Creek Bridge. On the way there, we noticed that the Russians had cleared the highway of vehicles and other obstacles. As we got closer to where the highway divided, we also noticed that the Russians had blocked off the northbound side of the highway and were only using the southbound side.

Sam and Bobby took their load of meat to the south side of the highway and were as close to the bridge as they could get without being spotted. Susan and I took our load of meat to the north side of the bridge. On the hill near the power lines, I took out my binoculars and surveyed the bridge and the Russian guard post. The Russians had road barriers and abandoned vehicles blocking the northbound side of the bridge, making it impassable. On the north end of the bridge, they had a guard shack, machine-gun placements surrounded by sand bags, road barriers blocking the road, and a truck blocking the single car opening in the barriers. Two guards were walking around near the guard shack and two more were walking the bridge. The south side of the bridge had the same set up with four more guards. We set our zombie dog bait and left.

When we were safely away, I said, "I'm real happy that we got lucky and didn't run into any Russian patrols on the highway between 400 and the bridge."

Sam said, "I wasn't too worried, because this late in the evening, the Russians are not likely to have any patrols out. With night coming, the zombie dogs will be out."

Susan said, "This looks like it was a populated area. Do you think all the people living around here died from the canine flu?"

Sam shook his head. "Most of the people that were living around this area were taken to FEMA camps by Homeland Security or captured by the Russians."

I said, "The ones that did get away have probably joined up with the hillbillies in Clermont."

Bobby said, "I hope the hillbillies in Clermont are friendlier than the ones in Dahlonega!"

Sam said, "I know quite a few of the mountain families around the Clermont area, and along with that note from Poppa, we should not have any problems in Clermont. For now, we need to stay focused on the Russians and the bridge."

After eating dinner, we loaded the rubber raft and gear onto Sam's bass boat. We brought the 308 Remington just in case we absolutely had to snipe out the guards. But we believed it would be too dark to see anything through the scope. Sam had two pairs of night vision goggles. One he gave to Susan so she could see to drive the boat. The other he used to help her navigate around the coves and islands. We each had AR15s, except for Sam, who took his trusted modified fully automatic AK 47. It was a bit unnerving and slow-going, traveling in the bass boat after dark through all the twists and turns. Luckily, it was a clear night and we could see by the moonlight. The bad part was that a clear moonlit night made it easier for the Russian guards at the bridge to spot us. By the time we reached Viewpoint Peninsula, Susan was comfortable at operating the bass boat.

At Viewpoint, we anchored the bass boat and unloaded the raft. With the bridge in sight, we loaded all the explosives into the raft and cautiously started maneuvering our way toward the bridge.

I whispered to Sam, "We're almost to the bridge, and I don't hear any zombie dogs."

Sam whispered back, "If there are any in this area, they will smell that meat and be around."

"I hope they get here soon and start making lots of noise. I don't want those guards seeing us before we get there."

Sam said, "So far so good; no guards on the bridge looking this way. We'll keep going."

We made it underneath the bridge without the distraction of the zombie dogs and without being spotted. We started attaching the explosives to the bridge supports. As we were attaching the last one, I heard water dripping into the river.

We both froze. I whispered to Sam, "What the hell is that?"

Sam listened and looked around for a minute, then whispered, "Damn, be quiet! One of the Russians is taking a piss off the bridge."

We waited until the Russian finished his duty. Then I said, "We're done, let's move out of here."

As we cautiously moved from out under the bridge, we heard the Russian that was on the bridge yell a warning to his comrades.

Sam said, "Shit, we've been spotted! I'll cover you. Give that trolling motor full throttle and head for the bass boat!"

I gave the little 40-pound thrust trolling motor full throttle, but I was afraid that wasn't going to be enough to get us out of range of the Russian weapons. Sam and the Russian on the bridge exchanged gunfire. I was ducking the hot, spent shell casings coming from Sam's AK-47 and gunfire from the Russian on the bridge.

I was about to call Susan and Bobby to come in for backup when I heard barking, growling, howling and screams from the Russians' direction. When the Russians came out of their guard shack onto the bridge to attack us, the zombie dogs that were in the neighborhood, attracted by the meat that we'd put out earlier, took the opportunity for some fresh Russian meat. One of the two Russians on the bridge was down from the exchange of gunfire with Sam. The other one retreated from the bridge to help his comrades in battling the zombie dogs. Sam and I were not wounded by any of the gunfire, but the raft had taken a few hits. It was quickly deflating.

I called to Susan and Bobby on the walkie-talkie, "Alert three, alert three we're going for a swim. We'd appreciate a rope and a tow."

Bobby replied, "Alert one, we are coming to get you!"

Just then, our raft fully deflated. Into the water we went. Susan, with the night vision goggles, was able to spot us. Bobby threw us a rope and pulled us aboard. Then we headed for the compound as fast and safely as the bass boat would take us.

Sam said, "It sure would be a lot easier and faster if the GPS on my fishfinder still worked, but the damn EMPs took out most of the electronics. I was lucky just to get the motor working again."

I said, "That's okay. We have a good boat pilot here to bring us in safe and sound!"

Susan was proud, "I never could've done it without Sam's help, and I sure hope I don't have to do that again!"

Bobby asked, "What about the bridge?"

I said, "Oh shit! Susan, turn us around, we need to be closer to the bridge in order for the detonator to work!"

Susan turned the boat around and as we approached the bridge, we saw that the guard shack was on fire, and we heard the zombie dogs barking and feasting on the Russian guards. We also saw the guard's and some other Russian vehicles from the Gainesville side of the bridge crossing over to help their comrades who were being attacked by the zombie dogs. I waited until most of them were completely onto the bridge, and I pushed the button on the detonator, igniting the explosives on the bridge supports. There was a large explosion, several big fireballs from underneath the bridge. But it looked like the bridge was still standing.

Bobby said, "Damn, for that big of an explosion, the bridge is still there!"

Sam was confused. "I don't get it. I know that's a big bridge, but that should've been enough explosives to take it down. That's all I had."

I said to Susan, "Well, let's get us out of here." Then we heard a loud rumbling noise and looked back toward the bridge. The explosives had weakened the bridge and the weight of the vehicles on the bridge finished the job. It collapsed, dropping what was left of the Russians and zombie dogs into the water. Susan gave the bass boat full throttle and we sped away, back toward the safety of the compound.

After we were all safely back inside Sam's house, we sat at the kitchen table. Sam said, "Well that was the last of my explosives. Hopefully we will not need any more. Job well done, people. Step one of the mission, complete."

We poured ourselves a drink, cleaned our weapons, and put away our gear before heading off to bed for a good night's sleep.

Meeting in Claremont.

In the morning at the breakfast table, Sam said, "We have to pack up all of our supplies that we're going to take with us to Savannah into both trucks today. We have to get ready and move out of here as soon as possible because the Russians are gonna be looking for a new route north to Dahlonega. That may take them into Claremont. The Claremont hillbillies may not know that the Thompson Bridge has been destroyed and will not be prepared for the influx of Russian troops through their area. So we need to get there and warn them as soon as possible."

We already had most of our supplies and gear separated and ready to load on the trucks, so it did not take us long to load up and ready the vehicles for the trip to Claremont.

I had been teaching both Susan and Bobby how to drive a standard shift, so if needed, either one of them could drive the old Chevy truck or Sam's Ford F150.

After locking up and securing the compound, we headed out in the trucks for Claremont. Susan was driving the Chevy truck. I was armed with the AR15 riding shotgun. Sam was driving the Ford F150, and Bobby was armed with an AR15 riding shotgun with him. We decided to keep the 30-caliber machine gun, which Sam had mounted in the back of his truck, locked up out of sight for now.

We drove up Route 400 to Long Branch Road, following it to Dahlonega Highway going south toward Claremont. We had to maneuver around several disabled vehicles, downed trees, and power poles. Just before Shoal Creek Road there was a large tree blocking the highway and we had to stop.

We got out of the vehicles to look over the situation. We'd have to find a way to move the tree or get around it. The tree was too big to easily move with the vehicles, and there didn't seem to be a passable way around it.

I suggested, "We have two working chainsaws. We can cut it up and move the pieces out of the way."

Susan said, "Did you notice all the farms and farm fields along the way here?"

Misunderstanding, I said, "Yes, there are many small farms in this area."

Susan said, "I didn't see any animals: horses, or cows, or anything."

Sam said, "Yes, now that you mention it, that is a bit unusual. Maybe we should check out one or two of them, because farm animals are a vital food supply. It would be good to know what's happening to them."

Bobby said, "I saw some old antique tractors a few miles back."

I nodded, "Good idea, Bobby. Maybe we can get one of those tractors started up and use it to pull this tree out of the road. At the same time, we could investigate the farm to see what happened to the animals."

Susan said, "Bobby has always been fascinated with old tractors and other farm equipment."

Sam said, "Okay, let's go back to those tractors and see if we can get one going."

We drove back, looking for the old tractors Bobby had seen. We spotted some outside a barn at one of the smaller farms. We drove into the barnyard and got out to look at the tractor. The tractor was a 1929 John Deere D with a two-cylinder engine.

I was familiar with this tractor; my grandfather had one when I was a kid. We used to skid logs out for firewood. This tractor started on gasoline by hand, spinning a large flywheel on the side. Once started, you switched a valve over on the carburetor and then it ran on kerosene. This tractor looked like it had been restored for one of the local antique tractor shows that were common in this area. With some luck, we should be able to get it started. It had three quarters of a tank of kerosene, but no gasoline in the gas tank. That problem was easily solved, seeing we had extra gas with us.

I said, "Before we start messing with this tractor too much, let's look around the farm and see if we can find out if there are any animals."

Sam said, "Good idea, but stay alert. Keep your weapons ready."

I said, "Susan and I will go check out the farmhouse. Sam, you and Bobby go check out the barn and barnyard."

The farmhouse was an older two-story structure with an enclosed porch going around the house. As we approached the house, we noticed the Homeland Security symbols painted on the house. The house seemed to be closed up, but in good condition.

Susan said, "Hold it, I think I see movement in an upstairs window."

We approached the house with more caution. Reaching the side door, I knocked and shouted, "Hello, is anyone home?"

No reply or sound of movement came from inside the house. I looked at Susan and shrugged. I tried the door and it was not locked, so I opened the door and entered the house, moving quickly to the right, scanning the room for any threats. Susan quickly followed me into the house moving to the left, also scanning the room for threats. This room seemed to be a large, old-fashioned kitchen. The house was neat and orderly, but the most unusual feature was that it was clean: no dust or debris anywhere. We went about clearing the downstairs of the house, finding no people or threats. We decided to check out the upstairs.

We were standing at the bottom of the stairs, talking in low voices about how clean the house looked, when suddenly, from the top of the stairs we heard a voice. "Who the hell are you, why are you in my house?"

Looking up at the top of the stairs, we saw a shotgun pointed in our direction. It's not a very good feeling, having a 12 gauge pointed at you at close range and seeing the large opening of the shotgun barrel pointed at you and knowing that a death of 00 buckshot could be coming in your direction at any moment. Susan and I quickly ducked to the side. Susan went to the right of the stairs. I went left. There were walls on both sides of the stairs, so we were out of direct sight from the top of the stairs now.

I yelled back, "Sorry, we did not mean to trespass. We are only passing through and stopped here to investigate the disappearance of all the farm animals. Maybe you know something about that?"

A woman's voice said, "Daisy, I've got these two. Signal the family."

We heard movement upstairs and then the woman's voice again. "Put your weapons on the stairs where I can see them, and then we can talk a bit."

Susan and I gave each other a nod and then we complied with the woman's wishes, laying our rifles on the stairs where she could see them.

I said, "My name is Mark Antonio and over there is Susan Miller. We mean you no harm."

Again the woman's voice, "You look like soldiers, and soldiers are trouble, American or Russian."

I said, "We are not soldiers, we're only wearing camo uniforms for defensive purposes, in case we should run into any of the Russian soldiers."

The woman hesitated. Then, "Stand where I can see you and keep your hands clear of any weapons."

Susan and I moved into her view, holding our hands out to our sides, away from our weapons. We looked up the stairs, seeing a woman with gray streaks in her hair, a husky build, possibly in her 50s, and holding a pump 12 gauge shotgun. She was coming down the stairs toward us. The woman was wearing a long-sleeved plaid shirt with the sleeves rolled up, jeans, and work boots. She was confident and appeared to know how to use that shotgun if she needed to.

She said, "I am Florence Henderson. You can call me Flo. This is my farm. The sickness killed my husband and two sons. I've been holding out here ever since. I'm not going to let you, the Russians, Homeland Security or anyone else take me away from here."

I said, "We have no intentions of trying to take you away from here or take anything from you."

She was doubtful, "I seen you two and the other two looking over my tractor out there. That don't tell me you're not here to take anything."

"We're only looking at the tractor to see if we can use it to move the large tree out of the road, so we can continue on to Claremont."

Her eyes narrowed, "What business do you have in Claremont?"

I said, "We're looking for any organized groups of country folks in this area to warn them that large groups of Russians may be coming through here soon."

Flo said, "The Russian soldiers do come through here occasionally, but most of the time they end up as dog meat, so they do not come here very often. What makes you think a large group would be coming here anytime soon?"

I answered, "Because we destroyed the Thompson Creek Bridge to prevent them from making a large-scale attack on Dahlonega."

Flo didn't believe me. "Poppa and the mountain people control Dahlonega. You do not look like you are part of their group. So why should I believe you?"

I said, "Yes, we are familiar with Poppa, and I used to live on Crown Mountain, and we're all Americans: mountain people or flatlanders, we're still Americans and need to work together to send them Russian bastards back to Russia. That's why I helped Poppa, destroyed the Thompson Creek Bridge, and now I'm looking for the leaders of the country folk here in the Claremont area."

Just then, we heard several vehicles and lots of shouting outside. We heard Sam's voice on our ear radios saying, *"Alert one, alert one, single flare has been fired and we now have lots of company, be aware!"*

I did not answer because I didn't want to make Flo aware of our earpiece communications.

Flow said, "Okay you two, put your hands on your head and let's go outside and meet the rest of the folks."

While all this had been going on, Sam and Bobby had gone the barn to investigate.

On the other side of the barn, they saw a working windmill and a large water trough, full of water. Sam said to Bobby, "That windmill pumping fresh water is a valuable resource. It seems to me that if anyone were around here it would be guarded."

Opening up the barn door and going inside, they saw a milk tanker trailer inside the barn, other farm tools, and empty animal stalls.

Bobby said, "There's nothing much of interest in here nor any sign of animals."

Sam said, "It's interesting that that milk tanker is parked in the barn here. Let's check around the outside."

Hearing a noise coming from the direction of the farmhouse, Bobby asked, "What was that?"

Sam looked up and saw a signal flare. "That means were going to have company! Back into the barn and take cover!" Then Sam tried to contact Mark and Susan.

Bobby was worried. "They didn't answer. I have a bad feeling about this."

Hearing several vehicles coming to the farm, Sam said, "Let's just stay hidden and see what happens. We've got company coming, and a lot of it!"

Peering through the slats in the barn, they spied Flo escorting Mark and Susan outside at gunpoint.

Once outside, I saw several pickup trucks with five or six people in each, all armed. They all got out of their vehicles and looked to Flo.

Flo said, "There's two more in the barn." They surrounded the barn and started calling for Sam and Bobby to lay down their weapons and come out. Seeing that they were outnumbered and their position compromised, they had no choice but to comply. The farmers disarmed them, bringing them over to where Flo had Susan and me.

The four of us were standing abreast of each other, facing in the direction of the farmhouse and Flo. From around the house came a young woman, 18 to 20 years of age, with long blonde hair. She was barefoot, wearing really high cutoff jean shorts and a low-cut light blouse that was tied off just under her chest. She was carrying a double barrel 20 gauge shotgun. Bobby looked at her wide-eyed, mouth hanging open.

I elbowed Bobby. "Put your tongue back in your mouth and pay attention to what's going on." Bobby blushed and looked at us, then back to Flo.

Flo said, "This is my daughter Daisy, and we run this farm. We supply drinking water to the families around here and any who need it. The rest of this group we call our family. They are the other farming families and neighbors who have survived the sickness and avoided being taken away by Homeland Security or the Russians."

Sam spoke up, "Happy to meet you all of you. I am Sam Jay from Dawson County and this here young man is Robert Miller, but we just call him Bobby. I guess you've met my other two associates: Susan Miller, Bobby's mother, and Mark Antonio from Crown Mountain, Dahlonega."

Flo said, "Are you the leader of this group of thieves?"

Sam was quick to deny that. "We're not thieves nor do we officially have a leader or spokesperson. We're just survivors of the recent catastrophe, passing through and doing whatever we can to help the friendly people whom we might meet on the way."

Flo still wasn't sure. "On the way to where and why?"

I spoke up then, saying, "We are on our way to Savannah to meet up with a group of friends who have started a refugee community there."

Flo said, "So I take it you're coming through here to avoid the Russians in Gainesville?"

Sam said, "That's correct."

Then Flo decided that we were telling the truth. She started talking to her people, telling them about us destroying the Thompson Creek Bridge and wanting to meet the family leaders in the Claremont area to warn them about the Russians. She went on to say that she believed us to be good people and trustworthy. After some more discussions, they returned our weapons to us and decided to escort us to Claremont, where there would be a farmers meeting to discuss the problems of the Russians, zombie dog and other survival issues.

Claremont town hall

The farmers sent out messengers to the other groups and families in the surrounding area to tell them about the town hall meeting in Claremont. Flo and some of the others escorted us into Claremont. On the way there, we noticed that the large tree had been pulled out of the road and a log skidder was parked alongside the road, with an armed farmer sitting on it, watching us pass.

Entering Claremont on Main St., Route 284, we passed a school or rec-center with a tennis court and basketball court on the right. Just past Dean Street on the left there was a large open field. We were guided into this field. Vehicles were beginning to pull into the parking area.

As people started to arrive there, they began setting up tables and chairs, assembling a fire pit and building a wooden platform. Flo told us that they usually had town meetings in Cleveland. This being a larger meeting with information from outsiders, they decided that this field would be better to accommodate everyone.

Everyone was setting up what appeared to be a feast. We talk with Flo and some of the others, exchanging what information we knew. Flo told us that Homeland Security tried to evacuate everyone from all the small towns in this area. The farmers, being protective of their livestock, land and family farms, banded together and drove Homeland Security away. Then the sickness, came killing off large numbers of the families and neighbors. As they were still grieving over their lost loved ones, they were under nightly attacks by wild dogs, killing their livestock and anyone who were caught outside. After the initial shock of dealing with these mutant dogs, they had banded together to pool their resources and livestock. What animal they had left were placed at farms under 24-hour guard where they could be protected and out of sight from the main roads. Barely recovering from the shock of the wild dogs then came the next challenge: Russians trying to steal their livestock and other food supplies.

Then Flo took us around, introducing us to some of the people. As the gathering got underway and we made friends, we were offered food and drinks. There was plenty of meat, vegetables, and even homemade bread. As we sat down for the meal, the local preacher said grace, blessing the food before anyone started eating. Everyone had stories to tell about their struggles with the wild dogs, the loss of loved ones, and battles with the Russians. After the meal, Mason jars of moonshine, pipes packed with tobacco, and joints of marijuana were passed around to any who wanted to indulge.

Flo and another woman, an older woman whom we were introduced to as Mama Grover, took up a megaphone and introduced us to the crowd. Then she handed the megaphone to Sam and asked him to bring everyone up to date on any outside news that we had.

Sam handed me the megaphone. "It's all yours, I have stage fright in front of this many people." I stood there, holding the megaphone and looking out at the crowd. I saw a crowd of 400, maybe 500 people, all looking at me and waiting to hear what I had the say. I was a bit weak in the knees myself.

I took up the megaphone and started speaking. "As you all know, the Russians are in control of Gainesville. What's left of our government is operating off the East Coast aboard the USS Ronald Reagan. Those dumbasses are still blind to the fact that the Russians are not here to help us. We know that the Russians are here to conquer us and control the country. Our government and other governments around the world have now gotten back some control and figured out the disease that they are now calling the 'canine flu' has run its course, and we the survivors have some resistance to it now."

"So other governments like the Russians and the Chinese are flocking here under the disguise of coming to help us. They are backed by the United Nations. In reality, they are coming here to conquer us. The small groups of families and neighbors from the little towns around here, like yourselves, are too few in number to stop them. And now they are flying in equipment and reinforcements."

The crowd started to mumble and ask what they were supposed to do, just surrender?

I said, "No, we can never surrender! We have to band together, work together, stick together and fight together, even if that means dying together as Americans for America!" This got a cheer from the crowd.

Once they quieted down, I took the note from Poppa out of my pocket. "Here I have a note from the leader of the mountain people in Dahlonega, Poppa. If a messenger from your group were to take this note to Poppa and inform him about the Russians getting reinforcements and the Thompson Creek Bridge being destroyed, you may be able to make an alliance with the mountain people, and together you should be able to hold the Russians in Gainesville."

Someone in the crowd yelled, "Maybe, but for how long?"

"I believe long enough for loyal Americans forces to push the Russians back to Russia."

After some cheers and hoots I continued. "My friends and I are traveling on to Fort Stewart in Savannah to meet up with a refugee community there. The plan is to arm and train the refugees and meet up with the Texas Rangers and take back this great country of the United States of America. The Texas government knows that the Russians and the Chinese are not here to help us and have put together their own forces of resistance, along with some help from Oklahoma and New Mexico. The more Americans we can band together and inform about the truth, the greater our chances are of putting America back together again."

With more cheers and hoots, I put the megaphone down and left the stage. Sam came over. "Hell of a speech there."

We noticed Flo, Mama Grover, and some others were having an intense conversation. Sam said, "Well, I don't know if it's going to work, but you sure stirred up a hornet's nest. We'll just have to wait and see how it all turns out I guess."

Susan said, "The bits and pieces of conversation that I've overheard sounds like the farmers and the hillbillies just might get an alliance going. By the way, did you see where Bobby went?"

Sam said, "I saw him down by the vehicles with that Daisy girl."

Susan and I looked at each other. I said, "We better go get him."

Sam said, "Don't come looking for me right away. Flo offered me some of that good moonshine. See you in the morning."

Susan agreed, "Yes, it is getting late. We're going to need a place to stay, away from the zombie dogs."

I said, "You go round up Bobby, and I'll ask around about a place for us to stay tonight. Meet you over by the trucks in about an hour."

Some of the local guys greeted me, and as we talked, they gave me the address of an empty house in town where we could crash for the night. I then went to the truck to wait for Susan and Bobby.

I heard some yelling. "Ow, mom, ow! I'm coming, I'm coming." I looked and saw Susan had Bobby by the ear, dragging him along toward the truck. I grinned. The gathering was breaking up and everyone was heading out to find sleeping quarters for the night. It was too late for most of them to make it back to their homes, so everyone would be crashing in the empty homes in town and then meeting back by the town hall for breakfast in the morning.

We went to the address of the house where we would be spending the night. Susan and I found a bedroom and settled in for the night. Bobby picked out his room, also.

Susan frowned. "I didn't see any children under the age of about 14, did you?"

I said, "No I didn't, but I did see a couple of women that were pregnant."

Susan said, "I wonder if the canine flu killed off all the young children?"

"It looks like the canine flu killed the young, the old, the weak, and the sick, leaving only the healthy people to survive. I guess in man's attempt to destroy himself, he gave nature a way to strengthen an otherwise contaminated gene pool."

Susan said, "Well, in nature only the strong survive, so you may be right."

Chapter 10

Morning breakfast in Claremont.

At daybreak, someone knocking on the door awakened us. I got up and answered the door. One of the farmers was at the door, saying, "Rise and shine! Meet in the field to help with breakfast. Women prepare the food, and the men and boys gather firewood and do the cooking. See you there in 10 or 15 minutes." Then the man walked off to the next house.

Susan and I finished getting dressed. Then we woke up Bobby and got him moving. We took our weapons and gear and went to the field to get our assigned tasks for preparing breakfast. Then we sat down to pancakes, fresh eggs, sausage and bacon. We even had butter for our pancakes! Coffee and milk were also available. We sat with Sam, Flo and Daisy as the preacher said the blessing.

Flo informed us that the farmers were sending a messenger to Dahlonega today. The messenger was taking the note from Poppa and one of two Vietnam era long-range military walkie-talkies. The other one was being left here with the farmers so that Poppa and the hillbillies could communicate and organize with the farmers to battle the Russians.

Sam said, "Flo, Daisy, and some of the others want to come with us to Savannah."

I asked Flo about her farm and the water deliveries. She told me that they used the old 1929 John Deere tractor to tow the tanker full of water to the families and farms that didn't have any fresh water. But the supplies of gasoline they had were going bad. Kerosene and diesel were still holding up, but they weren't sure how long that was going to last either. Another family had agreed to take over her farm and the water deliveries. Flo continued telling us that representatives from the farmers should go with us to meet up with the GGF and then on to Texas to let them all know that other bands of Americans were working together to drive the foreign forces out of our country. Flo said she and two other families would be coming with us. The farmers would stock us with food supplies but couldn't afford to give us any gasoline, medicine, or ammunition.

I said, "This all sounds good, and I think we'll have enough supplies to make it to Savannah. If we leave early, we may be able to make it there before dark tonight."

Flo shook her head. "I think it'll take us a bit longer than that. The roads between here and Athens are not in very good condition. Also, Athens and Augusta, along with some of the other small towns in between, have been overrun with bands of gypsies who have been attacking and killing anyone they come across, taking anything of value and adding it to their collective."

Sam said, "We're not going near Augusta, but we do have to pass by Athens. We'll take back roads and give Athens a wide berth. We need to head down Route 80 to Milledgeville and Dublin. After that, we have Swainsboro and Statesboro. Those are the only towns of any size that we have to go through before Claxton and Glenville, which is where we'll be meeting up with George."

Flo said, "We haven't gotten any news or information beyond Athens."

I said, "With the added people traveling in our group, we'll be a stronger force, and if we are careful, we should be able to make it to Dublin or Swainsboro without many problems from the gypsies in Athens."

After breakfast, the meeting broke up and all the farmers headed back to their respective farms, homes, and chores. Sam went with Flo and Daisy to their farm to pack up their added supplies and gear onto Sam's truck. Susan, Bobby, and I waited at the field for the other two families. We all wanted to head out together.

Susan said, "It's good to have more people traveling with us; there's strength in numbers. But I'm not too happy about having Daisy along. Daisy and Bobby are a bit too friendly, and Bobby is only sixteen."

I said, "There's only two years between them. Daisy is 18. Flo and Daisy seem to be good people. As to Daisy and Bobby's friendship, it's inevitable that relationships between teenagers will take place, just as it always has throughout history in times of disaster and crisis. We'll talk to Bobby, and I'll have Sam talk to Flo about this issue."

The other two families arrived and introduced themselves. The first family was driving a red Ford pickup truck. Their names were John and Lily Haynes. They had two sons, John Junior and Steve. John Junior was 22 years old and Steve was 20. It was easy to see that the two boys were John's sons. All three were tall and slender. John's hair was receding, and you could see evidence that the two boys would also be going bald in the near future. They were armed with bolt-action deer rifles and 12 gauge pump shotguns, each also carrying a large caliber revolver holstered on their hip.

The second family was Ralph and Betsy Beaver. They had no children and were driving a Dodge Dakota. Ralph looked to be in his 40s. A rather short man, he had gray hair and lots of it. He wore farmer jeans that had seen a lot of working days. Betsy was even shorter than Ralph and still slender. It was easy to see how beautiful she had been when she was young. Ralph had a Thompson WWII replica .45 auto and Betsy a 30-30 Winchester rifle. Ralph had a 1911 45-auto pistol holstered at his hip and Betsy had a Colt .45 revolver holstered on her hip.

Sam arrived with Flo and Daisy and we all prepared to leave. Flo was driving Sam's truck with Daisy riding shotgun. Sam was in the bed of the truck with a 30-caliber machine gun mounted and ready. I followed Sam in the Chevy truck with Susan riding shotgun and Bobby in the bed overlooking the cab with his AR15. Ralph's Dodge was behind us with Betsy riding shotgun. John and Lily took up the rear with their two boys armed in the bed of their truck.

We left Claremont heading south. The road had some abandoned cars and downed trees on it, but with some maneuvering it was passable. As we came into the village of Maysville there was a dead horse in the road. We were maneuvering around when it when Bobby started banging on the roof of the truck. The others behind started blowing their horns and Sam came on the radio saying, "We've got company in the air! Split up the vehicles and take cover!"

We split up our convoy and parked our vehicles so as to blend in with the other abandoned vehicles. We all got out and took cover among the trees and buildings. We heard large airplane engines and looked up. There was a large transport plane coming in low on a course for Gainesville. As the plane passed our position, we saw the markings on the wing and side of the cargo plane: a red flag with hammer and sickle.

Bobby exclaimed. "That's a Russian plane!"

I said, "Yes, it looks like the Russians in Gainesville are getting their reinforcements."

Sam gave the all clear and we all met back on road to talk a bit about the new development. I said to Sam, "Looks like the Russians got their reinforcements."

Sam said, "Not reinforcements of personnel. I saw parachuted boxes dropping from the plane into the Gainesville area, so I believe this was only a supply drop, but that does mean the reinforcements will be coming soon."

Flo said, "I hope the farmers in Claremont saw that plane and are getting ready for a possible attack soon."

Ralph assured her, "The farmers up there have lookouts keeping an eye on the Russians in Gainesville all the time, so I'm sure they know."

"There's no way for us to contact them," said Sam. "We need to get moving."

We climbed back into our vehicles and continued south toward Athens on Route 52. We came to the town of Jackson. It was completely destroyed. Most of the homes, buildings, and businesses were burned to the ground. The shells of burned and abandoned vehicles cluttered the streets, and we had to make several detours to get through the village.

Susan looked around with sadness. "What happened to this town? The people, there's nothing left."

I replied, "I'm not sure if it's a result of the attacks from the terrorists, or if maybe panicked people and looters set the town ablaze. In any case, it does not look like there's anything left."

We left Jackson, and as we approached Interstate 85, Susan suggested, "The ramp to 85 look clear. Wouldn't it be faster to take the interstate?"

I said, "No, because the ramps may be clear here, but I'm sure the interstate roadways are congested wlth abandoned vehicles, and it may be impassable in some areas. We might have to backtrack for miles in order to exit the interstate. It's better to stick to the secondary roads where we have lots of options for alternative routes if our path is blocked."

As we came into the city of Commerce, we saw that it had been burned and looted, the same as Jackson. After moving a few obstacles, we continued out of there and down south on Commerce Road toward Athens.

Sam stopped the convoy at Sandy Creek Park to discuss our route around Athens. We were just a few miles out.

Pointing, Bobby said, "I think I heard gunfire, and I see smoke over there."

I nodded, "Yes, I believe I hear gunfire also."

Sam was looking where Bobby was pointing. "The smoke and gunfire seems to be coming from the Athens bypass highway."

One of The Haynes boys suggested, "Maybe it's the Russians and the gypsies having a battle."

Sam said, "We can take some of the back roads and go around Athens, but with the amount of abandoned vehicles and debris in the road it's going to take us a long time. However, we would be out of sight of this battle, and we'd completely avoid Athens."

I said, "However, on the secondary roads, our visibility to see what's ahead will be drastically reduced, leaving us open to a surprise ambush. Also, if the gypsies are battling the Russians, it could be that the reinforcements are headed to Gainesville. If it *is* their reinforcement unit, we may be able to slow them down. It would also be good, tactical information if we knew the extent of the expansion of Russian control in this area. I propose that we get closer and investigate the situation."

Sam looked again toward the smoke. "Whoever they are, they seem to be involved in an intense battle. We may be able to get close enough to see who's fighting who without being spotted."

Susan cautioned, "We are a small group, and it might be best to avoid any fights or battles if possible. But if you all believe we can get close enough to see what's going on without actually having to get involved, it's okay by me."

Bobby said, "Any Russians or bad guys we get a chance to take out, we should."

Flo said, "If it *is* the Russian reinforcements heading for Gainesville, I would like to know."

John and Ralph agreed that we should investigate the battle and take advantage of any opportunities that should present themselves to take out any of the Russians that we could.

We approached the bypass on high alert. We continued down Jefferson Road to the country club where the highway splits. Stopping there, we could see some of the fighting going on at the bypass. Through our binoculars, we saw that neither of the groups involved in the fighting were Russians. One group on the bypass was attacking another group on the street level. The group on the highway looked like a motorcycle gang or some type of gangbangers. They reminded me of the Mad Max movie. The group at street level was more organized and holding their own. They were also oddly dressed, wearing brimmed hats that looked like they were from the 40s (homburgs, fedoras, and porkpies), with small colored feathers in the bands. Their clothing didn't seem to match. I assumed this group to be the gypsies that the farmers had told us about. Our best guess was that there were about two dozen fighters involved in each group.

The Mad Max group split up, driving their vehicles and motorcycles toward the exits to get to street level, to flank the gypsies. The gypsies on the south side of the bypass recognized the tactic and retreated into the city of Athens with most of the Mad Max group in pursuit. Two motorcycles and two pickup trucks from the Mad Max group exited the bypass on the north side (closest to where we were). There were small numbers of gypsy fighters on our side of the bypass, trying to retreat into an industrial complex. The Mad Max group on motorcycles were overtaking the retreating gypsies, and shot down two of them. The Mad Max group in their trucks arrived, shooting down two or three more of the gypsies and capturing two. The third vehicle operated by the Mad Max group was a tow truck, and it drove into the parking lot of the industrial complex.

Sam commented, "Things are not going very well for the gypsies."

I said, "That Mad Max group of highway warriors seems to be a more dangerous group than the gypsies."

Sam laughed at my Mad Max analogy. "Both groups seem to be well organized, and they have a few automatic weapons. What do you suggest we do?"

"Well, I say we try to rescue the two gypsies who were captured by the highway bandits. Sam… you, Flo and Daisy work your way around to the south side of the building near the parking lot and hold your position there. Me, Susan and Bobby will attack from the north side, working our way through the parking lot, using the abandoned vehicles for cover. Ralph and Betsy, take up position at the entrance to the parking lot, using abandoned vehicles for cover. Stephen and John Junior will take up sniping positions. John and Lily will be your spotters. Keep the gang members away from the prisoners. Ralph and Betsy, you open up on them first. Once you've got their attention, Susan and I will open up on them from our position and move in on them as quickly as possible. Sam, as soon as the gang members' attention is focused in another direction, come out from around the building and attack them from the south. They have us outgunned, but we have them outnumbered and we have the element of surprise."

As soon as we all got into position, Ralph and Betsy opened up on the gang. Then Susan, Bobby and I initiated our attack, alternating cover fire and positions, working our way closer to the road gang from the north. As soon as Ralph and Betsy opened fire on the road gang's position from the east, the road gang took cover and started returning fire. Some of them had automatic weapons, forcing Ralph and Betsy to take cover, pausing their firing. As the road gang members started to move in on Ralph and Betsy, Susan, Bobby and I intensified our attack, forcing the road gang to take cover and reposition. This left them exposed to attack from Sam, Flo and Daisy, who had been moving in close to the road gang's position from the south. After killing and wounding several members of the road gang, the rest saw that they were outnumbered, and they surrendered.

We all moved in to the road gang's position, disarming them and laying them out face down in the parking lot. The road gang members all had tattoos with the words 'Road Warrior' on their arms, and that was also painted on the doors of their vehicles. The two surviving gypsy members that they had captured were tied together and hoisted off the ground by the hook of the tow truck. We got them down and released them.

The two gypsies thanked us for rescuing them and introduced themselves as James and Robert Smith. We asked them if they were the gypsies who were robbing travelers and burning and looting the surrounding villages. They replied that they were not robbing anyone nor burning any villages. They said that they were the Boyash people from the tribe of Banat, and that they were in control of Athens and Augusta. They said the road warriors were the ones who had been robbing, raping, murdering, pillaging, and burning villages along all the major highways leading to and from Atlanta.

Suddenly, over a dozen vehicles rolled in on our position, full of heavily armed individuals. They quickly captured John, Lilly, John Junior and Stephen and then converged on our position, forcing us to surrender.

The two gypsies, James and Robert, waved their hats at their allies and then told them about how we rescued them from the road warriors.

The leader came over and introduced himself as Randolph Smith, leader of the Boyash tribe of Banat in Athens. He was a large man who looked like a cross between a cowboy and someone from the Mafia. He wore a cowboy hat, jeans, and chaps, but he had on a purple shirt and tan vest like something Jack Hanna would wear. He had a goatee and a handlebar mustache, and you just knew not to mess with him. The gypsies gathered up the road warrior prisoners, placing them in handcuffs and shackles. Randolph said, "We need to have a sit-down conference to discuss a covenant or us joining their collective."

They cleared out the middle of the parking lot, parking their vehicles in a large circle. They set up a small fire pit and lay out blankets and cushions for everyone to sit on. They handed out cigars to us, saying that they were thanks for rescuing their two brothers, James and Robert.

After the introductions, they asked us where we came from and where we were going. We were invited to a tribal meeting at Sanford Stadium. To avoid offending our gracious hosts, we agreed to attend the tribal meeting, even though we were anxious to get back on the road to Savannah and meet up with the GGF. The prisoners were loaded into their vehicles. Our weapons and gear were returned, and we followed the group to Sanford Stadium.

Sanford Stadium tribal conference.

At the stadium, we were told to leave our long guns in our vehicles. The only weapons allowed into the tribal meeting were sidearms and knives, which must remain holstered and peace-bonded. We were assured that our vehicles and equipment would be safe in the parking lot, which was well guarded. We were not comfortable with this situation, but Randolph and the gypsies had not left us with any other options.

As we were being escorted to the field in the center of the stadium, Flo and the other farmers said they were worried about our safety. Sam and I did our best to keep them calm.

The field was full of tables that were loaded with food and drinks. Other tables had been set up with chairs surrounding them in a manner for fine dining, including plates, silverware and wine glasses. There were hundreds of people on the field, cooking and attending the tables. The bleacher areas were mostly empty with the exception of armed men patrolling the festivities.

We were taken to a large group of tables set up in a horseshoe arrangement with all the seats to the outside. We were seated on the right arm of the horseshoe. Randolph took his seat at the center of the arch and several other well-dressed gypsies seated themselves on the left arm of the horseshoe. Once we were all seated, waiters and waitresses brought in platters of roast chicken, vegetables and rolls. Bottles of wine were brought to Randolph, which he examined, passing some to his right and some to his left. Each person poured their glass full of wine and then passed the bottle to the next person. Then, a gypsy dressed in black came to the open end of the horseshoe of tables and began to say a blessing over the food in some language that we did not recognize. As we started to eat our meal, Randolph explained that the blessing was spoken in their native Romanian language. We ate our meal and participated in small talk about our previous lives before 'the Happening' as they called it. Ralph and Betsy reached into a pack that they had brought with them into the stadium and pulled out a brown and tan pottery jug. From this they poured a clear liquid into their wine glasses.

Randolph saw this and asked them, "What is that you have there? You do not like the wine?"

Ralph replied, "This is an after-meal drink of our own recipe, which we prefer over wine." Then realizing he may have made a mistake, "no offense intended."

Randolph said, "Oh, I take it that is moonshine. If you have extra, I will take a glass."

Relieved, Ralph passed the jug to Randolph, who poured himself a glass of the moonshine. Taking a good swallow of the clear liquid, Randolph nodded approvingly, "Very tasty." Then his eyes widened and his face took on a bright red hue. "This stuff has a bit of a kick to it. If you have a quantity of this, we may be interested in making a trade. We'll work that out before you leave."

After our meal, the dishes were taken away, and more wine was passed around. Randolph asked us about the conditions of the town and people from which we came. We each described the turn of events that happened in our local area and how we had managed to survive it. Then it was Randolph's turn to tell us how Athens came to be under his control and what had taken place there.

Randolph said, "Just before 'the Happening,' Athens and Augusta were battling race riots. There was looting and widespread crimes throughout both cities. The local city, county, and state police forces were being overwhelmed. By the time the National Guard arrived for support, the local police forces had turned brutal in their attempt to control the civil unrest. The National Guard ended up trying to control the general population of the city and the local police force as well. Then Homeland Security moved in with their forces. Homeland Security started going neighborhood to neighborhood, evacuating everyone to FEMA camps and arresting those who resisted, putting them in detention centers. The National Guard did not approve of these actions and got into several skirmishes with Homeland Security. Sometime during all of this confusion, terrorists smuggled suicide bombs into the FEMA camps and detention centers and detonated them. The survivors from the blasts panicked and stormed the gates, overpowering the Homeland Security forces and scattering back out into the city. Once all of our power went out and electronic devices stopped working, the disease kicked in. There was not much left of the Homeland Security forces at this time, and they retreated out of the city. Some went to Savannah and some went to Atlanta. The National Guardsmen and most other military forces that were within the city limits deserted to parts unknown."

"Just as we were recovering from the disease which I'm told is called the canine flu, we began to come under attack nightly by mutant wild dogs. I've heard from our good friends here that they call them zombie dogs. We have good medical facilities here and have been trying to get the equipment up and functional again. We've been doing research on the zombie dogs and have learned that they only come out at night because their skin and eyes are sensitive to the sunlight. If exposed to sunlight, their skin burns and blisters, causing them so much pain that they die of heart failure. We sent hunting parties out at night to hunt them down and try to eliminate them. But the zombie dog's senses of night vision, hearing, and smell caused our hunting parties to become the hunted. The zombie dogs travel in packs. The largest packs that we've spotted number over 200. Each pack of zombie dogs is led by an alpha dog. This alpha dog can be male or female, and is much larger than the others, having a rust colored body. This alpha dog will not directly attack or engage armed humans. However, the alpha dog is like an army general, directing his troops. The alpha is very intelligent and will direct the subordinates and his pack in coordinated attacks on humans or animals. If there is a weakness in your defenses, the alpha dog will find it and exploit it to your doom. We've taken the bodies of zombie dogs that we've killed to our labs for testing. We have not learned much because once dead, the zombie dogs' blood and tissue deteriorate rapidly. What we did learn is that the zombie dogs are carriers of the canine flu. You can be infected with the canine flu after being bitten or if the body fluids of the zombie dog, dead or alive, contacts open wounds, eyes or mouth."

"We were just getting organized and learning how to deal with the zombie dog problem when the road warriors showed up. The road warriors are a ruthless, evil gang of bandits that travel the major throughways in and out of Atlanta. They have cleared the highways to make travel for them easier and appealing to unwary travelers. Any travelers using the highways are attacked and killed by the road warriors. Most towns within 50 miles of the exits off the throughway have been pillaged and burned by the road warriors. They use motorcycle men as scouts. They have tow trucks to clear the roadways and bring along cargo trucks to carry all the useful items that they pillage. The seven road warrior prisoners that you captured outside the north bypass will be hanged by the neck from the road signs overlooking the highway near the exit ramps where they were captured. This may sound cruel, but it is a message to the road warriors to 'stay away from Athens, or this will happen to you."

I was curious. "You have a lot of people here and have provided us with a bountiful meal. How is it that the road warriors or zombie dogs pose much of a threat to you?"

Randolph said, "The meal in the meeting here was a planned event which we were happy to share with you as our surprise guests. The zombie dogs have killed off most of the livestock and wild game for miles, so our food supply is running low. This was our last feast before a long, forced fast. The road warriors have many vehicles and a seemingly unlimited supply of petrol. We only have a limited number of working vehicles. We can't pursue them or maneuver into positions where they are looting and pillaging. The road warriors are able to move into an area and attack our people faster than we are able to respond, due to our limited number of vehicles. We have valuable commodities that the road warriors wish to take from us. We have petrol, both gasoline and diesel, in large quantities. We also have medicine, drugs, and one other commodity that the road warriors seem to be interested in: toilet tissue."

Susan agreed wholeheartedly. "I totally understand toilet tissue being a viable commodity, along with female hygiene items!"

Randolph said, "We have plenty of those also, and we'll make sure you girls have a good stock before you leave."

I said, "Couldn't you find the zombie dogs' lair and eliminate them during the daytime when they are most vulnerable?"

Randolph said, "We've been trying that. But most of our daylight hours are being committed to higher survival activities. Just simple things that we used to take for granted now consume a lot of our time, like disposing trash. And our sewage system no longer works, so we have crews setting up porta-potty's. Then, of course, the waste has to be disposed of somewhere. Food gathering and preparation is another full-time chore. Maintenance on the operating vehicles that we do have is a lot of work. We cannot pull into a gas station and fill the tank; we have to siphon or manually pump the fuel for our vehicles. And defending our city from threats. Human threats are not necessarily the most dangerous. Disease and pests are also a constant threat. All drinking water has to be boiled or purified before use. There is no refrigeration, so all of our food has to be prepared fresh. Everything has to be kept clean and orderly to prevent infestations of insects and bacteria. We have a good supply of medicines, but no way to replace what is used, so our doctors and medical staff have to be very diligent about how they administer medical treatment. In most cases, major surgery is impossible without the use of modern life-support equipment. It is true we have fuel for emergency generators, but the EMP destroyed most of the electronics that control the generators and the high tech medical equipment. We can generate electricity for basic things such as lights and simple pumping devices, such as small water pumps, but anything on a large scale is impossible at this time. And there is also the threat of gangs like the road warriors. We did find a few lairs of the zombie dogs in some abandoned buildings. We eliminated those. Nevertheless, there are many others scattered throughout the countryside in caves and wooded areas which are difficult for us to find."

Flow suggested, "The farmers may be interested in trading food for gasoline."

Ralph added, "The mountain hillbillies have junkyards full of older vehicles, which with a little work, could be made operable."

I said to Randolph, "Maybe your people could forge a trade agreement and an alliance with the farmers and hillbillies to pool your resources. The farmers and hillbillies have joined forces to keep the Russians in Gainesville penned up there so that they cannot continue their plot to take over the United States. The Russians are being supplied by the Chinese who control Hunter Airbase in Savannah. Both the Russians and the Chinese are expected to fly in supplies and reinforcements by way of Hunter. Some friends of ours at Fort Stewart are trying to convince the third infantry to attack the Chinese and the Homeland Security forces who control Hunter Airbase and most of downtown Savannah. But in the suburbs of Savannah, there is a brutal street gang called the Bloods that have been keeping the Chinese and Homeland Security tied up in Savannah and keeping the third infantry division at Fort Stewart out. The third infantry cannot launch an attack on the Chinese at Hunter without going through the territory controlled by the Bloods. If the third infantry were to attack the Bloods to eliminate this obstacle, then the Chinese would not be restricted in their movements either."

"If your tribes here in Athens and Augusta were to join forces with the hillbillies and the farmers, together you should be able to retake control of Gainesville. The Russians are holding large numbers of civilian hostages there. Those hostages could add to your collective along with the vehicles and weapons taken from the Russians. Once you have the those, along with the vehicles you already have, the members of the road warriors would no longer be a threat. With the Russians eliminated from Gainesville and your forces north and west of Savannah, the Chinese would be hard-pressed to gain a foothold here in Georgia. Your forces and the third infantry could eliminate the Bloods and really put the pressure on the Chinese and Homeland Security forces at Hunter Airbase."

Randolph nodded thoughtfully. "This is a novel idea. But we gypsies, as you outsiders call us, do not have a friendly relationship with the northern people, the farmers and hillbillies."

Flo said, "After meeting you and seeing all of this, I can see that you have been falsely accused of heinous actions committed most likely by the road warriors. I can write you a letter of recommendation to take to the farmers. If you send no more than a two-person message team to Clermont and ask for Mama Grover with this letter, you will be well received."

Randolph agreed, and Flo wrote her note: *I have met with the gypsies in Athens, and I spoke with their leader Randolph about a trade agreement between the gypsies and the farmers. The gypsies have not been killing travelers and burning villages as we first thought. The criminals of this deed belong to a gang out of Atlanta called the road warriors.*

-Your daughter, Florence Henderson

Randolph said, "It is getting too late for you to make it to Fort Stewart today, and it is too dangerous to travel after dark. You should stay here and enjoy our hospitality for the night. Then you can leave first thing in the morning."

We agreed to stay, and Randolph put us up in one of the hotels for the night. The more luxurious rooms of the hotel were on the upper floors, but we were assigned rooms on the lower floors. Randolph explained that this was due to the lack of air conditioning, making the upper floors uncomfortable. The newer buildings of the inner city were designed for air conditioning. Without electricity and air conditioning, the airflow was insufficient, making the interior of large, modern buildings hot and uncomfortable. Most people in Athens, and I assumed elsewhere, preferred to stay in the single-family homes in the country or suburbs where they could open the windows to allow natural airflow. The also provided a more comfortable shelter from the elements. In the big malls and department stores, the air was so stagnant that it made it hard to breathe.

After a good night's rest, we had breakfast out back in the pool area. The water in the pool was stagnant and not fit for swimming or drinking, but the patio was shaded and adequate for eating our breakfast and preparing to leave for our trip to meet up with George.

Road trip to meet George.

As we prepared to head out, Randolph showed up with several vehicles and told us that he was sending an escort along for our safety. They would go as far as Madison, at which point his people would return, and we'd be on our own. We thanked him for his concern and all the hospitality that he and his people had shown us.

The trip to Madison was smooth and uneventful. We continued south on 441 to Dublin. Along the way, through the countryside, we saw very little signs of human life. We saw the normal small animals, birds and squirrels, but throughout the whole trip, we saw very few farm animals, only an occasional horse or cow. These were very skittish and ran out of sight when they noticed our vehicles.

Entering the city of Dublin, the condition was much like most of the others we had encountered: an abandoned, burned out ghost town. We were delayed and spent several hours clearing vehicles and other debris from our path so that we could continue on to route 80 East which would take us to Statesboro. There we turned south on Route 25 to Claxton.

After taking the route 25 bypass around Statesboro and heading south toward Claxton, we were approaching the I-16 underpass when Sam said, "There's movement up on the highway. Put the pedal down and keep moving as quickly as possible."

As we passed under I-16, we saw moving vehicles and people up on the highway. Sam was then leading us south on Route 25 at a speed of about 60 miles an hour which was a bit reckless considering the road conditions (abandoned vehicles, debris and other obstacles were in the road). Looking back, we saw several vehicles leaving the highway to pursue us. Four motorcycles were in the lead and gaining fast.

John Junior and Stephen were exchanging gunfire with our pursuers, the road warriors. They were able to keep the motorcycle riders from overtaking us, but the rest of the vehicles in the road warriors group had now gained on us and were firing automatic weapons. The road opened up and I pulled over to one side, allowing Ralph and Betsy to pass. I then fell back with John and Lily, allowing Bobby a clear line of fire with his AR15 to support John Junior and Stephen's effort in slowing down our pursuers.

There was a large poultry farm complex just outside of Claxton. Sam used this area to guide us into a defensive position amongst the buildings and abandoned vehicles in the parking area of the complex.

Sam ordered everyone out of their vehicles and to take up defensive positions among the abandoned vehicles and other structures in the area. Sam stayed in his truck, manning the 30-caliber machine gun and laying down cover fire for us while we got into position. Sam took out two of the motorcycle riders with it. Bobby took out another of the motorcycle riders and Flo dropped the fourth one with a shotgun blast to the chest.

The remaining road warriors stopped their vehicles, taking up attack positions and sending a hail of gunfire in our direction. We were outnumbered 3 to 1 and outgunned. Sam was taking too much gunfire in his direction and he had to abandon his truck and the 30-caliber machine gun.

Sam called out, "Make your shots count and conserve your ammo!"

We were definitely running low on ammo, and the road warriors were preparing for a rush attack. Just then, we heard a loud rumbling of vehicles and heard more gunfire coming from the direction of Claxton. The road warriors stopped their advance on our position and turned to face the new threat. We saw several military vehicles headed in our direction. They were coming in fast, armed with heavy machine guns and armored vehicles. The road warriors, seeing that they were now the ones outnumbered and outgunned, made an attempt to retreat. We took advantage of the situation, advancing on the road warriors with full force. Between our aggressive attack and the advance of the military, the road warriors were annihilated down to the last man.

The military vehicles pulled to our position, training their weapons on us and demanding that we lay down our weapons and surrender. Sam saw the images on the doors of the vehicles and started laughing.

Sam called, "George, you son of a bitch, it's me, Sam!"

A man stepped out of one of the vehicles. He was a skinny man in his 60s, dressed in brown army camouflage. He looked like anybody's Grandpa. But the efficient air that surrounded him engendered instant respect.

"You can put your weapons down and relax boys," he said, "I know these people, they're friends of mine."

Sam and George greeted each other with a hug and a handshake. Sam turned to us and said, "I would like you all to meet Colonel George Snyder."

Sam introduced each of us, one by one. Then George said, "Let's load up and head back to post, it will be safer there for us to talk and catch up on current events."

As we were heading back to our vehicles, George said, "We do not have room for all your gear, but we may be able to tow one or two vehicles that don't have flat tires back to post."

Sam's truck had taken a beating; it was riddled with bullet holes, and the windshield was broken. Streams of antifreeze and oil were running out from underneath the truck. One front tire was flat. It was undrivable.

Sam said, "I think I can fix the flat tire rather quickly." He pulled a toolbox out of the back of his truck and took out a tire repair kit. A bullet had penetrated the tire but did not damage the rim. Sam put a plug in the bullet hole and inflated the tire with two cans of Fix-A-Flat.

"There we go. It can be towed now."

John and Lily's truck had taken a shot in the radiator. John said, "I think I can get our truck up and going here in a few minutes. John Junior and Stephen, go to one of the abandoned vehicles in the parking lot, pop the hood, and drain some antifreeze out into a pan."

John popped the hood his truck, took a pair of needle nose pliers, and pinched off three of the copper tubes going to the radiator that had been broken by gun fire. This stopped the leak. They then poured the antifreeze that John Junior and Stephen had taken from the abandoned vehicle into the radiator of the truck. John said, "It's a good thing these old trucks have copper radiators that you can repair. Not like the throwaway plastic junk of the newer models."

George and his unit of Rangers took us in to Fort Stewart.

Chapter 11

Conference at Fort Stewart.

Once at the fort, we were taken to a large conference room where we were offered refreshments. We brought George up to date on the developments of the alliances between the hillbillies, farmers and the gypsies. We also told him about the road warriors and the supply drop to the Russians in Gainesville. Then George informed us of the developments here in the Savannah area.

He said that things in Fort Stewart and across the country were on very shaky ground. The loyalties of military forces across the country had been changing hands, and there was no unified command structure between military departments or government. For now, acting President John Hager had a shaky control over the U.S. Navy and the Atlantic fleet. He had also been in communication with the British, who were trying to bring stability and control to the northeast and Canada. He had been able to coordinate some of the military ground forces. His loyal forces include Homeland Security, the US Marine Corps East Coast, the US Air Force and some regular Army units.

Most of all the local police forces have abandoned their duties and are not effective in enforcing local laws. Most of the National Guard units across the country have formed their own organizations and now control and defend their own local cities, towns and territory. Texas, Oklahoma, New Mexico, and now

Arizona have their own coalition separate from the United States, and they're involved in some intense fighting with Mexico. The Chinese have taken over and now control California and most of the country west of the Rockies.

The Pacific Fleet of the U.S. Navy in the Pacific are holed up in Hawaii and Southeast Asia, awaiting orders on how to proceed. The Russians have taken control of Alaska and most of Canada. Russia and China have formed an alliance to take over and divide North America. In our weakened state, President Hagar, under the advice from some military leaders, does not want to attack Russia or China. This is where the disagreements stem from. From the information I have acquired, I see the takeover being plotted and initiated by the Russians and Chinese. The Russians and Cubans have taken control of the Virgin Islands, Bahamas, Puerto Rico, and Florida. Our Air Force and military have annihilated North Korea and most of the Arabian Peninsula with tactical nuclear weapons. Only Israel, Jordan, and parts of other small countries in the northern area of the Arabian Peninsula still exist and support human life. But due to the radioactive fallout in this area, how much longer humans can exist has yet to be seen. There are scattered Russian and Chinese units in control of small cities throughout what is left of the United States.

U.S. Navy submarines in the Indian Ocean and South Pacific have detonated high altitude nuclear EMP bursts over Russia and China. The only thing preventing an all-out attack from Russia and China on the United States has been President Hagar's communication with their leaders, insisting that this was not a sanctioned attack by the government of the United States. That's the official word. I think the real story is that the EMPs devastated their countries as badly or worse than ours, preventing them from launching a full-scale modern warfare attack here on the United States. This is evident by the lack of invasion forces here.

The EMPs destroyed most of the world satellites and satellite communication equipment. There are still a few satellites functioning but communications and GPS coordinates are spotty and unreliable. They only function when the working satellites are in the correct position in their orbit to transmit the data. Only older aircraft that did not depend on satellite positioning would be able to fly long distances and arrive at their correct destination.

"The third infantry artillery division wanted to launch an artillery strike on Hunter Air Force base," said George, "to destroy the runway and prevent any Russian or Chinese planes from landing at Hunter Air Force base. But our surveillance is very limited, and higher ranking officers here at Fort Stewart do not want to drop artillery into downtown Savannah, killing innocent civilians. The Chinese are using the civilians in Savannah as slave labor and hostages. The Chinese have very little problems controlling and keeping track of the civilians inside the city. If they should escape, the Bloods would capture them. The Chinese and the Bloods have been fighting over the supplies in the warehouses around Savannah. The city, being a seaport, houses numerous warehouses containing import and export goods of every variety. We obviously have the correct coordinates, but we need spotters to guide our artillery. Without our high tech electronic surveillance equipment, we need boots on the ground in that area for spotters. We have portable communication equipment that'll reach out to about 50 miles, so we sent a squad of Rangers into Savannah to be our spotters. But that was yesterday, and we haven't heard back from them yet. We were attempting to sneak in the back door, approaching from Claxton. That's when we heard gunfire and we came upon you guys in a firefight with the road warriors. We assumed it was our squad of Rangers and possibly the Bloods who were having the firefight."

He continued, "One more bit of news on possibly a more personal note to you, Mark. Do you have a relative who is in the Army Rangers by the name of Brian Antonio?"

I was surprised, "Yes I do, is he here? What's happened to him?"

George said, "First Sgt. Antonio was the leader of the squad that was sent as spotters to Hunter Airbase."

I said, "I'd like to go with a squad into Savannah and find out what has happened to him."

"We would like nothing more than to do that, but we have limited fuel supplies for our vehicles and cannot make another trip there today. Most of the fuel in the Savannah area is under the control of the Chinese or the Bloods."

"We've brought enough fuel with us, so we could use our own vehicles to drive in to Savannah and search for Brian and the Ranger squad," I volunteered.

George said, "You people are not under my command, and I cannot order you not to go. But if you should decide to take this upon yourself, I'm sure you could get some volunteers from the Ranger unit. But that would have to be cleared with Major Higgins who is in command of the Rangers. I am only in command of the National Guard unit, now the GGF. Major Higgins commands the Ranger unit and Col. Whitmore is in command of the third infantry here in Fort Stewart."

Sam said, "My truck is toast, and I took a hit to my leg in that last battle, so I'm not able to come with you on this one. I'm okay, it's only a flesh wound. The medics have fixed me up, but I'll still just slow you down."

Ralph spoke up. "Betsy and I have a few years under our belts, but we both are veterans of the Iraq war and are still in good health. We would be honored to join you in the search for your brother."

Bobby chimed in. "I'm in, and I've got your six!"

Susan said, "I'm not normally one to volunteer to go into harm's way, but you risked your life for us more than once. So if you're going, Bobby and I are going too."

John said, "Right now my old truck is held together with Band-Aids and a prayer. I am sorry to say that we will not be able to join you, but we have some extra gasoline that you can use the top off your tanks."

George said, "Then I guess we need to go meet with Major Higgins and Col. Whitmore."

After talking with the two in command, we got detailed information and maps on the Ranger squad's assignment. Major Higgins said that he could not spare any of his rangers to go with us at this time. Major Higgins and Col. Whitmore wished us the best of luck. "We'll be standing by the long-range radio for word of your success."

The rescue mission.

The command at Fort Stewart either did not have or was not willing to supply us with a long-range radio, so all we had was the short-range earpiece radios that Sam supplied us with for communication between ourselves. Brian's squad was to patrol and scout the area from Claxton to Pembroke before heading on into Savannah. We now knew that Claxton was clear of enemy combatants, so we took Route 119 to Pembroke, then south on Route 204, and John Carter Rd. into Savannah, retracing Brian's steps. With only two vehicles and five people, we were less likely to attract the attention of the Chinese. But we were a vulnerable target for the Bloods. Brian was a sergeant in command of the six-man squad and two vehicles sent to Savannah. The squad was to split up into two three-man squads at vantage points overlooking the airfield at Hunter Airbase. The squads' call signs were Sierra 1 and Sierra 2. The artillery command call sign was Zulu 1. Third infantry call sign was Alpha 1. Our team would keep the call sign that we had been using of Alert 1. The Sierra squads were to maintain radio silence until they were in position or ran into an emergency situation. The Chinese had been monitoring all radio stations and frequencies. We didn't want to alert them to our presence or intentions. The Bloods controlled the area between Highway 95 and Veterans Parkway in Savannah. It was possible to encounter either the Chinese or the Bloods on patrol in this area. Beyond Veterans Parkway, all the way to the coast, was completely under Chinese control.

Our fuel tanks were topped off, and we unloaded everything except the essential gear and items needed for the mission. George supplied us with extra ammunition and light body armor. The road to Pembroke was mostly clear of obstacles, and we made good time. Route 204 and John Carter Rd. from Pembroke South was a bit more congested with obstacles, but still passable. As we approached the Brian County line and Morgan's Bridge over the Ogeechee River, we saw the husk of a burned out Humvee some distance up ahead. We stopped our vehicles and searched the area with our binoculars, looking for signs of Brian's Rangers or any dangers that might be in the area. I decided to have Susan take over the driving of the Chevy truck, and I took position in the bed of our truck with Bobby. Ralph also had Betsy take over the driving of his truck, and he took up position in the bed of his truck. We approached the Humvee slowly and cautiously. Leaving the girls in the truck, we got out and investigated the area on foot. We noticed bullet holes in the Humvee and lots of spent shell casings around the area. From the evidence, we had to assume the worst: that Brian and his squad were ambushed and killed or captured. But whether by the Bloods or the Chinese, we did not know. We decided to continue on slowly, keeping our eye out for any more evidence that might provide some answers. As Morgan's Bridge came into sight, we saw another Humvee blocking the roadway onto the bridge. We stopped the vehicles and parked them off to the side of the road, out of sight. We continued on foot along the tree line. Getting to within a few hundred yards of the bridge, we surveyed the area with our binoculars more closely. The binoculars showed the Ranger airborne symbol on the door of the Humvee.

We saw two black men wearing T-shirts and jeans: one leaning against the Humvee holding an AR15, and the other was standing over by the bridge railing carrying an Uzi.

We didn't see anyone else around. If we moved closer by going through the woods, I was sure we could get to within 100 yards of them without being seen. At that distance, we should have no trouble taking them out quickly.

We fell back into the woods and moved closer to the bridge. When we got to within 100 yards from the two Blood gang members, Bobby and I both found a good place with a steady rest and took aim. Using hand signals, I indicated that I would take the tougher shot of the one with the Uzi standing on the bridge.

Bobby took the one with the AR15 standing next to the Humvee. On a three count, we both fired simultaneously, dropping both combatants right where they stood. Not having suppressors on our weapons, and without the background of man-made noises, the sound of the gunshots echoed through the surrounding area. Before moving in we waited, listening and watching for any more threats. We neither saw nor heard anything more, so we exited the woods and approached the Humvee. Bobby and I checked our targets, confirming the kills and stripping them of their weapons. Susan and Betsy investigated the Humvee. Ralph covered our six. Other than a few bullet holes and a broken mirror, the Humvee seemed to be intact. Susan found a walkie-talkie on the front seat of the Humvee, but it was not the long-range military radio that was issued to the Rangers.

A voice came over the radio, *"Bubba, radio check."*

There was a pause. *"Bubba, radio check. You dumbass, you better not be sleeping!"*

We looked at each other and I said, "We better get this Humvee out of here because Bubba is not gonna make his radio check, and we're going to have company."

As we were dragging the bodies out of the road, we heard loud music and vehicles approaching from the Savannah side of the bridge.

I said, "Quickly, pop the hood on this Humvee!"

Susan and I detached the hood release and opened the hood. I used my tactical knife to pry the wires off the positive terminal of the battery, and we dropped the hood back down.

"Take cover in the woods!"

From where the Humvee was parked to the woods was approximately 50 yards. Just as we were entering the trees, three more vehicles came down John Carter Road right toward us. Now we had three vehicles approaching our position from the Savannah side of the bridge and three from the other side. The three from the Savannah side reached the Humvee first, blocking the bridge. They stopped and got out of their vehicles. Looking back, I saw six heavily armed black men standing on the bridge. The three other cars coming down John Carter Road reached our position and stopped. Six more heavily armed gang members got out of those vehicles. They started looking over the Humvee and around the area. It became quite apparent that they noticed the blood on the road, and it did not take them long to find the bodies of their fellow gang members. One of them, a large man with a red bandanna around his head, gave orders to the others to start searching the area.

I motioned for the others to follow me deeper into the woods to try to get out of sight and away from the gang members. Just then, a snake fell off a tree branch and landed on Betsy. She screamed loudly and threw the snake. Before we could do anything, the gang members opened fire into the woods. A hail of bullets came flying in our direction, buzzing like bees and ricocheting off the trees.

I shouted, "Everyone down! Take cover and prepare to face the enemy."

We all dropped down into the wet, soggy ground, taking cover behind trees and rocks, waiting for our pursuers to come into the woods after us. We heard lots of talking and yelling, but no signs of any of them entering the woods. We just lay there quietly, watching and listening. After several minutes, the yelling and sporadic gunfire stopped. We still heard the gang members talking but no more yelling. Apparently they were trying to decide if they should search the woods to find us or wait us out.

After about 30 minutes, Bobby moved closer to me and said, "I think the bloods are afraid to come into the woods. Maybe they are more scared of snakes then Betsy is."

I stifled a laugh and whispered to Bobby to be quiet and just wait. After another 30 minutes or more, we heard the cracking of twigs and branches. They had decided to pursue us. They were all talking loudly to each other and not wearing any camo. They came stomping through the woods in our direction. Half of them were wearing white T-shirts and the other half wore no shirts at all. The ones wearing white T-shirts would be easy targets, and we waited for them to get closer.

Then I said, "Fire!" We fired one volley of about 10 rounds each, dropping three or four of the gang members instantly. I yelled to fall back, and we got up, moving another 50 yards deeper into the woods. There we took up defensive positions again. There was more gunfire, and a hail of bullets was fired in our direction, all zipping by well over our heads. We heard a lot of yelling and screaming, then more gunfire. But this time we didn't hear any bullets zipping by. I considered this for a moment and then gave the order to move up. Staying low, moving from tree to tree, we moved up closer to the gang members.

Suddenly I realized that they were in a firefight with another threat. I stopped our group and said, "Someone else is attacking the Bloods; it could be the Chinese. If so, we want to avoid them. Let's move east and then north and circle around and see who it is."

We circled around and came back out onto John Carter Road, a couple of hundred yards west of where we had entered the woods. Looking east toward the bridge, we saw that the Bloods were having a firefight with another group of fighters on the other side of the road. We couldn't see their opponents, but the Bloods were definitely taking heavy casualties.

Bobby suggested, "If I climb this tree with my binoculars, I might be able to see who's on the other side of the road that the Bloods are fighting."

I nodded. "Okay Bobby, go for it."

Bobby climbed about 20 feet up and took out his binoculars to survey the fighting. After a couple of minutes, Bobby climbed down and said, "I didn't get a good look at the people on the other side of the road, but I did see what looked like Army uniforms, American Army uniforms."

I said, "Let's hit the Bloods from here and help them out. Whoever they are, I hope they're on our side."

We moved in on the Bloods along the tree line, flanking them. They were easy to spot. They were all wearing jeans and popping up out of the bushes like Jack-in-the-boxes and then dropping back down again. After observing this tactic, every time one or two of the Bloods pop up, we filled them full of lead. This firefight only lasted three or four minutes before the Bloods were eliminated. We stayed in the woods and observed the other side of the road, waiting to see who was over there.

After three or four minutes of silence, we heard a voice holler, "Sierra squad here." We knew Sierra was a call sign for Brian's squad of Rangers, but not being absolutely sure who was over there, I tried giving them some call signs to see what the response would be.

I hollered back, "Alert one here from Zulu." A few seconds later, a Ranger squad materialized out of the woods on the other side of the road. We exited the woods on our side, and then I saw that the lead Ranger was my brother Brian. Brian recognized me immediately. "I'm glad you came along when you did," he said, "But what the hell are you doing here?"

We gave Brian a quick update on why we were there. Brian said that they had been ambushed and outflanked by about 50 gang members the day before. They had been forced to retreat into the woods. The gang had been patrolling the area heavily, looking for the squad.

"There were too many of them for us to mount a counteroffensive, but when you guys showed up, that turned the odds more in our favor."

Including Brian, there were only three rangers left in his squad. Two had been killed in a firefight with the Bloods. Overnight, the zombie dogs got one more member of the team. Brian said it was dangerous being out on the streets. He said, "Soldiers, confirm those kills and dispatch any who are still alive. Grab their weapons and ammo. What we can't take with us we'll throw in the river. Mark, you people grab one of their vehicles and we'll take the Humvee."

I said, "We've got our own vehicles about 200 yards up the road."

Brian said, "Okay go get them and follow me in the Humvee. Let's get rid of the rest of these vehicles and move on out of here."

We pushed the vehicles that the Bloods had been driving off to the side of the road, flattening the tires and removing the spark plug wires from the engines. Brian and his two remaining rangers got in the Humvee and we followed behind them with our vehicles, continuing across the bridge toward Savannah, down Route 204. Just before we reached I-95, Brian pulled into a driveway leading to a large residence.

Brian got out of the Humvee and said, "This should be a safe enough place to take a break and put together our plans." Using the long-range radio that they found under the back seat of the Humvee, he said, "Alert one, rendezvous Sierra one complete. Bravo is a go, out."

Brian turned to me. "The plan is to take up observation positions on Veterans Parkway of the airfield at Hunter Airbase. The area between I-95 and Veterans Parkway is heavily patrolled by both the Bloods and the Chinese. We're going to have to make our way through that area without being spotted. Getting into a firefight with either the Chinese or the Bloods would compromise our mission. We'll park the vehicles here and go the rest of the way on foot. It's about a 5-mile hike from here. We'll be going down Abercorn Street to the railroad tracks. Then we'll follow the railroad tracks across the trestle over the swamp and then cut east to Veterans Parkway. At Veterans Parkway we'll take up observation positions in abandoned vehicles where we can overlook the airfield on Hunter Army base. Mark, are your people going to be able to handle this?"

I assured him, "Yes, these people are in good physical condition and have proven themselves many times over the last few weeks."

Brian said, "Okay, you stay with me. Susan and Bobby, you go with Cpl. Heinz. Ralph and Betsy will go with Sgt. Rossi once we get to Veterans Parkway. Fall in troops, and move out."

We started out at a vigorous pace, wanting to get into position before dark. We moved from building to building, keeping an eye out for any enemies as we went. A few times we spotted patrols of Bloods, on foot and armed, walking down the streets. We made it to the railroad tracks and up to Veterans Parkway without any incidents. There were plenty of abandoned vehicles to use as cover. It was too hot inside the vehicles, so we took up positions underneath them. Looking across from Veterans Parkway onto the airfield, we saw two cargo planes, one Russian and one Chinese. There was lots of activity, and soldiers were moving about near the planes.

Brian was about to call on the long-range radio when we heard vehicles coming. We all stayed quiet, watching as a Chinese APC and a Jeep made their way slowly up Veterans Parkway. They continued past us without spotting us.

Once they were out of sight. Brian made the call on the long-range radio. "Zulu one, Zulu one, Sierra one, Bravo is a go. I repeat, Bravo is a go."

We waited for what seemed like a very long time but was actually only a minute or less. Then we heard the artillery. We saw and felt the explosions. The other two soldiers yelled numbers back to Brian, who called the coded message into the artillery commander. Another barrage of artillery struck the airfield, destroying the cargo planes.

Brian said, "They got their Zero. Now it's time for us to get the hell out of here before this place starts crawling with Chinese and Bloods."

We packed up and headed out for the railroad tracks, retracing our steps back to Abercorn Street. Now the city streets were very much full of activity. We had to be extra cautious moving about because our appearance did not blend in very well with the Bloods or the Chinese. Brian and his other two soldiers had to physically and silently take out a couple of Blood gang members who were just hanging around in the wrong area. But we made it back to our vehicles without any major incidents. We could still hear the artillery barrage as we got in our vehicles and headed up Route 204 to Pembroke. It would be dark by the time we got there, so George was sending a squad of freedom fighters to meet us in Pembroke and escort us back to Fort Stewart.

In Pembroke at the intersection of 119 we saw an armored Humvee with the GGF symbol on the side. The Humvee had a heavy machine gun on the top which was manned by a freedom fighter. There were two freedoms fighters in the Humvee's front seat, one driver and one riding shotgun. In the back of the Humvee was Sam and Flo! They waved to us and instructed us to follow them back to Fort Stewart.

It was getting dark, and due to the obstacles in the road, we could only safely travel at about 30 miles an hour. We heard and saw several zombie dogs along the way. They quickly moved away from us and disappeared into the shadows. The guards at the gate opened the fence to allow us entrance into Fort Stewart. They quickly closed it behind us. All the guards patrolled inside the gate for protection from the zombie dogs.

We went to the same conference building where we had left from earlier that day. George and the other officers were there for a mission debriefing.

Rescue Debriefing.

Brian reported the destruction of the two cargo planes caught on the runway, but the full impact of the artillery barrage could not be known without visual surveillance at a later date.

After the debriefing, we talked with Brian and filled him in on the events over the past few weeks. Brian said his wife was here working at the refugee center, but his daughter was living in Florida before everything happened, and he feared the worst for her. His son had been in Atlanta, and he hadn't heard from him since.

Brian also told us that there were about 10,000 refugees in Hinesville and Fort Stewart. Feeding and caring for them was a 24/7 chore. Food and medicine were scarce and had to be rationed. There were about 500 rangers, 3,000 soldiers of the third Battalion, and 2,000 GGF freedom fighters at Fort Stewart. Most of the medicine and fuel were inside the areas that were controlled by the Chinese or the Bloods. Now that the airfield had been destroyed, it would be more difficult for the Chinese to get supplies and reinforcements.

After a bit more chitchat, we were shown to our quarters where we could get a good night's sleep.

Chapter 12

Fort Stewart.

We spent the next few weeks getting acquainted with the people and routine at Fort Stewart. Everyone was assigned tasks and duties that were needed to keep the community running smoothly. We attended daily briefings with the officers, getting updates from communications with other military units across the country. Acting President Hagar had declared the third infantry a 'rogue' military unit. President Hagar had lost the cooperation and full command over most of the Army nationwide. Gen. Richard Briggs now controlled most of the Army, including the third infantry there in Fort Stewart. Governor William Carey of Texas, who was in control of the Texas coalition, has been working closely with General Briggs to bring unification of the United States military forces, including the Air Force, Navy, and Marine Corps.

The larger cities across the nation were still in total chaos: New York City, Washington DC, Philadelphia, Atlanta, and Chicago. These cities were overrun by vicious gangs and zombie dogs. Within a few weeks after the event the food and water ran out. That started a mad rush by people to get out into the countryside where they thought there was food and shelter. But if they weren't able to find shelter, the zombie dogs forced them back into the cities. There they either joined the gangs or were killed by them. Upstate New York and most of New England, including Boston and parts of Canada, were being stabilized under the control of British forces under the command of Gen. Henry Van Horn.

Locally, the Bloods and Chinese had been involved in some fierce battles. The Chinese, receiving supplies from airdrops, had gained the upper hand and reduced the Bloods to a scattered group of street gangs. The zombie dogs remained a threat to humans and livestock. The zombie dogs had been making nightly attacks. The GGF had been tasked with protecting the refugees and the livestock farms. The Rangers had been finding the zombie dogs daytime lairs and eliminating them whenever possible. The third infantry had been engaged with keeping the Chinese from expanding their territory. The third infantry had daily skirmishes with the Chinese and the Bloods trying to move into Richmond Hill, Pembroke, and Claxton.

George told us, "You are welcome to stay here at Fort Stewart. Your skills and expertise would be helpful and greatly appreciated. But, being non-military, you would be given refugee status, or you could join the GGF. Everyone here has duties, responsibilities, and chores that they have to do every day. There are a lot of people here and it takes a lot of work to feed and take care of this community, no one has a free ride. The refugees work on the farms, in the galley, or in the public works department. The GGF rotate guard duty and security with the third infantry and Rangers."

"I would like to offer you all a membership in the GGF. Before you say yes or no, let me tell you a little bit about the GGF. The GGF is a militia organization that I started here in Georgia a few years ago before this all happened. The members are mostly ex-military personnel. Since the event, we've taken on a more active role in supporting 'a government for the people, by the people.' We had no intention of overthrowing the government. We only encouraged our members to vote out politicians who were trying to take away the rights of American citizens. We very rarely contributed to any political campaigns or supported any individual politicians running for public office. We did encourage our members to write their representatives in support of some bills that were before

Congress and not to support other bills which we felt threatened the freedom of Americans. We support the U.S. Constitution and the Bill of Rights as it was originally written and intended. Freedom of religion, free speech, and the right to bear arms, etc."

"The GGF has been working with Col. Whitmore and Maj. Higgins here at Fort Stewart. But the GGF is not officially under the command of the US military, nor do we take orders from the US government. The GGF is a private militia, which now operates with a military structure."

"If you should decide to accept our offer to join the GGF, your rank will be equivalent to the highest rank you achieved, in which ever branch of the military you served. If you are over 30 years old and did not serve in the military, you will start out at the rank of corporal. If you're under 30 years old and did not serve in the military, your starting rank will be private. All missions and duties are voluntary. Due to the harsh world that we now live in, some rules and duties are strictly enforced. As stated before, there are no free rides here at Fort Stewart. Discipline, if needed, would be in the loss of privileges and/or extra duties. Of course we all have to live by civilized laws which govern everyone, whether you are a GGF member, military service member, civilian or refugee."

I told him, "We've already discussed the possibility of joining the GGF. George told us a lot about your organization. I've been authorized to speak on everyone's behalf. We accept your offer and would like to become members of the GGF."

George was pleased. "There are no binding contracts or pledges. Everything is voluntary. If at some point you should decide that you no longer want to participate in the GGF activities, you do not have to quit or resign. You can just change your status from active to inactive. Before this all happened, we used to have monthly meetings. All members were welcome. Now we have weekly briefings and all officers and senior enlisted personnel are asked to attend. We still have the all member meeting once a month or as needed."

"Sam told me that he thought all of you might be joining,

so I took the liberty of having a package made up for each of you containing armbands with the GGF insignia and collar pins representing your rank."

"The map of the 48 states with Stars & Stripes like our flag represents our belief in the Constitution. The banner 'for the people, by the people' represents our belief in the Declaration of Independence. The pistol on the left represents our peaceful status with a relaxed hammer. The pistol on the right represents our state of readiness with a cocked pistol which we're in right now. This means that we are in a state of full readiness, taking on a fully armed mission."

Sam's rank is command sergeant major.
Flo's rank is corporal.
Daisy's rank is private 2.
Mark's rank is master sergeant.
Susan's rank is corporal.

Bobby's rank is private first class.
Ralph's rank is sergeant first class.
Betsy's rank is sergeant.
John Senior's rank is staff sergeant.
Lily's rank is sergeant.
John Junior's rank is private first class.
Stephen's rank is corporal.

Hinesville Guard Duty.

That night, our assignment was to patrol Hinesville and protect the farm animals from the zombie dog attacks. Our guard duty shift was from midnight to 6 AM. We were divided into four groups and were assigned a guard post area on the outskirts of Hinesville.

The refugees guarded the farms in the daytime and took care of the animals. Other refugees worked at produce farms, gathered and cut firewood, did the cooking at the chow hall, and took care of trash removal. Everyone had assigned duties and chores that helped support the community.

Alert 1 was Susan, Bobby and I; Alert 2 was Sam, Flo and Daisy; Alert 3 was Ralph, Betsy and Stephen Haynes; Alert 4 was John, Lilly, and John Junior.

Susan, Bobby, and I were assigned to guard the milk cows. Sam, Flo, and Daisy were to guard the beef cows. Ralph, Betsy and Stephen were to guard the chickens. John, Lilly and John Junior were assigned to guard the pigs.

At 10:30 PM, a messenger came to our barracks waking us up, giving us a duty roster and walkie-talkies. He told us that chow hall was open with fresh coffee and snacks that we could take with us to our assigned guard post. We got our gear together, along with extra ammo, and met the others at the chow hall. After eating a light meal, we each took a thermos of coffee and headed out to our assignments.

Alert Four At The Pig Farm.

John, Lilly and John Junior arrived at the pig farm. The farm was located on a 5-acre plot with a long barn-like structure in the middle of the lot, surrounded by a chain-link perimeter fence. At each end of the barn, there was a guard tower about 20 feet high with a ladder leading up to an observation deck. Each guard tower had a solar powered spotlight mounted so that it could be rotated 180°. The barn itself was 100 feet long and 60 feet wide with 10 pens along each side, each holding five pigs. The building had a roof, but the sides were open to allow airflow. The feed troughs ran along the outside and a watering trough along the inside. There was a 10 foot wide service walkway down the middle of the barn. In the center of the barn was a ladder leading up to another guard tower. The spotlight in the middle tower could be moved 340°. One person was to man each guard tower for the duration of the watch. The guard towers provide protection for the guards in case the zombie dogs should breach the perimeter fence. It also provided an offensive platform to fire on the zombie dogs or any other intruders. The guards who were being relieved gave John, Lilly and John Junior their duties and procedures.

"In case of a zombie dog attack, fire a flare to signal an army unit for backup. The walkie-talkies have a limited range, which you can use to communicate with each other between the towers on channel 3. Channel 1 is used to communicate to the other farms and barns to inform them of any zombie dogs that may be moving through the area. In the morning, some of the refugees will be coming to take over the duties at the pig farm. Grain and animal feed are in short supply, so the scraps from the cafeteria and the produce farms are brought here to feed the pigs."

John Senior was manning the east tower, Lilly was manning the west tower, and John Junior took the middle tower.

At 12:30 AM, Lilly heard noises along the fence line and saw some shadowy figures. She turned to channel 3. "I have noise and movement at the west perimeter."

Her husband John replied, "Use the spotlight to see what's happening there."

Lilly shone the spotlight in the area of the disturbance. There were several zombie dogs trying to dig under the fence near her location. Lilly fired two shotgun blasts at them. The dogs disappeared into the woods, yipping and barking.

"I drove them away. All's clear now."

John Senior turned to channel 1, "Alert two, alert two just had a small incident with the zombie dogs, and now they may be headed in your direction."

Sam came on the radio, "Thanks, John. We'll be watching."

Alert Three At The Poultry Farm.

As Ralph, Betsy and Stephen arrived at the poultry barn, they saw several zombie dogs in the road leading to the barn. They jumped out of their truck and attacked them, killing three and driving the rest off into the woods.

The poultry barn was a metal building 100 feet long and 50 feet wide, full of free-roaming chickens of all colors, shapes, and sizes. There were 4' x 4' windows cut every 10 feet along the sides of the barn. Each window had a shutter that was hinged at the top and a cable attached to the outer edge which, when pulled, would open the shutters upward or when released, would close the shutters. The shutters had nails sticking out of them. Toward the outside the windows were covered with chicken wire. There was a 20 foot guard tower at each end of the barn and an observatory tower sticking out of the middle of the roof. Each of the three towers was equipped with a solar powered spotlight. The middle tower/observatory was equipped with a hand crank and release to open and close the shutters. The guards who were being relieved thanked Ralph, Betsy and Stephen for their good job at driving off the zombie dogs and protecting the chickens. Then the guards gave them the same procedures as at the other farm.

"In case of a zombie dog attack, fire a flare to signal an army unit for backup. The walkie-talkies have a limited range, which you can use to communicate to each other between the towers on channel 4. Channel 1 is used to communicate to the other farms and barns to inform them of any zombie dogs that may be moving through the area. In the morning, some refugees will show up to feed the chickens, collect the eggs and clean the barn."

Before the guards left, Ralph reached in his cooler and gave each of the guards a small, glass-covered jar with clear liquid in it. The guards looked at the jars and one of them took the lid off, smelling the contents and then taking a sip. The guard was delighted. "Wow, nice moonshine! Thanks!"

Ralph and Betsy took the end towers and Stephen went into the barn and climbed a ladder to the middle tower. After Stephen familiarized himself with how to open and close the shutters, he sat down on the poo bucket, taking a baggie of marijuana out of his pocket and rolling up a joint. The night went smoothly and there were no incidents.

Alert Two At The Cattle Ranch.

Sam, Flo, Daisy, and one of the GGF soldiers, Charlie Pollen, arrived at the cattle ranch. Charlie was an older man, maybe in his 50s, but he looked strong and capable. He had a thatch of brown hair that was beginning to turn gray, and there were gray streaks in his moustache and beard. His blue eyes twinkled with mischief. The incidents of the last few months didn't seem to have dampened his spirits.

There were 50 head of cattle inside a 10-acre corral. The 6 foot high corral fence had 6 inch diameter wooden posts every 5 feet, 8 inch diameter posts in the corners, and 2 x 6 heavy planks between the posts. There was a 10 foot sliding gate at the front of the corral and the entire outside of the fence was zigzagged with barbed wire. There was a 20 foot high guard tower at each corner of the corral with a solar powered spotlight in each. The guards who were being relieved give Sam, Flo, Daisy, and Charlie Pollen their duties and procedures in case of a zombie dog attack. In addition to the same procedures as the other farms, they told them, "In the morning, some of the refugees on horseback will arrive to take the cattle to pasture."

At 2 AM, John Senior's voice came over channel 1: "Alert two, alert two just had a small incident with the zombie dogs and now they may be headed in your direction."

Sam answered, "Thanks, John. We'll be watching."

Fifteen minutes later, twenty zombie dogs charged at the corral, attempting to attack the cattle. Sam, Flo, Daisy, and Charlie Pollen trained their spotlights along the corral fence and opened fire on the zombie dogs. The cattle were frightened and started running around inside the corral. One of the zombie dogs managed to get through the fence. A big, Black Angus bull charged the zombie dog, slamming it into the fence and stomping it to death. Sam, Flo, Daisy, and Charlie managed to drive off the rest of the zombie dogs.

On channel 1, Sam said, "Alert all, alert all we just had a zombie dog attack at the cattle ranch. We managed to drive them off, but I'm not sure what direction they're headed."

The cattle were still very frightened about the dead zombie dog that was inside the corral. After searching the area with their spotlights, Sam and Charlie decided to leave the guard towers, and they dragged the dead zombie dog out of the corral in hopes of calming the spooked cattle. The cattle calmed down and the rest of the night continued quietly.

Alert One At The Dairy Cow Barn.

Susan, Bobby, and I arrived at one of the large barns that contained about 100 dairy cows. Fort Stewart's logistics command only kept about 100 farm animals at each location to reduce the losses of food supply in case one location was lost to the zombie dogs or enemy forces. The barn was a two-story structure with the cows in stalls on the first floor. There were kerosene lanterns burning at approximately every 10 stalls. There was a large door at each end.

The back door was closed and led out into the grazing pasture. The front door was open. The second floor was a hayloft with a large opening at each end.

One solar panel had been placed on the roof of the barn to charge a small battery bank. The power from the battery bank was used to operate two large spotlights, one at each end of the hayloft. In front of the barn was a fire pit and a stack of firewood. We were instructed to keep the fire burning all night. One person manned the hayloft and operated the spotlight whenever zombie dogs were spotted. They repeated the standard orders: "In case of a zombie dog attack, fire a flare to signal an army unit for backup. The walkie-talkies have a limited range, which you can use to communicate to each other on channel 4. Channel 1 is used to communicate to the other farms and barns to inform them of any zombie dogs that may be moving through the area. In an attack, the two people on ground level are to retreat into the barn and close the door to prevent the zombie dogs from entering the barn. Slots have been cut into the barn door to see through and shoot at the attacking dogs. Do not close the front door or the small windows by each cow stall. You need to keep these open for airflow to keep the cows from becoming overheated." They wished us luck and left.

At the barn, we rotated guard positions every hour. One person in the hayloft to man the spotlight, one person in the barn keeping watch of the cows so that they stayed calm and didn't hurt themselves in their stalls, and one person out in front of the barn, keeping the fire going for light and for a deterrent.

As Bobby climbed into the hayloft for his shift, he saw the guard dumping a powder into a bucket and removing a blue plastic bag from it.

"What's that?" Bobby asked.

The guard laughed and said, "This is your poo bucket, kid. If you need to take a leak or a crap, you do it in the bucket. When you leave, dump the poo powder in there, roll up the bag and take it with you. We don't want to contaminate our food supply with your waste." He held the bag up to Bobby's face, "be sure to take it with you when you leave. Poo powder absorbs, gels and deodorizes your waste."

Bobby waved his arms, "Yuck! Get that stuff away from me!"

At 3:00 AM, Bobby was in the hayloft looking out the back door at the pasture. Susan was in the barn petting and talking to the cows. I was out front tending the fire when we heard distant barking and howling. We all went on instant alert. I told Bobby not to turn on the spotlights unless the zombie dogs actually came in close to the barn for an attack. We needed to conserve the battery power. Susan and I stood by the front barn door, ready to close it immediately if the zombie dogs came in close for an attack.

As the howling and barking got closer, the cows became restless, pulling against their yokes. Susan was worried that the cows could get loose of their yokes or hurt themselves, and she went from cow to cow, trying to calm them down. Two large packs of zombie dogs exited the woodline heading straight for the barn. Bobby turned on the spotlight and tried to get a light on them, but the zombie dogs were wise to this tactic and avoided the light. They came at the barn from the sides where Bobby was unable to get the spotlight on them. I quickly closed and latched the front barn door. The zombie dogs were close to the barn and coming up to the side windows, barking and growling viciously. The side windows were too small for the zombie dogs to fit through, but their appearance at the windows further panicked the cows. I couldn't get a clear shot at any of them from the holes in the barn doors, so I sent Susan to the hayloft to take up a position at the other end of the barn. I told her to use the other spotlight and to try to shoot some of them. Bobby fired the signal flare out the back opening of the hayloft.

The cows were going into a panic. It was difficult for me to move around inside the barn to get to the windows and launch any kind of counteroffensive. Bobby and Susan fired their weapons at a few that they managed to get a light on. I fired a few rounds out the side windows of the barn. At the sound of the gunfire, the cows started breaking loose from their yokes and running around inside the barn. This created a dangerous situation for the cows and for me. The cows were breaking down the stalls, and I was unable to calm them down. I couldn't fight the zombie dogs because I had all I could do to keep from being trampled or squished against a wall by the panicking cows. The fear and chaos of the cows and the lack of deterrent sent the zombie dogs into a frenzy of barking and howling.

The cows broke down the back door of the barn and stampeded out into the pasture. The zombie dogs were on them immediately like a school of piranhas. The zombie dogs bit the legs of the cows which caused them to fall to the ground. Once the cows were down the dogs tore away their flesh in strips. They ran off with the meat, in most cases, leaving the cow still alive and thrashing on the ground. This was a brutal and evil scene.

Bobby and Susan fired madly at the zombie dogs, trying to keep them off the cows. I followed the cows that stampeded to the back door, firing at the zombie dogs and trying not to hit any of the cows. The cows were galloping across the pasture, and the zombie dogs were tearing them apart and killing them.

Just then, two Humvees with soldiers and heavy machine guns drove into the barnyard. They maneuvered around the barn and into the pasture, firing on the zombie dogs. I yelled to Susan and Bobby to keep the spotlight on the stampeding cows. I went out the front door and got in my truck to head off the stampeding cows, attempting to turn them back toward the barn. This endeavor was difficult: trying to maneuver through the cow pasture, avoiding the cows that had been taken down by the zombie dogs, and staying out of the line of fire of the soldiers in the Humvees. The soldiers managed to drive off the zombie dogs, and I was able to turn what was left of the herd back toward the barn with the help of the soldiers.

We were only able to save about 65 cows. The rest were either killed or severely injured and had to be put down. The soldiers called for reinforcements to bring trucks to either butcher or dispose of the dead cows. Susan was sitting on the ground, crying over the loss of the cows. Bobby stood next to her, staring in shock at the carnage. The reinforcement trucks arrived and started taking care of the cow bodies that were scattered across the pasture. Other soldiers in Humvees patrolled the edge of the woods, in case the zombie dogs should return.

It was daylight before all the carnage was completely cleaned up. The meat from the cows that were killed would be used for our meals in the next few days. A lot of the meat near where the zombie dogs tore into the cow's flesh had to be cut away and disposed of for fear of disease. The greatest loss was the milk that the cows produced. We were ordered to report to the conference hall for a debriefing on the events that occurred.

Debriefing.

At the conference hall we met with George. We were seated at a long table, and everyone gave a report of the events that happened at each one of our guard posts. George asked if we had any questions or suggestions to improve the protection of the farm animals.

Bobby spoke up. "Yeah, I have a suggestion." Placing a blue plastic waste bag on the table, he said, "We need trashcans at the farm sites so we can get rid of these poo bags, instead of having to carry it around with us."

"Bobby!" I said. "Get that off the table, take it outside, and put it in the dumpster!"

John Junior said, "I'll take Bobby and Daisy to the chow hall for breakfast, and then we'll head to our barracks for some sleep. See y'all later."

Sam agreed. "Good idea. We'll be doing the same thing once we finish up here."

I told them, "We need more fencing around some of the farms. It would be better if we could have one or two more guards at each location, also."

George shook his head, "Our supplies are quite limited. We've been taking down chain-link fences from unoccupied civilian homes and using that to protect the farm animals. However, with all the other duties that need to be done, our skilled work force is stretched quite thin. I have all the information from you in my report and will be discussing this at a staff meeting at 4 o'clock this afternoon. You are all invited to attend. Why don't you go get some breakfast and some rest? I'll see you this afternoon."

We all left and headed to the chow hall, then to our assigned quarters for some much-needed rest. Back at our barracks, Susan checked to see if Bobby was in his room.

She came back into our room, "I didn't see Bobby at the chow hall, and he's not in his room. We should go look for him."

"It's daylight now and there aren't very many dangers here on post. He's most likely still with John Junior and Daisy."

Susan frowned, "I'm more worried about him being with John Junior and Daisy that I am of the zombie dogs."

I grinned. "Okay, let's go see if we can find him."

As we were walking back toward the chow hall, we saw Bobby and Daisy walking in our direction. Bobby had his arm around Daisy and they were talking and laughing.

Susan called to him, "Come on Bobby, you need to get to the barracks and get some rest, we've been up all night."

Bobby's eyes were kind of glazed, and he had a large, goofy grin on his face. Daisy smiled, "See you later this afternoon," and she sauntered off to her barracks.

Bobby looked at me and said, "You know, I really like boobies, but you know what I would like more right now? Pizza! I think I could eat a whole 24-cut pizza right now."

Susan's jaw dropped, "Bobby, what the hell's the matter with you? Are you drunk?"

Bobby answered, "Nope, just tired. I guess."

My eyes narrowed, "Bobby, have you been smoking with John Junior?"

Bobby looked down at the ground, "I prefer to take the fifth at this moment."

Susan smacked Bobby on the back of the head, "Off to bed with you!"

At our barracks, Susan paced back and forth with her arms crossed. "That Daisy is a bad influence on Bobby!"

I snorted, but quickly sobered at the blistering look from Susan. "This has all been a drastic change for everyone, and we're living in hell most of the time. Bobby is young and needs some fun things to do with his peers. They are all good kids, and we need to cut them some slack."

Susan frowned. "I don't like it very much, but I guess you're right. As long as it doesn't get out of hand."

Daily Staff Meeting.

At the staff meeting, George told us that there were some big things going on. In a few days, Col. Whitmore would be having an official meeting to bring us up to date on all the latest news. George told us that there weren't any more building materials or chain-link fences to improve the protection of the farm animals, but that he might be able to provide an extra GGF soldier at the farms for the night watch. Food, ammunition, and other supplies were running low, so we needed to be conservative. The fishermen had a good catch that day off the coast, but had used the last of the fuel that we had for the fishing boats. "So everyone enjoy the seafood dinner tonight."

I asked if any progress has been made in eliminating the zombie dog threat. George told us that 17 zombie dogs had been killed, but it did not seem to matter how many were killed because more showed up the following night.

I said, "I have an idea on this. The people who live or have lived in the cities are now running out of food and coming into the country in search of more. The zombie dogs, like other predatory animals, follow the food. People are the main food source of the city zombie dogs. When those people leave the city for the country, the zombie dogs follow. That's adding to the zombie dog population, which is already here."

George said, "That sounds like a logical theory. But what do we do about it?"

Sam said, "The same thing we've been doing, only we need to be more aggressive."

George said, "The Rangers are doing the best they can. They haven't found any large lairs of zombie dogs recently but yet they keep coming."

Ralph thought for a second. "Maybe that's because Army Rangers are trained to hunt people, not animals like the zombie dogs."

"I see your point," agreed George. "What do you suggest?"

Ralph said, "Hook up some good trackers and hunters with the Rangers as scouts."

"Good idea, but Col. Whitmore has the Rangers tied up in some special missions at the moment, so it may be a few days before we can put this together."

I said, "Well, if you have other soldiers that you could put on farm guard duty tonight so that we can get some rest, tomorrow we could go on a zombie dog hunt. Ralph and John are the two best hunters and trackers that I know."

George agreed. "The zombie dogs are a high-level threat to our food supply and survival. There are going to be some unhappy GGF soldiers tonight, but I'm giving you guys the night off to rest up. Tomorrow, go zombie dog hunting."

Bobby was happy. "Cool, no more babysitting stinky animals or pooping in poo buckets."

John figured Bobby needed a wake-up. "That's right, Bobby. Tomorrow you get to walk around in the woods with snakes and bugs and alligators, hunting for zombie dog lairs where you may be torn apart and killed."

Bobby's grin disappeared. "Oh, crap. I didn't think of that."

George said, "Go enjoy the seafood dinner and meet back here at 2000 hours to plan our zombie dog attack strategy."

At the chow hall we enjoyed the seafood dinner of shrimp, fish, and oysters, along with vegetables, fruit, and baked goods from the produce farms. Stephen and John Junior told us that there was a youth dance at the Hinesville firehouse that night. Bobby and Daisy were invited.

Flo said, "That sounds nice. The young people need to have some fun and socialize with other young people their age."

Bobby looked at Susan, "Can I go? Please mom, can I go?"

I leaned close to her, "Let him go, Susan. He needs to have some fun too, and we're going to be tied up in that strategy meeting for God knows how long."

Susan wasn't sure. "When is this dance over, and how are you getting back to the barracks at night with the threat of zombie dogs in the area?"

Stephen said, "Everyone's going to be staying at the firehouse after the dance. Some of the GGF soldiers are the ones putting on the dance with the refugees and will be providing security and supervision. We'll meet you back here at the chow hall for breakfast at 6 AM. Dad is letting us use the truck for transportation."

Susan relented. "We live in dangerous times now. But Stephen, if you promise to keep an eye on Bobby and keep him out of trouble, he can go."

I cautioned, "Remember, we have a long day tomorrow, and it will be a lot longer if you have a hangover, so keep the drinking to a minimum."

Daisy put her arm through Bobby's. "Have you ever been to a hoedown before?"

Bobby was captivated. "No, and I don't know how to dance either. But it sounds like fun."

Daisy assured him, "Don't worry, I'll show you how to dance."

We all left the chow hall and went back to our barracks to prepare our gear for zombie hunting.

At 8 o'clock, we met George at the conference hall for strategy planning.

"Welcome everyone," he said. "We'll start this meeting by telling you what we've been doing, and you people can make suggestions on what we have been doing wrong or where improvements can be made."

"Each morning after the zombie dog attacks at the livestock farms, the Rangers have picked up the zombie dog trails and tracked them into the countryside. The Rangers have had good luck finding wounded zombie dogs and killing them. The Rangers have also found small packs of zombie dogs hidden in wild hog burrows. Nevertheless, the Rangers have not been able to find any large packs or alpha dogs."

John said, "A large pack of zombie dogs would need a large, dark place to rest and hole up during the daylight hours. Wild hog burrows are not large enough or numerous enough to support a large pack of zombie dogs. We know the zombie dogs have a top speed of about 30 miles an hour. I would venture a guess that when they are on the hunt they can travel at about 15 miles an hour. This time of year darkness lasts about eight hours. That gives the zombie dogs four hours out and four hours to get back to their lair. This gives them a hunting territory of about 60 miles. That's a lot of ground to cover."

Ralph said, "That's too much territory for us to cover. We need to narrow that down. The zombie dogs are creatures of opportunity. I believe they take advantage of any food supply that is available including humans, livestock, wild game, and the scraps left over from butchering livestock. George, what do your people do with the hides and innards of the cows and pigs that you butcher?"

"Most of the scraps from the butchered livestock are being used as fertilizer at the produce farms, and we've been working on how to cure and tan the hides. Curing and tanning the hides without modern day machinery has not been going too well. Therefore, the animal waste from the butchered livestock has been taken to a landfill, but we cannot bury it because we do not have the extra fuel for bulldozers."

Ralph nodded. "That landfill area could be a feeding ground for the zombie dogs. I recommend we start searching around that area first to get an idea of how many zombie dogs we're dealing with and from what direction they're traveling to and from the landfill area."

John disagreed. "The landfill area is most likely providing an easy, safe food supply for the younger and weaker packs of zombie dogs. The stronger animals and larger packs most likely prefer fresh, live food supplies like the livestock animals and humans."

Ralph insisted, "The young and the pregnant females are most likely the ones taking advantage of the food at the landfill. If we can find and eliminate them, that should keep the larger, more aggressive packs from increasing their numbers."

George was willing to try something new. "Everything we have been doing so far has not been having much success in reducing the zombie dog numbers or attacks. I think going with Ralph's idea of eliminating the young and the females is a good starting point. At 0600 tomorrow morning, I will have one of the GGF soldiers take you to the landfill to do your thing."

Sam said, "Be sure to pack a jar of Vicks and some insect repellent. We have our plan now. See you at the chow hall in the morning."

The Firehouse Dance.

John Junior, Stephen, Bobby, and Daisy arrived at the firehouse for the youth dance. The firehouse was a two-story structure with four large bays in the garage area downstairs and several rooms, offices, and sleeping quarters upstairs. The garage area had been set up to accommodate the dance. The band was set up at one end of the garage and tables were placed along the back wall, holding beer, moonshine and snacks. Oil lamps were placed along the walls and there were candles on the tables. The band was made up of guitar players, banjos, drums, a trumpet, and a saxophone. There were about 40 young men and women attending the dance, ranging in age from 16 to 25. Some were GGF soldiers and others were refugees and military dependents.

John, Stephen, Bobby and Daisy helped themselves to some drinks and snacks. After a bit of socializing, Daisy got Bobby out on the dance floor. Everyone was having a lot of fun. Daisy excused herself from the group to go use one of the porta-potties that had been set up outside. When Daisy did not come back right away, Bobby decided to go and check on her. Outside, Bobby saw two guys talking to Daisy. She saw him and tried to walk around the two guys talking to her, but they moved to block her way. Bobby approached and asked Daisy if everything was okay. Before she could answer, one of the guys turned to Bobby. "Get lost punk."

Bobby reached for Daisy's arm. "Come on, let's go back inside."

Daisy said, "Good idea Bobby," and tried to get past the two guys.

They were refugee farmhands, big guys with a rough appearance. As Daisy started to move past them, one of them grabbed her by the arm. "Where are you running off to, honey?"

Daisy tried to pull away from him, but he just squeezed her arm more tightly. "Ow! You are hurting me."

Bobby warned, "Let her go."

The other farmer pushed Bobby. "What are you going to do about it, punk?"

Bobby punched the guy in the jaw. It didn't even phase him. He laughed and said, "That was a big mistake." He punched Bobby hard in the face, knocking him to the ground.

Daisy screamed, "Bobby! You guys leave him alone!"

The two farmers turned to Daisy and one said, "You're coming with us, honey."

Just then, Stephen and John Junior came outside looking for Bobby and Daisy. Seeing Bobby on the ground and Daisy struggling with the two farmers, they rushed in and jumped the two farmers. With Bobby and Daisy's assistance, Stephen and John Junior were able to beat the two farmers and run them off.

Back inside the firehouse, Daisy took Bobby upstairs to check him out for injuries. "Thank you Bobby for defending me. I'm sure those two would've really hurt me if it wasn't for you."

Bobby said, "I didn't do anything except get punched in the face and lay on the ground."

"You may have some more injuries. We need to take off your shirt and check you out."

Daisy took off Bobby's shirt and started kissing him and rubbing his chest. Their kissing grew more intense, and Daisy removed her shirt.

Bobby said, "Wow, I need to get beat up more often!"

Daisy gently pushed him onto the bed. They spent the night together.

At the chow hall in the morning, John Junior, Stephen, Bobby, and Daisy meet up with the rest of the group.

Susan was looking at them, noticing that John Junior had a fat lip, Stephen's knuckles were red and bruised, Daisy had a large bruise on her arm that was shaped like a handprint, and Bobby had a black eye.

She exclaimed, "Oh my God, what happened to you guys?"

Stephen tried to pass it off. "It was a pretty good party, and we all had a good time until two farmer boys decided to give Daisy a hard time, but Bobby took care of it."

Bobby said, "Yeah right, I got my ass kicked real good. If it wasn't for you and John, things could have gotten a lot worse."

Susan said, "I can't turn my back on you for a second, Bobby."

John Junior reassured her, "Everything turned out okay, ma'am. We all looked after each other and it all turned out okay."

I said, "We'll talk more about the details later. Right now, we need to meet George over at the conference hall to get ready to go zombie dog hunting today."

Chapter 13

Zombie Dog Hunting / Landfill.

At the conference hall, we saw George standing outside by a Humvee talking with two other soldiers: Charlie Pollen and my brother Brian.

George told us, "Charlie and Brian will be going with you today. They have some explosives in the Humvee that they'll be taking along. Brian and Charlie will use them to blow up any zombie dog lairs that you happen to find. I only have five communication devices for your unit. Our communication department has been working hard to repair more walkie-talkies and communication devices. Our electric power and materials are low, so this process has been going slowly."

Charlie said, "The landfill is south of this position, about halfway to Jesup."

I said, "Well Brian, we get to work together on a mission. I guess you've been busy. I haven't seen much of you since I arrived here."

Brian said, "Yes, they've kept me pretty busy working with the Ranger units. This whole mess is a big shit sandwich. It's going to take a long time to get things back to normal."

Sam said, "We're burning daylight and need to get going. There'll be plenty of time for chatting later."

We got in our vehicles and followed Charlie and Brian to the landfill. The landfill was a large area filled with rotting animal bodies, trash, and human waste that was piled 6 feet high, stretching out as far as we could see. The odor was so strong that you could just about see it in the air. The whole area was covered with flocks of buzzards and crows, all picking over the piles of disgusting waste. Some late-model trucks and horse drawn wagons were bringing waste to the landfill. A dozen workers wearing hazmat suits and respirators were unloading the waste from the trucks and wagons, drawing it onto the pile.

Susan held her nose. "Oh my God! I think I'm going to be sick."

Bobby already had his head hanging over the side of the truck, turning green and puking his guts out. Most of the others in our group were just as bad.

I blew the horn on my truck and yelled as loud as I could, "Get out your Vicks and facemasks immediately!"

Brian and Charlie got out of the Humvee wearing respirators, watching us. After applying the Vicks and putting on our facemasks, we were able to regain our composure.

John gave instructions. "We'll split up into two groups, keeping about 100 to 200 yards away from the landfill. One group will go around the east side and the other the west side. We'll meet up south and report our findings."

Alpha one going east was Ralph, Betsy, Stephen, Sam, Flo, Daisy and Charlie. Alpha two going west was Mark, Susan, Bobby, John, Lilly, John Junior and Brian. We headed to our assigned search areas.

Ralph was leading team alpha one with Charlie bringing up the rear. John was leading team alpha two with Brian bringing up the rear. In the wooded areas, 200 yards from the landfill, the odor was more tolerable. We could still hear and see the buzzards and crows that were feeding at the landfill. The thick, wood foliage shaded us from direct sunlight, making the air feel a bit cooler. There were numerous small game trails zigzagging through this wooded area. Most of the tracks that we saw were from wild hogs, turkeys and deer. After two hours of searching the area we approached the southern end of our search area.

John said, "Here is a well-used trail that is full of dog tracks."

Alpha one team, with Ralph in front, approached our position. He said, "What you got, John?"

"There's a good trail here with dog tracks leading to the south."

Ralph said, "I was expecting a lot more trails and signs of the zombie dogs in this area."

John agreed, "Yes, I've seen mostly turkey and hog trails. This is the only dog trail I've seen."

Ralph said, "Let's go together and follow this trail to see where it goes."

John and Ralph lead us along the trail for about a half a mile when Bobby said, "I need a break for a minute."

"What's the matter, buddy?" asked Susan.

Bobby said in a low voice, "I have to take a dump."

I said to John and Ralph, "You guys keep going. We have to take a latrine call here. We'll catch up to you In a few minutes."

John Junior said, "I need a break myself. I'll stay here with you guys."

Brian, Susan and I hung back, waiting for John Junior and Bobby to take their latrine call. John Junior stepped off in the woods to the right. Bobby went to the left, just out of sight. After a minute or two, John Junior came back to join us. As we were waiting for Bobby, we heard him scream, and he came running from the bushes with his pants still half down and fell flat of his face.

We all went to full alert. "What's wrong," I asked.

Bobby got up and started pulling his pants up, his eyes as big as dinner plates. He pointed in the direction from which he had just come saying, "Snake, big snake, big ass snake!"

I started to get mad. "Pull yourself together Bobby and tell us what's going on!"

John Junior immediately walked off in the direction from which Bobby came. He found the snake and quickly grabbed it by the tail, whipping it through the air like a bullwhip. We heard a loud crack and the snake's body went limp.

Bobby was amazed. "Holy shit, yeah that's it!"

John Junior said, "This is a water moccasin, a pretty bad ass snake." He took the snake by the head, and when it opened its jaws, he showed the fangs to Bobby. "You see these fangs? There's enough venom in here to kill you in a matter of minutes. But this isn't the only bad snake in this area. Diamondback rattlers are the biggest and some of the most deadly that we're likely to see around here. Copperheads are around here also. What makes them dangerous is that they hide in the leaves in the dirt and will not move as you approach. If you step close to them they'll bite you. Coral snakes are another deadly snake in this area. Coral snakes try to avoid people. But if you put your hand on a bush or tree branch near one, he'll bite you in self-defense. Coral snake venom is the most deadly of all."

Brian said, "In this day and time, without a medevac to a hospital and anti-venom, if any of us gets snake bitten, we'll most likely die. So be extremely careful where you're stepping or putting your hands."

Susan was horrified. "Oh my gosh Bobby are you are right, you didn't get bitten did you?"

Bobby said, "No, but I think I'll need a shower and change of clothes when we get back."

I needed to get everyone back on track. "Okay, we need to catch up with the others. Let's get moving."

We caught up with the rest of the group at the coastline railroad tracks.

Sam asked, "What kept you?"

I said, "Bobby had a little snake problem. All is okay now. What did you guys find?"

Ralph said, "The trail goes south from here down along the railroad tracks toward Ludowici."

Charlie said, "I recommend we go back and get our vehicles and drive down Oglethorpe Highway to Ludowici to check out the buildings and the town."

We were a few miles from the landfill and decided that was probably a good idea. Brian lead us on an easier route back to the landfill by way of fire breaks which had been cut through the forest.

We got in our vehicles and quickly left the landfill area, glad to be away from the odor and sight of that nasty place. We headed south down Oglethorpe Highway to Ludowici. Just as we were coming to the town, we noticed a large building off to the left.

Ralph blew the horn on his truck and stuck his arm out the window, pointing to the building. We drove our vehicles into the parking lot, getting out to see what Ralph had to say.

Ralph told us, "The glass doors on this building are broken, and it's large enough and dark enough to make a good daylight den for a large pack of zombie dogs."

Sam said, "Okay, let's go check it out."

Charlie said, "Let's check around outside before we go in."

John lead the way up to the front of the building. It did not take an expert tracker to see signs that the zombie dogs had been using this building. Muddy tracks, leaves, and bones trailed right through the front door.

Brian said, "There are very few windows in this place, so it's going to be extremely dark in there. Make sure your flashlights are working. We'll have to be extra careful. I've had to deal with the zombie dogs in the dark before. We don't have any night vision gear, and the zombie dogs can see, smell and hear in the dark much better than we can."

I said, "We'll split up into our two groups, one taking the right side of the building, the other the left, clearing section by section."

Brian cautioned, "Once we enter the dark part of the building, stand to the side out of the light and give it a minute for your eyes to adjust before continuing."

It was a large industrial building, most of which was a warehouse area. Inside the building, once we passed the office area into the dark warehouse, we gave our eyes two minutes to adjust, and then clicked on our headlamps. Alpha 1 team went right and alpha 2 team went left. We proceeded cautiously in single file, about 10 feet apart. There was a strong, pungent odor mixed with the smell of death. The building was full of industrial racking, two stories high. There were some second-level landings and office structures scattered throughout the building.

As we are about halfway through the building, all hell broke loose. Howling, barking, growling and shadowy figures came at us from all directions. Daisy saw one shadowy figure coming in her direction, identified it as a zombie dog, and gave it both barrels from her 20 gauge shotgun, dropping it in its tracks. It was quickly followed by two more. Daisy didn't have time to reload her shotgun, so she drew her .38 special revolver and fired on the other two approaching her position. Flo moved in quickly to back her up with the 12 gauge pump, keeping the others at bay long enough for Daisy to grab her 20 gauge and reload. Sam had several zombie dogs moving in on his position and opened up on them with his AK-47. A zombie dog jumped off the second-level landing on Charlie. Charlie went down in a hail of gunfire, snapping jaws, and tearing teeth. Ralph and Betsy moved in to rescue Charlie. More zombie dogs were coming off the landing and Ralph opened up on them with his Thompson. Betsy was having a difficult time holding off another group of zombie dogs which were attacking her. Her 30-30 Winchester was not really up to the task. Just as Ralph reached Charlie, Charlie dispatched the zombie dog with his tactical knife. Charlie was injured badly. Sam yelled aloud over the radio, "Retreat to the exit!"

John and Lilly were jumped by several zombie dogs from the roof of one of the offices. Lilly gave one zombie dog both barrels from her over and under 12 gauge. Not having time to reload, she drew her .38 special, firing on the other dog approaching her position. John was laying down a deadly barrage of buckshot with his 12 gauge pump. John Junior's and Stephen's bolt action rifles were not very effective in this close-up combat situation. John Junior pulled out his .44 Magnum revolver and had better success at fending them off. Stephen followed this tactic and drew his .357 Magnum, dropping two zombie dogs immediately. Bobby had several zombie dogs moving in on him. With zombie dogs and bullets flying in every direction, Bobby decided to take a crouching position to fire on the zombie dogs that were coming toward him. I followed Bobby's example, crouching and firing my semi-automatic, striking several of the zombie dogs. Susan had her back against the wall, firing the Ruger carbine .44 Magnum at zombie dogs that were running on the second level, dropping two or three of them. Brian, being at the rear of our group and not being immediately threatened by any zombie dogs, yelled, "Retreat to the exit. I'll provide cover."

We all started backing out of the area in a crouched position as Brian provided cover fire over our heads. We all made it, stumbling and half running into the lighted front office area where we had entered the building. The zombie dogs did not follow but were still there. Lots of growling, barking and howling was coming from inside the warehouse area. Alpha-1 team came through the doorway just before we did. That was when we noticed Ralph and Betsy kneeling over Charlie. Charlie was laying on the floor, gasping for breath. His uniform was torn to pieces, one boot was missing and the flesh from his knee to his ankle was gone, leaving the exposed bone. He had chunks of flesh missing from both arms and a large hole in his side, just below his left armpit. His face was scratched and torn, and one cheek was ripped away, exposing his teeth. He was choking and coughing up blood. His injuries were too great and he had lost too much blood. There was nothing we could do for him. He coughed a few more times and died.

Susan and Daisy both screamed and started crying and hugging each other.

Sam was livid. "Evil son of bitches! We need to annihilate them."

Flo said, "We cannot go back in there again."

John asked, "Brian, can you call in an artillery strike on this building?"

Brian said, "No, our radios are not long-range, and I believe the artillery unit is currently set up and directed for another mission."

Ralph asked, "What are we going to do? We gotta do something!"

Bobby said, "Charlie was a good guy. I liked him a lot. We need to do whatever it takes to kill these evil, bastard zombie dogs. What they did to the cows was horrible, but what they did to Charlie is even worse!" He started crying.

Stephen had an idea. "Brian, what about the explosives you brought with you?"

Brian said, "I'm not sure that it's enough to bring this building down. We would have to go inside to set the charges on the beams and stanchions which hold the building up."

I said, "Maybe we could blow enough holes in the roof and walls to let in the sunlight, driving the zombie dogs out where we can kill them or the let the sunlight do its work for us."

John said, "That might work if we can get enough sunlight into the building."

Brian said, "We can try that. We can strategically place several charges on the roof and blow out a wall on each side of the building. That should allow a lot of sunlight to get in there. It'll at least irritate the hell out of those bastards."

I agreed, "With enough sunlight entering the building, we could go back in there and have the advantage this time."

Sam said, "Yeah, that just might work. If we get enough sunlight in there, the zombie dogs will have to come through the light to get to us. We'll be able to see better, and they'll not be able to ambush us from the darkness."

John, Ralph, Sam, Brian, Bobby, John Junior, Stephen and I said together, "Let's do it!"

Susan said, "I'm not sure Daisy is going to be able to handle going back in there again."

Sam said, "Flo, you and Daisy stand guard here in case any of the zombie dogs try to exit the building this way. Can you do that?"

Flow said, "Yeah, we can handle that."

I turned to Susan. "What about you, can you handle going back in there again?"

Susan said, "I want revenge on them for all the pain and suffering that they've caused all of us. I'm ready."

Bobby said, "For my dad, Charlie, and those poor cows. I want to kill every last one of those bastards!"

Brian got the C-4 explosive out of the Humvee. He showed us how to set the timers and blasting caps. We put seven C-4 charges on the roof, setting the timers for 10 minutes, giving us plenty of time to get down. Down below, Sam and Ralph set two charges on the back wall and one on the east wall. We all went to the vehicles, bringing Charlie's body with us. Then we waited. The explosions started going off one after the other, blowing 4 to 6 foot holes in the building.

Sam said, "That ought to light the place up pretty good!"

Brian said, "Now we'll be able to see much better and have the advantage. We'll enter in groups, same as before. This time alpha two team will take the right side and try to get to the shipping bay doors. Try to get them open to let in more sunlight."

We entered the building as before. Flo and Daisy remained in the outer office area. We heard lots of howling, barking, and yipping coming from the warehouse area. Sam lead Ralph, Betsy, John Junior and Stephen down the left side. Brian lead Susan, Bobby, John, Lilly, and me down the right side.

There were dead and wounded zombie dogs everywhere we looked. They were not interested in attacking us this time. They were barking, howling and running around, looking for dark places to hide. The sunlight was coming through the holes from the explosions, making it easy for us to see the zombie dogs. It was like shooting fish in a barrel. We made it to the shipping doors with very little problems. We shot the locks off the doors and opened them one by one, letting more sunlight into the building. We systematically started clearing the building's first level and then the offices. In one of the office buildings, Susan found the red alpha dog. She emptied her gun on him, dropping him without a whimper.

She came out smiling. "I got that red alpha dog son of a bitch."

We did a quick body count and second search of the building. Dead zombie dogs: 214, casualties: 1. We loaded up and headed back to post for our debriefing and report. Mission a success.

Mission Debriefing

George, Col. Whitmore, and Maj. Higgins all attended the debriefing. Maj. Higgins said, "First Sgt. Antonio, you are the senior officer on this mission. I expect a full detailed report surrounding Sgt. Pollen's death."

Col. Whitmore said, "Maj. Higgins, this is a new type of enemy. Even though they are only animals, they possess some superior abilities and pose a serious threat. I'm sure 1st Sgt. Antonio and Col. Snyder's men did the best they could to protect Sgt. Pollen. 1st Sgt. Antonio, we're ready to hear your report of the mission."

Brian reported, "After searching for trails around the landfill area, we found one mutant dog trail leading south along the railroad tracks to the town of Ludowici. We tracked the creatures to a large industrial building just outside of town. We entered the building in groups, Sgt. Poland being on team alpha 1. I was on team alpha 2. The building was completely dark inside, and we did not have any night vision equipment. Shortly after entering the building, we were attacked from all sides, outnumbered and outflanked. Both teams took out a dozen or more of the creatures before we were forced to retreat. GGF team members Ralph and Betsy did their best to defend Sgt. Pollen and brought him outside with them during the retreat. Once outside we were able to see the full extent of his injuries. Sgt. Pollen succumbed to his injuries shortly thereafter."

"After regrouping outside, we decided to set explosive charges on the building, allowing sunlight to enter the building. This turned the battlefield in our favor. The beasts were in pain and were blinded by the sunlight. With the improved lighting we were able to hunt them down and exterminate them to the last dog. GGF member Susan Miller located and dispatched the alpha leader. The enemy body count was 214 with a friendly forces casualty count of one."

Col. Whitmore said, "I'd call this mission a success, and I congratulate you all."

George asked, "Is there any other information to bring to the table before we close this briefing?"

I said, "It appears that the zombie dogs are using abandoned buildings as dens to hole up in during the daylight hours. I would recommend a systematic search of all abandoned buildings within a 60-mile radius, killing any and all zombie dogs and destroying the buildings so that they cannot be used by the zombie dogs again."

Maj. Higgins said, "The Rangers are going to be tied up on other missions for the next few weeks. As soon as personnel become available. We will consider pursuing this recommendation."

George said, "Due to the high threat level of the zombie dogs, the GGF will provide teams to start searching the abandoned buildings as soon as possible."

Maj. Higgins said, "A memorial service will be held for Sgt. Pollen tomorrow afternoon."

George said, "You are all dismissed. Get cleaned up, go to the chow hall, get something to eat, and report back to me at 0600 tomorrow morning."

The next morning there was a flurry of activity all across the post. Some of it had to do with Sgt. Pollen's memorial service. Mark and his group of survivors from North Georgia heard rumors that a large military mission would be taking place soon. They reported to the conference hall for their meeting with George and the rest of the GGF. George told the group to ready all of their equipment and weapons for an upcoming large military mission which Col. Whitmore would give the details of at 4 o'clock that afternoon.

Chapter 14

4 o'clock staff meeting. Final.

At 4 o'clock, we showed up at the conference hall for the staff meeting. All officers were there, including the highest ranking enlisted soldiers from the special units. Representatives from the refugee workforce were also attending.

Col. Whitmore, who was leading the staff meeting and was the highest-ranking officer at Fort Stewart said, "Welcome. We have a lot of information to cover, some good and some bad. As usual, I'll start out with what we know about the world news and then the national news before we get down to our local news and business. This is so that everyone knows the scope of the big picture and problems that we are facing. Small pockets of technicians, both military and civilian, have been able to restore power and communications in some localized areas. Our technicians here have been able to repair much of our communication equipment, allowing us communications with other military forces across the country."

"On the world news front, the continents of Africa and South America are the only ones who have not suffered EMP attacks and have full electrical and electronic device usage. This is a big promotion and power achievement for those Third World countries. We don't know how they're going to handle this new power advantage that they now have over some of the larger, more advanced countries that they have seen as bullying them. We believe that some of these countries will take advantage of their technological abilities to launch aggressive actions against their neighbors, including us or what was us, The United States."

"Numerous conflicts have broken out across every continent on the globe. Every country or group who thinks that they have a slight advantage are attacking their neighbors and trying to grab real estate and resources. For us, this is a two-sided coin. On one hand, that keeps our enemies busy so they're not attacking us. On the other hand, it's keeping our allies, who are able to help us, from doing so. This is why our allies have been slow in launching any kind of relief effort or assistance to us here in the United States. The other issue holding back our allies from providing any kind of relief efforts is the presence of the Chinese and Russians on United States soil. With communications being unreliable, the world has been getting mixed messages about the relationships between the United States, Russia, and China."

"On the national front, Texas Gov. Carry has been making progress in unifying the military and most of the states that still have any type of government. John Hager has dispatched Marine Corps and Homeland Security forces from Charleston to reinforce the Chinese in Savannah. The official word: this was due to the third infantry artillery division's unauthorized attack on Hunter Airbase. I know this sounds bad, and I'll get to more details on this in a moment. Army and National Guard units in Nevada, Oregon, Idaho, and Washington are now engaged in fighting the Chinese in California and west of the Rockies. The Midwest states have lots of farms and crops but no way to distribute the food to places that need it. It's basically rotting in the fields. The heavy populated areas from New York City south to Norfolk, Virginia, west to Cincinnati and north all the way up into Detroit and Wisconsin are in total chaos. What people do remain there have become like animals, starving to death, doing whatever they can to survive, no matter how horrible it may be. These are just the ones we know about. No information has been coming out of the northern Midwest from

Kansas to Wyoming and half a dozen other places. New England north of New York City is under the command and control of British Gen. Henry Van Horn. He's been getting relief shipments and support from Europe and Australia. Texas no longer has the threat of the United States on their borders, so they have been able to slam the Mexican army hard, detouring them from trying to invade the Texas border."

"Gen. Richard Briggs is now the highest-ranking surviving Army officer. He's been working closely with Gov. Carry to bring all the US Army units under one command, including the third infantry here in Fort Stewart. General Briggs is the highest ranking survivor at STRATCOM Omaha, Nebraska. He sees and understands the real reasons that the Russians and Chinese are here on American soil and wants them gone. Rear Adm. Taylor, who is in command of the Pacific Fleet, has deployed ships to the coast of California to engage the Chinese on the west coast and to Alaska to engage the Russians to take back Alaska. The Australian Navy is reinforcing Adm. Taylor. Sen. Samantha Simmons has relieved John Hager as acting president with the support of rear Adm. Ted Pickett of the Atlantic Fleet. Senators Simmons and Adm. Pickett are trying to regain control over the Marine Corps and Homeland Security forces which are on their way to Savannah to reinforce the Chinese. However, at this time we do not know the status or loyalties of this Marine Corps unit or the Homeland Security forces. They may see Senator Simmons and Adm. Pickett as enemies who have launched a coup to seize power from their last known commander-in-chief, John Hager. Regardless of the Marine Corps' loyalties, at sun up tomorrow morning, the third infantry is launching a full-scale attack on Hunter Airbase and invading downtown Savannah to retake control of Hunter Airbase and the seaport."

"The canine flu has basically run its course here in North America and is no longer a major threat. Anyone who's been exposed to the disease and has survived now has an immunity to it. But the mutated virus that has infected the canine species, mutating them into zombie dogs, still remains. The zombie dogs still remain a significant threat to humans and livestock worldwide. Ninety percent of all the metropolitan cities that we know of are infested with zombie dogs and uninhabitable at this time. Once electrical power is restored, we are hoping to eradicate the zombie dogs from populated areas. But our first priority is unification of our people, the military, and to reestablish our government structure. We are going to be doing this one town, one city at a time. Locally, we are starting with Hunter Airbase and Savannah."

"We are quickly running out of supplies here at Fort Stewart. We need the airport and the seaport. We only have enough fuel for our vehicles for this mission to retake Savannah. Win or lose, we are out of fuel. We only have enough food for maybe another one or two months. I am asking the GGF to be our reserve force and back us up on this mission."

Sam said, "The GGF and many of the refugees will be there to back you up as needed."

Col. Whitmore said, "We are low on guns and ammunition. Hell, we may be down to swords and bayonets before this is over. We'll work out all the details in the war room meeting at 2100 hours."

Bobby piped up, "I've got a samurai sword, if you need it, Sir."

Col. Whitmore laughed. "You hang on to that private, you just might need it."

Col. George Snyder of the GGF said, "I have a quote I would like to read."

"There is one fact that will bring notable relief to many survivors: the grim problems facing them will at least be completely different from those that have been tormenting them in the past years. The problems of the advanced civilization will be replaced by those proper to a primitive civilization, and it is probable that a majority of the survivors may be made up of people particularly adapted to passing quickly from a sophisticated to a primitive type of existence."

Roberto Vacca, The Coming Dark Age.

At the 9 o'clock meeting in the war room, Col. Whitmore informed us that a group of Rangers were sent around Savannah to meet up with the Marine Corps and Homeland Security force with updated information on the turn of events to try and persuade them to engage the Chinese in Savannah, not reinforce them. At 0600, a messenger detachment would be sent to Savannah, asking the Chinese to surrender Hunter Airbase and downtown Savannah to the third infantry. If the Chinese refuse, the third infantry would move in to attack Hunter Airbase and downtown Savannah. The U.S. Navy would be sending destroyers to retake the seaport in Savannah and Hilton Head, South Carolina. The GGF would attack from the west into Pembroke and Pooler, keeping the Bloods busy and out of our way.

Contact had been made with General Briggs at STRATCOM. He brought us up-to-date on the latest information. "I'll read you the following message from general Briggs as written:"

"As the protests and civil unrest increased across the country, Russia and China devised a plan to infiltrate and conquer the United States without ever having to go to war. They sent thousands of college students here on student visas with skills to keep the protests and violence going so that eventually Russia and China could come to the aid of the US with peacekeeper troops backed by the United Nations. Russia also sent scientists and engineers to NASA to work on the special deep space exploration projects. However, they were the ones who built and fired the EMPs. Of course, Washington has blamed North Korea. Sen. Kane was in Houston for the deep space launch by NASA. Sen. Kane and Gov. Carry of Texas now have two of the Russian scientists locked up in Texas at a secret location."

"All precautions are necessary, due to the circumstances. I find it appropriate to give Col. Whitmore a field promotion to Brigadier General. Congratulations Brig. Gen. Whitmore. I've been in contact with various military forces across the country, unifying our command structure. As a member of the Chiefs of Staff, I have full command of the United States military by Republican Sen. Thomas Kane. He's the only congressional representative that can be confirmed as loyal to the United States of America. Brig. Gen.

Whitmore and all officers and personnel under your command, you are under my orders not to give out any restricted information to any other congressional representatives without confirmation from myself, Sen. Kane, or some other confirmed and trusted source. Sen. Kane is also the Lieut. General in charge of the Southwest region of the United States. I'm taking personal charge of the Northwestern United States. Brigadier General Whitmore from Fort Stewart, Georgia, you are in command of the southeastern United States. Rear Adm. James Taylor is in command of the Pacific fleet and is taking control of Alaska and the western territories of the United States from the Rocky Mountains to the coast. Rear Adm. Ted Pickett, commander of the Atlantic Fleet, has command of all military forces in the Atlantic and is the senior officer on the East Coast. General Henry Van Horn of Great Britain has command of the Northeast and New England states under my authority. I will contact General Van Horn and inform him of your current locatlon and status. STRATCOM will continue to monitor this channel and all others for updates and status changes. Good luck to all of you and God bless America."

Attack On Savanna.

Col. George Snyder lead the GGF's 2,000 soldiers into Pooler. The GGF was met by a small group of Bloods who had two jeeps with .50 caliber machine guns mounted on them and about 50 gang members with light automatic weapons. The GGF quickly spread out into defensive positions. Several GGF soldiers firing 203 grenade launchers quickly took out the .50 caliber machine guns. Other units of the GGF flanked the Bloods' position, raining hell down on them from three directions. The Bloods, being outnumbered, outflanked and outgunned, were quickly annihilated. The GGF had control of Pooler and continued on to Savannah International Airport. Col. George Snyder received word from Brig. Gen. Whitmore that the Chinese had refused to surrender. The Army Rangers had made contact with the Marine

Corps detachment from the USS Ronald Reagan. Homeland Security troops disputed General Briggs' authority and orders, but United States Marine Corps Major Bowel acknowledged them. The Marine Corps unit disarmed the Homeland Security troops and sent them back to Charlotte, South Carolina. Major Bowel had agreed to take the Marine Corps unit and secure Savannah International Airport. Col. George Snyder and the GGF were tasked with securing the seaport area along West Bay Street.

At that time, a Chinese cargo plane arrived, escorted by two Chinese fighter jets, a Chengdu J-10 and a Sukhoi Su-35 Flanker E. The USS *Arleigh Burke* (DDG-51) called in the warning and fired SAM RIM-67 Standard ER (SM-1ER/SM-2ER) missiles, taking out the two jets before they could launch an attack. Using the 5-Inch/54-caliber (Mk 45), the USS *Arleigh Burke* (DDG-51) took out the transport plane as well. Under the cover of an artillery barrage from Fort Stewart, the third infantry moved in and took control of Hunter Airbase from the Chinese.

On the Savannah River side of W. Bay St., the GGF found a large concentration camp guarded by Chinese soldiers. They surrendered immediately upon seeing the 2000 GGF soldiers marching in on them. The USS *Arleigh Burke* (DDG-51) came up the Savannah River, blowing an air horn and playing victory music over its loudspeakers for all to hear.

In the excitement of the moment, I climbed the guard tower overlooking the concentration camp, speaking into the PA system which the Chinese had set up there. "You've been freed and liberated by the United States militia group GGF. You're free to leave and go about your lives to create a better United States government for the people, by the people. Go now and enjoy your freedom, never forgetting the atrocities that befell you and our country due to the blindness of our previous government leaders. There is a lot of work ahead of us to rebuild this great country, the United States of America. I encourage you all to join the fight and take up the task of rebuilding our country. Lawless gangs and warlord organizations are being eliminated to make it safe for you to return to your homes. Reconstruction of electrical power and communications are making progress throughout the country. Good luck. and God bless you all."

Rear Adm. Pickett loaned the USS *Arleigh Burke* (DDG-51) to the third infantry and the GGF to continue the fight to retake Florida and the Southeast all the way to New Orleans. Rear Adm. Pickett and the US Marine Corps continued taking seaports and cities along the East Coast northward to Washington DC. The Dahlonega and Claremont farmers and Athens gypsies captured Gainesville from the Russians, bringing the whole northeastern part of Georgia back under the control of US citizens. Rear Adm. Taylor, with help from the Australians, drove the Chinese and Russians out of western North America, retaking California to Alaska.

With the foreign troops eliminated, power and communications were soon reestablished across most of the continental United States. For the first three years, Sen. Thomas Kane and Sen. Samantha Simmons governed the United States of America and oversaw the rebuilding of the government structure. In November of 2024, the first presidential elections were held. I, Mark Antonio, was elected president with my vice president, Randolph Smith.

The zombie dogs continued to be a major threat to humans and livestock worldwide. Some metropolitan areas still harbored large populations of zombie dogs and were unsafe for human habitation. The elimination of the zombie dog threat was a continuous problem. Human beings were no longer at the top of the food chain and now had a predator that changed human life on planet Earth forever.

New Laws And Policies

The last four years of the hellish nightmare called day of the dog influenced new laws and policies of the United States government.

Office of the president of the United States.

- The president and vice president cannot be a member of a political party or be CEO or board member of a multimillion dollar organization.
- As leader of the executive branch of office, the Pres. and VP must have an unbiased and neutral association.

Elections of senior government officials, senators, governors and president.

- Special interest lobbyists and lobbying ban.
- Campaign contributions from any source, including personal, cannot exceed the total amount from individual constituents.
- "None of the above" ballot added to election booths. If the "none of the above" ballot count equals 50% or higher a new election must be held within six months.

Trade And Commerce.

- No restrictions of trade between states, including but not limited to insurance companies (automobile, health, home, and life).
- No export of natural resources / unfinished goods (logs, cloth, ore).

Firearms And Ammunition.

- Standardized laws and regulations covering all states, allowing all US citizens an equal right to possess, carry and transport firearms. Full automatic firearms and explosives are restricted to the military.

Bills And Laws Brought Before Congress.

- Bills and laws brought before Congress for a vote can no longer be bundled containing multiple laws of the same or different subject matter.
- All laws and changes to existing laws must be voted on separately.

Taxes.

- All income tax deductions, exemptions, and breaks are eliminated.
- 10% flat income tax on all income from any source for individuals, corporations and businesses.

Printed in the United States
By Bookmasters